PRAISE FOR LOUISE JENSEN

'The term pageturner was made for books lik
Andrea Mara

'A gripping, edge-of-your-seat thriller you
won't want to stop reading!'
Lauren North

'This book has it all! I was desperate to
know how it was going to end'
J.L. Blackhurst

'Creepy and compelling'
B.A. Paris

'Twisted and suspenseful'
Woman's Weekly

'A galloping pulse-pounder'
Heat

READERS ARE GIVING *THE FALL* FIVE STARS!

★ ★ ★ ★ ★

'Louise Jensen is the queen of thrillers!'

'Kept me on the edge right to the end'

'An excellent read'

'Absolutely brilliant! This book contained everything I look for'

'The plot was woven together masterfully'

'Louise Jensen has yet again shown us
what a brilliant storyteller she is'

Louise Jensen has sold in excess of a million English language copies of her international No. 1 psychological thrillers *The Sister*, *The Gift*, *The Surrogate*, *The Date*, *The Family*, *The Stolen Sisters* and *All For You*. Her novels have also been translated into twenty-five languages and are for sale in over thirty territories. Louise's books have been featured on the *USA Today* and *Wall Street Journal* Bestseller List and have been optioned for TV and film.

Louise's books have been nominated for various awards including the Goodreads Debut Award, *The Guardian*'s Not the Booker prize and best Polish thriller of 2018. She has also been listed for two CWA Dagger Awards.

When Louise isn't writing thrillers, she turns her hand to penning love stories under the name Amelia Henley. Her first two novels, *The Life We Almost Had* and *The Art of Loving You* have both been international bestsellers. *From Now On* is out now.

Louise also writes short stories which have been featured in various publications including *The Sun*, *Best*, *Candis* and *Hello* magazine. She has a monthly fictional column in *My Weekly*.

THE FALL

LOUISE JENSEN

ONE PLACE. MANY STORIES

HQ
An imprint of HarperCollins*Publishers* Ltd
1 London Bridge Street
London SE1 9GF

www.harpercollins.co.uk

HarperCollins*Publishers*
Macken House, 39/40 Mayor Street Upper,
Dublin 1, D01 C9W8, Ireland

This edition 2023

7

First published in Great Britain by
HQ, an imprint of HarperCollins*Publishers* Ltd 2023

Copyright © Louise Jensen 2023

Louise Jensen asserts the moral right to be identified as the author of this work.
A catalogue record for this book is available from the British Library.

ISBN: 978-0-00-850850-0
CA/ANZ: 978-0-00-850851-7

This book is produced from independently certified FSC™ paper
to ensure responsible forest management.
For more information visit: www.harpercollins.co.uk/green

This book is set in 10.7/15.5 pt. Sabon

Printed and Bound in the UK using 100% Renewable Electricity at
CPI Group (UK) Ltd, Croydon, CR0 4YY

For my cousins, Tori, Mark, Lee, Dean and Paul, who shaped my childhood with the hide-and-seek-den-building adventures that we shared.

PROLOGUE

The darkness is absolute.

A ragged breath.

The wait excruciating.

A whimper.

Light floods the stage.

Two little girls stand shoulder to shoulder, hands anxiously fiddling with their tutus, pink tulle stiff, before their fingers find each other, linking together.

The audience collectively sighs, hearts melting, as the girls edge forward, ballet shoes shuffling, chubby legs clad in cream tights. The hall smells like every other primary school – poster paints and lemon cleaner – but tonight it has been transformed into a theatre. Rows of grey plastic chairs stripe the shiny parquet flooring.

The girls look at each other for reassurance, so similar with their bright blue eyes and blonde, tightly wound buns that they could be mistaken for twins instead of the cousins they are.

They're the best of friends.

From the speakers, the first strains of Tchaikovsky's *The Nutcracker*. From the wings the frantic whisper of their teacher.

'Come on. Everyone's waiting.'

The lower lip on one of the girls juts out before it begins to tremble, her eyes filling with tears. On the front row, her mother grabs the arm of her sister.

The desire to go and rescue the girls is immense.

'Shall we go up there and—'

'Give them a minute,' her sister says in a low voice. Although she's concerned about her niece, she knows her own daughter will take care of her. 'They've got each other. They'll be okay.'

The first girl steps into position, raising one arm in a perfect arc above her head. The other stays by her side, still tightly gripping her cousin's hand. The first girl squeezes her cousin's fingers, three times in the way she knows her mum does to her aunt when she is stressed about something.

The second girl wipes her eyes, mimics the move.

They begin to dance, their moves clumsy at first because they never once let go of each other until beaming smiles replace worried frowns.

Then, they break apart, each spinning pirouettes that are only fractionally out of time. Even then you could see they had rhythm, talent. Too young to go on pointe, they run, graceful, circling the perimeter of the stage, arms outstretched as though they are flying, hair escaping their buns.

Their mothers relax. One sister placing her head on the shoulder of the other.

A family united. A family who love each other. Support each other.

A family full of secrets.

As cameras click and bright flashes fill the auditorium, no one could have ever guessed that ten years later one of those girls would be in a coma, fighting for her life. Everyone close to her hiding . . . something.

That the two sisters, so proud of their daughters, would be at war, trying to uncover the truth, conceal the truth.

Protect their children.

The entire family forced to take sides, torn apart.

It was impossible to predict as they sat watching the show.

But in the years to come, they wouldn't be the only ones watching those girls.

PART ONE

CHAPTER ONE

Kate

Hands cover Kate's eyes. She shuffles forward, uncertain. Heart pounding in her chest. Adrenaline surging through her veins.

'Are we—'

'No questions.'

Pressure from behind forces her to take another tentative step, stumbling on unfamiliar heels.

The cold bites at her legs, inadequate sheer tights offering no protection against the damp winter weather.

She longs for her jeans and wellies. Her thick, padded jacket.

The surface changes underfoot. Harder. The air warmer. They're inside now.

But where? She'd been spun around three times and has completely lost her bearings.

Her mouth is dry. She licks her lips, running her tongue over the sticky pink gloss. She isn't used to wearing make-up. She can feel it sitting on the surface of her skin.

'Ready?'

She isn't sure she is, but she croaks out a yes anyway.

Her daughter's fingers fall away from her face.

'Surprise!' Caily says but it's not only her voice Kate hears.

She blinks, her mouth stretching into the broadest of grins. She glances to her left, at her twin sister, Beth, who had been led here by her own daughter, Tegan. She looks equally shocked.

There's a chorus of 'Happy Birthdays' while around twenty-five guests simultaneously fire party poppers at them. Laughing, Caily scoops up a handful of the brightly coloured streamers and drapes them around Kate's shoulders.

Twix, their chocolate Labrador who had been sitting patiently, smart in a new tweed bow tie, bounds towards her, ears flapping, tongue lolling.

'You were in on this too, then?' Kate strokes him as she looks around.

The barn they usually use for storage twinkles with dozens of fairy lights. It's magical. There are trestle tables groaning with a buffet, the smell of Mum's homemade apple pie battling with the scent of the hay bales stacked around the walls as makeshift seats.

'I thought we said no party,' she gently chides Caily but she can't stop smiling and, as she looks at the 'Happy 40th' banner strung between the rafters, she thinks it is, perhaps, something to celebrate after all their recent hardship.

She hugs Caily tightly. The floral perfume her daughter had begun wearing at fifteen filling her throat.

'Thank you.'

'It wasn't all me. Dad, and Grandma and Grandad helped.'

'A conspiracy.' Kate waves across the barn to her parents.

She had thought Mum was cooking them a quiet family dinner at their farmhouse.

'No wonder you and Tegan insisted Beth and I dress up.' Kate tugs down the hem of her black dress, unused to showing her knees.

'That's why we wanted to do your make-up. You both look great.'

Kate feels great as she gazes at her closest friends, family. She feels loved.

'Happy birthday, wife.' Matt, her husband, gives her a gentle kiss before pushing a glass into her hand.

'My hero.' She takes a sip, bubbles fizzing. 'I can't believe this.' The sparkling wine is cold but she no longer feels the chill of the outside. It isn't only the portable heaters dotted around that are providing the warmth, it's the waves of affection as she's hugged and kissed.

Kate tries to reach her parents, slowed by well wishes, thanking everyone for coming, promising to have a proper chat with them soon.

'You two.' She stands before Mum and Dad, hands on hips. Beth is already with them. 'I can't believe you kept this a secret.' She opens her arms and embraces her mum first, kissing her cheek, the loose skin brushed with powder. Her hair stiff with Elnett. 'How on earth did you set all this up without me knowing?' She hugs Dad.

'He's good at keeping secrets,' Mum says.

'Hello, stranger.' There's a light tap on her shoulder.

Kate turns and the years fall away.

'Nicola?' Kate hears the question in her voice but it isn't really an 'Is that you?' but a 'How are you here?' 'Why are you here?'

She hasn't seen her childhood friend since . . .

'Toast!' Matt shouts, popping open another bottle and splashing wine into glasses that Caily and Tegan offer around. He stands on a hay bale.

'Kate, my beautiful wife, and Beth, my sister-in-law who's obviously beautiful as well, have turned forty.'

Kate momentarily covers her face, feels a blush creeping around her neck. Not because she's embarrassed about her age, but because everyone is looking at her and she's never liked being the centre of attention. Not like Caily and Tegan, who thrive on a stage.

Beth takes her hand and gives it three gentle squeezes. It's an 'I'm here for you' and has always been their 'you are not alone' gesture because Kate has a special language with her twin and it isn't always comprised of words.

'Kate and Beth share many traits, not just their looks or being identical twins, or their generous hearts, but also their sense of loyalty.'

Kate groans, sensing a story coming.

'When I first knocked on the door of the farmhouse, looking for work, I was welcomed wholeheartedly by Patrick and Mary,' he raises a glass towards Kate's parents. 'They provided me a cottage to live in, often inviting me to eat with the family.'

'There's nothing like my wife's apple pies,' Dad calls out.

'There isn't. I loved Mary's baking and before long I also began falling for Kate. We'd hang out in this very barn—'

'Oi, oi,' shouts Travis, their farm manager.

'I'm not sure I want to hear about my parents in a barn.' Caily looks mortified.

'And it wasn't long before I invited her out to dinner. I'd expected Patrick and Mary to be cautious, but it was Beth I needed to prove myself to. On the day of our date,' Matt runs his fingers through his hair, 'man, I was so nervous. We'd arranged to meet at Pizza Hut.'

'Very romantic, Uncle Matt,' Tegan cuts in.

'I stood outside, clutching a bunch of flowers, rehearsing what I was going to say as I watched her through the window, leaning over the menu, blonde hair twisted up off her neck, and I knew. I knew then.' He pauses.

'That it was true love?' asks Travis.

'That it wasn't Kate. Beth had taken her place.'

'I wanted to see how much you really liked my sister so I made her swap with me. Most people get us confused until they really get to know us.'

'I thought about playing along with it, getting my own back somehow, but I knew they'd always be one step ahead of me. Would always keep me on my toes, and they have. I've been part of the family for over twenty years now and . . .' Matt breaks off, suddenly serious. He lowers his head and takes a deep breath before he raises his face and his glass. 'I couldn't love you all more. To Kate and Beth.'

'Kate and Beth,' everyone repeats. Glasses are drained.

'Speech.'

'Oh no,' Kate begins but Beth is already dragging her towards Matt.

'It's wonderful to see you all here tonight. I'm Beth, by the way.' Everyone laughs. 'As you all know, it's been a really challenging time for us.' She covers her chest with her palm as she looks at their parents. Kate takes a sip of her drink to swallow down the emotion that's risen in her throat. 'But we've come through it. As we always do, as a family. Tomorrow our daughters are facing another challenge and I know they'll make us proud.' Caily and Tegan both form hearts with their hands. 'What I really want to say,' Beth's slurring slightly. She turns to Kate. 'What do I really want to say?'

'Eat, drink and be merry?' Kate suggests.

'Yes. All of that. And a toast to our parents, who really are the glue that holds everything together.'

'To Patrick and Mary.'

Music begins to stream.

Kate hugs Matt tightly, before drawing Beth into their fold, conscious that she's on her own without Sean, but she won't think of him today.

She won't think of any of it.

The Spice Girls invite everyone to tell them what they want. Beth whoops and grabs Tegan's hands, Kate does the same to Caily and they begin to dance, both daughters smiling despite rolling their eyes. Twix weaving around their ankles, occasionally darting off when he notices someone has dropped a morsel, hoping it's a sausage roll.

Kate is warm, breathless by the time she takes a break. The lights are lowered, everyone singing 'Happy Birthday' as the cake is carried towards her and Beth. The candles are baby pink, pushed into pale buttery icing. Just as they have for every single birthday, Beth and Kate hold hands and blow out the flickering flames together. Kate experiences a moment of total peace.

Of total happiness.

Then, somehow, she's drunk another couple of gins, and

is again balanced precariously on a hay bale with Beth, both of them kicking their heels off.

Matt hands them a microphone and fires up a portable karaoke machine. He doesn't need to ask what song they want because he knows.

They sing, unselfconsciously, through the fug of alcohol about surviving and not being able to live without you by my side.

Kate hopes she survives the hangover that tomorrow will bring because tomorrow, for Caily and Tegan, for the entire family, is going to be a life-changing day.

But not in the way she thinks.

CHAPTER TWO

Kate

Kate can't think clearly, her hangover raging. How much did she drink last night at the party?

'Matt?' Where is her husband? She can't see him. Can barely see anything.

There's something about fog that makes her shudder. The way it snakes towards her before coiling its damp fingers around her neck, her eyes, her mouth until it's all she can see, taste, feel.

It reminds her of that day, all those years ago, when she'd almost died. And even now, when it rolls in over the expanse of fields, she feels the same fear she did then.

But she is safe now, and even if she doesn't feel like one, she is an adult at forty years old, not a terrified child.

'Matt?' She calls again as she edges towards the barn, barely able to see where she is placing her feet. The bleating of the sheep guides her until she is safely inside under bright white light, but outside the mist still swirls around the outbuilding as though trying to swallow it.

There's a clatter behind her. She breathes in sharply – the

stench of manure catching the back of her throat – but the noise is only one of the sheep kicking against a metal gate. She isn't really expecting Matt to be here. The sheep, unable to graze outside at this time of year, have already been given their hay and grain – she knows this because she is the one who fed them – but he isn't ploughing the fields as he'd planned, the tractor is still in the yard. She's glad of that, it could be hazardous in these conditions.

It's so easy to get hurt.

Where is he?

Kate tries his mobile again, peering outside into the gloom. She should be able to see the main farmhouse from here but, although it's only three o'clock, it's almost dark. A chill snakes down her spine. Winters on Marsh Farm are brutal and, while the remoteness and solitude can be idyllic in the summer months when a beaming yellow sun smiles over the fields, now, in December, it can be grim.

Lonely.

Once more, Matt's phone goes straight to voicemail, but the signal here is weak and he's probably out of range. Still, she checks the second barn to her left. The remnants of last night's party linger inside. The 'Happy 40th' banner still hanging from the rafters. At the far end, the makeshift stage constructed from bales of hay where she and Beth likely made complete fools of themselves. Her memory is hazy. Still, it was their party.

The tight band around Kate's head tightens, the aftertaste of gin sour in her mouth. Matt's probably off somewhere nursing his own hangover.

The hens cluck, every noise a jackhammer in Kate's skull.

She calls Travis, the farm – it seems too grand to call him 'manager' when he's responsible for much of the hard labour, but that's the title they gave him, in part to make up for the meagre wages they offered, when he'd knocked on their door, looking for work, at the end of the summer.

He doesn't pick up.

Kate scurries across the cobbled courtyard towards the farmhouse, slipping through the back door into the kitchen. Her parents are sitting at the huge pine kitchen table, spines stiff, atmosphere heavy. It's unusual that there isn't a teapot cocooned in a green knitted cosy.

Matt isn't here.

'You okay?' She glances between her mum and dad. Mum's eyes are rimmed red, Dad's too. They're not used to late nights, drinking, and with Dad still on strong painkillers, two years after his accident, he shouldn't touch alcohol at all but she'd seen him knocking back the whisky.

'Thanks again for last night,' she says, feeling awful. A surprise party was a lovely idea but it's worn them out, hosting. No doubt cooking breakfast for Beth and Tegan who had stayed overnight. Her parents wanted everyone to enjoy the champagne, although that's perhaps too fancy a name for Tesco fizzy wine.

'About last night—' her dad begins.

'We loved it. Really. Look, have you seen Matt?'

Mum gazes at her, eyes unfocused, and Kate wonders if she's having one of her memory lapses before she shakes her head, 'sorry,' and Kate hurries back out of the door with a 'see you at the school later' and a wave.

The mists envelop her as she walks briskly around the edge

of the farm, head down, hands stuffed into pockets, sticking close to the hedges. She'd walked rather than driven to clear her head but now she wishes she were in her car, driving around their land to reach her cosy cottage, which is impossible to make out in these atrocious conditions but muscle memory and the sound of the water guides her towards it. The wind whips her hair around her face. She's pushing against it as she turns a sharp left, now walking parallel to the river. She shudders at the sound of the water angrily bashing itself against the rocks.

She hates that river.

Hates it.

Somewhere in the gloom is the bridge where she, Beth and her friend Nicola used to play pooh sticks. Before . . .

She reaches her cottage. Matt's ancient Land Rover isn't parked in their courtyard next to her car.

Back in the warmth of her kitchen, the age-battered pine table is still laden with breakfast things. Egg yolk dried onto plates, and she was sure she'd left a sausage.

Twix gazes at her with guilty eyes.

'I don't blame you for giving in to temptation.' Everyone does sometimes, don't they? She scratches him behind his ears and his tail wags, swishing against the flagstone floor.

She clears away a bowl containing a few stray Rice Krispies, soft in a puddle of milk. At fifteen, Kate's daughter is always in too much of a hurry to wait for the bacon to fry, the tomatoes to grill.

Thoughts of Caily drive her to grab a pen and notepad and scribble a note for Matt.

Taken the costumes to Beth's. Meet you at the school at 7.30. Don't forget to pick up Mum and Dad on your way x

She refills Twix's water bowl and promises him another walk before bed and then hurries back out into the cold, climbing into her rusting Ford Fiesta, which splutters before the engine turns over and it grumbles to life.

The headlights of the car illuminate, rather than cut through, the thick soupy fog, the grey whirling mass like ghosts from the past tap-tap-tapping on the windscreen – *let me in, let me in.*

Kate crawls down the rutted track, onto the lane that encompasses the perimeter of the farm, knowing that when she gets into the village the fog will likely disappear as though it was never there at all.

She passes the main entrance to the farm. There's a Range Rover parked on the verge. She hesitates. It's unusual to see a car out here. Since the bypass was built, this road is infinitely quieter than it used to be. She thinks she's seen it here before and wonders whether she should ask what they are looking for.

Who they are looking for.

She tries to make out the driver but can't and the thought of someone staring back at her makes her shiver.

As she waits to turn right, the school bus trundles past. Normally Caily would be on it but this afternoon she has stayed behind for one last rehearsal before tonight's performance.

While she thinks of it she punches out a good-luck text. **Break a leg!** She adds an **I love you** before deleting this last part. Caily thinks Kate is too slushy, doesn't like it when she fusses and she's already horribly stressed about the musical later that evening.

She shouldn't be, she'll be great. She always is.

A warm glow of happiness massages the knots in Kate's shoulders at the thought of seeing her daughter on the stage again, in the pre-Christmas production of *La La Land*.

It is going to be the perfect, perfect evening, or so Kate thinks.

Kate had nipped into town to use the cashpoint because the school is likely to be passing a bucket around for donations for something later. Now, she stamps her freezing feet, breath billowing in front of her. Beth's front door remains unanswered. Her car isn't on the drive but it could be in the garage.

Footsteps on the path behind her cause her to swing around.

It's Beth; her twin's face, identical to her own, looks flustered. 'I wasn't expecting you yet.' Her hair is damp, cheeks pink. She adjusts the tote bag on her shoulder. 'I've just been to the shops. We were out of biscuits, imagine that.'

'I'd rather not, I need my sugar fix to soak up the gin that's still in my system. I came early because I didn't want to rush in this weather. Besides, thought I'd give you plenty of warning that I'm staying for dinner.' Kate kisses her sister on the cheek. 'Is that okay? The weather's so vile I'd rather not drive home only to come back this way again later.'

'You don't need an invitation,' Beth says.

'Good job. I never bloody get one lately,' Kate smiles as she shrugs her coat off and hangs it on the brass hooks by the front door, before following Beth into the kitchen.

Beth's home is everything that Kate's is not. Light and modern. White walls and clean lines.

Rented.

Sometimes Kate feels a twist of guilt that their parents let her and Matt live in the cottage on the edge of the farmland while Beth still hasn't taken that first step onto the property ladder, but her sister has no interest in working the farm permanently, although she helps out when she can. She was always the wild one, the yin to Kate's yang, but that's why they're so close. Kate is calming and Beth encourages her sister to take risks. They balance each other out.

'You look as rough as I feel.' Kate watches Beth fill the kettle, noticing the tremor in her hand. The lack of colour in her cheeks.

'I wish Mum had waited until the weekend for the party. The poor girls having to perform tonight,' Beth says.

'You know she likes to celebrate things *on the day*. Besides, it wasn't too late a night and they've bags of energy at fifteen. It's not as though they touched the alcohol either, lucky them. I shouldn't have mixed my drinks. Gin, fizzy wine and what *was* in the punch?'

'It'd be easier to list what wasn't.' Beth pulls a face, leaning back against the worktop, waiting for the water to boil.

'No wonder my memory is murky.'

'Yeah, when I saw you knocking them back, at first I was afraid.' Beth covers her heart dramatically. 'I was petrified.'

'Oh stop it. Karaoke is not my friend.'

'Speaking of friends—'

'Nicola.'

'Nicola. Guess Mum invited her as a surprise?'

'It was certainly that. Never thought we'd see her again, did you?'

'No,' Beth says. 'It seems like another lifetime ago that we'd all hang out together, doesn't it? Me and Sean, you and Owen. Nicola and Aaron.'

Three couples and none of them had stood the test of time.

They fall silent for a minute.

'Let's have a look at these costumes, then,' Beth says, a little too brightly.

Kate unzips the storage bag and is flooded with a warm glow of pride as Beth sharply inhales.

'You've done an amazing job.' Beth fingers the iridescent pearls and shimmering sequins that Kate had painstakingly stitched onto Tegan's costume, while Kate hangs up Caily's bright-yellow dress on the back of the kitchen door. It is the second one she's made, because of what happened to the first dress, but she doesn't want to think about that today. It's horrible and everything is fine for Caily now.

Isn't it?

'Sorry it took so long. I'd hoped Tegan would have hers before the dress rehearsal but you know how busy this time of year is on the farm.'

'Is there ever a quiet time?' Beth places a cup of steaming coffee in front of Kate, pushing aside a pile of post. A letter flutters to the floor. Kate picks it up, noticing the red 'Final Demand' from the landlord.

'Beth?' she asks tentatively. She knows things have been tough for her sister since she lost her job last year but Beth had told her she had savings to fall back on, and there are benefits she was entitled to. She doesn't get any financial support from Sean, her ex.

'It's fine.' Beth plucks the letter from Kate's hands. 'It's all under control. Anyway, you never know,' she says lightly, 'Caily might have the lead but Tegan might be the one scouted tonight and on her way to fame and fortune and then she'll be able to keep me in the manner in which I'd like to become accustomed.'

The school isn't a performing arts academy but West End sensation Eloise Parks had once been a pupil and the school, eager to take credit for her success, staged more than their fair share of productions. Many of the kids aspire to follow in Eloise's footsteps, Caily and Tegan included. Eloise, when between roles, often returns to the area to spend time with her parents and if it coincides with a school performance she goes along to watch. Tonight is even more special, with Eloise actively seeking out talent to nurture. What will be Caily's last dance at this school could be the beginning of a career.

'Ha. Eloise might take them both.' Kate keeps her tone equally light. 'Imagine the peace and quiet if she did.' She cups her hands around her mug, blowing steam from the top of her drink before she looks around the kitchen. 'Where are these biscuits you've just bought, then?'

'Let's not spoil dinner.'

'But I'm so hungry. Okay, okay,' Kate says as Beth raises her eyebrows. 'I'll wait if I have to.' She grabs the salt pot from the centre of the table and holds it in front of her mouth like a microphone. 'I will survive.' She shoulder bops as she sings.

Beth's mobile rings, vibrating across the table. She answers it and then mouths, 'It's Miss West.' Kate rolls her eyes, wondering what Caily and Tegan's drama teacher is complaining about this time. The kids didn't nickname her 'Wicked Witch'

22

for nothing. But Beth, rather than grinning at her in return, looks serious, her eyes full of concern.

'She's checking everything's okay for tonight because the girls didn't turn up to the final rehearsal,' she says when she's rung off. 'They did as much of a run-through as they could without them but it must have been a shambles without one of the leads and the understudy.'

'But they must have been there . . .' Kate trails off. The show is so important to them both, it doesn't make sense.

Then there's the sound of the front door opening, slamming shut. Shoes being kicked off onto the mat.

The sisters rush into the hallway.

Tegan's face is tear-stained, cheeks blotchy, eyes swollen.

Beth draws a breath but, before she can speak, it is Kate's phone that rings.

She's expecting the same call from the same teacher but it isn't the school.

It's the police.

CHAPTER THREE

Beth

'It's the police,' mouths Kate.

Beth's stomach flip-flops as she watches her sister pace, agitated, palm against her forehead. Whatever the person on the other end of the line is saying, Beth knows it's bad.

Very bad.

Because of the deep bond between them, sometimes Beth thinks she feels what Kate feels. A memory of that night all those years ago slams into her. She remembers suddenly being unable to breathe, lungs burning as she tried to suck in air. Experiencing all the things her sister was experiencing. Again, Beth feels that same tightness in her chest, a constriction in her throat. She stands behind Tegan, resting her hands on her daughter's shoulders, reassuring herself that she is here.

She is safe.

But where is Caily?

Tegan tries to bolt for the stairs but Beth tightens her grip.

'What is it? Is it Caily?' Beth asks in a low voice, not really wanting to disturb Kate but desperate for some clarification.

She is aware that it is two hours since school finished, neither of the girls had showed up for rehearsal and now Tegan is here, crying.

Briefly, Kate's eyes meet hers but she doesn't answer. Beth's mind hops. 'Is it Mum and Dad?' Their parents haven't been in the best of health lately: Dad had an accident a couple of years ago that led to his leg being amputated. It was around the time that Mum was first diagnosed with cognitive impairment. A shock to them all. Oh god, has she got confused and wandered into town in her nightie or left the gas on or something? She is definitely getting worse.

'What's wrong?' Beth asks again, urgently. Not knowing what the police are saying causes a cold wash of fear to drench her and she feels the physicality of it so keenly she grapples to even out her breathing.

'Matt?' Beth tries again: the machinery at the farmyard can be lethal. Look at what happened to Dad.

Rather than answering, Kate's hand drops to her side, still tightly clutching her mobile. As though the bones in her legs have been suddenly whipped away, she sinks to the floor, crouching, head on her knees.

Beth kneels next to her twin, wrapping her in arms that tremble.

For a few moments Kate clings to her but then she's pushing her away, staggering to her feet.

Beth rises too, taking Kate's hands in hers, angling her head until their eyes meet. Kate's are wide, full of panic.

'There's been an accident.' Her words are thick. She licks her lips. 'Caily.'

That one word causes Beth to instinctively squeeze Kate's fingers three times.

'Where is she?' Beth asks gently.

'At the hospital. She was found . . . she was by the river. Under the bridge. She'd fallen.'

'But she's all right? The bridge isn't very high.' Beth envisages shock, perhaps, at the worst a broken limb. She remembers as kids that Aaron would run and jump off it into the water, drenching them. Sean would sometimes follow but Beth never did. Her parents had raised her to respect nature, not just the things you could see but the weather, the currents.

'Apparently it isn't the height she fell from but the way she landed, near the bank, directly onto the rocks. What was she doing there? She was supposed to be at rehearsal.' Her frightened eyes land on Tegan. 'You were *both* supposed to be at rehearsal.'

'Is she . . . is she dead?' Tegan whispers.

'No. She's unconscious, though.'

'But she'll wake up soon?' Tegan asks.

'Of course she will,' Kate says firmly as though saying it will make it true. 'I don't understand, though. She should have been at school.' She repeats herself but doesn't wait for an answer, an explanation. Instead she hurries into the kitchen and scoops up her bag, fishes out her car keys.

'I've got to go and—'

'You're not driving in this state.' Beth plucks her keyring from her hand. It's a clear photo holder and on one side there's a photo of her and Beth as children, identical faces beaming at the camera. The other side is one of Caily and Tegan at their first performance. They must have been around six. Tegan had been in tears and Beth had longed to rush onto the stage to whisk her daughter away from the scrutiny but Caily had held her cousin's hand tightly, never letting go as they began to dance, until a smile had spread over Tegan's face. At the end of the number they had both taken dramatic bows instead of the delicate curtsy they'd been taught, bending deeply at the waist, blonde hair loosened from tight buns, tendrils of hair framing heart-shaped faces, beaming smiles brighter than the spotlight. They were both so similar, are still so similar, but now Tegan is here, healthy, and Caily is lying in a hospital bed with goodness knows what wrong with her.

Beth feels sick at the thought. 'I'm going to fetch my bag and coat. Sit down for a minute. Do you want to call Matt?' Kate nods, numb, but then stares at her handset as though she's never seen one before.

'It's okay. I can phone him from the hospital,' Beth reassures her as she runs towards the stairs, thundering up them two at a time. Her mind full of the people they need to inform – her parents for one, the school – but she doesn't quite know what to tell anyone yet.

She passes Tegan's bedroom. Her daughter has come upstairs and is sitting on the edge of her bed, turning her first-ever ballet shoes over in her hand. The pale-pink satin is scuffed at the toe. The ribbons, a deeper hue, trail over Tegan's wrists. They're so small, so light.

Fragile.

Tegan carries hers for luck, the same as Caily.

They hadn't brought Caily luck today.

Kate might be waiting downstairs but Tegan needs her. Growing up, Kate might always have come first, timid, fragile, whereas Beth was louder, braver. Reckless. But now Beth is a mother, her priorities have shifted.

'Tegan.' Beth crouches before her, places her hands on her daughter's knees. 'Do you want to come to the hospital with me?'

Tegan shakes her head, her eyes are dry. 'No. I've got to get back to school.'

'School?'

'The show.' Tegan's expression is blank.

'I don't know if it will go ahead now. With Caily—'

'But I'm the understudy.'

'Tegan,' Beth says gently. Her daughter is in shock. 'Do you feel up to it? Caily is hurt.'

'But Aunt Kate said Caily will be okay?'

Beth takes a second. 'We . . . we hope she will but we just don't know how serious it is at this stage.'

'So it might be . . . bad?' Tegan whispers.

'We just don't know.' It's an inadequate answer but the only one Beth has.

Tegan covers her face with her hands and begins to cry.

'What happened? Why weren't you at school?' Beth can't help asking, but Tegan buries her face into her neck the way she used to when she was small and wanted to hide.

Disappear.

Beth's hand doesn't feel like her own as she turns the key in the ignition. It takes three attempts before the car splutters to life but then the engine cuts out.

Not now.

Her car is old, unreliable, but she can't afford to replace it.

She'd told Kate her finances are under control but she has not been honest about how bad things have been, how desperate she has felt because debt is a lonely place to be. She feels ashamed that she hasn't quite got her life together since she became a single parent after Sean was sent to prison, seven long years ago. Sometimes she feels she's only just getting over the shock of it.

She's done the best she can. She loved her job running the café of her local theatre but they hadn't been able to afford to reopen after the third lockdown and she hasn't managed to find any work since then, despite applying for almost 220 jobs. She doesn't even get a reply for most of her applications.

She had thought the constant, gnawing worry about how to feed her child, how to keep a roof over their heads was as bad as it could get, but this, this situation with Caily is far worse. She glances at Kate, her sister's chest heaving with shallow breaths.

She twists the key again. This time the car starts and she quickly pulls away.

During the drive Kate has periods of silence where she stares blankly out of the window, chewing on her thumbnail, peppered with bouts of frenzied questions about what might have happened to Caily. Why she might have skipped rehearsals.

Beth tells her that she is as much in the dark as Kate, and this placates her for a while until the endless speculation begins again. It's a relief when they reach the hospital, Kate opening the car door before Beth has properly parked.

She's close behind her sister, hesitating as she passes a parking ticket machine, knowing she cannot afford a fine if she doesn't pay but also knowing she doesn't have the £4 in change and if she tries to pay on her phone the transaction will probably be refused due to lack of funds. Her overdraft at its limit.

It is hot inside. Stuffy. The smell of chemicals is cloying. They run, paces perfectly matched, through the corridors with pale grey walls and a darker grey vinyl floor. Beth catches glimpses through the windows of the car park.

Black tarmac and concrete bollards.

Already, the world has lost its colour.

Kate stumbles, Beth grabs her hand, transported back in time to when they'd race around the park in the matching dresses they had insisted on. Their mother had wanted them to have some individuality, but Kate always preferred to look the same as Beth, have the same things as Beth, adoring her big sister even though she was only older by twelve minutes. Relying on her again, now.

Inside their small local hospital they are told that Caily hasn't regained consciousness and is having tests, they can't see her yet. The relatives' room is occupied so would they mind waiting in the corridor?

'What sort of tests?' Beth is the one to ask because beside her, Kate is shaking so hard she can hear the rattle of her teeth. She guides her sister to a chair so Kate can sit before she falls.

The nurse gives a sympathetic smile. 'Don't worry. She's in good hands. The doctor will talk to you as soon as he can.'

As she turns away Kate grabs her wrist and says, 'Please don't let her die.'

The nurse gently uncurls Kate's fingers: 'She's in good hands,' she says again and then they are left – porters streaming past them pushing wheelchairs, visitors hurrying towards wards, the odd patient in a dressing gown, clutching cigarettes and a lighter – feeling completely alone.

Beth rings Matt on her ancient Motorola pay-as-you-go. From under the cracked screen a photo illuminates, the selfie he'd tried to take of him and Kate, Twix pushing in front of them both, nose close to the camera, pink tongue lolling out of his mouth. It looked like Twix was laughing and it usually made Beth smile.

Not today.

Matt picks up straight away, and she tells him where they are. 'I'm on my way,' he says. He sounds breathless as he asks her questions she cannot answer, as though he's already running towards his car, but perhaps it is pure terror squeezing the air from his lungs the way it is from hers.

'Shall I tell Mum and Dad?' she asks Kate, who nods and then shakes her head before shrugging. Beth hesitates for a moment before making the call.

Mum bursts into tears before Beth has finished speaking, crying so hard she cannot speak. Dad takes the phone and asks a million questions in a stricken voice that Beth cannot answer. In the background, Mum is distraught. 'Tell Kate I'm so sorry,' she says. 'Tell her to be strong.'

'She *is* strong,' Dad says. He sounds weak, old, frail. She had once thought her parents were invincible but now she knows no one is indestructible. Dad's disability and the deterioration of her mum's memory have diminished them, aged them. They are only in their sixties and it seems too young for the health challenges they've faced, but then Caily's only fifteen. Sometimes life isn't fair, is it?

Beth berates herself for relaying the news over the phone. She's rushing because she knows she is almost out of credit, not giving her parents time to process the news. She cannot imagine the shock of learning your grandchild is unconscious, seriously ill; it defies the natural order of things, doesn't it?

Stop it.

Caily isn't dead.

When she's reiterated to her parents that they are better off waiting at home until they can see Caily, she explains to the nurse about the performance and asks her if she wouldn't mind notifying the school that Caily has had an accident and neither she nor Tegan will make it in, and then she sits next to Kate.

'The people in the relatives' room—'

'Don't.' Beth cannot bear to think of the news that is being relayed. She takes Kate's hand and squeezes it three times and then they sit, in silence.

Beth is reading the group text that she has received from the school – 'Due to unforeseen circumstances tonight's performance of *La La Land* is cancelled' – when Matt rushes towards them.

'Where is she?' He looks up and down the corridor as though Caily might materialize.

'She's still having tests,' Kate reaches out her hand towards him but he doesn't notice.

'Still?'

'Do you think that's good or bad?' Kate wrings her hands together on her lap while Matt paces.

And paces.

And paces.

32

It is several hours later when Dr Rogers stands before them, looking as exhausted as Beth feels. He's positioned in front of the window; behind the glass the moon casts a silver glow upon him, giving the impression that he is heavenly. Almost as though he can save Caily if he chooses to do so.

Has he saved her?

'Caily is in a coma. She sustained a head injury—'

'Is she brain damaged?' Matt asks at the exact same time as Kate questions, 'When will she wake up?'

'We're not sure but the CAT scan and MRI haven't shown any reason why she won't wake up but I'm afraid I can't guarantee anything. It's frustrating with comas that we can only make a best guess based on experience but there is no definitive answer. It's a matter of waiting. The scan has shown some swelling, although that's not uncommon with a fall. There isn't any bleeding, so that's encouraging. There's no need for neurosurgery right now.' He pauses. 'Caily also has a broken arm and a fractured pelvis.'

Beth covers her mouth with her hands. Beside her, Kate whimpers.

'We've set the arm, the pelvis we're leaving alone for now. We'll be keeping a close eye on Caily but leaving her sedated to give the brain a chance to recover.'

'But . . .' Kate falters.

'She'll be all right, won't she?' Beth finishes the sentence her twin began.

'We'll do our absolute best.'

'Can we see her now?' Matt asks.

'Of course. I'll leave you with Nita.' A smiling nurse steps forward and Dr Rogers hurries away, checking his watch as he leaves.

'It's two visitors only, I'm afraid,' Nita says.

'But—'

'It's okay.' Beth cuts Kate off. 'I should get back to Tegan anyway. It's so late.' She is exhausted both mentally and physically.

'Why don't you say a quick hello to Caily first,' Matt offers kindly. 'You've waited all this time.'

'Thanks.' Beth is both grateful and nervous.

At the ICU the nurse prepares them for the sight that awaits them but Kate is impatient, rubbing antibacterial gel into her hands, tying on a plastic apron she's been given to help prevent infection: she's halfway through the door before the nurse has finished talking, Beth right behind her.

Kate's knees buckle at the first glimpse of Caily looking so small, so pale, eyes closed as though she could be sleeping but the machines in the room, the tubes and wires, don't let them forget for a single second that this is not a sleep.

They don't know if she'll ever wake.

Beth supports her sister around the waist, feels a violent juddering. She isn't sure whether it's emanating from Kate or from her.

'Breathe,' she whispers, reminding Kate, reminding herself.

They inch closer to the bed, Kate fumbling for Beth's hand, her other stretching out to touch Caily lightly on the cheek, the arm, the hand, reassuring herself that she is solid, here.

'Beth?' Kate utters one word. It's a question and in return Beth squeezes Kate's fingers three times – you are not alone.

She doesn't offer reassurances that Caily will be okay because she does not know that. She doesn't say anything because when they were small the girls had made a pact to always be honest with each other and, although there are things Beth has kept secret from her sister, particularly recently, she has never looked her directly in the eye and lied to her face.

Until today.

CHAPTER FOUR

Kate

Until today Kate has never known her daughter so still, so silent. Even in sleep she is always moving, rolling from one side to another, elbows drawn into her chest, hands clenched into fists. It's the way she'd always lie in her cot as a baby, the position she kept as she grew.

But now there is no shuffling of covers, no soft sighs. She's deathly quiet. Kate berates herself for joking earlier that she wished Eloise would whisk Caily away to the West End. Teasing that she'd love the peace and quiet.

She didn't . . . doesn't want . . . *this*.

Caily is flat on her back. Electrodes hooked up to her chest. Breathing tube coming from her mouth. A catheter snaking out from under the thin sheet. Something for goodness knows what taped to the back of her hand. She's wearing a pale-green hospital gown, nothing like the bright eye-catching outfits she favours. She'd hate it. She was always so full of colour, Caily.

So full of life.

Is.

Is full of life.

Nita runs through the equipment. Explaining the numbers showing on the monitors for Caily's oxygen levels, blood pressure and heart rate. Kate watches these figures in bold black letters with no idea if they are good or bad.

Normal.

With no idea what normal even is anymore.

'An alarm will sound if there's an emergency,' Nita explains. Kate doesn't ask what kind of emergency. She knows from Nita's low voice, from the sympathy in her eyes that she's referring to if Caily should stop breathing. If her heart should fail. 'She'll get lots of attention; we've only got four beds here, we're such a small hospital, any cases we feel may require urgent neurosurgery are transferred to Lakeside. They have over thirty beds in their ICU and that wasn't even enough during the height of the pandemic.'

Kate cannot imagine thirty beds. Thirty worried families. She glances around. There's an elderly man in the bed in the corner but the other two are empty. She doesn't know whether that is reassuring or terrifying. Whether the previous occupants have disappeared or . . .

'Kate,' she feels Nita's soft touch on her arm. Realizes she is swaying on her feet. 'Would you like to come outside and have a cup of sweet tea? You can't eat or drink in here because of the risk of infection.'

'I don't want anything,' Kate says, not needing anything in this moment except for Caily to sit up, roll her eyes and tell Kate she's making a fuss over nothing again. 'I'm okay.' She sits heavily on a chair.

Beth approaches the bed, leans over and whispers something in Caily's ear before kissing her gently on the forehead.

When she straightens up, she is crying and Kate feels her own tears welling again.

'You know where I am if you need me, Kate,' Beth says as she heads towards the door, and Kate feels a swell of panic. She fights the urge to grab Beth and tell her that she needs her here, now, but that wouldn't be fair. Matt is Caily's father and should be here, even if he can't calm Kate in the same way that Beth can.

Beth slips out of the door and Kate watches her sister through the glass as she says something to Matt before they hug. Sometimes it feels strange, watching her husband with her twin, the mirror image of her, seeing what her and Matt must look like together for other people. She wonders if Matt ever finds it uncomfortable, looking at someone who is so like his wife but not. Whether he understands that although he should be Kate's other half, he isn't. Although she loves him deeply, Beth will always be her missing part the way she is for Beth.

He enters the room. Not with his usual confidence and speed but slowly, hesitantly.

Nita shows them both how best to touch Caily without dislodging any of the equipment.

Sitting either side of the bed on matching hard, blue chairs, Matt takes one of her hands, Kate the other. Matt raises his eyes to Kate's, draws a breath as though to speak but instead gives a sad, sorry shake of his head as though apologizing for the inadequate words that rest on his tongue.

'Patients under sedation sometimes recall conversations that have happened around them once they wake up,' Nita says. 'So do talk to Caily. Is there anything you'd like to ask me?'

Kate says no. She has so many questions, so many worries,

but she doesn't want to voice them here, now, in case Caily can hear.

'I'm going to be sitting on that stool by the door for the rest of my shift,' Nita says. 'There will be a member of staff in the ICU all the time.'

'What if you leave to go to the toilet?' Kate finds the thought of being alone in this unit terrifying.

'Then someone should come in and cover.'

'But what if there isn't anyone free? I've read about how short-staffed the NHS—'

'It isn't something you should worry about, but we're only human. On the very rare occasion the nurse on duty is momentarily absent for any reason, there is an alarm you can press. Look.' She shows them a button. 'If you have any concerns. If there's any change in Caily's condition do press it. Okay?' she asks gently.

'Yes.'

'And, as I've said, if Caily needs urgent attention the machines will sound. There's a whole team ready. Okay?'

Kate nods and Nita heads back towards the door and settles herself on the stool, studying a screen in front of her intently. The silence is deathly. Kate's palms are sweating. She lets go of Caily's hand to wipe her own on her jeans, forgetting about the apron she is wearing, jumping as her skin touches the warm plastic.

Kate swallows hard.

'Sweetheart,' she whispers. 'Please wake up.' She's not sure why she's keeping her voice so low. Whether it's ridiculously so she doesn't disturb the man in the other bed or because she's self-conscious pleading for her daughter to defy the

39

doctors in the presence of Nita. But even though Caily is sedated, there's a chance Caily could come around, isn't there? Her daughter is young, strong.

She glances at Matt. He looks at her helplessly so she tries again, keeping her voice bright and breezy this time, speaking of things that might seem inconsequential but are important to Caily. Twix, who will be waiting for her to come home, head on his paws, sorrowful eyes trained on the door, wondering where everyone is.

'The minute you get home he'll bring Duck to you, wanting to play tug of war.' Twix's favourite toy is little more than a scrap of material nowadays, having long since lost its stuffing and, thankfully, its squeaker, but he adores it.

She promises to hang up the bright-yellow dress Caily was to have worn as Mia so it won't crease and then she pauses. A hard lump swelling in her throat. Will Caily ever dance again? Does a broken pelvis mean broken dreams? She should have clarified this with the doctor but it hadn't seemed important then but now it feels imperative that Caily has something to wake up for. Some hope.

Eventually there is nothing left to say.

She and Matt sit in silence, not a companionable one but one that is heavy with fear, both jumping when the door creaks open, so lost in their own thoughts.

It's Owen.

Kate's heart still lifts at the sight of her first boyfriend, first love, but of course he's not here to comfort her, but in a professional capacity. Sometimes she can't believe the boy with whom she shared her first taste of alcohol, aged fifteen in the local park, is now in the police force, an inspector.

He speaks briefly to Nita before he approaches Caily's bed.

'Kate.' He kisses her cheek. 'Matt. I'm so sorry.' He clears his throat. 'Sorry I wasn't here when you arrived.' Owen's job is to remain detached but his voice is thick with regret because he cares for Caily. He cares for them all.

'It's okay. You're here now.' Kate is grateful. With his high ranking, she doubts informing families of accidents is something he'd usually do. 'Do you have Caily's things? Her school bag?' Kate hadn't thought of this before. Hadn't thought to ask the policewoman who telephoned her with the news any questions.

'We've recovered her rucksack. There were only a few books in it.'

'What about her phone?' On it would be the last text Kate sent her daughter – **break a leg** – how she wishes she'd added the **I love you**. If there's one last thing her daughter had to hear, she wants it to be that. Would the confirmation that she was loved have brought her any comfort as she toppled from the bridge, crashed onto the rocks on the riverbank below? Kate hopes her fall was too sudden to register. That she wasn't scared.

Stop it.

Kate straightens her spine from the defeated curve it has settled in. Caily is alive, here. She strokes the back of her daughter's hand with her thumb. She won't give up hope.

'Her handset was on the bridge.' Owen says. 'Someone had used it to call an ambulance.'

'Who?'

'We don't know. We're trying to trace them.'

'Wouldn't her phone have been locked?' But even as she

asks this, Kate knows it likely wouldn't have been because her daughter would probably have been glued to it as she usually was. Is that why she fell? 'She must have been using it.' She answers her own question.

'And they *left her*? This person?' Matt says with contempt.

'Yes.'

Kate feels a tightening in her stomach, how could anyone be so callous? Had Caily been conscious then? Alone and frightened. What had she been thinking as she'd tumbled from the bridge? About her family? The performance she'd give later that night? How had she lost her balance anyway? She'd crossed that bridge near the cottage a hundred times. A thousand.

The fog.

She must have been running and had skidded. The wooden planks were old, covered in moss, lethal when damp, and the bloody railings were broken. Matt had asked Travis to fix them but Kate had said she'd report it to the council, Travis had enough to do and strictly speaking, although the river bordered the farm and their cottage was next to it, it wasn't their land. But she had never reported it. It had slipped her mind. If she had made one simple phone call they might not be here right now. Is this all her fault?

'Her coat was on the bridge,' Owen says. 'We think she was probably carrying it rather than wearing it.'

'But it was freezing.' Kate shivers with the thought. 'Although I guess she'd only just have got off the warm bus.' Neither Caily or Tegan seemed to feel the cold with their short sleeves and cropped tops. Neither of them ever stood still long enough to. There's a crack in Kate's voice as she asks, 'Do you have her ballet shoes?'

The soft, small, ballet shoes Caily had worn for her first-ever performance all those years ago with Tegan had become a good-luck charm. Kate had watched her pack them in her bag only that morning so that she would have them with her during *La La Land* later that evening.

'No. There weren't any ballet shoes.'

Kate feels her face fall and knows Owen must have seen it because he says, 'I can ask someone to take another look. We've cordoned off the area under the bridge. I take it she was on her way home?'

'I guess so but she shouldn't have been. She was supposed to have been at school for the final rehearsal. She's the lead in the musical. Was.'

Kate can't figure out her tenses.

'The thing is,' Owen pauses. 'There is some bruising to the top of Caily's arms consistent with being grabbed with some force. There's also the position she was found in. Flat on her back, on the bank. Her clothes were sopping wet though, so she had been in the river. It's doubtful she would have been able to crawl out with the injuries to her arm and pelvis, and there weren't the scratches to her palms that you might expect if she'd dragged herself over the rocks. I've asked for some samples to be taken.'

'Samples?'

'Scrapings from under the fingernails, that sort of thing. Anything that might provide some DNA.'

'Why do you . . . What exactly are you saying?' Kate can

hardly bear to think it, to say it. 'You don't think someone . . . touched her.'

'We don't believe she was sexually assaulted,' Owen clarifies quickly. 'But I'm saying . . .' He runs a hand over his stubble. 'I'm saying that I, we, don't think this was an accident. There's a strong possibility that someone deliberately hurt Caily. We think she was pushed.'

CHAPTER FIVE

Matt

It was as though Matt had been pushed, physically stumbling when Owen voiced his suspicions that Caily's fall hadn't been an accident. Then he felt a flash of temper. He has a poker-hot rage that rises quickly nowadays, almost coming out of nowhere.

He stalks after Owen into the corridor, aware of Kate's worried eyes on him, his fist tightly clenched, knowing that he is directing his anger towards the wrong person but unable to help it anyway.

It's not as though he has ever got on with Owen, not really. Kate had ended things with her first boyfriend when she had met Matt and, although it was all amicable on the surface, Matt had experienced months of hostile looks. Then, for Kate's sake, they had fallen into, not friendship but civility, and over the years when their paths had crossed, as they often do, they greet each other with a smile, a handshake that is just a little bit too firm.

And now Owen is what exactly? The knight on a fucking white horse who can uncover what happened to his daughter? It's his job as a father to protect Caily.

His.

He shouldn't feel so woefully inadequate but he does.

'What now?' He squares up to Owen, asking more aggressively than he should but he's tired. Helpless.

Hopeless.

'As I said a moment ago, we'll be making enquiries.' Owen is polite, guarded. Professional.

'But what does that mean?' Matt hears the hint of despair in his words, hates himself for it. If ever he needed to be strong for his family, it is now.

He'd thought being a parent of a baby was terrifying, the never knowing what she wanted when she cried, frightened of dropping her, scared she'd never sleep through the night, petrified when she finally did that she wouldn't wake up. Frequently standing over her cot, watching the reassuring rise and fall of her chest. But as Caily passed through the stages of childhood, Matt realized that each age had its own challenges.

Perhaps the teenage years the worst of all.

Never being certain where Caily is, who she's with after she's breezed out of the door in a cloud of perfume with a promise to be home by curfew and a bright 'Don't worry, I'm old enough to look after myself.' But Matt did worry. Although at forty-two he isn't old, it's a different world to the one he grew up in. Every time he hears of a teenager being stabbed on the news his blood runs cold. How do the parents cope? But now Caily has been the victim of a crime and it gnaws at him that he can't remember the last time he hugged her. Can't remember the last time he told her that he loved her. Sometimes he barely sees her with the unsociable hours farming pins him to, and it's almost as though she's grown up overnight. Not needing him in the same way. Not running to him in her pyjamas – Daddy, Daddy – bare feet speeding across the carpet as she hurled herself into his arms because there was a 'monster' in her room. Covering his cheek in kisses after he'd evicted yet another large moth, wings trembling as he'd gently ushered it out of the window.

'Matt.' Owen brings him back to now and Matt can see genuine sympathy in his eyes. 'I can promise you. I'll get to the bottom of this.'

He walks away. Matt's jaw clenches. What promises had Owen made his wife once upon a time before she shattered his seventeen-year-old heart?

And then Matt thinks of the promises he has made Kate. The type of husband he has turned out to be, and he knows she deserves better than both of them.

He slumps against the wall, waiting for his breath to slow, his legs to stop shaking before he can go back into the room and face his wife, his daughter, his sense of his own failing.

It is the small hours before Matt stumbles from the hospital. Caily's accident has changed the earth beneath his feet and he doesn't feel he'll ever regain his footing. The air is frigid, a slap to the senses, his breath billowing in front of him as he unlocks his car. He starts the engine and then allows himself a moment to rest his forehead against the steering wheel and let the tears roll unchecked down his cheeks. It's a wrench to leave Caily but farming waits for no man. He needs to check the pregnant ewes and feed them as well and make sure Mary did close the hen houses as she'd promised so the foxes haven't savaged them. He phoned and asked her but she was so flustered, so upset, he's not sure that his request sank in. Bit late now, he supposes, if she hasn't, but it will put an additional strain on the farm, on his shoulders, if anything has happened to his hens. He's already lost half of his brood early in the year and hasn't been able to afford to replace them.

He can't afford anything.

He's had to diversify because they can't rely solely on some healthy litters of lambs in the spring and the crop planting was such a disaster in the autumn. But although he was devastated about this several weeks ago, going out of his mind trying to figure out how the farm could possibly survive another year with a meagre income, it doesn't seem important right now.

Nothing is as important as Caily.

The moon is full and round. His headlights sweep the verges, which glisten with frost. It appears the whole world is swathed in silver.

Rather than driving around the other side of the farm to his cottage, he pulls up outside of the farmhouse, his headlights shining through the windows. He's not worried about waking his in-laws at this ungodly time, knowing that years of farming have programmed them to be early risers, but when Matt steps inside the Aga-warm kitchen, it doesn't seem like they've slept at all.

'Matt.' Mary steadies herself against the table as she stands before wrapping him in a hug. He holds on tightly to her, telling himself that he is comforting her when really it's the other way around. 'I'm so, so sorry. How is Caily? And Kate?' She steps back and looks into his eyes. Hers are swollen, rimmed red. 'And you?'

48

'Caily's in a coma.' The words fall from his tongue but they don't feel real. Despite the doctor's explanations, he doesn't think he fully understands the implications of this yet. 'Kate's bearing up. The nurse tried to persuade her to come home and get some rest but she wants to be there when Caily wakes.'

He says this because he can't bear to think of the alternative. Of Kate's fear she had voiced when he tried to persuade her to come home and get some sleep, that their daughter might slip away alone, no one holding her hand.

He slumps onto a seat and takes the mug of tea that Patrick pushes towards him. It's ridiculously strong and almost cold, the pot has probably been sitting for hours, but he's grateful for it.

'I need to be getting on,' he says, but Mary is already clattering pans, chopping mushrooms, sizzling bacon. Her response to every crisis is to fasten her apron and roll up her sleeves. Patrick's solution is to get out his tools and fix things.

He feels a rush of love for this couple who took him in as a farmhand at the tender age of nineteen when he was lost and alone following the death of his own parents.

His stomach rumbles. He hasn't eaten since yesterday's lunch.

'You'll be wanting a hand while Kate is out of action,' Patrick says. 'Can we take on a lad from the village?'

'Thank you but I should be okay.' Matt smiles at the old man. Even if they could afford someone, he doesn't have time to train them. 'I've got Travis. Let's see how we manage.'

But the truth is that he will not manage. Pure desperation flows through his veins whenever he thinks of the farm and what he needs to do to sustain it. Frequently he has chest pains. He has to stop what he's doing and cover his racing heart with his hand while he reassures himself that he is fine. That it has to be solely anxiety because there are so many people relying on him that he just doesn't have time to be ill.

He is not fine.

Farming was already tough enough before the last few years made everything a million times worse. They had to write off so many crops during the pandemic because of the overwhelming demand for haulage and the lack of drivers. Watching helplessly while the results of their back-breaking work spoiled was akin to watching money burn.

It wasn't only this, though. Thanks to Brexit, they had lost their seasonal workers and now their EU Basic Payment Scheme is being phased out. It's still not entirely clear how much money they'll get through the government's replacement schemes, or the complicated hoops they'll have to jump through to get it.

There are so many man-made challenges without throwing climate change into the mix. Changing rainfall patterns and soil conditions are becoming more apparent with every passing year.

Matt isn't the only farmer who feels discouraged and despairing, but mental health isn't something they discuss. Whether it's because farmers are supposed to be 'real men' who just get on with it or whether it's because they don't have the opportunity to talk about their feelings, Matt doesn't know. Besides, who would he talk to anyway? His family are realists, they've been farming for generations, but Matt still tries to shield them from just how bad things are. If he opens up he's scared he'll drown them all in a tidal wave of fear.

'I shut the chicken coop,' Mary says as she quickly pulls together his meal. Not hesitating to remember where things are kept or how to work them like she frequently does now. It's as though shock has filled her mind and she's on autopilot, her face pale and haunted, her hands operating almost of their own accord.

His breakfast appears in front of him and his stomach growls in appreciation. He forks beans into his mouth. Tries not to grimace when he realizes they are cold, Mary has forgotten to heat them.

'Lovely,' he says. He shares a look with Patrick who has also scooped beans into his mouth. A silent conversation.

Don't upset her.

I won't.

Soon he is mopping up the last of his egg yolk with thickly sliced bread.

'I'd better get off.' The legs of his chair scrape against the floor as he pushes it back. 'Thank you.' He leans to kiss Mary and shake Patrick's hand, knowing the old farmer isn't usually comfortable with physical displays of affection but Patrick bats his hand away and pulls him tightly into a hug.

'You'll all be okay.' Patrick claps him on the back before releasing him. Matt straightens up, wanting to feel those arms around him again. It has been so long since he was held by his own father and right now he needs to draw strength from wherever he can. But Mary has opened the back door and the cold air gusts in. With a final wave of his hand Matt hurries outside into the world, which suddenly feels enormous or perhaps it is he who is too small and insignificant.

His car bumps along the track, not to the farmhouse but skirting around the fields to the top-left corner of their land. He needs to see Travis.

He thinks back to when he last saw his farmhand at Kate's birthday party, the way they had argued. He needs to apologize.

Travis lives in the two-up, two-down cottage that Mary and Patrick had first given to Matt after he knocked on their door, battered suitcase in the boot of his car, looking for work and, he supposes, a refuge. His arrival had been timely; their full-time help had just resigned. It felt meant to be.

Kate had reminded him of this when it had been Travis rapping on the door last September. But it was remembering how he and Kate had fallen in love, in lust, the things they had got up to in the barn, that had made him hesitant about welcoming Travis in. Was he too young? Too good-looking? He had a teenage daughter and niece to think about.

Mary had invited Travis inside, poured him tea and cut a thick wedge of carrot cake and Matt knew the decision had been made.

The cottage is in darkness. Travis should be up by now. Matt bangs on the front door. The cold sucking the colour from his hand.

'Hello?' he shouts through the letterbox before stepping back and scanning each window in turn.

He strides around the perimeter. Cupping his hands and peering through each pane of glass. There's nothing, no one. No dancing flames in the empty fire grate, no early news on the TV.

Something isn't right.

Through the lounge window he can see the front door mat. Usually there are muddy wellies on the rack. Trainers. Boots. Now the space where Travis keeps his footwear is empty.

Matt experiences a sudden lurch in his stomach.

'Travis?' He runs back to the door and this time pushes the handle down, leaning his weight against it. It's always been stiff but now there's a creak, a loosening. It swings open.

'Travis?'

Matt calls his name as he dashes from room to room, all the while knowing it is fruitless.

Travis's things have gone.

So has he.

Matt is gripped by a fierce dread. How is he going to manage?

He should have been more understanding last night, not snapped at his farmhand, but it wasn't the time or the place for the discussion Travis wanted to have. It was his wife's fortieth birthday party, for Christ's sake. Wasn't he entitled to relax for once?

How is he going to manage, though?

He asks himself the same question over and over as he leans against the doorframe, hand against chest, breathing deeply through the stabbing pain until it subsides. Then he ignores the tiredness in his bones, the sting in his eyes as he begins his working day.

Before he nips home to let Twix out he'll collect the eggs. Supplying the local pubs and hotel is a small income but every penny helps.

When he approaches the chicken coops he sees them. His

beloved hens scattered over the ground, torn apart, crimson blood coating a scattering of feathers.

Mary can't have secured the hen houses.

He looks around for a fox but there is nothing to be seen. Still, he feels he's being watched.

CHAPTER SIX

Kate

She's being watched. Kate becomes aware of eyes on her as she wakes. Her body aching from sleeping in a chair, her neck cricked at an awkward angle. She is cold, stiff.

'Morning,' the nurse, one she hasn't seen before, whispers. 'I'm Tara. We're just changing shift.'

Kate stretches, trying to quash her rising disappointment that Caily still looks the same. A mass of tubes and wires and machines that are there to monitor, to reassure, but that, if she's honest, scare her.

Last night both Matt and Nita had tried to encourage Kate to go home and get some rest. There wasn't anywhere she could sleep at the small hospital but she had been unable to bear leaving Caily.

'I'll keep a close eye on Caily if you want to get some breakfast?'

Kate is desperate for a coffee, and she should probably have some toast or something, but she doesn't want to go to the canteen at the other side of the hospital and she cannot eat or drink in ICU.

The monitor beats are metronome-steady, reminding Kate of years past when she would sit at the piano, Caily fidgeting on her lap as she guided her daughter's chubby fingers over the keys. Caily never wanted to play, she wanted to dance and she would wriggle to the floor, where she'd leap and spin as Kate bashed out 'The Sun Will Come Out Tomorrow'.

Linking her fingers through Caily's now, she begins to sing in a soft voice about days that are grey and lonely and then of clearing away cobwebs and sorrow and, although her voice is thick with tears by the time she has reached the end, Caily hasn't stirred, so she begins the song again.

And again.

And again.

She switches to 'You Are My Sunshine', which brings back memories of her own mother singing it to her. She wishes she hadn't told her parents not to come. She needs them both.

'Please.' She draws Caily's hand to her mouth and kisses it. 'Please wake up.' Her tears drip-drip-drip onto Caily's skin and Kate gently dabs them with her sleeve the way she had at the tears Caily had shed when she was small and had fallen over and hurt herself. Then she would promise her wailing toddler that the Mr Bump plaster she'd smooth over grazed knees and elbows had magical properties.

Caily's eyes would widen and, after a few minutes, a cuddle and a bag of chocolate buttons, everything was right in her world once more.

Now Kate can't fix things but she makes another promise as she runs her finger lightly over the bruises on Caily's arm.

Her phone buzzes, a text from Owen.

Can I speak to you and Matt at ten o'clock. Either at your house or at the station

There isn't a question mark.

It isn't a question.

She hesitates, reluctant to leave Caily but knowing there is no private space where they can talk here. She replies they'll come to the station. It's only five minutes from the hospital.

Then she takes her daughter's hand again.

'I promise we are going to find out who hurt you,' she whispers to her daughter. 'And why.'

In this moment to know the truth is all Kate wants.

Because she does not yet know that it will tear her family apart.

Be careful what you wish for.

CHAPTER SEVEN

Caily

Three months ago

Caily wished that things didn't have to change. It was unsettling to think that today was the beginning of her final year at school. She'd have to decide whether she wanted to stay on and sit A levels, go to college or find an apprenticeship. So many decisions. She wasn't ready to adult yet. What she really wanted was a career on the stage but what were the chances of a girl from the middle of nowhere making it? Eloise Parks had, but perhaps she'd taken all the luck.

'You okay?'

Caily raised her head from the bowl of Rice Krispies she'd been spooning into her mouth and met her mother's worried eyes.

'Yeah, fine.' She wiped a dribble of milk from her chin with her sleeve. 'Was just thinking about whether I want to sit A levels next year. Go to uni.'

'No.' Her mum laughed as she wrapped her arms around Caily's neck, pressed her face against hers. She smelled of soap and home. Everything familiar. 'I won't let you leave.

You have to stay here with me for ever. Even if I have to tie you up.' Mum dropped a kiss on her cheek.

'Get off.' Caily wriggled free. Just because Mum didn't wear make-up didn't mean she had to ruin hers. 'I'm not staying here for the rest of my life,' she said, even though she kind of wanted to. She loved the cottage with its uneven stone floors and gurgling pipes and the thatched roof that sometimes leaked. And then there was Twix. As usual, he lay patiently at her feet, nose resting on his paws. She reached down and stroked his silky ears. He licked her hand.

Mum clattered the frying pan she'd used for Dad's bacon into the sink and Caily quickly stood, swinging her rucksack over her shoulder before she could be asked to wash up.

'See you at Grandma's after school?'

It wasn't really a question. Monday-night dinners had been a thing ever since she could remember.

'Yeah. Laters.'

'Wait.' Kate dashed over to Caily and smoothed her hair before pulling her into another hug. 'Have a good first day.'

'Mum.' Caily gently pushed her away. 'Stop being so slushy. I'm fifteen not five.' She noticed Mum's face fall so she relented and gave her a quick squeeze before hurrying out of the door. The bus was only twenty minutes away.

It was drizzly. Dull. She followed the river until she reached the bridge, smiling to herself as she did every morning, remembering how she and Tegan would scare themselves silly here when they were younger – *who's trip-trapping over my bridge* – squealing as they pelted across the slats, imagining a troll grabbing hold of their ankles, tripping them up.

She climbed the rickety wooden steps and crossed the

river before turning right towards the road, not left into the woods. It had been there, and only this summer, when she had tried her first taste of alcohol, her first cigarette. Sitting under the shade of a tree, the bark hard against her spine. The stolen vodka had burned her chest, the Marlboros stung the back of her throat.

'Why do people do this for fun?' Tegan, recovering from a bout of choking, had wiped the tears streaming down her cheeks.

'Dunno. No wonder it was hidden at the back of the kitchen cupboard,' Caily had said as she screwed the cap back on the bottle.

It was only a few minutes before she reached the lane, sloshing through newly formed puddles. Feet dripping water as she climbed aboard the school bus, almost losing her footing as the driver pulled away before she'd found somewhere to sit. She shook the rain from her hair and untangled the wires of her earbuds before losing herself in her favourite playlist until they reached Tegan's estate and her cousin swayed towards her down the aisle, using her hands to steady herself until she reached the back seat.

'I see you.' Tegan sat next to her. Her damp rucksack against Caily's legs.

'Saw you first,' Caily grinned. It was the way they'd always greeted each other ever since forever. Mum said it dated back to the days they'd toddle around Grandma and Grandad's house playing hide and seek. Whatever, it had stuck.

'What are you listening to?'

'An Andrew Lloyd Webber playlist.'

'You're so uncool,' Tegan said, waving at Billy who was making his way towards them, a feather boa draped around his neck.

Since joining their school three years ago, Billy had somehow fused with her and Tegan in a way that nobody else had ever been able to do, making them laugh until their stomach muscles hurt.

'I see you,' he sang, squeezing between them. If anyone else had tried to say that to them they'd have closed ranks, but Billy was different. Family almost.

'Saw you first,' Caily and Tegan chorused.

'What do you think?' Billy looked at each of them in turn. 'New school year, new image.'

'You look like you've fallen face-first into the cosmetic counter in Boots,' Tegan said, blunt in a way you can only be with your best friend.

'Boots? Honey, please. This is all MAC.' He made a 'v' with his hands and placed them under his chin, fluttering his eyelashes. 'You can't make a statement with cheap shit.'

'What's the statement? That you don't know how blending brushes work?' Tegan rubbed at a strip of blusher on his cheek until it softened. 'There. All gorgeous.'

'Is it too much?' Billy asked in a low voice, brow creased in question.

'Yeah. But you can totally carry it off,' Caily reassured. Billy might appear loud and confident but she knew that deep down he was insecure.

'Of course I can. I'm fucking gorgeous.'

Very deep down.

'But . . .' Billy hesitated. 'My parents said . . . they said

61

that I'm . . . it isn't like when they were young, is it? We don't have to fit ourselves into a box, do we? Conform?'

'Of course not. It's different times now, they'll come round.'

'When Dad saw me this morning he snatched my make-up bag and stamped on it. Everything's smashed.' Billy shrugged as though he didn't care but there was a quiver in his voice as he said, 'Dad demanded I take it all off. Said it gave the wrong impression. "What impression is that, then?" I asked. "People might think you're not normal. That you like boys." And then Mum whispered, as though it's really shameful, "or that you want to be a girl".'

'Christ. What did you say?'

'I told them that their views would set the LGBTQ community back by like a zillion years and they could shove their prejudice up their arses.'

'Did you actually?' Tegan asked.

'Nah. I locked myself in the bathroom and had a little cry until they'd left for work because I've been over the way I feel with them but they just don't seem to hear it or try to understand. Fuck 'em.'

Caily didn't know what to say and so she fished around in her bag until she found her black eyeliner and she pressed it into Billy's hand. Tegan did the same with her mascara.

It was lunch time and the drama club were gathered in the hall.

'What do you think Wicked Witch has in store for us?' Tegan asked.

'Dunno but if you don't like it,' Billy rose to his feet and loomed over them, face screwed up, 'then I'll get you, my pretty, and your little dog too.'

'William Vaughan,' Miss West slammed the door behind her. 'Something to say?'

'I was just about to channel my inner Dorothy in case you've chosen *The Wizard of Oz* for the next production.'

'As much as I admire your imagination and commitment to playing *all* the roles, there is a room full of people here eagerly waiting for a chance. Now, not only is this your last performance at this school—'

'Unless we stay on for sixth form,' Billy said.

'Well yes, but otherwise it's the very—'

'Or if we come back as a teacher,' Billy cut in again.

'Yes. Thanks, Billy, but realistically—'

'Or unless,' Billy held up both hands, fingers spread – *wait for it* – 'Unless we become super-famous like Eloise Parks and return to gloat in the faces of—'

'Eloise doesn't gloat. She's too pretty,' Tegan said.

'You think *she's* pretty,' Dani said, flicking her hair back over her shoulder.

'Stop it. Everyone, I have some exciting news.' Miss West pressed her palms together, raising her fingertips to her lips, prolonging the moment.

'What's up with her face?' Billy whispered.

'I think it's a smile?' Caily whispered back.

'Eloise Parks is coming to watch the show. And . . .' Miss West pauses. 'She's forming her own academy and setting up a scholarship fund. She'll be actively looking for a student with enough talent to take part. Of course, that doesn't mean it will be someone from this school, but it would make for some fabulous publicity, what with her being a former pupil.'

'What does that actually mean? Scholarship?' Caily asked.

'It means she's offering the chance for one of you to join her academy. To move to London once you've sat your GCSEs, where you'll be given a part in her next production, due to start next Christmas, and you'll—'

'But I thought we had to stay on at school or go to college until we are eighteen?' Kofi asked.

'What about our A levels?' Tegan exchanged a glance with Caily.

'Why?' Billy asked. 'Why would she do that?'

'Bet there's some sort of tax incentive,' Dani said. 'She's bought shares in that theatre in the West End so.' Because Dani claimed her dad was a rich businessman, she thought she knew everything.

'Quiet.' Miss West clapped her hands. 'It's an amazing opportunity. And of course one you don't have to take if you're chosen. I've outlined everything in a letter we'll be emailing to your parents, and if you don't think the scholarship is right for you I suggest stepping back if you're offered one of the roles.'

'No chance,' Billy grinned. 'Anything to get away from here. Can you imagine my dad's face if I told him I was going to wear make-up for a living! It could be my ticket out of here. Away from them.'

'What I'd like,' Dani said through glossy red lips, 'is to actually get a chance at the lead rather than the usual suspects.' Caily and Tegan exchanged a glance. Dani might be beautiful but she couldn't sing in key and she had no

64

rhythm. 'If we did *West Side Story* I'd make an amazing Maria.'

'This is what I've chosen.' Miss West fiddled with her phone and then 'Another Day in the Sun' blared out of the Bluetooth speakers on the stage. She made an upward motion with her hands and then everyone was on their feet, unsure whether this was part of the audition.

'*La La Land*,' Billy raised his arms above his head, hips swinging.

Laughing, Caily took Tegan's hand and their eyes met. There was no need to say anything, dance was a language of its own. Their feet began to move, falling into a rhythm with the music and each other. They jived effortlessly before Tegan joined Billy in a fast waltz around the room. Everyone was up now, the group longing to be performers, dancing unashamedly.

As the soundtrack sang of happy summer days, everyone faded to a blur. Caily was no longer consciously hearing the music, feeling it instead, her ballet training kicking in, arms in a perfect arc as she span pirouettes, legs stretched as she leaped through the air.

This was when she felt most alive.

When the song finished she was exhilarated, poised for more, but Miss West switched off the speakers and asked them all to sit.

Caily sank down onto the parquet flooring, panting, grinning at Tegan.

'So was that part of the audition, Miss?' Kofi asked.

'No,' Miss West said. 'I've already decided on the cast. Kofi, you'll play Sebastian.'

Caily felt Tegan take her hand. She gave it three gentle squeezes.

'Caily, you'll play Mia. Tegan and Billy you'll have parts in the chorus as well as playing Alexis and Keith but you'll also be Caily and Kofi's understudies.'

Dani rose to her feet, hands on hips. 'That's not fair—'

'Caily's the most talented,' Tegan said. 'Well done, cuz.'

'Thanks.' Caily didn't quite know how to feel. She was pleased, but also guilty because the fact that she got the part meant that Tegan hadn't.

'*La La Land* only has two leads, everyone else is background.' Billy's disappointment bubbled under every word and, suddenly serious, he said, 'Miss . . . I've actually been writing something myself.'

'I don't think th—'

'You literally just said you admired my imagination.'

'Billy, I'm sure it's very good but the audience will expect something they know.'

'They'll never know my work if it's never performed anywhere.'

'Billy's a good writer,' Tegan said.

'I'm not saying that—'

'Toby Marlow and Lucy Moss wrote *Six* while they were at uni,' Caily chipped in.

'Billy, I'd love to look at what you've written, but for our next performance we're going to perform something established.'

'Okay, but does it have to be *La La Land*? If we did something more inclusive, like *Everyone's Talking About*

Jamie, there'd be more roles and it'd show how progressive the school is.'

'We are diverse—'

'Is that why you've chosen Kofi?' Dani challenged. 'Because we all know he's not the most talented boy.'

'I've chosen Kofi because he's right for the role of Sebastian. He might not be the strongest singer but he's a fine actor and a talented pianist.'

'Thanks, I think,' said Kofi.

'And Caily's the safe bet? Again. It's always her or bloody Tegan.'

'I've chosen the right people for the roles,' Miss West repeated.

'Yeah, you keep telling yourself that,' Dani said.

Miss West told them all what she expected them to do to prepare, before saying, 'Go and have your lunch now and I'll see you all at the first rehearsal.' As she left the room everyone huddled in splinter groups, muttering. Caily's cheeks burned. She knew they were talking about her.

'You totally deserve to play Mia,' Tegan said, reading her concern. 'But Billy is a far better singer than Kofi.'

'Yeah, but I can't play piano,' Billy said. 'And Kofi and Caily look good together. I'm shorter than Caily, so perhaps Miss West thought that would look odd. I bet I'd have been Sebastian if you were playing Mia, Tegan. We're the same height.'

Caily's stomach churned with guilt. 'Are we okay?' she asked her cousin, suddenly insecure. 'You want a career on the stage too.'

'Yeah. I do but I need to sort my nerves out somehow. I still have a meltdown before every single performance.'

But this was not any other performance. It could be life-changing. What would the rest of the family think of Caily getting this opportunity while Tegan missed out?

'Everyone in the family will be so proud of you. We all love you.'

Caily hoped that this was true. Their family had been torn apart once before, and then it had all been Caily's fault. She'd hate for anything to come between them again.

As she thought this, Dani barged between her and Tegan, separating them.

She glared at Caily before her mouth twisted into a smile. 'Take care, won't you.'

'Are you threatening me?'

'No. Just advising you to watch your back, farm girl. You've pissed a lot of people off today.'

Caily ignored her, not knowing then that Dani was right.

She should have watched her back.

She should have been more careful.

Not everyone loved her.

CHAPTER EIGHT

Kate

'Everyone loves Caily,' Kate tells Owen, speaking loudly, awkwardly, for the benefit of the tape. 'She has charisma. An indefinable quality that draws people to her. That's why she glows whenever she's on stage. She has . . . had . . .' Kate glances at Matt for both guidance and reassurance before she switches back to the present tense. 'She has a great career ahead of her.' Kate won't entertain the thought that Caily may never wake from her coma, tries not to speculate whether her injuries will prevent her from dancing again. There is no reason to think this way, but still, it's hard to stay positive when all she feels is confusion and despair. She doesn't want to be dramatic and say performing is all Caily has, but it does bring her the most joy. 'I don't know of anyone who would want to hurt her.' She says this firmly but her voice still wobbles. Matt takes her hand. Both their palms are slippery with sweat. The interview room in the police station is small, windowless. A radiator blasting out heat.

She fidgets in her chair, longing to get back to Caily.

'So there's been no cause for concern? No problems?'

'No,' Matt says but Owen, whether through his police training or because he has known her for so long, has picked up on Kate's hesitation to answer. His eyes are full of questions as they meet hers.

'Well, there has been a little jealousy within the drama club but it's kids' stuff,' Kate concedes.

'Nothing serious,' Matt says.

'Well, there was the issue with the costumes.'

'Please,' Owen leans forward, elbows on the table, steeples his fingers together. 'You must tell me everything, no matter how trivial it seems.'

Kate quickly fills him in. Matt shifts his weight in his seat next to her. They are both desperate to leave. She wants to go back to the hospital. Matt too, although of course he has to keep the farm running. She glances at her husband. His shoulders are also rounded. The weight of his responsibilities crushing.

'If there's any change in Caily's condition we'll be notified right away,' Owen reassures, reading her again. 'Tell me where you both were between 3.30 and 4pm yesterday.'

'I was . . .' Kate can hardly bear to say it, think it. 'I was driving. The school bus actually passed me. I didn't for a second think Caily would have been on it.'

Guilt is a constant itch she cannot scratch. If she'd only realized. Waited.

'And then where did you go?' Owen brings her back to the present.

'I went to the cashpoint on Green Street and then I took the costumes to Beth. I arrived there around 4.15.'

'Okay. And Beth can confirm the time?'

'Yes. Well, no. She was at the shop when I got there but she arrived shortly afterwards. Owen, I'm not ly—'

'No one is accusing you of anything. I'm just trying to build a picture. Matt, where were you?'

Matt casts his eyes to the ceiling as though he might find the answer there.

'It's difficult to be precise because I had no need to keep checking my watch, but I'd noticed some damage to one of the drystone walls and I spent a good couple of hours fixing it.'

'I thought Stan usually repaired everyone's drystone?'

'Yeah. Well.' He sighs, ashamed. 'We can't afford him right now.'

Kate squeezes Matt's hands. It isn't his fault the farm is struggling, but if it wasn't for the government grant they wouldn't even be able to afford to feed themselves. Their profit for the last financial year had been a paltry £478. Soul-destroying for 365 days of work. This year is set to be even worse.

'I'm sorry. I know farmers are having an awful time of it right now.'

'Yes, and with this year's wettest autumn on record we're not going to fare much better.' Matt's voice creaks with strain and Owen gives him a moment to gather himself. 'Still, it doesn't seem so important now. I've felt so . . . so bloody desperate, so frantic to find a way to keep the farm but . . . but Caily's accident has put everything in perspective. Family. It's all that matters really, isn't it?' His gaze meets Kate's. His eyes damp with tears.

'She'll be okay,' Kate reassures him and he swallows hard, nods, taking that reassurance even though he knows it doesn't mean anything, but sometimes wanting something so badly is enough to bring comfort.

'So, Matt.' Owen steers him back to the interview. 'You were repairing the wall between 3.30 and 4pm?'

'Yeah. Kate had tried ringing me just before that but it kept diverting to the answer service, didn't it?'

Kate nods. 'You know what the signal's like on the farm.'

Owen jots this down, 'Okay. Thursday night, at the party? How did Caily seem?'

Although it has been almost two days since she's drunk, Kate can still detect gin on her breath. She will always now equate the taste with the hours that have gone since.

'We danced together at the beginning and she seemed happy, but after that I . . . I didn't spend much time with her.' Kate feels the stain of regret colouring her cheeks. 'Beth had drunk too much, we both had really, and we spent a lot of the night together.' Kate casts her mind back, remembering how light she had felt as she'd watched her twin laugh. The worry that seemed to permanently etch Beth's face had melted away. Beth had been so tense lately, but at the party they'd reverted back to being teenage girls, not the forty-year-olds they had become. 'We sang karaoke.'

Owen's eyes meet hers and Kate feels something pass between them, thick and private, both back in the past, Owen's arms looped round her shoulders, singing 'Summer Nights', him with his John Travolta hips and her with a halo of blonde hair. But then she'd met Matt.

'And then I mingled, chatted to . . . it's all a bit of a blur, but everyone who was there, I guess.'

'I need a guest list for the party.'

'Of course. It was family really, a few friends, you know,' Kate says before remembering that Owen didn't know at all. He wasn't there and she guesses from the flush creeping around Matt's neck that he hadn't been invited either. She'd thought any petty jealousies had been laid to rest long ago and Owen really should have been included. Along with being one of her oldest friends, he needed support right now. His wife had left him last year because they had been arguing endlessly. Owen wanted children and she didn't. Recently Owen had discovered she was in a new relationship. Pregnant. Happy about it. Kate can't imagine how devastated Owen must be, but she's been so caught up with the farm, with Caily, that she hasn't really been there for him.

'Oh, Nicola came,' Kate recalls. 'Nicola Crosby. That was a surprise.' Kate can't figure out if it was a good one. She and Nicola had been so close once, before that awful, awful night. She hadn't heard from her again since then, but there she was, at the party, looking both pleased to see her and embarrassed, as though she shouldn't be there somehow. By the time Kate had sung with Beth and cut the cake and waded through the other guests who all wanted to wish her well and tried to find her old friend to talk to her properly, she had gone.

'I didn't know you were still in touch with her?'

'I invited her,' Matt says. 'I'd been through your parents' old photo albums and your mum gave me Nicola's name. I tracked her down via social media.'

'Take me through Caily's movements that day.'

'It was . . . normal.' The word feels strange on Kate's tongue. It seems such a long time since anything has felt normal. Was it really only yesterday that she received that devastating phone call? Twenty-four hours since she was excited about watching Caily on stage. Certain that her daughter's life would change that day. It was unbearable to realize she was right about that at least, only it hadn't change in the way they'd expected. 'Caily ate her breakfast and went to school.'

'And you didn't hear anything from her all day?'

'No, but then I didn't expect to.' Kate thinks of the text she sent – **Break a leg** – the **I love you** she deleted. Had Caily even opened her message? Suddenly it seemed important to know.

'Caily's phone, when can we have it back?'

'It's with our tech guys right now.'

'You'll read her messages?' Tears spring to Kate's eyes that someone will read private things her daughter has sent. Received. A stranger.

'Yes. We'll be going through her social media accounts too. Try to piece together a picture of what life looked like for Caily.'

Kate knows what life looked like for her daughter, she knows all of her hopes and dreams. What she doesn't know is what the future looks like now for any of them.

Caily's broken bones.

Kate's broken heart.

She mentally shakes herself and focuses on the question she hadn't finished answering. The sooner they can finish here the sooner she can get back to the hospital. 'Caily was supposed to be staying at school for the final rehearsal. I've no idea why she got on the bus. Have you spoken to Miss West, her drama teacher?'

'We have and she wasn't aware Caily was leaving the

school premises. She was still expecting her at the rehearsal along with Tegan.'

'Of course, with everything else I'd forgotten Tegan arrived at Beth's just before you rang that day. Around 4.30, I suppose. Or was it later? She seemed upset. Shall I ring Beth?' Kate offers, already reaching for her bag, her phone.

'No need. I'll be speaking to Tegan and Beth later today. I think that's everything for now. Thanks for both coming in.'

'Can I get back to Caily?' she asks in a small, sad voice.

'Of course.'

'Before we go,' Matt asks. 'If this wasn't an accident, how . . . how will you find out who did it?'

'We'll piece things together. We're conducting door-to-door enquiries, although there aren't many houses around the area of the bridge other than yours. We've also put out "incident" signs appealing for information along the roadside and also on our social media accounts. You know, asking if anyone saw anything and if the person who made the 999 call can come forward. Is there anyone else you think we should talk to aside from her teachers and school friends and of course Beth and Tegan and your parents?'

'No. There's no one I can think of.' Matt is already scraping his chair back, standing. They all follow his lead.

'There's Travis,' Kate says as she's looping her handbag over her shoulder.

'Travis?'

'Travis Miller. He's our new farmhand. I say new, it's been a few months. He lives in the cottage that backs onto Lady's Lane.'

'Right. We'll—'

'You can't,' Matt blurts out. 'He left. We had an argument at the party. He wanted more money and I couldn't afford it and so,' he finally pauses for a breath. 'He cleared out his things and he's gone.'

'But he was at Kate's party on Thursday, so he left some time yesterday? The day of Caily's accident?' Owen raises his eyebrows. 'Tell me more about this argument,' Owen says at the same time as Kate asks, 'Why didn't you mention this earlier?'

'It just slipped my mind. There's been such a lot to process. Sorry, Owen.'

'It's okay. But the row you had—'

'That makes it sound more dramatic than it was. It was nothing really.' Matt shrugs. 'He asked for a raise and I couldn't give him one. He said he thought he could get more money elsewhere and I said go if that's the way he felt. I was annoyed, I guess. It was Kate's party, not the time or the place, and,' Matt casts his eyes down to his lap, 'he was right. I paid him less than he deserved, but I genuinely gave him as much as we could.'

'It seems drastic to leave before he had another job lined up. Do you know where he's gone?'

'No. He didn't leave a forwarding address.'

'Right,' Owen stretches the word out. Taps his pen on the table while he thinks. 'What did he drive?'

'A van of some sort, I think?' Kate says. She's no interest in vehicles. 'I don't know the registration. Do you?' She turns to Matt, horrified that they've let this man they barely know into their home, into their lives.

'No, sorry. But yes, he drove a van, a white transit.'

'There are a thousand white vans. It's not much to go on. Can you think of anything else that might be helpful?' Owen asks.

'No. Nothing,' Matt says.

But just above his collar his skin is flushed, and that's when Kate knows.

He's lying.

He must have a good reason for keeping things from Owen.

As soon as they get outside, she'll find out what it is that makes him seem so guilty.

CHAPTER NINE

Matt

'I feel guilty, as though I've done something wrong.' Matt welcomes the bitter breeze that slaps his cheeks as he steps outside of the police station. 'I never thought I'd be questioned in a police station. I've never been so aware of my body language. It's frightening.'

'It is but not as frightening as Caily being in hospital,' Kate says.

'I know. Christ, this whole thing is unbearable. Come here.'

He holds Kate tightly against his chest and in turn she clings to him. He rests his chin on the top of her head and wonders if she feels they have survived something just the way he does.

When they break apart she says, 'I can't believe Travis has left. What are we going to do?'

'We'll be okay.' Beneath his thick jumper his heart races.

'But if I'm at the hospital with Caily, I can't help out either.'

'I have everything under control, I promise.'

He doesn't have anything under control but, although Kate

is a wife, a sister, and a daughter, first and foremost she is a mother and she needs to be at Caily's side.

There's a real chance they'll have to let go of the farm but he can't tell her this. It's been in her family for generations.

'Everything's okay,' he reassures her again and the worry in her eyes softens. Under different circumstances he knows that she'd question how can everything possibly be okay. She knows how tough things can be but he's always tried to shield her from their problems as much as he can, and right now her head is full of their child.

He loves Kate completely.

He has always held the steadfast belief that they could weather any storm as long as it was together. Why then has he cast her adrift? He's created a rough and choppy sea of lies and he's drowning in them. If only he wasn't so proud. He feels so utterly lost and alone, a failure in so many ways.

He pulls Kate into another hug – his anchor – and breathes in the smell of her, the outdoors and the natural musky scent of her skin. She's never been into fancy perfumes.

She raises her face to his and asks, 'Are you coming to see Caily?'

Matt is despairing that he cannot go with Kate to the hospital. Despairing that he cannot wake his daughter up with a gentle kiss akin to those in the fairy tales he used to read to her before bed, when she'd smell of innocence and apple shampoo, curled up on his lap in pink unicorn pyjamas.

'I can't. I need to make the most of the daylight, I haven't even begun spraying the cereal and maize yet, but I'll be in later. Sorry.'

'Don't be.' Kate stands on tiptoes and presses her lips

against his. 'I'm sorry that everything at home has fallen to you. It's a lot.'

Everything is a lot.

He sees Kate safely to her car, opening her door for her the way he always has and then he climbs into his own battered Land Rover.

He drives too fast, in a hurry to check the drystone walls are intact in case Owen checks.

There are 248 acres of farmland. For now, nobody knows he wasn't where he said he was.

For now.

CHAPTER TEN

Caily

Three months ago

'Dani talks rubbish. Don't worry about her,' Tegan reassured Caily as they splashed down the lane. Caily in her sensible Clarks school shoes Mum insisted on, Tegan in a cheap plastic pair from the market, the soles already falling off, avoiding muddy puddles they'd once have jumped into with wellington-booted feet. 'You should be thinking about how to tell everyone you're going to be a superstar.'

'Dunno about that,' Caily said although it was what she wanted more than anything.

The farmyard was deserted, the sheep quiet for once. The rain had coaxed a damp earthy smell from the surrounding fields.

They skirted around the red tractor that was always breaking down, abandoned on the cobbles, and tumbled through the door of the farmhouse, hungry, ready for Monday-night dinner. The smell of beef stew greeted them.

'Yuck. Even my socks are soaked.' Tegan kicked off her shoes, droplets of rain splattering the flagstone floor.

Twix bounded towards them, Duck in mouth, as though he hadn't seen Caily for seven years, not seven hours.

'It's cats and dogs out there,' she said. Twix pricked his ears up at the word 'cats'. She grabbed hold of the scrap of material his jaws were gripping and played tug of war.

The kitchen was empty but, as usual, there was a pot of tea covered by a green knitted cosy in the middle of the huge pine table. At the head of the table, in the comfiest chair – the one with arms and the extra padded seat – curled Custard the tabby cat. He momentarily stared at them – *quiet please, I'm sleeping* – before closing his eyes again, too old and too lazy to rush towards them as he once would have, long past the stage of wanting to play with sticks and feathers, wind-up mice.

'Hello? We're home.'

Caily hung up her wet coat. Grandad's wheelchair was folded underneath the hooks next to the door of the basement. Years ago, after she and Tegan had become obsessed with *The Lion, The Witch and The Wardrobe*, Grandad had covered the door with a wallpaper to look like the wardrobe door in the book. An entrance to Narnia. Often, when they'd play hide and seek, the one doing the hiding would sneak through the door and down to the basement where they had squashy beanbags and their teddy bears arranged in a circle around a plastic tea set.

'I see you,' the seeker would say as they clattered down the stairs.

'Saw you first.'

When they grew too old for toys, Grandad had built them a small stage down there where they'd practise their plays before performing them for the rest of the family in the lounge.

They hadn't been in the basement for ages. The door was kept locked now because it kept springing open and Grandma was worried someone would fall down the steps.

'Grandma?' Caily called her now.

'I'm starving.' Tegan prised the lid off the cake tin and lifted out a homemade chocolate-chip muffin.

'You'll spoil your appetite, young lady,' Grandma said from behind them, making them jump.

'You're like a ninja.' Tegan kissed her cheek. 'Silent and deadly.'

'Sounds more like a fart,' Dad said, pulling off his wellies and stacking them on the boot rack. He ruffled Caily's hair before he reached for the pot of tea.

'Dad.' Caily pulled a face. 'You're *so* embarrassing.'

'You don't know the lengths us dads go to so we *don't* embarrass you,' said Grandad as his crutches click-click-clicked across the stone floor. He had a prosthetic leg but often he chose not to wear it. He sank onto a chair. Caily took his crutches and propped them up in the corner.

'Right,' said Mum, wandering in from the lounge, 'so when you said my primary school class could visit the farm when we were learning about where food came from and we stood in front of a field where two sheep were mating and you told everyone *exactly* what they were doing, *that* wasn't embarrassing at all?' She winked at Caily.

'You can't grow up on a farm and be all coy about the birds and bees,' Grandad said.

'Most of those kids hadn't seen—'

'Not telling the sheep-having-sex story again?' Aunt Beth grinned as she stepped into the kitchen and shimmied out of her raincoat.

The teasing continued until the kettle whistled it was hot enough, and the teapot was refilled. This was where Caily felt happiest. Here, surrounded by her family. It was times like these she thought she never wanted to leave.

Could she really go to London if she was offered the scholarship?

'You two lay the table.' Grandma handed the placemats to Tegan and the cutlery to Caily. Together they began to set each place.

'There's one too many mats here,' Tegan said.

'And an extra knife and fork.'

'No.' Grandma frowned. Pointing as she named each empty chair in turn. 'Caily, Tegan, me, Patrick, Kate, Matt, Beth and Sean. That's right, isn't it, Caily?'

Caily hesitated, on the brink of speaking but for a moment unsure how to tactfully tell Grandma that she'd had another memory lapse, slipped back into the past because Uncle Sean wasn't coming to dinner.

He couldn't.

Tegan's dad hadn't been around for seven years.

The memory of the last time she had seen him looped again, as it often did.

They had been playing hide and seek in this kitchen. It had been Sean's turn to hide. He'd been quiet all day, hadn't really wanted to play, rubbing his eyes and saying he had a headache, but they'd begged him until he agreed. Caily and Tegan had stood in the middle of the kitchen, arms slung over each other's shoulders, eyes closed, counting. Caily heard the creak of the basement door open. The groan of the third step. She had grinned to herself. She was going to find him first.

They'd reached 100, were just *coming ready or not*, when, with a light tap, the back door opened. Caily had opened her eyes, smiled as Owen stepped inside the kitchen, not really noticing the other policeman behind him.

'Where's Sean?' he'd asked.

'He's hiding down the basement,' Caily had said, laughing, but then there was that drop in her stomach as, unsmiling, Owen had disappeared into the basement, leading Sean back upstairs in handcuffs. Beth crying as though her heart had been broken, and it probably had.

Perhaps if the police had been strangers they'd have knocked on the front door, rather than the back, and Sean would have had the chance to run away and things would have been different.

Perhaps if Caily hadn't blurted out where he was Owen would never have known and things would have been different.

'What if' was a game she frequently played because, despite her parents and grandparents reassuring her that she had done nothing wrong, she had always felt responsible that Tegan had lost her father, and Beth her husband. She felt like the cause of the many arguments that followed between Beth and her grandparents. Her mum and Beth. Beth defending him. Trying to excuse the inexcusable.

He had taken part in an armed robbery.

Caily found it hard to equate her uncle who let her ride on his back around the kitchen – *giddy up, horsie* – with the criminal he admitted to being. She couldn't imagine how hard it was for Tegan and Beth.

Although Beth said she didn't blame her it had taken weeks for her to be able to look Caily in the eye again. It had somehow brought Caily and Tegan closer. They had both been too young to properly understand, and then Tegan was adamant she never wanted anything to do with him again. She hadn't seen him since that day. After endless heated discussions, Beth had promised that she wouldn't go and see him. Wouldn't take Tegan into the prison. As it turned out, he never added them to his approved visitors' list anyway.

Once, when Caily had asked Tegan again whether she felt it was her fault he had been taken away, Tegan had cried and said, 'It's not your fault, Caily, it's mine.'

'Yours? Of course it isn't. Why would you think that?'

'Because . . .' Her face had creased with the strain of trying to put what she felt into words. 'If he loved me enough . . .' Her voice had broken. 'If I was lovable enough, then he wouldn't have risked leaving me, would he?'

'That's not true.' Caily had gripped Tegan's hand tightly, wanting the squeeze to convey all of the things she wanted to say but wasn't quite sure, at her age, how to.

They had talked about him endlessly at first, Tegan sometimes confused, sometime angry, always sad, but eventually she had said, 'I don't want to talk about him anymore. It's as though . . .' She'd tilted her head to the side, like Twix, in the way she always did when she was thinking. 'You know when you had a toothache and you kept poking it with your tongue and complaining it hurt and I'd tell you to leave it alone?'

'Yes. It was painful until I got my filling.'

'That's what it's like with Dad. Thinking about him is like poking a bad tooth with my tongue. The more I do it, the more it hurts, and I don't want to do it anymore. If I stop talking about him that will be like my filling. An end to it hurting perhaps?'

Caily wasn't convinced it would be as easy as that, but she respected Tegan's decision and they'd never spoken of him again. She wasn't even sure when he was due for release. Not sure what she'd say if she ever saw him again.

Her feelings surrounding him were muddled.

In a way she had mourned him, like a loss.

It had been impossible for them to forget him, though. Grandma clearly hadn't.

'Silly me, of course Sean isn't coming.' Grandma realized her mistake before anyone could speak and rattled the spare cutlery back into the drawer.

There was a moment of awkward silence before Tegan clapped her hands. 'Caily has some news.'

'Oh, do tell.' Mum looked at her expectantly.

'I've been cast in the musical.' Caily glanced at Tegan, tried not to sound too excited.

'She's not just *in* the musical,' Tegan said proudly. 'She's the lead *and* Eloise Parks is coming to watch.'

'Oh Caily, that's amazing.'

'There's more,' Tegan said when Caily didn't offer any further information. 'Eloise is launching a scholarship and if she likes Caily, then Caily might move to London.'

'What?' Dad's face fell. 'You're only fifteen.'

'I know, but it wouldn't be until next year, after my

GCSEs,' Caily said quickly. She'd done nothing wrong but she still felt, somehow, that she was disappointing him.

'Yes, but what about A levels? Education is important and what would I do if you weren't here to help out on the farm after school and at weekends?'

'Dad! I don't want to be a farmer.'

'I know but . . .'

'I think what your dad means is that London is . . . Caily, you're too young to go,' Mum said.

'You can't stop me,' Caily's temper flared. Why couldn't they be happy for her?

'Nobody is trying to stop you,' Grandma said in her soothing voice. 'We're delighted you've got the part and when, if, you're offered this scholarship, we can discuss it.'

'You okay, Tegan?' Grandad asked. 'You in this play too?'

'Yeah. It's cool. I'm happy for Caily. I wouldn't want the lead, I'd have to be so fit—'

'Umm so will you, you are my understudy.'

'Yeah, guess so. Grandma, we'll be getting you to teach us some yoga moves.'

'You joke but yoga might do your performance anxiety good, Tegan. Is it a paid thing? This scholarship?' Aunt Beth asked.

'I thought we weren't discussing the scholarship?' Grandma said in a firm voice.

'We're not. I just wondered, with it being London, you'd think there'd be a fair bit of money on offer, the price the West End theatres charge for tickets?'

'I dunno. Miss West is emailing a letter . . .' Caily trailed off. The sound of a vehicle crunching across the yard pulled her away from what she was about to say. Outside the window a white van reversed, parking next to Grandad's old Land Rover.

And then, just like it had before Sean was arrested, came a knock on the door that would change their lives. Change her life.

Change everything.

If she had known what was to come, would she have begged her family to ignore the door? The person outside?

She thinks, perhaps, she would.

CHAPTER ELEVEN

Beth

There's a knock at the door of the interview room in the police station and it's a welcome relief when Owen momentarily leaves the room.

'Are you okay?' Beth whispers to Tegan but she knows that she isn't. Her daughter is clearly distressed at the myriad questions Owen has been asking her and, although she wants what's best for her niece, talking won't change what happened to Caily. Words cannot help her wake up.

Words cannot help Caily wake up.

And it is Tegan who is her primary concern, her knees pulled up to her chest, feet on the seat of her chair, sleeves of her jumper yanked down over her hands as though she can make herself disappear.

'Did anything happen between Caily and Travis?' Beth asks in a low voice. Tegan has already told Owen that as far as she knew, Caily had a crush on the farmhand but it was unreciprocated, but then Tegan has always protected her cousin. Beth makes a mental note to search for Travis on social media. To see whether he might have posted any photos of him and Caily. She's sure the police will do this too but she feels so helpless, she wants to do *something*.

Before Tegan can answer Owen returns.

His face soft as he gazes at Tegan's pale face. 'We could have done this at your house, you know. It's just an informal chat. I know police stations can be quite intimidating.'

'I'm fine,' Tegan says. 'I want to help.'

'Okay. Tell me about school. Any problems there?'

Tegan tilts her head to one side, thinking. 'There's been some stuff since Caily was cast as Mia. Some posts on social media.' Tegan tells Owen about it. She doesn't know for certain who was responsible.

'Cyberbullying,' Beth says when Tegan has finished. She's read a letter about that from the school but really hasn't given it much thought. 'Does Kate know?'

'No. Caily didn't want to upset her.'

'What do you think triggered the posts?'

Tegan shrugs. 'Dunno. Suppose it's because Caily always . . . shines. She's always picked for stuff and she's always perfect.'

'You're just as good and you get picked for things too.' Beth offers reassurances.

'I'm not saying I'm not. It's just Caily is better and that's cool. Everyone might as well be invisible next to her. Everyone fades into the background when she walks into a room. She . . . she's brilliant. Will . . . will she be able to dance again?' Tegan begins to cry.

'Of course,' Beth makes a promise she can't keep. 'Caily's lucky, you know that.' Beth winces at her poor choice of words. What is *wrong* with her? There are many things her niece is but right now lucky isn't one of them.

'She thinks she's good because of those ballet shoes. Remember, Mum? The first time we danced? I was so scared and Caily held my hand and . . .' Tegan collapses into sobs. 'Who's holding her hand now?'

Beth leaves her chair, dropping to her haunches in front of Tegan. Rubbing her calves while she soothes her. 'Kate will be with her. Shh, it's okay.'

'Are you going to visit Caily today?' Owen asks gently.

'No,' Tegan wipes her eyes with her forearm. 'I can't. I just can't.'

'It might be good for you. Good for both of you.' Owen smiles but Tegan is not looking at him. She is staring into her lap. Her eyes puffy. She's done nothing but cry for twenty-four hours. It was a complete bombshell for everyone that the police believe Caily might have been pushed. Beth wonders whether, as well as shock and worry, Tegan carries a semblance of guilt the way Beth had when Kate had almost drowned and she wasn't there with her.

Owen leaves a pause but Tegan doesn't fill it.

'Tell me about the day of Caily's fall. There was the final rehearsal but neither you nor Caily went to it or let Miss West know you were leaving the school premises. When was the last time you saw Caily?'

Tegan chews the edge of her thumbnail, thinking. 'Probably in English, after lunch.'

'Why didn't Caily go to the rehearsal?'

'It wasn't like we needed one. Everyone has practised so much we could literally perform it in our sleep.'

'But it doesn't seem like Caily to not show up to something when she was supposed to.'

Tegan shrugs.

'Why didn't you go to the rehearsal, Tegan? Where were you?'

'I went into town. I knew there wasn't going to be a rehearsal without Caily.'

'How did you know Caily wasn't going to the rehearsal?'

'I . . .' Tegan hugs her knees closer to her chest. 'I saw her leaving school.'

'But you said you hadn't seen her since after lunch?'

'Not to talk to properly.'

'But you must have asked her why she was leaving?'

'Owen,' Beth says firmly, 'can't you see how upset Tegan is? Is this really necessary?'

'We're nearly finished here but it's important we know everyone's movements for that day so we can get to the bottom of what happened to Caily.'

'Caily's . . .' Tegan blushes. Falters.

Beth takes her hand. 'Whatever it is, you can say it.'

'I feel like I'm betraying her, though. Embarrassing her.'

'Tegan, it isn't my intention to embarrass anyone. I'm just trying to understand Caily's movements that day.'

Tegan nods. Head bowed as she speaks. 'Her period had started early and she didn't have . . . she wasn't prepared.'

'Aren't there any machines in the toilets for sanitary products? No one else Caily could have asked for something?' Owen asks.

'It wasn't just . . . she needed to change her underwear.'

A flush of pink creeps around Tegan's neck, stains her

cheeks. 'I would have come with her but I was getting really freaked out about the performance so I decided to go to the chemist and get some Rescue Remedy. Billy had tried it before and said it really helped with nerves.'

'What's Rescue Remedy?' Owen looks blank.

'It's . . . I dunno. Liquid herbs or dried flowers or something. You put it on your tongue and it calms you down.'

'Tegan gets performance anxiety,' Beth cuts in. 'She gets so emotional before she goes on stage. She's great when she's on it, though.'

'Which chemist did you go to, Tegan?'

'Watts on the High Street. I was gonna hang around town until the performance but the Rescue Remedy tasted horrible and I still felt nervous so I wanted to come home and see Mum. She knows how to calm me down.'

Beth longs to soothe her daughter now. To gather her into her arms and sing the same song that she's been singing to her since she was a baby. The song her own mum used to sing to her and Kate, which had taken on new meaning since she became a mother. Because Tegan is her sunshine who always makes her happy. With the passing of time into teenage years it has sometimes seemed as though the thread of connection between them is fraying and Tegan is slowly slipping away from her. But when Tegan is panicking and Beth holds her, cutting through the heaviness of her stress with her voice, as light as organza, all the pieces she thought had been lost flutter back together and their relationship is whole once more. Unbreakable.

'What time did you get to Watts?'

'I dunno exactly.'

'Don't worry. We can check the CCTV for precise timings if we need to.'

'Do you think I'm lying? That I had something to do with Caily's fall? I love my cousin. I wasn't anywhere near the bridge. I . . . I . . .'

Beth sweeps her daughter into her arms.

'Enough,' she says to Owen. The distress pours out of Tegan, into her. 'Tegan, go and wait outside for me.' Nobody speaks while Tegan scurries to the door.

'I know you want to find out what happened to Caily,' Beth says, crossing her arms. 'We all do, but Tegan's just a child. She's dealing with such a lot, and being interrogated in an interview room is—'

'I'm just doing my job,' Owen says. 'I know it's difficult but I'm not picking on Tegan. I'm asking everyone who knew Caily to explain where they were at the time of the accident . . .' he splays open his hands. 'For Kate.'

Suddenly deflated, Beth slumps down in her chair, a balloon losing air. 'Sorry.'

'Don't be. If we can quickly run through your movements now that will be enough for today.'

'Sure. I was at home. Kate came over with the costumes around . . .' She screws up her forehead, trying to remember. '3.15 maybe?'

'Kate says she arrived around 3.45 and you weren't in.'

Beth tries to keep her face neutral. 'I'd popped to the shop to buy some biscuits. You know how hungry my sister gets.'

Remember us, that phrase means. Remember me. We are friends. Were almost family.

95

Owen doesn't comment, instead asking, 'Which shop did you go to?'

Beth feels herself begin to sweat as she gives him a name, rising to her feet as she does. 'There's nothing more I can tell you. Can I take Tegan home now?'

'Of course. Thanks. You've both been really helpful. Beth?'

She looks at him as she slings her handbag across her body.

'I'm on your side, you know,' he smiles.

She nods a thank you before she wanders, dazed, back out into the corridor, where she gives Tegan a hug but her daughter's body is stiff, unyielding, not wanting comfort, not from her mother anyway, or perhaps feeling she doesn't deserve it.

Exhausted, Beth fishes her keys from her bag. She feels as though she hasn't slept for a week.

A month.

A year.

In the dull, grey reception area they wrap themselves in their winter layers before they step out into the biting cold.

'Mum, I really wasn't anywhere near that bridge,' Tegan says earnestly.

'I know,' Beth says, because she does know. She does believe her.

The wind whips Tegan's hair around her face. She stuffs her hands into her coat pocket, immediately pulling her left hand out again. Offering the bottle she's holding to Beth.

'This is the Rescue Remedy. Should I go and show Owen?'

'I don't think that's necessary.' Beth reads aloud from the bottle. 'Comfort and Reassure.'

'It didn't do either,' Tegan says sadly.

Beth gently sweeps Tegan's fringe to the side with her fingers, thinking how much she resembles her cousin, and then she can't help thinking of the last time she saw Caily.

The disappointment on her niece's face.

The horror.

The shock.

CHAPTER TWELVE

It's going to be a shock facing you. Facing what I've done. I know this as I slip inside the building, take a moment to collect myself.

The hospital has a smell, a taste, disinfectant catching in the back of my throat.

I shouldn't be here.

Perhaps there's part of me that wants to be caught. Wants to confess.

But then it would all be over, wouldn't it, and I refuse to believe that this is how it ends. Not here, not now.

Not like this.

Scanning for security cameras, I wind my scarf around my mouth, tug my hood down lower. Winter clothes hide a multitude of sins. You never know who is under all the layers, the hat, hair hidden, eyes shrouded.

Even if the CCTV is working, which you can't rely on nowadays, I'm unidentifiable.

A ghost.

I wend my way through the corridors, head down, certain

that if anyone looks into my eyes they'll see who I really am, what I've done.

The police.

Adrenaline surges through my body as I catch sight of the officers heading towards me. Quickly, I turn to the notice board, studying it intently, holding my breath as they pass me, body tense as I steel myself for a clap on the shoulder. But I am invisible, and here's the thing: if you don't want to be noticed, it's easy to blend in.

From my peripheral vision I watch them until they disappear from view, wondering what they are thinking, what they know, what they think they knew. They can speculate all they want to, there are only two people who know what happened on the bridge: me and you.

I won't talk.

And you can't.

That much is apparent as I stand at the foot of your bed, unsure what to do now I'm here.

When I first arrived, I'd heard the nurses talking. You'd been taken for another scan and so I waited, not sure how long you'd be, loitering in the corridor, pacing up and down, biding my time. Eventually I heard the squeak of wheels. I lingered by the vending machine, pretending to count coins, until you had been pushed back into the unit.

After a few minutes the nurse and the porter left and then the other nurse, the one who sits by the door like a guard dog, nipped across to the toilets, a guilty expression on her face. I waited a second but no one came in to cover her so here I am.

Here we are.

How quiet you are, Caily.

How still.

What secrets you hold.

Your face is so pale, hair already lank. A million miles away from the girl on the bridge who'd been so full of life, waving your arms, shouting.

Struggling.

Anyway, as much as I'd love to stay, I think it's likely that the nurse will return any minute so I'll leave you this little gift on your bedside table.

I hope you like it.

I'm reluctant to leave you.

But I'll see you again soon.

That's a promise.

CHAPTER THIRTEEN

Beth

I promise I'll be more careful if you let my debit card work. Beth offers up a plea to the universe as she chucks things haphazardly into her shopping basket. She hasn't checked her banking app but her benefits should have been paid into her account this morning, which will have freed up a little of her overdraft.

She can't believe that this is her life. All those years ago when they'd sit cross-legged in the field, her and Sean, Kate and Owen, Nicola and Aaron sharing what they wanted their future to look like, it was never . . . *this*.

This constant, gnawing anxiety that there isn't enough makes Beth feel that she isn't enough. She has said no to Tegan so often that her daughter has stopped asking for anything. Beth can see that she is outgrowing her clothes again, the hems of her jeans brushing the tops of her ankles, but Beth hasn't acknowledged it because if she does, then what? She can hardly take her daughter on a shopping spree: even the cheaper shops are out of reach.

Since the sudden sharp increase in the cost of living, Beth

is often forced to choose between a nutritious meal and heat. Usually she skips lunch so Tegan has enough. She is fanatical about switching off the lights. Unplugging the appliances before she goes to bed every night in a futile attempt to save what? A few pounds a year.

As well as the guilt, Beth feels a rush of anger whenever she watches the smug politicians on the news. Reads in the papers that they are finding it almost impossible to manage on their six-figure salaries when her reality isn't a seven-week holiday in the summer but charity shops and food banks. Although she shouldn't feel ashamed, she does.

She had cried frustrated tears last week when she'd read on social media that during an interview a politician had advised those struggling to manage to find a better-paid job or take on a second role. Beth can't find any job, well paid or not, and it isn't for lack of trying.

She rushes to the checkout. Usually she's selective about what she buys. Before she lost her job she used to go with a list, a fixed idea with what she'd be cooking that week, but since she became unemployed she goes first to the reduced section, picking through the produce marked with yellow stickers, figuring out what meals she can make with limp leeks. Browning salad. Bread that doesn't spring back into shape when she squeezes it. Despair has become an ever-present weight in her stomach.

Today, recklessly, she is stocking up on all of her daughter's favourites, Jaffa Cakes, pickled-onion Monster Munch, the foods Tegan devoured as a child, as though through these familiar tastes and smells Beth can bring back that sense of safety Tegan used to feel when she was small.

She had looked so forlorn when Beth dropped her home after the police station. Beth had tried to persuade her to come to the supermarket but Tegan tugged her sleeves over her hands, yawning.

'I didn't sleep much last night. I'm going to have a nap.'

Beth had taken the opportunity to run a few errands before going to Asda, but now, as she packs her items into her canvas bags, exhaustion suddenly slams into her. Her heart accelerates as the cashier swipes her debit card. It's okay. She slowly releases the breath she had been holding.

She pauses at the exit. There's the usual charity collection trolley and she places in it the tin of baked beans and tomato soup she had bought especially. It might seem odd to some, donating to the food bank when sometimes she is the one relying on it, but there is always someone worse off and honestly, she's spent less than fifty pence on those two items. It's a drop in the ocean compared to what she owes, not only on her overdraft and credit card but on the loan she had foolishly taken out before realizing that the mounting interest would jab her awake at night, drench her in a cold sweat. If her car was worth anything she'd sell it. As it is, she barely uses it, won't be able to afford the MOT and tax when they come around.

How could she ever have thought that ringing the phone number on the leaflet that had been stuffed through her letterbox was a better option than swallowing her pride and asking her own family for help? But it wasn't only pride stopping her. She'd seen the worry etched onto Kate's face. Noticed the threads of grey peppering Matt's hair now he was running the farm without her dad by his side and knew that, although he downplayed the financial challenges the farm was facing, they were in trouble. Her brother-in-law forgets sometimes that she and Kate are the daughters of farmers. They can't be fooled.

That bloody loan, though.

She's still not paid off any of the original balance, could weep when she thinks of how much one panicked decision had cost her, but she'd thought it would be okay. Short term. That she'd quickly find another job and be able to pay it back in full after a month, but then she couldn't even get to interview stage, her car had broken down, Tegan had grown out of her school shoes and she was short of one payment, not even by much, but . . . god, that interest. It had all spiralled out of her control.

Perhaps she should have been honest with Kate, shared with her sister how much trouble she was in, but she can't now because Kate is going through something that no parent should ever face.

The prospect that she might outlive her child.

Beth had never really thought about life and death before. Both sets of her grandparents had passed away, she barely remembers the ones she had met. The sepia photographs her mum used to show her and Kate never triggered any memories despite Mum telling them of happy Christmases when they had apparently helped their remaining grandmother, Dad's mum, make the plum pudding, stirring a five-pence piece into the mixture, making wishes.

Beth's shoulders ache, her shopping bags weighted with too much food she can't afford and guilt. Still, Tegan will enjoy the Jaffa Cakes. Beth pictures how she eats them, stuffing them into her mouth, whole. But then her thoughts turn to Caily. How she would always lick off all the chocolate on the top before nibbling the orange jelly away from the sponge.

She is overcome with sadness and tries to think of something other than her niece as she hurries back to the car, the handles from the bags carving grooves into her fingers, but she can't.

Last night she had fired up the old laptop and endlessly googled. Reading with horror about patients who never wake up from comas, or how those who do who are irrevocably altered. Suffering from some form of brain damage that, whether mild, moderate or severe, ensures the patient is never quite the same again.

She could not bear it and had slammed the lid shut. Before she went to bed she had stood in the doorway to Tegan's room and watched her sleep, the way she had when Tegan was small.

Then Beth had tumbled into her own bed, but every time she closed her eyes she saw Caily's face, sometimes as a toddler, a baby, a teenager. Her memories mixed up and back to front and always, always, out of order.

All night, all of today, she has forced herself not to think of the last time she saw her niece.

It's just too awful.

No one must ever find out.

The house is quiet. Still. Beth dumps the shopping in the kitchen and quietly climbs the stairs, wondering if Tegan is napping. From the creak of Tegan's bed frame last night Beth knows her daughter had a restless night too.

Beth gently opens the bedroom door. Tegan's quilt is half on the floor, the bed empty.

'Tegan?' Beth calls, worried. Her pulse rate rising as she checks the other rooms, an ominous feeling rising from deep within her. A primal instinct. A mother's knowing.

Something is wrong.

Normally she wouldn't worry if Tegan wasn't home, but this is not a normal day, is it?

'Tegan?' she shouts, knowing that her daughter will not answer.

The sound of the front door opening and slamming drives Beth back down the stairs.

'Where have you . . .' she trails off when she notices the tears in Tegan's eyes. The tremble in her lips.

'Mum,' Tegan rushes into Beth's arms. If she was worried before, now she is frantic. She can't remember the last time Tegan wanted to be held, not by her anyway.

'Sweetheart?' Beth asks gently. 'What's wrong?'

'I think . . . I think somebody followed me.'

Tegan twists her neck to look at the front door with frightened eyes as though she expects it to fly open.

'Tell me everything,' Beth says firmly, calmly, although she is already striding to the front door. Drawing the chain across it.

'I couldn't sleep so I walked to the post office to buy a get-well card for Caily and . . . I don't know. I just felt like . . . you know when you go all goose-bumpy and your neck feels tingly like someone is staring at you from behind.'

Someone walked over your grave.

The old expression slithers into Beth's mind and she shudders. 'Yes.'

'I felt like that. I cut through the cul-de-sac and I could hear these footsteps behind me and I began to leg it through the alley and they . . . They were *right* behind me and I . . . I was so scared, Mum. I ran all the way home.'

'Did they follow you here?' Beth cricks her neck to try and see through the kitchen window.

'I dunno. I stopped hearing footsteps and all I could hear was . . . like a whooshing in my ears. I literally thought I might faint. I didn't stop running, though. I didn't look around.'

'You did the right thing. You must have been very scared.'

'I was. Oh god, you don't think that whoever has hurt Caily is coming for me, do you?' Tegan's voice rises in pitch.

'Of course not.' She brings her daughter in for a hug. 'Try not to worry. I *promise* you, Tegan, I won't let anyone hurt you.'

Beth will do whatever it takes to protect her daughter.

She already *has* taken drastic measures to protect her daughter.

CHAPTER FOURTEEN

Kate

Sitting by Caily's bed wouldn't protect her daughter from whatever is to come, wouldn't make her wake up. Kate knew this yet it had still been such a wrench to tear herself away from the hospital for the second time that day, but while Caily was taken for more tests there wasn't anything she could do. It was frustrating that her scan hadn't been carried out this morning while Kate had been at the police station with Matt and Owen. Anyway, she had let Nita usher her out of the door, had reassured the nurse that yes, she would go home and have a shower and something to eat.

Still, as she left, Kate had made a pact with God, or the universe, or some sort of higher force to look after Caily while she was at home, in return vowing that she would be a model citizen, a perfect mother. It wasn't like she'd ever been a believer, but she wished she had faith in something, wished she could place her daughter's recovery in the hands of something infinitely bigger than this hospital, these doctors, science. Longed for that utmost certainty that her prayers would be if not answered then at least listened to. But her plea – to keep

Caily safe until she returned – must have been heard because Caily is back in her bed, in the unit, the machines all displaying figures that are reassuring, for Kate is a fast learner. She has picked up more in these past two days about oxygen levels and blood pressure, danger signals and encouraging changes, than she had during years of watching *Casualty* and *Holby City*.

'What did the scan show today?' Kate asks, for another thing she has learned is that the wait for results is not always seemingly interminable. Here, everything is almost instantaneous.

'The swelling to Caily's brain has gone down.'

'That's good. So . . .' Kate's question dries on her lips but Nita reads her.

'She's still sedated so we don't expect her to have woken up. The doctor will talk this over with you later.'

Kate's stomach hops and skips at the thought the doctor might withdraw sedation now. She knows, *knows*, that this does not mean Caily will instantly wake, be herself – the doctor has already explained that once sedation is withdrawn, waking could take days for Caily to fully come back to them – but this is a good sign.

She hurries over to her daughter.

'I think they might wake you up soon, Caily,' she says, walking around the bed so she is nearer the window. Frowning when she sees what is on the seat of the chair.

She picks it up.

A gift. Wrapped in green paper and tied with a red bow. Kate can't imagine where it came from.

Has Caily had a visitor while Kate was away? Did they buy her a present?

She glances to Nita, holding the box in her hands, unsure what to do. The rules on infection control are stringent. No flowers. No food. No drink. Plastic aprons to be worn at all times.

What germs might this wrapping be carrying?

She runs the satin of the ribbon through her fingers as she examines it from all angles, looking for a card, some sort of clue.

The hopeful part of her wants to leave it exactly as it is, for Caily to open when she wakes, but it could be something from a friend to aide her recovery. A CD of music she'd loved, a favourite smell, something to spark her back to life.

Carefully Kate unwraps the gift, slowly peeling away the Sellotape, preserving the paper so she can parcel it back again afterwards if it isn't something that will be helpful right now.

The box is on her lap as she lifts off the lid. A scream catching in her throat.

It isn't anything helpful.

It isn't any of the things she thought it might be.

It's Caily's missing ballet shoes, covered in blood.

CHAPTER FIFTEEN

Caily

Three months ago

The blood rushed to Caily's head as the man standing outside her grandparents' back door knocked on it again. Through the window she could see not just any man but *the* most gorgeous person Caily had ever seen.

Beth was still asking questions about the scholarship but the chatter in the kitchen fell away from her as Mum answered the door.

'I was wondering if you had any work going,' he asked hesitantly. His voice as rich and comforting as one of Grandma's homemade cookies.

Twix ran up to him and nuzzled his leg. The man reached down and stroked him, his brown wavy hair that hung past his collar falling over his shoulders.

That hair.

She had never felt like this before. Not with any of the boys at school. Not this instant, struck-by-lightning, earthquake-beneath-her-feet reaction.

'Well, you've got the seal of approval from Twix,' Mum laughed. 'Come in.'

'Thanks.' He stepped inside, much to the delight of Twix who gangled across the kitchen, paws skidding on the tiles, returning seconds later with Duck in his mouth.

'What have you brought me?' He gave a shy smile as he leaned forward and took a scrap of Duck's material, played tug-o-war.

That smile.

She touched her lips with her fingers, checking her mouth wasn't hanging open, imagining him kissing it.

Kissing her.

Catching her staring as he straightened up, he gave a little wave. Caily was transfixed by his bright blue eyes, by his hands, almost feeling them on her skin. She rubbed the top of her arms as goosebumps speckled her skin.

'I'm Travis.'

Travis.

She rolled his name silently around her mouth, tasting the sweetness of it.

Travis.

'I'm sorry,' Dad said. 'I really don't think we can afford to hire anyone yet. Maybe in a few weeks—'

'But Dad,' Caily cut in. 'You've so much to do and you're always so tired.'

'And I ain't a lot of help nowadays,' Grandad said, so sorrowfully that Caily wrapped her arms around his neck. He gently removed them. He wasn't one for hugs.

'This is your dad?' Travis's gaze flickered between Dad and Grandad.

'Father-in-law.'

'Patrick Marsh,' Grandad said, introducing everyone else with a wave of his hand.

'Must be nice to have a big family,' Travis said wistfully.

'When you showed up on the doorstep all those years ago we listened to what you had to say,' Mum said to Dad.

'Come in. Come in.' Grandma ushered him over. 'You look a little familiar.' She studied him. 'I think you have a touch of the Cary Grant about you. I loved him in *An Affair to Remember*. Do you want a cup of tea? Something to eat?' Grandma ushered him over to the table. Cut him a huge slab of carrot cake. Poured the tea with a shaky hand, splashes speckling Travis's arm, but he discreetly wiped them away and scooped up a forkful of sponge.

'You're very kind. This is amazing.' He smiled.

'So, you local?' Dad asked.

Travis shook his head, his mouth full.

'What brings you to these parts, then?'

'It was a pin-in-the-map, spur-of-the-moment decision.'

'And do you have farming experience?'

'No, but I'm a fast learner.'

'It ain't all about shovelling shit,' Grandad said. 'It's back-breaking graft and can be dangerous too. Gotta keep your wits about you.' Grandad patted the top of his thigh. Caily watched the expression on Travis's face change as he realized that Grandad's leg was missing from just above the knee, but his face displayed shock and then sympathy, not the revulsion they had sometimes seen over the past couple of years.

'What happened to your leg?' Travis asked and Caily

knew that Grandad would appreciate his directness. Not averting his eyes, embarrassed.

'I was cleaning out a blockage from the combine harvester and stupidly, because I did know better but it was the fifth time it had blocked, I didn't turn it off. My foot slipped and got trapped in the auger. Know what an auger is, lad?'

'No.'

'Know what a combine harvester is?'

'I know the song by The Wurzels.' Travis shrugged helplessly.

Grandad laughed, and launched into the story of how he'd met one of The Wurzels in the local pub, 'Not drinking cider as you'd expect after having a hit with "I am a cider drinker",' his disability, his accident seemingly forgotten, although the family could never forget that day two years ago.

Twix barking as he barrelled into the kitchen to find Dad who was taking a quick break, howling as he pawed Dad's leg. Running back outside, checking Dad was following before running across the fields. Leading Dad to an unconscious Grandad.

Caily and Tegan had learned this later, after they'd arrived home from school to find a fire engine and an ambulance in the wheat field. It had taken three hours to free Grandad. They'd all cried, thinking they'd lost him, but he survived. If he'd been younger perhaps he'd have been back to manual work after the amputation, but he was sixty-five and he hadn't regained enough strength for the things he used to do. He'd taken over from Mum dealing with the endless paperwork, instead leaving her to be more hands on. Not only because it's less physical, they all thought, but to be close to Grandma. The accident happened shortly after her diagnosis and Caily had overheard Kate and Beth speculating whether it was this that had been on Grandad's mind, caused him to make a mistake doing something routine he had done a million times before.

'I'm not sure I have time to teach you what everything is,' Dad said, steering the conversation back to now. 'This is one of our busiest times. If we can't get the land cultivated then we can't drill and plant the winter wheat.'

'I'm sure I could—'

'Make the sun shine?' Dad nodded towards the window, fat raindrops flinging themselves against the panes. 'Because that's what we need to happen. We can yield 3½ tonnes an acre if planted on time but at this rate we'll be down to 1½ tonnes.' A pained expression crossed Dad's face. He had been trying to be more cheerful these past few days but Caily knew how worried he was. He'd been relying on a good crop. 'I'm sorry.' He shrugged. 'I'd love the help but—'

'Remember when you first came here, lad,' Grandad said softly.

Dad nodded.

'He knocked on the door like you,' Grandad told Travis. 'I didn't have an awful lot of cash – we'd been through a rough patch – but he worked for his lodgings and board. That cottage is empty now, isn't it, Matt? We haven't found any new tenants yet?'

'Not yet. There's been a couple of viewings but it's cold and damp and—'

'I really don't mind,' Travis said. 'I . . . I've recently

lost my grandma and there's nowhere else I need to be. The great outdoors and some manual labour is exactly what I need.'

Grandma reached out and squeezed his forearm. 'I'm so sorry for your loss.' Her eyes filled with tears and when she removed her hand her fingers automatically found the silver locket that she always wore. It contained photos of her and Grandad on their wedding day and it was as though the memory soothed her.

'I taught you everything, remember?' Grandad said to Dad. 'How to hitch the equipment to the tractor. How to—'

'I'm good with machinery,' Travis interrupted.

'It isn't just machines. Farming's a lot of paperwork nowadays. With grant applications and health and safety checks and—'

'Please,' said Travis. 'I know this is new to me but perhaps I can think of ways for you to diversify. A farm shop? This delicious cake would sell, I'm sure.'

'We looked into that but we can't afford the start-up costs,' Grandad said. 'It's ridiculous all the hygiene standards and planning permissions and whatnot. We should be able to do what we want with our own land.'

'Then there was packaging and advertising, and not to mention where we'd have the shop. There wouldn't be enough customer parking this side of the farm and the outbuildings across Lady's Lane aren't fit for anything,' Mum said.

'We thought about bees too. The Aldridge farm tried hives to produce local honey and bees' wax polish and someone came and nicked them. Imagine that? Stealing bees?' Grandad was getting upset.

'It was unBEElievable,' Beth tried to lighten the mood. She had been stressed herself lately but seemed happier today.

'It's a big place. 248 acres,' Grandad said. 'This was once two farms. This part, with the house and the empty cottage, was the biggest. Across the way, to the east, is the cottage Matt and Kate live in. The river runs by it. Very pretty. You access their place by Lady's Lane. The land across from Lady's Lane is ours as well. We don't do a lot over there, though. We get paid per hectare to rewild the land. You know, encourage wildlife, that sort of thing. Parts of it are really overgrown. We make more from subsidiaries now than we do from agriculture.'

'Yes. There wouldn't be anything for you to do over there. It's just empty fields.'

'And the remains of the old farmhouse and the red barn,' Grandad said.

'The farmhouse is a shell,' Dad explained. 'And the red barn is empty. We used to store machinery in it when we used the fields for barley and oats too but now we keep everything we need in this yard. It's more accessible. You mustn't go to the red barn because—'

'The roof is dangerous, it's a death trap,' chorused Caily and Tegan, used to Dad fussing, not that they had any interest in playing in a barn. It's not like they were five.

'Does this mean you're giving Travis a job?' Mum asked.

'If you're sure you're okay with food and lodgings and the pittance we can pay, then—'

'I am. Thank you!' Travis grinned, his whole face lighting up. He was the sun and the moon and the stars.

And, best of all, he was staying.

She knew, even then, he would change her life.

Only not in the way she had thought.

CHAPTER SIXTEEN

Beth

Life has already changed immeasurably and Beth can't think about, can't possibly predict what's going to happen, but nevertheless wakes with a sense of dread. Expecting the worst because her family seems to be stuck in some kind of warped Groundhog Day. The events may change but the feelings, the feelings stay the same.

Exhaustion.

Despair.

Fear.

She rolls over. Away from the first light that trickles in beneath her curtains. She used to look forward to Sundays when Sean was here. It was her breakfast-in-bed, lunch-cooked-for-her, favourite day of the week but then he was sent to prison, she became a single parent and there was no such thing as a day off, an hour off.

She misses waking up with him. Falling asleep with him.

Sean had promised to love her for ever. They were only fifteen when they started dating but she'd known, undoubtedly, unequivocally, he was the one. She'd been mad for him in the same way that Kate had been for Owen. That Nicola had been for Aaron. How grown up they had felt, the six of them. Sprawled on the haystacks in the barn, swigging sweet, fizzy cider, their futures spread out before them, paved with hope. Even then Owen had wanted to be a policeman, waving away their jokes about them underage drinking. Making his own joke that his first arrest would likely be Aaron. He was always getting into trouble, shoplifting.

'It's not my fault I didn't have a family to teach me right from wrong,' Aaron had said, looking wounded, and Beth had felt awful. She couldn't imagine growing up in foster care. It wasn't like Aaron had been mistreated – he said the homes he was placed in were largely nice – but none of them lasted long enough to form an emotional attachment. He never felt loved.

'You have us now,' she'd nudged him. 'We're your family.' She hadn't always liked Sean hanging around with him, was afraid he'd get Sean into trouble, but it's kind of what they had felt like, a dysfunctional family.

They'd chat for hours about everything and nothing.

Beth's fingers linked through Sean's. Owen's leg slung over Kate's. Aaron's hand on Nicola's stomach. Never envisaging a time they'd be separated. Sean's arrest. Kate's head turned by Matt. Nicola leaving suddenly, the day after the row that night.

The night that Kate nearly died.

Whatever Kate says, Beth still isn't entirely convinced that Nicola hadn't been to blame.

It had been a shock to see her at their birthday party.

Beth is roused from her thoughts. Through the thin wall

she can hear Tegan crying. Immediately, Beth swings her leaden legs from the bed, stuffs her feet into slippers before she shuffles into Tegan's room.

'Hey.' She climbs into Tegan's bed. Holds her daughter's shaking body. Strokes her hair gently while she cries it out.

When her sobs have subsided she asks, 'Do you want to talk about it?'

There's a beat, Tegan's breath ragged, but then she says sadly, 'I wouldn't know where to start.' She sniffs. Dries her tears with her pyjama sleeve. 'It isn't just worry about Caily. I've got my period today. Really bad cramps.'

'Then you need a hot-water bottle, paracetamol and some chocolate.'

'Yes please to the first two. I'm not hungry, though.'

'Since when do you need to be hungry to eat chocolate?'

'I'm not a kid anymore,' Tegan's voice is tight.

'No, I suppose you're not. I'll go and put the kettle on.'

'Thanks. And Mum? I could do with some sanitary towels. The thick ones.'

'Okay. Let me get you settled and then I'll go to Asda and buy some.'

Beth drops a kiss on top of Tegan's head before trudging downstairs to boil the kettle.

When she's seen to Tegan she pulls on yesterday's clothes. She's reluctant to leave the house after Tegan was followed yesterday but she'll lock the door behind her while she goes to the shops.

Tegan will be safe.

Won't she?

With a shiver she realizes that that's what Kate would have assumed about Caily.

Downstairs, Beth dials her parents' landline. While she's going to Asda she can collect any bits they might need. She's going to pick them up later, take them in to see Caily. Kate has been shielding them from the sight of their granddaughter immobile in her hospital bed, but Caily hasn't woken up yet and Kate is hopeful that some familiar voices might rouse her.

Her mum answers the phone with a cautious 'hello'. As though she's expecting bad news.

'Hi, Mum. It's Beth,' she says cheerily. 'Don't worry. Everything's okay.'

She states her name because, although once her mum would have known which of her daughters was on the phone, her cognitive impairment is worsening. She has an appointment with the neurologist again next week but, until there is an official diagnosis of dementia, Beth clings to the hope that her mum will recover. That 'impairment' is solely a weakening that can, perhaps, be strengthened. And the whole family have tried to reverse the changes. Caily and Tegan pretending they once more enjoy the matching cards game they had grown out of years ago – *I've found two cats that look like Custard* – and Mum going along with it, a sadness behind her eyes as she played, knowing deep down what they were trying to do.

Beth and Kate reminiscing over happier times. Something the nurse told them would be comforting, stimulating.

Her dad ordering two copies of the same novel from the library so they can read together, their own book club of two, hoping Mum can follow the plot, remember the characters.

It broke Beth's heart to see this. Her once-active father forced into stillness by his accident, his ensuing disability, his age a factor too, taking up a hobby he doesn't enjoy because he loves his wife so much.

They all know in their hearts that Mum will never be quite the same again, just as they know that Dad will never be as mobile as he'd like, despite the endless, sometimes painful, physio. If he'd had his accident when he was younger, stronger, it's hard to know how differently he'd have adapted.

They have all been through so much.

'How's Caily?' Mum asks.

'The swelling has gone down.' Beth repeats the same information that Kate will have relayed to Mum yesterday. Her sister's text first thing this morning had said there was nothing new to report.

'I still can't believe it happened. Has Owen been in touch?'

Beth takes a second to think. For a moment unsure what to say. Whether Kate will want to tell their parents about those ballet shoes covered in blood. The broken CCTV in the hospital meaning they cannot tell who left them by Caily's bed.

Her mum fills the silence with a stream of worries about Caily, ending with,

'And how are you coping, Kate?'

'It's Beth,' Beth says gently, squeezing the bridge of her nose to stem her tears. The family have been advised to make eye contact when talking to Mum, to give her time to respond, but this is impossible on the phone. She wraps up the conversation.

'I'm going to Asda this morning. Do you and Dad need anything?'

She waits. Can tell her mum is struggling to think.

'Can you get something I can take in for Caily? Some flowers?'

'She won't be allowed them in ICU because of the risk of infection,' Mum has been told this twice already, 'but I'll think of something she'll love when she wakes up.'

'Thanks. I'll give you the money when you get here.'

'Okay,' Beth says but she will not ask for it, remembering the last time she had picked up shopping for them. The distress on Mum's face as she tried to count out change from her purse, staring at the coins as though she'd never seen them before. Telling Dad she could manage when he tried to help, although she clearly couldn't.

The second Beth hangs up, her phone rings. She picks it up, thinking it's her mum again having thought of something else she needs.

But it isn't.

It's Matt.

With bad news.

CHAPTER SEVENTEEN

Caily

Three months ago

Since the good news, Caily had tried to picture herself as Mia, but Travis kept encroaching on her thoughts. Today, she didn't have to try to imagine herself in the role because it was the first rehearsal. Rather than start at the beginning, they were launching straight into the 'A Lovely Night' scene. The group might complain about Miss West because she pushed them hard, but really they were fond of her. She knew how to get the best out of them. Caily knew that it was this scene that would form a real connection between her and Kofi. If they could nail this iconic dance then the rest of the show would come, perhaps not easily, but naturally.

They began by strolling around the perimeter of the hall, past the other members of the drama group who were sprawled on the floor. Kofi was self-conscious, stilted as he told Caily to hold her phone against her chin to turn it into an antennae. He didn't have Ryan Gosling's sense of comic timing, not yet, but this was only day one.

Caily was wearing black yoga pants and a white cropped top, trainers on her feet, but in her mind she tried to imagine she was in heels, that sunshine-yellow dress. That her view was not of the wooden gym bars fastened to the walls but of LA spread before them, endless possibilities.

Kofi began to sing. Caily glanced at Billy, who had a much stronger voice, but Kofi would wow the audience with his piano playing.

Then she caught the glare of Dani and this threw her off. She missed her cue.

'From the top,' Miss West shouted.

Caily shot an apologetic look at Kofi, trying to ignore Dani's sniggering.

This time they got to the bench before she messed up. It was unrealistic to think they'd know the choreography off by heart already but Miss West had told them to study the dance on YouTube and, although she had watched it, her head had been full of Travis since he arrived a couple of days ago and she hadn't taken any of it in.

'Let's take it from the bench,' Miss West said.

This time Caily moved her feet the wrong way.

'You're doing great, Caily,' Tegan called out encouragingly.

'She's bloody not,' Dani shot back.

'Third time lucky,' Billy said, giving Caily a thumbs-up.

After a few deep breaths she cleared her thoughts, allowed her heart to lead rather than her head. She had watched this film a million times with Tegan.

She knew it.

Her feet moved of their own accord. Suddenly she was Mia. An aspiring actress chasing her dreams in Hollywood. A barista. A seductress.

This is what she loved most about dance. It was so much

more than solely movement. It was the telling of a story. It had heroes and heroines, tragedy and hope. True love, unrequited love.

She linked her fingers behind her back, hips swaying as she sashayed across the hall. Momentarily she fell out of step as she imagined Travis's hands on her hips. She recovered. But when Kofi took her hand to spin her around, all she could think of was Travis's hand in hers and she snapped out of character, shook her head, 'Sorry.'

'This is going to be a shitshow,' Dani said. 'There's no way that farm girl can cut it.'

'Take five,' said Miss West and clapped her hands.

Caily scurried over to the corner of the hall to retrieve her rucksack, pulling out her ballet shoes, fingering the pink silk ties, the familiarity and softness of them reassuring. It was hard to believe her feet were once so small. So delicate.

'Remember what happened the first time you wore those,' Tegan nudged her gently. 'I cried and you took my hand and we danced together. You didn't have any fear.'

'Yeah but . . .' Caily shrugged. When they were five there was nothing to worry about. There wasn't a famous performer in the audience who could decide her whole, entire future. Who held everything Caily wanted in one hand and could snatch it away just as easily.

'Hey,' Tegan nudged her. 'It's supposed to be me who can't take the pressure. But this is what we want to do, remember? This is what we love.'

'But what if . . .' Caily stared down at the floor. Fingers of sunlight poked through the window, casting tiger stripes across the parquet. She couldn't let her fears leave her lips but Tegan heard them anyway.

'You'll get the scholarship, make a name for yourself and then I'll join you. We'll have made it. Remember how you slayed as the lead in *Annie*? Do that again and "We'll have clean sheets every month".' Tegan quoted Miss Hannigan from the show and that's what Caily wanted more than anything. Not the clean sheets bit but her and Tegan. Together. 'We'll have a great time.'

'You will,' Billy grinned. 'I'll write the shows. Tegan will cry and vomit before every performance—'

'And the industry is so competitive we'll be broke and out of work most of the time,' said Tegan, smiling too.

'And on a constant diet.' Caily patted her stomach.

'And still look like pigs,' Dani muttered from where she'd been eavesdropping behind them.

Caily and Tegan ignored her, turned to each other, laughing, 'But we'll have a great time.'

'You'll be living your dream,' Billy said.

Miss West clapped her hands. 'Back to it. Caily. Kofi.'

Caily put her tiny ballet shoes carefully back in her bag. Tegan took her hand and gave it three squeezes. 'You've totally got this. It isn't the shoes that make you fabulous, you know.'

Miss West clapped her hands again.

'She's like a fucking seal,' said Billy, shaking his head sadly.

'I see you,' Billy jogged behind Tegan and Caily at the end of the day, slapping a hand on each of their shoulders, breath rasping. 'Christ. I'm so unfit.'

'Saw you first, and why don't you stop vaping, then?' Caily couldn't understand why he did it. Billy had never smoked.

'But I love the smell of the caramel one. It makes me feel I'm eating a Mars bar.'

'I'd rather have the chocolate.'

'I'd rather have your hips.' Billy patted the top of his thighs. 'But we can't always get what we want.' Pouting, Billy began strutting like Mick Jagger, singing the Rolling Stones song as they all climbed on the bus.

Conversations drifted around Caily, Miss West was going to read Billy's musical over the weekend, Dani was complaining about something, Kofi laughing, but mostly, she was in her own world, thinking not about the rehearsal but about Travis. He was moving in to the cottage today. Joy spread through her like the brightest spotlight. Already she was thinking up excuses to see him.

Billy saying goodbye brought her back to now. Tegan's stop would be next.

Soon Caily was the only one left. She lived furthest out.

She rested her head against the window. Summoned up an image of her and Travis, sitting on the bench from the *La La Land* movie with LA spread out beneath them. He would take her hand, their eyes would meet and . . .

Her phone vibrated. She pulled it from her bag.

She'd been tagged on Instagram.

It was a photo. A pig. Caily's face superimposed where its face should have been. Its fat, pink body draped with a bright-yellow dress.

She glanced around in case someone was watching her, waiting for her reaction.

Her chest tightened as she turned her attention back to her phone.

She clicked on the profile – it was a new account. This the only photo. Their handle @PigsCantDance.

Pigs can't dance.

Bile rose in her throat.

She was the pig.

And so it began.

CHAPTER EIGHTEEN

And so it begins.

The police investigation. The questions. The endless speculations.

They can't know anything or they'd have made an arrest by now.

But what will happen if you wake up?

Will you keep my secret, Caily?

Do you know how much is at stake if you tell?

Do you know what will happen?

CHAPTER NINETEEN

Matt

Travis had a secret.

It was unimaginable. Unthinkable. Unspeakable.

On the phone, Matt tells Beth everything he knows while Owen and his team search the groundskeeper's cottage, his knuckles white as he grips his handset.

After he finishes the call, his face burns again as he recalls the way Owen had asked, 'So you didn't carry out a background check?' before the search began but Matt hadn't answered him. The news had shaken the earth beneath his feet. He had folded in half. Hunched over, hands on knees, feeling the sickness rise as though he's been punched in the stomach.

'Matt?' The weight of Owen's hand on his shoulder. A bottle of water waved in front of his face.

He straightened up, legs as unstable as wisps of straw. He was unbalanced, swaying, the ineffectual scarecrow in the upper field. He drank deeply from the bottle of Evian and then wiped his mouth.

'A background check?' Owen prompted.

Matt shook his head, 'Travis was . . .'

Trustworthy.

Cheap.

Dangerous.

Matt had thought he'd found a good thing, a worker who didn't need paying much, happy with accommodation and pin money. Travis had reminded Matt of himself when he'd first arrived at the farm all those years ago. But now he knew.

They are *nothing* alike.

Travis is scum and Matt had invited him into their lives. Put his daughter in danger, he who was once her hero. There was a time Caily would place her small feet on his after her bath, her arms circled around his waist, and he'd walk, exaggerated stomps from the bathroom to the bedroom while she clung on tightly.

'Fi, fi, fo, fum,' he'd growl in a deep voice and she'd shriek with laughter, shaking her head. Droplets of water dripping onto his arm, apple shampoo fresh.

'Daddy, you're not the giant. You're supposed to save us from the giant.'

'You think I can save us from the giant?'

'Of course you can. You're my daddy.'

And that was her simple truth then. That Matt was strong and brave and could conquer everything. The opposite, in fact, to now, where he is weak and timorous and has let her down.

Fi, fi, fo, fum.

He has never felt so small.

After Matt ends the call with Beth, he hovers outside the cottage, while inside drawers are pulled open, cupboards flung wide. Matt knows there is nothing there. He has already looked, scrabbled around for clues himself, desperate to find out where Travis has gone, desperate for a way to fix things.

Is Travis still in the area?

Yesterday, somebody had left Caily's ballet shoes by her bed, shoes that Owen had carefully sealed inside a plastic bag and taken away.

Matt scans the horizon, his hands bunched into fists.

If he thought he'd been angry with Travis before, now he is incandescent, bubbling with a rage he has never felt before.

Why hadn't he insisted on any sort of background check?

'We've found something.' Owen carries out a singed envelope. 'It was in the fire grate.'

The one place Matt hadn't thought to look.

Inside are local newspaper cuttings, crumpled and yellowing with age, of Caily and Tegan. Their first dance recital. Holding hands under the bright lights, Tegan close to tears, Caily beaming at the camera. Later, one of a young Caily singing at the care home in town at Christmas, Santa hat at a jaunty angle. There's a school photo, the first secondary school production of *Annie*, Caily playing the lead in a red curly wig. Tegan, Miss Hannigan, tangerine lips pursed. The paper had called Caily 'a star in the making'. There are red circles ringing Caily and Tegan's faces.

Matt's throat burns again with a hot bile that rises suddenly. He drops to his haunches, arms crossed over his stomach, retching. Travis knew who the girls were before he turned up on the farm. He'd been watching them for years.

Why?

Matt cannot bear to think of the things Travis might have subjected Caily to.

His daughter. His beautiful, trusting, innocent daughter.

But then Matt thinks about what he had asked of his daughter himself.

Don't tell.

He'd asked too much.

'Matt?' Owen asked. 'You know what we need to do now?'

Matt nods. He does know. But he doesn't want to do it.

It's *all* too much.

CHAPTER TWENTY

Kate

It's all too much to process.

Kate had invited danger to their home. Not only invited danger but given it a key.

'Travis is . . .' Kate can't bear to say it but she tries again. 'Travis is . . .' her voice is too high. Too loud. She breaks down into noisy sobs, covering her face with her hands. 'He's on the sex offenders register?' she asks into her palms as though her hands can absorb the horror of her words.

'I'm so sorry, Kate.' It is Owen who speaks but Matt who wraps her in his arms and, although it's unfair, although he must be hurting too, she pushes her husband away, irrationally angry with him for hiring Travis even though she had suggested it, suggested giving him the groundsman's cottage.

She had welcomed him into their home.

Their lives.

She glances towards the ICU. The doctor has told Kate that the swelling to Caily's brain has reduced, not enough to withdraw sedation yet, but he will assess this every day. Now Kate is scared that sedation will be withdrawn and Caily still won't wake up because she is traumatized. Her mind might keep her under so she does not have to deal with what her body might have been through.

What Travis might have put her through.

Her parents are visiting today. How can she tell them . . . this? It will break them. It has broken her. But Owen holds her together with kind words and reassurances.

'We didn't discover anything when we found Caily that led us to believe she had been sexually assaulted.'

'But now? Now you know that Travis has . . . Travis is . . .' Kate has never felt so sick, so helpless, such a failure as a mother.

She had laughed with him. Laughed.

Her knees violently shake. She sinks onto a chair, wishing she'd followed Owen to a private room as he'd suggested.

'What did he do . . . before?' Kate both wants and doesn't want to know.

Owen sits beside her and takes her hand. She doesn't know if he's allowed to tell her but she knows he will anyway. He's her oldest friend and it is a friend she needs more than anything right now.

'He had a relationship with a fifteen-year-old girl. He claims she told him she was eighteen. The girl backs this up, says it was consensual, but her father wanted to press charges. He was influential, pushed for a conviction. Travis didn't serve jail time but he is registered.'

'Fifteen,' Kate says dully. The same age as Caily.

'Kate, there's something else.'

Owen pauses, and Kate can tell he's searching for the right words. Knows that whatever he is about to say is bad.

Very bad.

'Just say it,' she whispers.

'Travis had newspaper cuttings of Caily in the cottage. It is possible he came here to pursue a relationship with her.'

Kate inhales so sharply her breath actually sticks in her throat, bringing a rush of light-headedness that clears her mind of everything except one burning question.

'Why?' It's all Kate can think of to ask. It doesn't make sense. Her chair rocks beneath her, swaying from side to side. She grips Owen's fingers tighter because she is falling, falling.

'We don't know that yet.'

Kate glances at Matt. There is confusion and despair on his face but, more than that, she has never seen him look so scared.

'What happens now?'

'The tech guys are going to speed up looking at Caily's phone and see if there's any texts from Travis—'

'If he's so much as laid one finger on my daughter—' Matt's voice breaks.

'I can't imagine how you both feel,' Owen says.

'No you can't,' she says and the words sound spiteful spoken aloud, given a concrete shape and sharp edges, but it is true. Owen can't know how it feels. That the anguish of failing your child is a sharp-toothed, pointed-clawed creature devouring you from the inside out. He can't know because he has never had a child of his own and Kate knows this is unfair because he desperately wanted one, but none of this is fair.

Still she says 'sorry', quietly. Tears leaking down her cheeks. Knowing that the person she wants to apologize to most of all cannot hear her.

'It's okay.'

She takes the tissue he passes her and roughly wipes her cheeks.

Owen waits for a woman to pass by carrying a 'Get Well Soon' balloon, her overpowering perfume coating the roof of Kate's mouth with a bitter taste. When her heels have click-clacked away from them he says, 'There's a specialized nurse on her way who will examine Caily carefully and then we'll have more of an idea what might have happened.'

'But it's been forty-eight hours,' Matt says.

'We're aware of that. Time is imperative.'

'And we'll know, straight away, if . . . if anything?' Matt's voice creaks under the strain of the implication. Kate stands on legs that feel too weak to support her, stumbles to his side. They wrap their arms round each other and Kate can't tell who is supporting who.

'We might find out something today, but perhaps not everything. Swabs will be taken.'

'But when Caily was brought in swabs were taken.'

'They were, but not from that area.'

Owen doesn't elaborate. He doesn't have to.

'Will you find Travis's DNA on her if he has a record?'

'It isn't that simple, or that quick. Nothing is like on TV, I'm afraid, where the results seemingly come back in minutes, but there is faster new technology now and I do have someone in the lab who owes me a favour. I can promise you I am doing everything I can to speed things along.'

'I don't want some stranger touching Caily.' Kate wants answers, of course she does, but it's still her daughter's most intimate parts.

'It isn't a stranger. Sorry, I should have said,' Owen begins but before he can elaborate he adds, 'Oh look, here she is,' smiling at the nurse bustling towards them.

Owen is right. It isn't a stranger.

It's Kate's former friend.

Nicola.

'Nicola?'

Before her and Beth's surprise fortieth birthday party she had not seen her old friend for years, but now she is here.

Again.

'You're the nurse?'

'I am.'

'Thanks for coming at such short notice,' Owen says. 'The doctor is just in with Caily. As soon as he comes out she's all yours.'

Nicola opens her arms. While she is not the one Kate wants, in the absence of Beth she falls into her old friend and allows herself to be held. Kate feels the onslaught of tears, stinging her eyes, clogging her throat, but she swallows hard and extracts herself from Nicola's embrace.

'Do you know what's happened? The farmhand, Travis—'

'Try not to panic. It's easy to jump to conclusions,' Nicola says kindly, offering Kate a tissue.

'But Travis has a record and he's disappeared.'

'That doesn't necessarily mean he's guilty.'

'He had clippings of Caily in his cottage. He's on the sex offenders register.'

'I know. And I'm not defending him for that, but Owen said Travis dated a girl he thought was eighteen, didn't you, Owen?'

Owen nods.

'It could have been completely harmless. Don't assume he's a monster. Do you remember when we were fifteen? The short skirts. How much make-up we wore to try and make ourselves look older? You wanting to impress Owen, me with Aaron, Beth and Sean.'

Kate is uncomfortable with Nicola bringing this up in front of Owen and Matt, even if she is trying to calm Kate. You can't compare first love to a . . . to a sex offender.

'It's a different situation. We were all in the same school year. The boys knew our ages.'

'In an ideal world perhaps everyone should ask for ID when they go on a date but it doesn't work like that, does it?'

'You can't defend Travis—'

'Kate.' Nicola holds her hands up. 'I'm not. I'm just trying to reassure you, that's all, so you don't think the worst. We'll know soon enough but . . . innocent until proven guilty and all that.'

'I know. Sorry. I'm just so tired and so scared and so . . . everything.' Kate can't find the words. 'I miss the old days. Everything seemed so simple then. We thought we'd all be friends for ever. Why did you leave, Nicola?' What Kate really wants to know is why she never made contact again. Whether it was because of the things that Kate had told her.

'I left because . . . Mum.' She shrugs helplessly. 'And I should have stayed in touch but . . . I don't know. I couldn't bear to think of you all still together without me. Funny how we can think things will never change but then everything does.' They both glance at Owen.

'You never settled down?'

'You know Mum, she was always so demanding and . . . I suppose I never really got over Aaron. He may have been my first love but . . . I know he was . . . troubled and, well, you know? Part of me thought he might still be here.'

'Is that why you came back?'

'Not entirely,' Nicola's brow creases into a frown. 'I'd have come for your party anyway. I've thought about you and Beth a lot over the years. I'd forgotten how identical you are. I thought Beth was you when I arrived. Your girls are so similar too, aren't they? They could be sisters. Sorry, I'm rambling.' She takes a breath. 'But . . . I've felt lost lately. My job takes me all over but I wanted something to come home to. Something solid. Returning to my roots, wanting a sense of family.' Nicola's eyes welled with tears. 'I've been estranged from Mum for a number of years and . . .' She sniffs. 'I realize things have changed here. You don't need me anymore.'

'Oh, Nicola.' Kate put her arm around her friend. 'You were practically family. My parents adored you.'

'I know they did once, but that was before.'

'Before? You're not talking about that night, are you? Honestly, it's all forgotten now.'

The door to the ICU opens and the doctor steps out.

'Right. I'll get on.' Nicola gives Kate one last, swift hug, and then she's inside the room with her daughter. The door closes against her and Matt, and all they can do is wonder what happened to Caily.

And wait.

CHAPTER TWENTY-ONE

Caily

Three months ago

Caily couldn't wait.

It was Travis's welcome dinner.

Mum had arranged it over a group WhatsApp. Caily had already memorized his phone number.

As she carried bowls heaped with minted peas and a garlicky roast chicken over to the table, she sifted through storylines in her head, creating multiple narratives of their future lives together, discarding them just as quickly as they appeared.

What was wrong with her? She didn't even know him yet.

But she wanted to.

Even then her emotions were tangled because, in truth, although she allowed herself the indulgence of imagining that this was their house – that she was his partner – the pull of London, of the stage, was stronger than anything else.

She felt his eyes on her, felt the burn in her cheeks.

What would he think of her if he knew she'd been day-dreaming about him when they'd only just met?

He'd think she was a child.

'Caily?'

At the sound of her name, soft on his tongue, she clattered down the dish of new potatoes. One slipped from the bowl and rolled off the table, leaving a buttery trail. Twix swallowing it whole before she could retrieve it.

'Sorry, I . . .' Flustered, she wiped her clammy hands on her jeans.

'I was asking about Twix. Whether you've had him from a puppy?' He ran Twix's silky ears through his fingers as he spoke.

'Yes.' She slid into the seat next to him. 'Almost six years now. As you can see, we're still training him.'

Twix licked his greasy lips.

'I'd have loved a puppy growing up.'

'I tell you who didn't love him,' Tegan said, forking a ball of stuffing onto her plate. 'Custard.'

On hearing his name, the cat sat up, yawned widely. Grandad fed him a titbit of chicken.

'So, how did the first rehearsal go?' Mum asked, sloshing water into everyone's glass.

'Rehearsal?' Travis asked.

'Caily is playing Mia in *La La Land*,' Grandma said.

'Tegan is the understudy.'

'That's amazing. You must both be so talented,' Travis said.

'They are.' Grandad beamed. 'They get it from me.' He gave a little shimmy.

'You must both enjoy performing?' Travis drowned his dinner in thick gravy.

'I love it when I'm doing it, and the high afterwards is

incredible, but before the performance I'm always a mess,' Tegan said.

'But you feel the fear and do it anyway? That's incredible. Do you get nervous, Caily?'

Caily basked in the glow of Travis's interest, leaning into him, a flower to his sun.

'Not usually no, but this time I am. There's a lot riding on it.'

'I'm sure you'll be as fabulous as you were in *Annie*. "A star in the making".' He smiles reassuringly.

'How did you know I was in *Annie*?' She frowned.

'I . . .' An expression she can't read crossed his face.

'Did I tell you?' Grandma said. 'Travis, you should know I'm having problems with my memory lately. So please forgive me if I repeat myself or don't always remember the things you tell me.'

Momentarily, Grandad rested his hands on hers.

'Of course. Thanks for being honest,' Travis said.

The chatter around her subsided as Caily fell back into the memory of playing *Annie*. Not the fun of rehearsals, a two-year-old Twix playing Annie's dog, Sandy. Chasing his tail in joyful circles when he was supposed to be sitting looking sombre, sad. But remembering it was the time that everything changed. The definitive moment she knew she wanted to make a career out of the stage.

It wasn't that the choreography was in a different league to the shows she'd taken part in at primary school. Although she found it effortless keeping time with the music and the other kids. Belting out 'It's a Hard Knock Life', dancing around a broom. But it was while singing 'Tomorrow' that something ignited inside her. She'd become that orphan who had been through so much and yet still retained so much hope. She sang with everything she had and, when she'd finished, the audience rose to their feet, clapping, even though the performance wasn't finished. If she could bottle up one feeling and carry it with her for life, it would be that. The applause. The . . . the love, although love is not something she has ever lacked. It was more the shared experience. She was feeling something and passing that feeling on and she knew, undoubtedly, as her eyes scanned the audience and she saw not only her own family but other people's mothers and fathers all clapping for her, that it was what she wanted to do for the rest of her life.

Outside her bedroom window the moon was a crescent in a navy sky, popping with stars. Caily couldn't stop thinking about Travis. His bright blue eyes, the curl of his hair where it brushed against his collar. She knew if she'd reached out to touch it, it would have been soft in her fingers.

She was sitting at her dressing table, wiping her face with washable cotton pads drenched with micellar water when her phone beeped with a WhatsApp message.

Travis.

Tonight was lovely. You're so inspirational. Looking forward to getting to know you better :-)

She smiled at her reflection, saw the light in her eyes, the glow of her skin.

Did he like her too?

Perhaps he did. Perhaps he'd been asking Grandma questions about her and that's when she'd told him about *Annie.*

He'd only just moved in so they can't have had a chance to talk much, and the fact that when they had it had been about her must mean something, mustn't it?

She turned the words of his text over and over in her mind, looking for hidden meaning, rereading them until they blur and skip and morph into something else entirely.

You're beautiful.

But then Tegan shared a photo with her, a screen grab of a message Travis had sent her.

Exactly the same message she had received, obviously copy and pasted.

And then she didn't feel special at all.

Another alert.

An Instagram tag.

A pig dressed as Annie this time, in a red curly wig, red dress.

Caily tried to brush it off. It must be Dani. Before the account was set up she'd overheard Caily worrying about her weight, called her a pig. She'd been eavesdropping when Caily and Tegan had reminisced over their roles in *Annie*. But knowing who was doing this didn't make it hurt any less.

She clutched her phone tightly, stared at her reflection, the mirror telling her something different now. She wasn't pretty at all. She was fat. Ugly. She lowered her eyes to her phone again, stomach churning as she studied the picture, read the caption.

Tomorrow. Tomorrow. You'll get slaughtered, tomorrow.

She felt sick.

CHAPTER TWENTY-TWO

Kate

Kate's stomach spins nauseous circles as she stares at the closed door, Nicola on the other side of it. What will her examination reveal?

'How long will Nicola take?' Kate asks Owen.

'I'm not sure. Why don't you head over to the canteen? When did you last eat, Kate?'

'I don't know.' The minutes are blurring into each other, the hours, the days.

'You need to keep your strength up. I'll come and find you the second there is news.'

Kate nods once, sadly.

'Look, here's your family.' Owen is looking over her shoulder.

Kate turns.

Beth is pushing Dad in his chair. Mum slightly behind. Both her parents are wearing the same shocked and anxious expression that Kate feels on her own face.

'We can't go and see Caily just yet,' Kate says. 'Nicola is with her.'

'Nicola Crosby?' Her mum's fingers automatically seek out her silver wedding locket.

'What's she doing here?' Dad asks.

'She's a nurse.' Kate doesn't expand on that, putting aside her own stress and looping her arm through her mum's. 'Let's go and get a drink.'

'But we wanted to see Caily. Don't you want us to see her?' Her mum's voice is thick with tears.

'Of course I want you to see her. I'll fill you in when we get to the café.'

'Come on, Mum.' Beth leads the way, settling them all at the table, removing one of the chairs so Dad can stay in his wheelchair, then offering to fetch the coffee. Kate goes to the counter with her. They pass platters of greasy, golden chips, the smell of oil turning her stomach.

'Matt called and told me about Travis being on the sex offenders register,' Beth says while their drinks are being made.

'That's why Nicola is with Caily. They think . . . Caily might have been sexually assaulted. Nicola is a forensic nurse.' Kate detaches herself from her body, her voice, hearing herself whisper the words but not allowing herself to feel them. Not allowing herself to fall apart. 'Did Matt tell you about the newspaper cuttings?'

'No. The police were searching the cottage when he rang, though.'

Kate fills her in.

'My god.' Beth lowers her voice as the barista brings their order. 'And Tegan's face was circled too? That's terrifying. What does Owen say? Did Travis target Caily? Was he after Tegan too? Do you think she's safe? Fuck.' Beth is garbling. 'Tegan thought she was followed yesterday.'

'Followed? By who? Did you report it?'

'No. Tegan didn't actually see the person, and once she'd calmed down she wasn't sure if she'd just imagined it. We're all on edge.'

'You have to tell Owen.'

'Of course. We *have* to find Travis. This is really creepy. He must be the one who pushed her. I've been checking social media but I can't find any trace of him . . . do you have any idea where he might have gone?'

'No.'

'He must have mentioned where he grew up? Anything?' Beth's face creases in desperation.

'He didn't. Beth, I know you want to help but it's not your job to find Travis. We have nothing to go on. Matt's been the same. Wanting me to recall conversations with him. Trawling through Google. The police were already trying to track him before they found the cuttings. Hopefully now he'll be even more of a priority.'

'I know. I just . . . I wish we knew where he was, that's all. Are you going to tell Mum and Dad about him?'

'I don't know if they'll cope with the thought of a sexual assault.' Kate throws a worried glance towards her parents. Already they seemed to have shrunk. Skin hanging looser, shoulders infinitely more rounded. She stacks one cardboard cup on top of the other, steam billowing from the plastic lids. Beth scoops up the remaining three.

'Hang on,' Beth says as Kate begins to walk off. 'There's something you should probably know. When Owen interviewed Tegan and me yesterday she said that there had been some sort of online bullying.'

Kate feels her hands begin to shake, hot coffee splashing out of the hole in the lid. What else has her daughter been through that she didn't know about?

Matt's suddenly by her side, taking the drinks from her.

'Is everything okay?' He's frowning, his eyes flitting between her and Beth.

Kate nods, her throat too tight to talk. Wordlessly, they all head back to the table.

Kate tells her parents that Nicola is here in a professional capacity as a nurse, checking Caily over, she doesn't say for what, but they'll be able to see their granddaughter soon.

'Is she living back here, then?' Beth asked.

'When I invited her to the party a few weeks ago she said she was in the process of relocating. I did do the right thing inviting her, didn't I?' Matt's question remained unanswered. 'I thought you were best friends once?'

'Beth's always been my best friend,' Kate says tactfully. 'But there was no big falling-out so you haven't done anything wrong.'

Nobody speaks. Dad blowing the heat from his coffee. Mum staring at the cup as though she has never seen one before, reaching out tentative fingers to touch it. Perhaps her muddled mind is playing tricks on her again so she has to focus on her drink rather than this terrible situation they have found themselves in. They are so far removed from the independent, capable parents who had run the farm, led the Monday-night family dinners.

It is Monday tomorrow and when Kate pictures all their

empty chairs around the table she wants to cry. Will they ever share a meal as a family again or has Travis ruined everything for ever?

She invited him into their home.

What will Nicola discover when she examines Caily? Her thoughts turn to her former friend.

She and Nicola had met in secondary school when, for the first time, she was placed in a separate class to her twin. They'd grown close, not as close as her and Beth of course – no one could replace her sister – but she had enjoyed having another friend. Once the three of them began dating it was fun hanging out together. Her and Owen, Nicola and Aaron, Beth and Sean. They were all sharing the same experience, first love and it felt . . . It felt like everything.

She remembers the evening of her accident clearly. They were fifteen.

Nicola's mum had dropped her at the farmhouse for a sleepover, as she often did before she went on a date with her current boyfriend.

She had a lot of boyfriends.

It had been dark, rain hurling itself angrily around the farm. Recently, Kate and Beth had discovered where their parents kept the key to the cottage that Matt and Kate live in today. It had previously been rented out but the tenants had moved on and so, while they looked for other occupants, it was empty.

Beth, Sean, Owen and Aaron were already there. Aaron likely telling stories in flickering candlelight, trying to terrify Beth. In truth, neither of them liked him much. Kate had waited at the farmhouse not only to walk across with Nicola but also to tell her that she had seen Aaron outside the off licence yesterday, kissing another girl.

Kate had deliberated whether to tell her friend. Questioning whether she'd want to know if it had been Owen with his arms wrapped around some red-head. However much it hurt, she knew that she would. Beth thought that if Kate told Nicola tonight and she decided to confront Aaron they'd all be there as back up. He had an edge to him. She didn't know why Sean was such good friends with him. One day he'd get Sean arrested, Kate was sure. Aaron was what her grandfather called a wrong 'un.

The wind was brutal, snatching their breath as they slipped out the back door of the farmhouse. The mist swallowing them.

Rather than taking the shorter route across the fields they turned right, hoping the hedges that ran along the perimeter of the farm would offer them some protection from the weather, guide them through the swirling fog.

The girls walked quickly, hoods pulled over heads that were bowed against the wind. Cold rain still lashing against their faces, trickling down their necks.

When they reached the river, they turned left, trudging forward, wet jeans plastered to their tired legs.

They began to chat.

'Wish we had a torch,' Nicola said. There was scant light emanating from the crescent moon. But the change of direction had brought respite from the wind.

'Won't be too long.' The cottage lay in shadows in front of them.

'I'm going to look such a wreck for Aaron,' Nicola said.

'I've got something to tell you about last night,' she said tentatively. 'About Aaron.'

'You know?' Kate was surprised and relieved. 'And you've forgiven him? I'm not sure I would if it were Owen. I can't bear the thought of him kissing anyone else.'

'What?' Nicola stood stock still. Her arm falling from Kate's. 'I don't know what you're talking about.'

'I thought . . .' Kate trailed off. The gentle speech she'd prepared to tell Nicola redundant on her tongue. She'd messed up.

It happened in tandem. The sudden whip of lightning making them jump. Kate losing her footing. Arms windmilling as she lurched backwards.

The feel of Nicola's fingers tight around her wrist and then a release as she fell, feet slipping down the rain-sodden bank.

She screamed.

She had never learned to swim. Wanting them to have separate hobbies, Beth had taken swimming lessons while Kate learned to horse ride, something Beth wasn't interested in.

'Nicola!' Her friend's name tore from her throat as her feet scrambled for traction, screaming again as she slid into the freezing water.

At the memory, she shivers, wraps her arms around herself. She'll never forget the terror as she was sucked under the surface, her legs kicking frantically, her body quickly tiring.

'Kate!' Nicola had yelled but Kate could not see her through the water and the darkness and her own blind panic and, although she called for help, her friend did not come into the river. Did not try to save her. But, after what felt like hours, even though it was apparently only a few minutes, Beth was there. Hoisting her to safety.

Beth had heard Kate's screams from the cottage, although she said later that even without them she would have sensed something was wrong. Whether that was true or not, Kate didn't know. All she knew was that, if it hadn't been for Beth, Kate would be dead.

They all knew it, although nobody voiced it.

When they got back to the farmhouse, Kate supported by Beth and Nicola, crying, Dad had been ashen. Still, he had consoled Nicola, it wasn't her fault. Kate had told her friend the same thing before they went to bed. She really didn't blame her, but had woken from a nightmare still feeling her friend's fingers around her wrist.

In the morning Nicola had barely spoken to her. Hadn't come back to school on Monday and shortly afterwards Kate had stood outside her rented house, which was now empty. She never knew why Nicola moved away, only that she missed her.

Dad had still been upset the following day.

'I'm fine. It's okay.' She had made him a cup of tea, guessing that he probably felt he'd failed in his role as a father, a protector.

'It isn't okay. You could have *died* last night. I don't want anyone staying again.'

As it turned out, after Nicola had moved away she hadn't anyone to ask anyway. She hasn't really thought about Nicola for twenty-five years now. Aaron neither, she can't even remember his surname. It is sad and strange how people who once brought the colour into your life often fade away.

But now Nicola is back.

There's a throbbing inside Kate's head. She cannot think of the past anymore but she physically cannot make conversation. Her tongue feels thick, her mouth is dry. She is terrified and so she waits silently while Matt and Patrick fill the silence with talk of the farm. They discuss whether it's time to let the sheep go.

'Financially they're not viable. We've lost so much money this past year. Even with the grants we're entitled to—'

'But we've always had sheep,' Dad says. 'My father and his father and—'

'I know, but they're costly enough normally with the vaccinations and the six-week checks for foot rot and the parasites. And now,' Matt takes a deep breath, 'almost half the ewes aren't pregnant.'

'How can that be?' Patrick leans forward. 'You hired the rams from Reg Aldridge's place?'

'No,' Matt fiddles with the packets of sugar on the table. 'Chris Chandler's were cheaper.'

'Oh, lad,' Dad says, but he doesn't make Matt feel any worse than he clearly already does. Dad is infinitely kind.

'Here's Owen,' Beth interrupts.

Kate's heart misses a beat as Owen strides across the canteen, Nicola at his side.

She feels the slow thud, thud, thud in her ears as he slides into the empty chair next to her mum, Nicola hovering awkwardly behind him. Her worried glance shifting between Kate's mum and dad. To Kate, to Matt and then back to Owen.

Kate holds her breath, senses rather than sees Matt's hand

stretch out towards her. Their fingers automatically linking together.

It is not the place for news. There are no other customers, a couple of staff behind the counter some distance away, but still.

It is not the place for news.

CHAPTER TWENTY-THREE

Beth

While they wait for Owen to impart the news, Beth feels a tightness in her chest, a burn.

'Nicola hasn't found any evidence of trauma or injury.' Owen doesn't say where to, he doesn't have to.

Beth releases the air from her lungs in one relieved breath.

'We can go and see Caily now.' Kate scrapes back her chair before their parents can ask any questions.

At the ICU Beth isn't sure they'll all be allowed in together, but Nita looks sympathetically at her parents and tells them it's okay. There are no other visitors right now but if one comes some of them will have to wait outside. Kate explains to Mum about the risk of infection, and the procedures they need to follow. Beth had already told her on the way but she still looks blank as though she's never heard them before. Concerned.

Mum and Dad clean their hands, loop plastic aprons around their necks. Grandad self-propels his chair, there's a squeak with each rotation of the wheel. 'She'll hear me coming,' he tries to joke, but his voice is thick with tears.

Mum begins to cry the instant they reach the bed. Linking Caily's fingers through hers, not wary of the tubes and wires the way Beth had been on her first visit. Almost unaware of them.

'I'm so sorry, my darling,' she turns to Kate, her face tearstained. 'She can hear me, can't she?'

'I like to think so.'

Mum talks softly to Caily. 'I was thinking about the first day Twix came to the farm. When he bounded into the kitchen at eight weeks old, his paws skidding across the floor. He crashed into the table leg. He'd only ever set paws on carpet before and looked so bewildered, a bit like Bambi learning to walk, do you remember, Caily? Custard was on the windowsill, staring at him with complete disdain. Twix saw the expression on the cat's face and hung his head, dropped his ears. I still think he felt silly.'

'One scathing look from Custard can make you feel like that,' Matt says.

'Then you and Tegan began skidding across the floor on your knees until Twix joined in racing alongside you,' Beth adds. 'Tegan wore a hole in her tights that day,' she says but with no hint of annoyance.

They rake over old memories, the whole family. Sometimes they laugh, sometimes tears come, but whether the stories are laced with humour or sadness they are all coated with a thick layer of love.

Matt is the first to leave, he needs to return to the farm. Beth walks him out. They have a worried chat and a hug and then she returns to the ICU, where Kate is pulling on her coat.

'Do you want me to take you home when I drop Mum

and Dad off?' Beth says. The bags beneath Kate's eyes have grown larger, darker. She's worried her sister is too exhausted to drive.

'I'm not going home. There's someone I need to talk to.' Kate pinches her lips together in the way she always has when she doesn't want to talk about something.

Later that night, there are hands around Beth's throat, squeezing. She moans with pleasure, her hips rising, spine arching, grateful to lose herself in the physical sensations. To not, for a short time at least, have to worry about the other news Matt had given her on the phone. The news that no one else knew about.

Afterwards, she lies panting on the crumpled sheets, heart slowing from a gallop.

'We have to stop meeting here, doing this.' She's gripped by a spasm of guilt. Not only for what just happened but for the way she enjoyed it. For allowing herself to forget all about Kate and Caily. To, for a brief period, not worry about her mum's memory and her dad's disability.

Shamefully, she isn't considering her daughter.

But then she's alone and back in reality, back where she and Matt have made a mess of everything.

Where Caily could wake at any moment and tell everyone what they've done.

And Beth would have to fight to save everything.

CHAPTER TWENTY-FOUR

You *fought so hard to save yourself that day.*

Your mouth open in a scream as you lost traction, your hands grasping at nothing, feet scrambling for purchase but by then you were already falling.

You looked so beautiful.

Just as you did on stage.

You'll never be on stage again, Caily.

Never dance.

You're a bird with clipped wings.

You'll never fly.

CHAPTER TWENTY-FIVE

Caily

Eight weeks ago

It felt like flying, the sensation of love. The giddiness Caily felt whenever she thought of Travis. It was only when she let him fill her mind that she could let go of all the Instagram posts that were chipping away at her confidence.

Sometimes she couldn't help lying in bed, scrolling on her phone, torturing herself, pinching the flesh of her stomach – was she fat? – but then she'd force herself to focus on Travis. Recalling the brush of his hand against hers, the intensity in his gaze. He was interested in her too, in her family, in a way the boys at school weren't. He was deeper.

Intense.

And if he was interested in her then the posts didn't mean anything, did they? She wasn't that plump, clumsy pig but someone else.

Someone desirable.

Dad had kept Travis busy, then finally it had stopped raining and there had been a rush to plant the crops, knowing it was too late for the yield they needed to survive. Still Dad seemed not happier – he still walked with a stoop as though he had the weight of the world on his shoulders – but he'd stopped talking about giving up farming, suggesting that Patrick sell the land.

The buttery sun was melting over the fields, brushing everything with a golden light. Caily walked with purpose, Twix at her heels, their long shadows matching them step for step. It was late afternoon but still warmer than usual for this time of year.

Crazy weather.

Crazy feelings.

Travis.

She was almost at the farmhouse.

Every day since he'd come home after his accident she had helped Grandad with his physio exercise, trying to keep his muscles strong.

Sometimes he tried to wave her away, 'You've got better things to do than help an old man,' he'd say and she'd smile and tell him the exercises were exactly the same ones she needed to do as a dancer. 'You're doing me a favour,' she would say. 'Keeping me on track.' Which wasn't true, but she loved the time with him. Knew that, without her, he'd be so focused on Grandma he'd likely slip out of the habit of stretching his muscles. And he needed to at his age. After a lifetime of manual work, his body wasn't used to stillness, his muscle mass decreasing rapidly. Anyway, it wasn't like she didn't have the time. Since her parents couldn't afford her dance lessons anymore, she didn't have many other places to be and there was only so much on the farm she could help with.

Travis was right, Caily thought, as she pushed open the

door with an 'it's only me'. She was lucky having family so close by.

As though she'd conjured him with her thoughts, there he was, sat at the table.

Travis.

'Hi, Caily. Your grandma's tempting me again.' He gestured with his fork at the mound of homemade fruit pie heaped on the plate in front of him.

'You need feeding up,' Grandma said. 'Looking after.'

Caily noticed the protrusion of Travis's Adam's apple as he swallowed hard and she knew he was thinking of the loss of his own grandmother. How he didn't have anyone to look after him.

'It's bribery,' Grandma said. 'The rats are out in force again and the nights haven't got colder yet. They're too brave. Too big,' she shuddered. 'Custard isn't up to catching them.' At the sound of his name, the snoozing cat opens one eye, closing it again when he realizes there aren't any treats on offer.

'I'll lay some poison,' Travis promised.

Caily filled up a bowl with water for Twix before she helped herself to a glass of lemonade.

'Want me to refill the teapot?' she asked while she was up.

'Please, save my old legs,' Grandma said.

'At least you've got two of them.' Grandad grinned.

'You're not old!' Caily never thought of her grandparents as elderly.

'I certainly feel it. My daughters are turning forty in a few weeks. Forty! I remember the day they were born.'

'So do I,' Grandad said. 'You gave birth in the early hours and then by late afternoon you were feeding the sheep.'

'Farming stops for no man, or woman, and that was such a cold winter.' Grandma smiled. 'Anyway, they were good babies. Even then.'

'I bet you've a few tales to tell, though. Twins must have been hard work?' Travis asked.

'They certainly contributed to a few of my grey hairs. Double trouble.'

'Double everything,' Grandad said. 'Prams, cots, car seats.'

'Sounds expensive.' Travis pulled a face.

'We managed, and with babies there is always someone wanting to pass on clothes, buy them gifts. We had a lean period when they were teenagers, wondered whether we'd be able to keep the farm, but they never minded sharing, did they, Patrick? And we pulled through. They were so content.'

'We need to do something for the girls' birthday,' Grandad said. 'A party?'

'I can make a pink blancmange shaped like a rabbit, they love that. And we can play pin the tail on the donkey and—'

'Mary,' Grandad said gently. 'Remember they're forty.'

For a moment Grandma's eyes glazed over with a thin film of tears but then she said, 'Yes, of course they are.'

'But that's something to celebrate,' Grandad said. 'We don't know at our age how many more birthdays we'll see.'

'You're 67, not 107.' Grandma shook her head affectionately.

'I know—'

'With your mind and my body, we can be grateful we make one complete person between us.' Grandma took Grandad's hand, and there was such love in the gaze that passed between them that Caily felt a pang of longing for someone to look at her the same way they looked at each other.

'You guys are inspirational,' Travis said. 'How long have you been together?'

'A lifetime. We met when I was fifteen and Patrick was twenty-one. It was different times then. Age gaps didn't matter and we didn't go on dates with multiple people like nowadays with all the swiping whatnot Tegan was telling me about. It was simple. Patrick was my one and only sweetheart.'

'Wow. Where did you meet?'

'At my father's greengrocers,' Grandma said. 'Patrick used to supply the shop with the vegetables, and one day in the school holidays I was helping out and—'

'Love at first sight?' Travis leaned forward, a smile on his face.

'Not exactly. Patrick said to my father he could have this week's delivery for free if he could have a date with his daughter.'

'I thought it was romantic.'

'My dad hit the roof.' Grandma frowned at the memory, fiddling with the locket around her neck. 'Other people wouldn't have batted an eyelid at the age gap, but he did. He called Patrick a pervert and said I was still a child and I wasn't for sale.'

'I hadn't meant it like that, and I hadn't realized Mary was still at school. I felt awful.'

'It wasn't your fault,' Travis said sympathetically. 'It can be hard to gauge a girl's age.'

'I felt terrible too,' Mary said. 'Patrick was so sweet. I gathered up every ounce of courage I had to come here, to the farm, to apologize for the way my father had spoken to him. We ended up talking for hours, didn't we?'

'We did, my love. I was completely smitten. Still am.'

'And your father came round?'

Grandma's fingers tightened around her locket. 'No. Patrick and I met in secret for months, but Dad found out and forbade me to see him and . . . I couldn't picture me without him, and I'd turned sixteen by then, so I moved in here and . . .' Her eyes watered. 'I don't regret it for a second, although I missed my dad. We never did make up.'

'And your mum? What did she think?'

'She died when I was small.'

'I'm so sorry.' Travis paused. 'But what an incredible story. It just goes to show, you can't fight true love.'

Caily's phone buzzed, Mum telling her that dinner was in half an hour.

'I should be getting back.' Caily set her empty glass on the table. 'Come on, Twix.'

Travis stood and said, 'I'll walk with you.'

Caily couldn't look her grandparents in the eye as she said her goodbyes.

This was not a date.

But she couldn't help the feelings zapping around her body.

'It's so beautiful here,' Travis said as they reached the river. He stood still, shielding his eyes against the low sun. He was right next to her, so close, her shoulder almost against his arm. She was overcome with a desire to throw herself against him so she took a step away. 'I wonder why anyone would ever want to leave?'

She didn't know if he knew about the scholarship, if he

was referring to her, but he was gazing into the distance and she looked around, seeing what he saw, what she took for granted. The sun glinting off the water. The patchwork fields. The sky stretching clear and wide, limitless. She wanted to explain the pull of London inside her, but she didn't know if the longing she felt in that moment was for the bright lights of the big city or if it was for him.

She couldn't help wondering whether Travis's skin would be warm and soft if he took her hand in his, feeling she was about to cross something, step away from the child she was towards the woman she wanted to be. Not knowing if she was ready but wanting it, wanting him, all the same.

'Travis,' she was uncertain as she gazed at him, willing him to kiss her. When he didn't move she lunged forward, pressed her lips against his.

It was unexpected.

Sudden.

Frightening.

That shove.

She'd barely been aware of his hands against her chest until she was flying backwards, twisting, landing awkwardly, her cheek slamming against something hard. Her jaw clamping together. Blood filling her mouth.

But then Travis was crouching down, helping her up, apologizing profusely.

And she let him hold her, feeling the blood dribble from the corners of her mouth, trying her hardest not to cry.

The moon bathed her bedroom with a soft creamy light.

Caily's stomach grumbled. She'd skipped dinner. Calling

to her mum that she had a headache and was going to bed as she had rushed up the stairs.

She lightly touched her cheek with her fingertips: it felt sore, swollen.

Still, it didn't hurt as much as her pride.

Was she that repulsive?

She squeezed her eyes closed but she could still see the horror on Travis's face as she'd tried to seduce him.

Seduce?

She'd thrown herself at him like an animal.

Caily picked up her phone, wanting to tell Tegan what had happened, but she hesitated. She'd always shared everything with her cousin, always, but perhaps not this. Travis was still sometimes sending them identical messages, 'Playing you off against each other,' Billy had said, but why would he? Travis obviously didn't find her attractive or he'd have kissed her.

She opened Instagram, knowing that she shouldn't. She was tagged in another photo.

The same pig. The same yellow dress. But this time the backdrop was LA. The same bench where Ryan Gosling and Emma Stone sat, gazing at the lights spread before them, full of hope and possibility.

Caily is full of neither.

Pigs can't dance.

She swallowed hard, not brushing this off the way she had before.

She *was* useless, ugly, and in that moment she felt unloved and unwanted.

Afraid.

What if it were true?
She couldn't kiss.
Couldn't sing.
Couldn't dance.

CHAPTER TWENTY-SIX

Kate

'She just wanted to dance.' Billy sobs. Black make-up streaking down his cheeks. 'She was so beautiful.'

'Is so beautiful, Billy. *Is*.' Kate takes a breath and tries to calm herself. She's come to see Billy to find out about the cyberbullying Tegan mentioned to Owen. She'd called Owen and he said they'd be looking into it but Travis is their priority, as he should be.

Kate could have gone to Tegan but didn't because Tegan and Caily have always protected each other and Caily clearly didn't want her or Matt to know about the problems she was having.

Billy's parents had sighed, complained that she was interrupting their Sunday lunch and Kate had bitten her lip so she hadn't snapped at their insensitivity. What wouldn't she give to be sitting around the table with her daughter tucking into a roast. Twix lying under the table, pressed against Caily's legs, knowing that she would slip him morsels of chicken.

No wonder Caily had said Billy was desperate to get away from his parents.

They are in Billy's garden, she hasn't been invited inside the house.

'Was she seeing Travis?' Kate asks again, softer this time, handing Billy a tissue.

'I don't know.'

'You must know whether anything happened between them?'

Billy blows his nose noisily.

'Caily won't get into trouble. Neither will you, but . . . you know the police think someone pushed Caily from that bridge on Friday?'

'What?' Billy dissolves into tears again. 'She was pushed? She didn't jump?'

'Why would she jump? Did something happen between her and Travis?' Kate is losing patience. Wants to take hold of Billy's shoulders and shake the truth out of him.

'I don't know. Caily really fancied him. She wanted something to happen. Please don't be mad at her.'

'I'm hardly likely to be mad at her, Billy. She's in a *coma*.' Kate covers her mouth with her hand, remembering that this is one of Caily's best friends. Remembering he is only fifteen. 'I'm sorry for being short with you. But, please, tell me what you know.'

Billy looks at her helplessly. 'She's been so quiet these last three weeks. We haven't been hanging round together as much. I think she was getting nervous about the performance. She wanted that scholarship. Really wanted it, but she was losing confidence.'

'Because of the cyberbullying?'

Billy shrugs.

'The police have her phone and will be checking her social media and emails and everything—'

'Do they think the posts have something to do with whatever went down on the bridge?' Billy stares at her with wide eyes.

'I don't know. But a crime has been committed and they need to explore all avenues. Can you show me the posts?'

There's a beat. Billy looks at the ground, the sky. At everything but her before finally whispering, 'Are you sure you want to see them? They're horrible.'

'I'm sure,' Kate says, although she isn't sure at all but she needs to see what Caily has been going through.

Billy opens the app and lands on a profile. The grid is full of pictures of Caily, or rather Caily's face, superimposed onto pigs in various locations.

'Who did this?' she hisses. She is incandescent with rage, she feels the heat of it under her skin.

Billy shrinks away from her fury.

'Billy? You must have some idea?'

'Dani had been giving her a really hard time in rehearsals. Daniela Kent. She'd wanted the lead in *La La Land*. The scholarship.'

'Do you know where she lives?'

'Umm. Yeah, but—'

'Tell me.' Kate's hands shakes as she digs a piece of paper and a pen from her bag and passes them to Billy, who scrawls down an address. The second the pen leaves the paper Kate snatches it, runs towards the car.

*

'I don't understand why you want to do this,' Matt says, grumbling when Kate picks him up from the farm. 'Let Owen handle it. After what the police found in Travis's cottage, it's not likely that this kid, Dani, pushed Caily, is it?'

'I want Owen's focus to remain on finding Travis. I don't for a second think Dani had anything to do with Caily's fall, she's a child, but I want to tell her parents what she's done. There are no consequences for kids these days. Imagine if someone's mother knocked on the door and said Caily had been trolling someone.'

'I think I'd be more worried if the police knocked on my door.'

Kate pulls the car against the kerb. There is a light on in the house. It is big. Imposing. But she will not be intimated. She climbs out of the car and locks it. Begins to crunch up the long gravelled driveway. Past the tacky nude statue on the perfectly manicured lawn.

Somebody must be home. Somebody must be home, there's a Range Rover parked outside.

'What did you say this girl's name is again?' Matt grabs her arm as she rings the bell.

'Daniela.'

'Daniela?'

'Daniela Kent.'

'Kate, let's go. I think . . .' Matt falls silent as the door swings open. A stocky man shadowed in the doorway.

There's something in his gaze that flickers between Matt and Kate. He licks his fleshy lips.

'I'm Matt and this is my wife, Kate.' The words fall out of his mouth in a rush. 'My *wife*,' he emphasizes, glancing at Kate, taking her hand, as though she needs protecting against this man.

'Are you Dani's father?' she asks.

'Yes. I'm Victor Kent.'

'We'd like to speak to her about an Instagram account.'

'Oh you would, would you?' He leans against the door-frame, runs his hand over his bald head.

'My daughter has been tagged into some photos.' Matt says, almost apologetically. 'We don't know for certain that Dani posted them—'

'I think we do,' Kate cuts in.

'But you don't have any proof?' Victor asks.

'No, but I'm certain she did.' Kate is so exhausted she can't think of a diplomatic way to phrase her accusations. 'You should call her down. Ask her to apologize.'

'Should I?'

'Or I'll let the police deal with it.'

'I'll tell you what I will do.' His face twists into a smile. 'I'll give you five seconds to get off my property.'

Matt roughly begins to pull Kate back down the driveway. She tries to shake him off but something in Victor's eyes chills her.

Like father, like daughter?

Who exactly are the Kents and what are they capable of?

CHAPTER TWENTY-SEVEN

Matt

Victor fucking Kent.

Victor Kent is Dani's father.

Victor, who Matt had telephoned earlier, offering stuttering apologies and foolishly asking for help.

As Matt hurries Kate back down the driveway, brushing away her questions, telling her that no, he doesn't know Victor but he doesn't get a good feeling about him.

It's only when he is safely inside his car he glances towards the house.

Victor raises his hand, draws his finger across his throat in a slashing motion.

CHAPTER TWENTY-EIGHT

Caily

Four weeks ago

It was slashed. Her beautiful yellow dress was in ribbons. It had taken her mum two weeks to recreate Mia's iconic costume and now somebody had ruined it.

Somebody.

They all knew who it was.

'You fucking bitch,' Tegan flew at Dani.

'I see you.' Billy sauntered into the hall, assessing the situation, face dropping, instantly grabbing Tegan around the waist and pulling her back. Caily should have been the one to help her cousin but her legs were trembling and she could not move.

'Look,' Tegan shouted. 'Look what she's done to Caily's dress.'

'It wasn't me.' Daniela held her hands up. 'Perhaps Caily ripped it when she wore it last? It was rather . . . *snug.*'

Words can't hurt me.

But it wasn't words that had sliced into her beautiful dress, was it? It was something sharp and pointed and dangerous.

She wanted to scream.

CHAPTER TWENTY-NINE

Your screams tore thorough me as you plummeted to the ground.

I'll never forget the sound, the terror on your face.

You hadn't wanted to die.

I could see that thought flicker across your face as you began to fall.

The horror.

The panic.

'Caily,' I whisper into your ear, along with my secrets, my fears and my hopes because who else can I talk to?

You'll never tell.

What if you don't recover?

You're so vulnerable right now.

Unaware.

Unable to call for help.

My eyes travel down your body to the plaster cast cocooning your broken arm. Your pelvis is shattered. Your heart would be too, if you knew.

You'll never dance again.

Never make it to the West End with the gruelling rehearsals and punishing schedule. Never step onto a stage on Broadway.

What kind of life will you have?

What kind of life will I have if you tell?

CHAPTER THIRTY

Matt

'Tell me.' There is fear on Mary's face as Matt steps inside the kitchen. Her left hand seeks out Patrick's, the fingers on her right wrapping itself around her pendant.

'There's no change in Caily's condition,' he quickly says and instantly he sees the drop of their shoulders, the slackening of the skin across their forehead. They're permanently poised for bad news. Everyone is.

'So they haven't withdrawn sedation yet?' Mary drags him out of his thoughts, frowning again, fiddling with her locket.

'No, but it's looking likely that they will soon. The scans are promising. When they do, the doctor said she might not wake instantly. It could take several days for the sedation to leave her system. This is . . .' He doesn't want to say normal. Perhaps normal in the world of ICU, but not here. Not on the farm. 'Okay,' is the best he can manage, although it isn't okay. It isn't okay at all.

He steps forward, throat parched, but there is no teapot on the mat between Mary and Patrick. There is no delicious smell drifting from the Aga.

Usually Mary would be prepping the Monday-night meal by now, playfully slapping Patrick's hands away as he dips into the bowl of carrots she's sliced, peas she's shelled. Smiling affectionally at him as he crunches, saying there wouldn't be enough food for dinner even though she always makes enough to feed the county.

'Can I make you some tea?' Matt asks.

'I'll do it.' Mary rises to her feet, slower than usual, boils the kettle, tips the scalding water into the pot. Wraps the cosy around it. It's familiar. Reassuring.

'The rats are worse,' she says as she lifts mugs out of the kitchen. 'They're scratching all day and all night too. It's unbearable. I hear them all the time.'

Patrick's face creases with worry and Matt understands from his expression that, although there are rats on the farm, the problem is not nearly as bad as Mary thinks. Kate says this is something do with cognitive bias. Matt hadn't really understood the science but he understands the desperation on Mary's face as she asks, 'Can't you hear them now?' She's longing to be believed.

'I'll lay some more poison,' is the only answer Matt can give.

What are they going to do when Mary gets worse? Will she need a carer? Is there funding for that? Matt shouldn't be thinking like this. His in-laws are not a burden and he loves them deeply, but he already pays for Patrick's physio, the NHS no longer providing it as resources are limited and Patrick isn't someone they can 'fix', but with the general loss of muscle mass that comes with ageing it's important that he has help, on top of Caily coaxing him into doing his daily exercises.

Something inside Matt's chest contracts. He picks up the pot and swirls it around before pouring out the tea, only the liquid isn't strong and dark. It's water. Mary has forgotten to put the leaves in.

His phone buzzes.

An unknown number but it will be from a burner phone.

Victor fucking Kent.

Matt's fingertips tingle. Heart begins to race.

He can't open the message. He can't believe that he and Kate turned up on Victor's doorstep with their demands and accusation and fucking naivety. If only he'd known whose house it was.

How stupid he has been in so many ways.

Victor is the kind of man you don't want to get involved with, and yet Matt had because he was trapped in a kaleidoscope of debt and worry and exhaustion, churning, churning, churning, everything mixing up but the underlying feelings remaining the same.

Desperation.

There's a sharp twinge in his chest. Matt rubs against it with his hand, and one of the buttons from his patched-at-the-elbows shirt pings off, rolls across the floor. Custard twitches his ears, tracks it with his eyes. When he was a kitten he'd have bounded after it. Now he's too bone-tired to move.

Matt feels a fleeting kinship with the ageing cat.

'You okay, lad?' Patrick asks gently. He's sipping his mug of hot water, not wanting to upset Mary by pointing out her mistake.

'Fine.' Matt forces a smile because if he admits to the chest pains he's been having he'll be forced to acknowledge they are real, get them checked out, and then what? What would happen to the farm, the family, if the doctor orders him to rest? What if he needs an operation and can't do any heavy lifting for months? There are so many what-ifs, the biggest of them all, the one where Matt ignores the pains and they lead to the worst possible scenario, is one that he cannot contemplate because everything is on him. He carries the weight of the entire family and their livelihoods on his shoulders, and his knees have buckled so much under the strain he can't see a future where he can walk upright again. Lighter. Proud.

His mobile is a magnet drawing his hand, opening the message when he really doesn't want to read what it says.

Tick tock.

The edges of Matt's peripheral vision darken as he reads. 'Matt?'

Matt's head jerks up. He's disorientated. Dizzy. Patrick swims into focus. He's studying him carefully. He knows he could tell his father-in-law how stupid he has been. What a mess he got himself into when the pressure got too much to bear, but he is scared and ashamed and he does not know where to start. When did it all begin? When the oil seed rape failed? When the rain prevented him from cultivating the fields on time? Covid? Brexit? There are a million reasons he could give but none of them excuses what he has done.

Tick tock.

What is he going to do?

If one thing could go right, just one thing. He pleads with higher beings he doesn't fully believe in to give him a break. Let something go his way.

Everything he knows feels precarious. He is on the edge of a crumbling cliff, looking down. Wondering whether to jump.

Let something go his way. Just one thing.

His phone vibrates again. He hardly dares look, a tremor in his hand as he lifts his mobile, but then he reads this new message, from the police station this time, stark and formal, lacking in information and yet saying everything it needs to.

Just one thing.

An arrest has been made in connection to Caily's case.

CHAPTER THIRTY-ONE

Caily

Three weeks ago

Nothing was going Caily's way. She was barely holding it together. Viscous raindrops chased each other down the windowpane as tears streaked down her cheeks. She jammed another cookie into her mouth, staring miserably at the pile of discarded clothes heaped on her bed. She hoped the sweetness of the chocolate chips would dilute the sadness she felt, but instead they fuelled the self-loathing she now wore every day along with her school uniform.

You are disgusting, she told her reflection. *Disgusting.* She pinched the skin that hung over the top of her pants, her nails digging into the flesh.

Pig.

Pig.

Pig.

The Instagram posts were frequent and ferocious. Under different circumstances Caily might have been able to ignore them, laugh them off even, but no matter how often Billy and Tegan told her to ignore them or that she was amazing, she knew they must hold an element of truth because Travis had found her repulsive, hadn't he? He hadn't even rejected her kindly. Her tears are back as she recalls the horror on his face, the way he had pushed her away.

The pain of it.

It didn't matter that the next day he had given her a hand-picked posy of wildflowers, apologized again – *I can never be with you, Caily*. But he hadn't said if that was because he already had a girlfriend, or because she was too young or anything else. So it must be her.

She caught him watching her sometimes. She'd catch his eye only for him to look away. He was probably worried she'd launch herself at him again.

Oh god.

Her humiliation coupled with those bloody Instagram posts was making her life unbearable. Everyone had seen them at school.

Everyone knew her dress had been slashed.

Dani's @PigsCantDance account had started a chain reaction. Sometimes she walked down the corridor to the sound of other kids oinking at her. She was incredulous that a few weeks ago she was on the path to a bright and glittering future but now had instead been thrust towards a journey of self-doubt and insecurity.

She was messing up over and over at rehearsals. Not feeling light and free as she usually did when she danced, but clumsy. Heavy.

Pig.

Pig.

Pig.

Everything she had ever wanted, everything she had worked for was slipping away, and the tighter she tried to hold it the more it slid from her grasp. She was trying to keep it together because rationally she knew that if she could impress Eloise Parks and bag that scholarship then none of this would matter, but when you're called names often enough they begin to take on a shape, a form.

Her shape, her form.

Pig.

She wouldn't go to Kofi's party that night. She didn't know why she'd been invited anyway. Probably so everyone could laugh at her.

She swept all the clothes she used to feel so good in off the bed and onto the floor. Threw herself on top of the mattress and messaged Tegan and Billy.

Can't make party.

You must!! came Tegan's instant reply.

Got a headache.

Take some paracetamol! Don't leave me alone with bitch Dani.

Alone? Billy messaged. **Babe I'm about to climb out my window so the 'rents don't make me change.**

Wearing something sparkly?

You'd better be wearing sunglasses!

Have a great time both of you!!!

She closed the chat but immediately another message sprung onto the screen. This time solely from Tegan.

I don't have to go to the party. Sleepover?

Honestly, I do have a headache. Go. Have fun!

Caily let her mobile slip from her fingers as she turned her face into her pillow and wept.

Later, she was in the darkened kitchen eating leftovers in the yellow glow of the fridge, a hopeful Twix leaning against her legs.

He barked.

'Shush, you'll wake up Mum and Dad.'

Twix omitted a low growl towards blackness beyond the window.

'It'll only be a fox. Here.' She passed Twix a slither of ham.

As she ate, she opened Instagram. On Tegan's grid was a photo from Kofi's party. Her face pressed against Billy's. Both of their eyes bloodshot. Neither of them used to drinking. On Billy's grid a grinning selfie, Tegan in the background, kissing a boy from the drama group that Caily knew her cousin wouldn't look twice at if she was sober.

Caily had been tagged in another photo from that bogus account.

This time, the pig with her face was in front of Cinderella's pumpkin carriage, the footmen reverted to mice, dress in tatters.

There wasn't any caption. There didn't need to be.

Caily felt lost and lonely and scared. Everyone was having a good time except her.

She felt so alone.

I can never be with you, Caily.

The pain of it hurt so badly.

She stuffed another piece of quiche into her mouth to stifle her scream.

She felt she wanted to die.

Two weeks later they were late leaving school after rehearsals.

The toilets stank of berries, sickly sweet, as though some-body had been vaping out of the window. Caily finished washing her hands and studied her reflection. Tegan handed her a paper towel.

'Caily. I've something to tell you—'

'Do you think I'm fat?' Caily turns sidewards to the mirror, breathing in and then relaxing her stomach muscles.

'No, I don't think you're fat. Listen—'

'It's getting worse. Instagram.'

'Then tell someone. Or don't. But stop obsessing over it.'

'I'm not obsessing.'

'You totally are. There are more important things th—'

'I know.'

'I don't mean bloody Travis.'

'I wasn't thinking of him,' Caily lied.

'Really? Because it's all you talk about lately. Travis, Travis, Travis, Instagram, Instagram, Travis—'

'What's up with you?' Caily was hurt.

'Me? Oh, you've noticed I exist? That the world doesn't revolve around you?'

'Tegan?' This wasn't like her. Them. They never fought. 'I've been trying to tell you something for days and you . . . you . . .' Tegan's voice cracked.

'What is it?' On the sink, Caily's phone buzzed and she glanced at it for a split second but that was all it took.

'Fuck's sake,' Tegan shouted, slamming the door as she left.

Caily grabbed her phone and bag and hurried out after

her into the empty corridor. Tegan was leaning her forehead against the noticeboard.

'I was listening. I just—'

'Thought it might be Travis, or an Instagram alert.'

'I'm sorry. You have my full attention now. I promise. What do you want to tell me?'

Tegan turns to her, doesn't answer and Caily wonders if she's going to say anything at all, but then she says, 'Promise you won't tell anyone. This has to stay a secret.'

'Ooh secrets,' Billy said, appearing behind them. 'Do share.'

Tegan bit down on her lip.

'Do you want me to bugger off?' Billy asked.

'No, it's . . . I've found a stack of bills that Mum had hidden in the drawer. Unpaid bills.'

'We're behind on our electric,' Caily said. 'Dad cancelled the direct debit, said he'd rather pay what we owe when we owe it, but I know it's because he can't pay. The cost of living is—'

'This is more than electric. There's an arrears letter from the landlord. What are we going to do if we're kicked out? We're really behind on the rent.'

'It'll be okay.' Caily touched her arm.

'Okay for you, you're off to London to a ready-made career.'

There was a bitterness to Tegan's voice that Caily hadn't heard before. 'That's not fair.'

'Isn't it? You'll probably forget we all exist. I barely see you nowadays anyway.'

'I see you every day.'

'Not outside of school unless it's at rehearsal.'

'That's kind of true,' Billy said, but not unkindly. 'We miss you, is all. You're behind on all the goss. Miss West has read my musical and said it showed promise. She's given me some notes for the next draft.'

'That's great and I'm sorry I haven't been very present. I've had a lot on my mind.'

'Dani? It's hardly comparable to getting kicked out of your bloody home, is it?'

'Tegan—'

'Sorry. I'm just . . . I'm so freaked out. One of the letters said about eviction. Eviction!' Tegan placed her hand over her chest. 'I literally feel like I'm having a heart attack. I can't breathe.'

'Here.' Billy fished a bottle out of his bag and pushed it into Tegan's hands.

'What's this?'

'It's Rescue Remedy. A few drops under your tongue and it will calm you down. Want some air?'

Tegan rose to her feet. Billy's hand on the small of her back as they headed towards the front door. Neither of them asked her to join them.

Everything was falling away from her.

CHAPTER THIRTY-TWO

Kate

Kate feels as though she is falling off the edge of a tall building as she reads the text.

An arrest has been made in connection to Caily's case.

She's dizzy, sick. Relieved.

Seconds later Owen rings.

'I've got the message from the station,' she garbles. 'They've found Travis?'

'I thought I'd better ring and warn you. It isn't Travis who has been arrested,' he replies grimly.

Before he's even given a name, Kate is hit by a sense of foreboding.

CHAPTER THIRTY-THREE

Caily

Five days ago

Caily felt a sense of foreboding. She wasn't looking forward to her mum and Beth's surprise party later that night. Not just because she was nervous about her performance in *La La Land* the following day but because Tegan had barely spoken to her since their row in the toilets.

Caily rooted through her wardrobe, trying on and discarding dress after dress before settling on baggy jeans and a loose shirt. It wasn't as if there'd be anyone to impress. Besides, despite all the heaters, the barn would likely be freezing.

Downstairs there was the slam of a door. Mum and Beth were getting ready here. They thought they were having a meal at the farmhouse, but she and Tegan were giving them a makeover. Grandad had been trying to keep Mum out of the way all day while Grandma and Travis set up the barn.

'I see you,' she said to Tegan as she walked upstairs.

'Saw you first,' Tegan muttered, not looking at Caily. At least she answered.

'Right, let's get you two ready.' Caily brandished hair straighteners and a make-up kit.

'Don't do anything too fancy. We're only having a family dinner.'

'I know but it's your birthday so you should dress up. I've chosen something out of your wardrobe.' She held up a black dress.

'That's a bit much,' Mum said.

'It isn't.' Tegan pulled a sparkly jumpsuit out of her bag. 'This is for you to wear, Mum.'

Beth laughed. 'You're only forty once, right?'

Caily and Tegan worked as a team, passing each other eye shadow, trading lip gloss.

It should have felt like old times.

But it didn't.

It hadn't seemed that long into the party when most of the adults were drunk. She had had fun at first, dancing with Mum, but now she was on her own.

'Beth!' Mum stood on a bale of hay, swaying, microphone in hand. The first strains of 'I Will Survive' began and Beth whooped and ran over to Mum, clambering up on the bale, looping her arm around Mum's neck.

They began to sing, if you could call it that, about being afraid and petrified and not wanting to live without you by my side, and Caily realized that was the way she felt when she thought of her life without Travis. Oh god, why was she so dramatic? She glanced at Tegan. Normally they'd exchange an eye roll, a sarcastic comment, but she kept her sight fixed ahead. Caily turned to scan the throng of people, half of whom she didn't recognize.

Travis was in the corner, talking to an older woman. Not just talking, it looked as though they were arguing.

'Who's that?' she asked Grandma.

'That's Nicola Crosby. Your mum was good friends with her at school.' Grandma was distracted. Caily slunk miserably away and poured another glass of coke.

Mum and Beth had stopped singing. Beth jumping down from the hay bale. Mum carrying on alone. 'Don't Go Breaking My Heart' began. Mum doing both the high and low parts.

She was *so* embarrassing.

Caily looked around for Dad, afraid Mum would fall. She couldn't see him, but noticed Beth slipping outside.

She followed.

Travis was leaning against the wall of the house, the red glow of a cigarette dangling from his fingers. She didn't know he smoked.

'What was all that in there?'

'What? Your mum murdering music?' He gave a weak smile.

'No . . . that woman. Nicola. It looked as though were fighting. You know her?'

Travis took a deep drag on his cigarette before blowing the perfect smoke ring.

'Caily,' he sighed, flicking his cigarette butt to the ground before stamping on it.

She watched him walk away, amazed that he didn't turn around at the sound of her heart breaking.

Caily wandered back into the barn, but suddenly it all felt too much. Twix pushed his nose into her hand with a soft whine. He'd had enough too. She wished that they were back home.

'Come on, boy.'

Without telling anyone she was leaving, she shoved her hands in her pockets, out of the biting cold, and began to stalk across the fields, by the river.

Here she used to play with Tegan when everything was simple and uncomplicated and summer days stretched endlessly ahead. She stared down into the swirling blackness of the water, wondering how it would feel if she let it carry her to somewhere else entirely. Another place. Another town.

She wanted another life because in that moment she hated her own.

By the time she reached the cottage she was a swirling mass of emotions that felt too complicated to understand. All she knew was that she was too wound up to sleep. She wanted to keep walking.

She carried on towards Lady's Lane, into the land they used for wilding. Twix caught the scent of something. Darted into the undergrowth. She chased him.

In the distance she could see a faint light. There weren't any buildings here other than the derelict barn and old farmhouse. She shivered.

'Twix,' she hissed, nervous. There was a rustle, a shadow. Twix.

She tried to grab him but then his ears pricked and he raced across the fields.

Towards the light.

She followed.

The glow was coming out of the old red barn. The barn that nobody used because the roof was dangerous.

'Twix?' she whispered. The door was cracked open. Slowly, tentatively, she peered inside. Was met by the guilty faces of Dad and Beth.

'Caily, it's not what it looks like.' Dad's cheeks burned bright red but she knew what it was. It was *exactly* what it looked like. 'You won't tell anyone, will you? You won't tell your mum?'

Caily didn't know what to say. She didn't know if she could keep it a secret.

CHAPTER THIRTY-FOUR

Beth

Secrets will be her downfall.

Beth has never felt so scared. She thought things were bad enough when she received that text.

Tick tock.

Victor fucking Kent.

But then, shortly after the message on her phone there had been a thudding at the door. She jumped, scuttled over to the window and peeked out, terror banging a loud drum in her chest.

It was the police.

Her hands shook as she undid the chain on the front door, slid open the locks before twisting the key – it had been such a long time since she'd felt safe.

There were two uniformed officers, and Owen.

'Mum?' Tegan said uncertainly, hovering at the top of the stairs. Unnaturally pale but then she was still suffering from terrible period cramps.

Just as Beth was about to tell Tegan to go back into her

room, to reassure her daughter that this was nothing to do with her, the officer spoke and Beth felt the floor fall away from under her feet.

'Tegan Marshall, I am arresting you on suspicion of Grievous Bodily Harm. You do not have to say anything . . .'

'Mum?'

'No. You can't do this.' Beth stepped in front of the police-woman who was making her way up the stairs. 'Owen?' She turned to him. This had to be a mistake. *Had* to be.

'I'm sorry, Beth. We've found some evidence—'

'What? What evidence?' Beth shifted her gaze to Tegan, who was now quietly crying.

'We can sort this out at the station.'

'No.' Beth shook her head. 'You can't take her, you—'

'We have to.' Owen took her arm and gently pulled her aside. 'I've come to make this easier—'

'Easier?' Vomit rose in her throat. This couldn't be happening.

It couldn't be. And yet it was.

She watched helplessly as the woman guided a shaking Tegan down the stairs.

'Don't . . .' Beth swallowed hard. 'Don't handcuff her.' Beth could still hear the clink of the steel fastening around Sean's wrists before they took him away. Not her daughter too.

'That won't be necessary,' Owen said.

She followed Tegan outside.

'Mum.' Tegan reached out to her. Beth's heart broke as all she could do was watch helplessly as a hand was gently placed over Tegan's head and she was guided into the back of the police car.

'I'm going to drive you to the station in your car,' Owen told her. 'Then it'll be there when you leave.'

Beth wanted to ask if he thought they'll both be leaving, her and Tegan. But she didn't dare.

'Can we go now? They'll be there before us.' Beth was frantic. Her hands wringing together. Her whole body jittering with nerves.

'I can promise you Tegan won't be questioned until there's an adult with her,' Owen said kindly, but he kept his distance, not hugging her the way he might do in any other situation, as a friend. And yet he probably didn't have to be here today but he'd come for her.

For Kate.

Although Tegan didn't leave in handcuffs, Beth pictures her daughter's hands clamped together, her languishing in a cell.

She is half out of the car before Owen has properly parked in a space directly outside the door of the police station. Running into reception, panting, looking frantically from left to right. Seconds later Owen is guiding her elbow, leading her towards a room with Perspex glass instead of bars, where Tegan is sitting on a wooden bench, head hung low, cradling a cup in her hands that, even from here, Beth can see trembles.

'Can I?' She is already reaching for the handle.

'Let's bring her out and book her in,' Owen says.

The second Tegan spots Beth she hurls herself into Beth's arms, almost knocking her over with the force, clinging to her in a way that she hasn't since she was small and she'd had a nightmare or fallen over.

Beth wishes she can make Tegan feel better as easily as she

had then, with a cuddle and a song. All she can offer is a brief hug and so she puts everything she has into this embrace. Her love, and her support, and her unwavering belief that Tegan has done nothing wrong. She half expects Tegan to be wrenched from her arms. To be told physical contact isn't allowed, but Owen stands by and watches and Beth thinks she has watched too much TV. This isn't like one of the gritty crime dramas on BBC. Tegan is spoken to gently, kindly. Beth is allowed to stay with her as they approach the desk.

In a shaky voice Tegan gives her name, address and date of birth to a sergeant who tap-tap-taps it into a computer.

'We're going to take a mouth swab from you, Tegan, before we interview you, along with your fingerprint and a photo,' a policewoman says.

'Swabs?' Beth asks. 'Like DNA? Are you allowed to just do that? Keep her on file when she hasn't even done anything wrong?'

'If Tegan is released without charge you can apply to have her DNA removed from the database. Now, Tegan, you will need to have an appropriate adult with you while you're questioned.'

'I'll be with her,' Beth says.

'Tegan might want to choose someone else,' the police-woman says, but not unkindly.

'I want my mum.'

'Okay. And you can have an independent solicitor, free of charge, if you'd like.'

'A solicitor?' Beth knows she is repeating the things she is hearing, but even then she cannot make sense of them.

This world of fingerprints and swabs and DNA samples and solicitors she has suddenly been thrust into.

Tegan has asked for her to be the appropriate adult. But an adult is the last thing she feels like as she watches helplessly while Tegan is swabbed. More than anything, she wants her sister with her. She wants Kate to hold her so badly she could cry, but Tegan has been arrested for hurting Caily and she knows that Kate might never hold her again.

Speak to her.

Look at her.

Beth's throat aches to cry but she swallows down her fears and her distress and her own selfish longings and she follows her daughter into the interview room.

Owen is leading the interview. Beth didn't know if he'd be allowed, with his friendship with the family – with Kate – but he introduces himself for the tape along with PC Khan, who Tegan doesn't once look at. She, like Beth, is keeping her eyes on Owen, on his familiar, reassuring face.

He asks Tegan questions. Who else she is friends with. Who else Caily is friends with. If she knows anyone who might want to hurt Caily. If Caily's behaviour has changed recently. He's asking her all the same questions he had when he interviewed her before, and this exacerbates Beth but it also fills her with hope that they'll be free to leave soon.

'You already know this,' Beth sighs.

'Beth. You're sitting in as an observer,' he chastises her for interrupting and then he pushes the interview in a different direction.

'Tegan, you said that Caily had skipped the rehearsal because her period had started and she needed to change her underwear.'

'Yeah.'

'We know that isn't true.'

'But . . . that's what she told me.'

'The tech guys have unlocked Caily's phone and we've been going through her social media accounts. There are people she follows who I believe are part of your drama group?' He reads out some names but the confidence in his voice indicates he already knows the answer.

'Yeah.'

'There was a party, not long ago. Everyone seemed to be there except Caily?'

'They weren't joined at the hip,' Beth cut in.

'Beth. You're here to listen. Please stop interrupting. Tegan?'

'It was Kofi's party. Caily was invited but she had a head-ache.'

'We've looked into the cyberbulling you mentioned in your previous interview. You said you didn't know who started the account "Pigs Can't Dance".'

Tegan shrugs.

'Can you answer for the benefit of the tape?' Owen's sits up straight, serious, reassuring smile gone.

'No.'

'No?'

'I've an idea but I haven't said because I don't know for certain. Most of the group were jealous of Caily, the girls anyway.'

'Were you jealous? Did you set up that account, Tegan?'

'No.'

'Of course she didn't,' Beth mutters.

'We *will* be able to trace the person responsible. Who do you think it might be?' Owen waits.

'It was probably Dani but I dunno for sure.'

'Dani?'

'Daniela King. Lots of the girls in the group wanted a shot at the scholarship and have been bitches but Dani has been the worst. She was so jealous.'

'And you? Were you jealous?'

Tegan shrugs before quickly following it up with 'I was happy for her but . . . yeah, a little.'

'That doesn't mean anything—'

'Beth. I'm afraid I'm asking you for the last time to let Tegan speak for herself or I'll have to suspend the interview and wait for another appropriate adult.'

A heat creeps around Beth's neck, into her cheeks, borne out of both frustration and humiliation, but she cannot bear the thought of Tegan being questioned in this dull, soulless room without her, so she purses her lips together in a bid to stop the words from popping out.

'Did Dani ever, to your knowledge, threaten or hurt Caily?'

'She wouldn't have dared do anything when me and Billy were with her. Although she cut Caily's dress up. I nearly punched her for that. I mean, I didn't.'

Dani cut up Caily's dress.

Dani was cyberbullying Caily.

None of this explains why Tegan has been arrested.

'It seems like Dani is the one you should be speaking to,' Beth says.

She's blocked the previous reference to 'evidence' out of her mind.

Until Owen brings it up.

'The tech guys have also found a couple of texts on Caily's phone from you,' he says. Beth leans forward in her chair, squinting to read the printouts he pushes across the table, turning to Tegan to make sure she can see them. Noticing all the blood has drained from Tegan's face.

'It says "You'd better not say anything" and "If you tell anyone, I'll kill you". What was that about?'

'I didn't mean literally.' Tegan is stricken. 'It's just a phrase. Everyone says it, right?' She turns to Beth, her eyes wide. Beth squeezes her hand.

'What were you referring to?'

Tegan glances at Beth and Beth gives her a nod and smile of encouragement.

'I don't remember. It was nothing.'

'Do you know what a conditional threat is, Tegan?'

Tegan shakes her head before remembering to speak, 'No.'

'It's when you say something like, if you tell, I'll kill you and then that person tells so—'

'I didn't mean it. I didn't.' Tears roll down her cheeks unchecked.

'But you wanted Caily to keep a secret?'

Tegan doesn't answer.

'For the benefit of the tape, I'm showing Tegan the footage we found in Caily's WhatsApp drama group.'

Beth grips the table to steady herself as she watches the footage. Tegan pushing Caily, hard, 'You silly cow, I hate you.' Someone had made a boomerang of it so it repeated on a loop, Tegan's face twisted with anger as she shoved her cousin.

'This is dated the day of Caily's fall. Where were you when she fell, Tegan?'

'Umm. Dunno. Walking.'

'On your previous statement you told us that you went to Watts the chemist for the Rescue Remedy?'

'Yeah. That's right.'

'And yet we've checked the CCTV and there's no sign of you anywhere. Where were you really? Did you follow Caily?'

'Stop.' Beth's voice cracks. 'She doesn't . . . I don't . . . please.' Owen has stopped the video but Beth can still see it in her mind. 'Is it too late to request a solicitor?'

She's never felt so out of her depth.

CHAPTER THIRTY-FIVE

Matt

Matt is completely out of his depth.

A thousand needles piercing his chest as his phone buzzes low and urgent, an angry wasp.

Why is Beth's car in front of the police station?

Matt's hands are clammy as he replies that Beth is there because of her daughter, it's entirely unrelated to Victor.

His breath is laboured as he waits, watching as the three dots indicate an imminent reply, and when it comes he shivers.

Unless she wants an accident she'd better not say anything stupid.

CHAPTER THIRTY-SIX

Beth

This is stupid.

Ridiculous.

Beth doesn't care how many bits of paper Owen pushes towards them, how many fragments of video he plays them, Tegan is not a monster. Where's the rest of the video anyway? Showing how Caily reacted? Whether she had even started it.

Already Beth is shifting the blame. The battle lines have been drawn and she is firmly on one side with Tegan, Caily on the other. And Kate? Kate who has always had her back, always been the other half of her, twins meaning so much more than sisters, she'll be on Caily's side, won't she? As a mother she couldn't stand anywhere else.

Beth wants to weep when the solicitor arrives, in her hands the future of her daughter, her family.

Jocelyn introduces herself. Her eyes are tired behind silver-rimmed glasses but Beth hands her a version, their version, of the truth, and prays that she can transform it into a solution, a way out of here.

Outside the door, Beth hears a deep voice ask Owen who he's got.

Got?

Owen answers, 'Tegan Marshall, sir. She's been accused of assaulting a fifteen-year-old girl. Police were called to Waterford Bridge last Friday and found Caily Granger, who looked as though she'd fallen from the bridge. Since then we've discovered evidence of injuries to Caily that indicate third-party involvement. We've found video footage and a text. There's been a direct threat.'

'How long has Tegan been here?'

'Three hours, but about an hour of that was waiting for the solicitor.'

'Okay. Still time, then.'

Time? For what?

'How long can he keep us here?' Beth anxiously asks Jocelyn.

'Up to ninety-six hours, but that's extremely rare with someone of Tegan's age. The duty inspector has authorized for the first twenty-four hours and then an independent police officer will review. An inspector will look over the case every six hours. They won't hold her for longer than they have to. She is, for all intents and purposes, still a child.'

The door swings open and Owen and PC Khan take their seats. The tape begins to record and virtually the same questions are asked again, although reframed in different ways.

For the most part Jocelyn gestures at Tegan to offer a 'no comment' and Beth begins to feel not relaxed but the way she had when she was small and her father had been her hero.

A grown-up stepping in, taking charge. She's no longer alone but a part of something. A team.

At least Owen says they are releasing Tegan under investigation pending further enquiries.

'That's much as I was expecting,' says Jocelyn, putting her notes into a Mulberry bag. 'You're not off the hook, young lady, but they don't want to charge you, yet.'

Yet.

The car always used to be filled with noise. Tegan hated travelling, claimed she felt sick before every journey, and Beth would distract her with music. They'd sing loudly along to Tegan's favourite songs. The Wheels on the Bus turning endlessly round and round.

Later, pigtailed and Disney-obsessed, Tegan would throw herself into performing 'You've Got a Friend in Me,' jiggling in her seat, pointing at Beth, covering her heart. And that's what they always felt like, friends, only now Beth realizes that this is so far removed from the truth. That she does not know her daughter at all. Recently the speakers have blasted Orla Gartland but today neither of them switches on the stereo. Tegan stares straight ahead but, from her faraway expression, Beth doesn't think she is seeing the brightly coloured fruit and veg stacked outside the grocers or the blue and white striped canopy framing the bakers. Instead, Beth wonders if she is back in that day, watching Caily fall.

Pushing . . .

Stop it.

Whoever her daughter is, she is not a monster. But she is, perhaps, the daughter of one.

Everyone makes mistakes.

It's a gradual awareness, realizing she is being followed. The black Range Rover close to her bumper, not keeping its distance. Not caring about being discreet.

Oh god.

It's *him*.

Not Victor personally perhaps, but one of his cars, one of his henchmen.

She thought they had more time. Matt told her they had more time. Hysteria rises in her throat.

Beth tightens her grip on the steering wheel. Tries to recall whether the car was behind her when they left the police station and thinks it probably was. Owen had parked her car right in front of the entrance, visible and exposed.

Victor must think she had gone to report him.

They're heading out of town now, the roads curving around green fields. Beth's foot squeezes the accelerator, the other driver effortlessly increasing their speed too. Beth's battered old Corsa is no match for a sleek Range Rover.

She is no match for them. She's been out of her depth from the start.

But still she tries to throw them off her tail, these country lanes familiar.

She swerves down a rutted track. Each time they violently dip down a pothole her spine jars with pain.

'Mum? Is everything okay?'

'Fine. Just a detour.' Beth glances in the rear-view mirror. The Range Rover right behind her. She accelerates, faster and faster, taking the corners wide, knowing if they meet a vehicle coming from the opposite direction, a tractor, she's going too fast to avoid an impact.

She hares around the bend and then takes a hard right, a hidden track into the woods, and there is an uplifting, glorious moment, when she thinks she's lost them, but then headlights cut through the gloom of the trees and—

'Mum!'

'Don't panic,' Beth says, her voice tight. 'He's just some idiot with road rage. I must have cut him up or something.'

They exit the woods, a flash of red to their left.

An approaching car.

Beth yanks at the steering wheel and Tegan screams as they veer off the road. Beth's teeth rattle inside her skull as they bump over the rough ground before the engine stalls and they come to rest in a ditch.

The driver of the red car blasts its horn before it disappears over the horizon. In her mirror Beth watches with inexorable horror as the Range Rover slows to a crawl. She is so, so scared, sweat already forming and cooling on her skin.

Don't hurt my daughter. Don't hurt my daughter.

But nobody gets out of the car. Instead, when it's level with Beth, when her eyes lock with the driver's, he places his index finger against his lips.

Shh.

'Mum?' Tegan says uncertainly.

'It's okay. We're okay.' Beth repeats this over and over as though saying it can make it true.

She tries to smile when all she really wants to do is cry. To rest her hot forehead against the cool window and weep.

She has to draw several deep breaths and shake her

trembling hands before she can restart the car. For a second, as she tries to pull away, the wheels spin fruitlessly, and she grits her teeth and leans forward as though she can propel the car by sheer willpower alone.

She does not want to ring Matt to tow her. It has been difficult enough to face him lately, knowing the mess she has got them both into, when it was she who persuaded him to get involved with Victor. It is entirely her fault.

But just as she's about to lift her foot from the pedal, fearing she is making the situation worse, the car lurches forward and then they are back on the road. She drives too fast, telling herself to slow down, telling herself that the worst part of the day is surely over now.

Telling herself lies.

Because when she pulls into her street there is a car outside her house.

Someone waiting for her.

CHAPTER THIRTY-SEVEN

Kate

Kate has been waiting outside Beth's house since Owen texted her to let her know that Tegan has been released. She was sure that Beth would bring Tegan straight home, they both must be exhausted, but the journey from the station shouldn't take this long and Kate is almost giving up when Beth's Corsa rounds the corner.

A cocktail of emotions swirls into one indescribable mix inside her.

Indecipherable.

She's been through shock, disbelief, rage and now, although she wants to shake the truth from Tegan, she feels a glimmer of compassion as she watches her niece climb warily out of the car. Pale face lowered, not meeting her eye, but then Kate remembers what Tegan has been accused of and she feels anger flare once more. She swallows it down, stepping forward, her arms hovering awkwardly at her sides, not wrapping Beth in her usual hug.

'It's not a good time,' Beth says defensively.

'Not a good—'

'We're tired.' She turns and slips her key in the lock, dismissing Kate but Kate will not be dismissed. She grabs Beth by the shoulder and spins her around.

'I'm sorry you're *tired*. I'm pretty *tired* myself. Tired of all the lies.' She raises her voice, glaring at Tegan who scuttles into the house, pounds up the stairs.

Kate pushes her way through the front door.

'Leave her.' Beth grabs her arm, fingertips bruising.

'Don't fucking touch me. Or is it like mother, like daughter?' Images of the yellow and purple angry marks on her daughter's fair skin coming to mind as Kate shakes her arm free.

'Tegan didn't—'

'Owen said there's evidence, Beth,' Kate says quietly.

The sisters stand close enough to touch but oceans apart, worlds.

Beth shrugs, resigned, and trudges into the kitchen. Kate follows, freezing in the doorway as she spots the table. Remembering the last time she sat at it. Those last few blissful moments before the police rang to notify her that Caily had fallen. When life was routine.

Normal.

Good.

Kate recalls how fraught she had felt that day – really, she had no idea how easy she had it – how hungover. She is transported back, to her and Beth's fortieth party. Gin sharp on her tongue. Her arm looped around her twin's neck as they sang 'I Will Survive'. She straightens her spine.

They will come through this.

They *have* to.

'I don't want to fight.'

Kate takes a seat. Beth perches stiffly in the chair opposite.

'You know when we found out we were pregnant, what we said?' Kate asks. They'd taken a test days apart. Squealing with joy. Unable to believe their luck, amazed that although they'd both been trying, they'd fallen at the same time.

'A lot's changed since then.' Beth won't be drawn in to the emotion.

'Has it? You promised you'd always be there for my child, I promised I always be there for yours.'

'And are you? There for Tegan?'

Kate hesitates a fraction too long. 'Yes. But I need to know the truth.'

'We chose their names together, remember?' Beth says.

Kate nods.

'Because they both meant beautiful, we wanted them to have that connection.'

Kate thinks of Caily now, shrinking in her hospital bed, her light dimmed.

'Tegan . . . some of her recent behaviour might have been ugly but she is still beautiful, on the inside. To me.'

'I know.' In her lap, Kate's fingers contract into three gentle squeezes but Beth's hand is not touching hers and her sister cannot feel them. But, despite wanting them to be okay, Kate has to know. She has to ask.

'Did Tegan push Caily?'

Kate expects denial, but Beth's face fills with sorrow and Kate sees how she is torn. Tegan is her daughter but Kate is her sister.

Her twin.

She waits, not filling the space, knowing there is power in holding the silence.

'I don't know,' Beth says helplessly. 'There was a video. I've never seen Tegan like that. So . . . angry. So desperate.'

'Do you know why?'

'No.'

'Can I talk to her?'

'I can't let you do that. Her solicitor has instructed her not to speak to anyone.'

But Kate is not just anyone. She is Tegan's aunt, her second mum.

But, perhaps, not her ally.

'I'd let you talk to Caily if it was the other way around.'

'If you think that you don't know yourself as well as I know you.' Beth's gaze is challenging and Kate knows that she is right.

She is a sister, a twin. But first and foremost she is a mother and Caily does, must, will, *always* come first.

'I thought you'd help me.' Kate holds her last hand, deals out guilt to Beth.

'Then you don't know me as well as you think,' Beth says.

'You're wrong. We're the same—'

'We are not the same. We may look the same. Have the same mannerisms but . . .' Beth's fingers wrap around her throat as though trying to release the words that might be stuck there. 'You don't know me,' she whispers. 'You don't know the things I've done.'

'What? What have you done?'

'Please, just leave.'

Beth has clammed up in the way she always does when she's defensive, scared.

She gazes helplessly at her sister. Beth's features a mirror of her own and she knows that her own eyes will also display the same deep sadness, are also damp with tears that threaten to spill.

When she arrived she didn't know how she felt, but now she knows.

Sad.

Sad for Beth and Matt, Caily and Tegan. Her parents who will be caught in the middle. And for herself.

Sad for all of them.

She is not going to find out the truth today, if Beth even knows the truth, and so she turns and slowly, silently, stumbles back to her car. Her footing unsure against the uneven terrain. Her relationship with her twin irrevocably damaged.

Kate is no longer half of a whole. She is insubstantial. Incomplete.

She glances at Beth's house one last time as she puts the car into gear.

Beth has already shut the door.

Kate is numb as she drives, turning Beth's words over in her mind.

You don't know the things I've done.

What has her sister done?

CHAPTER THIRTY-EIGHT

Beth

What has Tegan done?

Beth has to protect her daughter. Clear her name, but she does not know where to start.

Her eyes are gritty with tiredness, hands cupping a mug of cold coffee. The hours slide by, shadows creeping across the walls in the creamy moonlight until, finally, outside the kitchen window dawn streaks the sky peach and lilac.

Above her, the floorboards creak. Tegan is awake. Probably hasn't slept either. How could she after the trauma of her arrest yesterday? And it is the ache for all that her daughter has been through that brings some clarity to Beth's exhausted, muddled mind and she knows exactly what she needs to do today.

Find Travis.

He's the one with the record. The one who has disappeared. Why aren't the police focusing on him?

Find Travis.

But she doesn't know how. It isn't as though she hasn't searched online. Asked at the local pub. Is this what the police have done? They have more resources than her. Have they located him yet? She doesn't think so because, if they had found Travis, there is a good chance they would want to talk to her and Matt because Tegan isn't the sole reason that she needs to find Travis.

He's screwed them over.

Not just them.

Victor Kent.

A man you definitely didn't want to mess with.

A man who is running out of patience.

Beth's stomach violently plummets again the way it did when Matt told her the news – the worst news – on the phone. It was during that call he also told her that Travis's cottage was being searched. Her vision tunnels as she remembers encouraging Matt to be honest with Victor on Sunday afternoon, naively thinking that Victor might help them find the farmhand. Beth grips the edge of the table, taking deep breaths to steady herself. Sometimes she feels she is hanging on by her fingernails, just seconds from falling.

She tells herself that Victor would have found out eventually, but if only they'd kept quiet they'd have bought some time to find Travis.

But how?

Think.

Travis doesn't have social media accounts.

Think.

No one in town has seen him.

It seems impossible to find someone who doesn't want to be found but it can't be. Not in this digital age where everyone leaves a footprint.

Think.

When was the last time she saw him? At her and Kate's fortieth birthday party. She opens up the photo app on her phone. She had asked Tegan to take pictures but, with everything that has happened since, she hasn't looked at them yet. Could they hold a clue somehow? Could Travis be wearing something with some sort of logo indicating where he came from? A local football team or . . .

Something.

Desperately, Beth begins to scroll through shot after shot.

There she is, balanced on a hay bale, face pressed against Kate's, cheeks gin-rosy. Her parents sitting by the Bluetooth speaker, anxious expressions on their faces, probably worried it would stop streaming and then what would they do? Technology is so beyond them. There's Caily. Beth's breath catches. This is probably one of the last photos of her niece before her fall. She's gazing to her side. Watching someone. And then there he is, Travis. But he's not alone. He has an angry expression on his face. His mouth open as if in a shout.

He isn't alone.

He's with Nicola.

She has a pleading expression on her face.

Beth's pulse pounds as she studies the picture. This does not look like a casual conversation.

This is an argument between two people who know each other very well.

Nicola gave Beth her phone number after she'd examined Caily at the hospital. She calls it now.

'Hello.'

'You knew Travis before the party. Before you came here,' she blurts out.

'I don't know wh—'

'Don't lie to me, Nicola. My niece is in a coma—'

'Travis wouldn't hurt anyone—'

'You'd only be able to say that if you know him well,' Beth fires back.

There's a beat. Beth's fingers tighten around the handset. 'Who is Travis? Where is he?'

There's a silence.

A sigh.

An answer.

CHAPTER THIRTY-NINE

Kate

Kate needs answers. Yesterday, after Tegan's arrest, emotions were running high and, on reflection, Kate can understand why Beth wouldn't let her speak to Tegan.

Today, though, she intends to try again.

She sits in her parents' kitchen, Custard on her lap, Twix by her feet as though she's trying to build a team because, although the last thing she wants is for her family to turn into an 'us and them', she is so scared that it might be too late for that already.

She's trying to explain how she feels to her parents. Her words are muddled but there is no mistaking the desperation in them.

'I know you're conflicted.' She frantically strokes the cat, trying to calm herself down. 'But please, if either of you are protecting Tegan—'

'Sweetheart, we're not,' Dad says, shaking his head, the skin on his face, his neck, looser. Is it possible to have aged in five days? Kate feels that she has.

'I'm going to tell the police,' Mum stands, shakily. Swamped by her cardigan.

'Tell them what?'

'That . . . that Tegan wouldn't hurt anyone. It was only a few weeks ago that she found the baby bird that had fallen from its nest. You remember, Patrick, you made a box for her and we put some hay in the bottom and she nursed it back to health.'

'Mum.' Kate's heart cracks. Tegan had found that bird ten years ago when she was five. The narrative inside Mum's mind is mixed up, back to front, out of order.

Dad rises to his feet, gripping the table. He winces as he puts weight on his leg. 'I'll come with you to the station. It's preposterous that they think one of our granddaughters could hurt the other.'

It's ludicrous that, with everything going on, Kate experiences a stab of hurt, of jealousy, that her parents seem to be on Team Tegan. Twix leans against her legs. At least he'd never let her down.

'Mum. Dad. I'm sure Beth appreciates your support.' Her voice is thick, words barbed.

'Kate, love. We're not taking sides.' Her mum's face creases in pain. 'It's just that we *know* Tegan wouldn't have hurt Caily.'

'I thought they were after that Travis? He's the kiddie fiddler.'

'Dad! You can't call someone that. Besides, Caily wasn't . . . fiddled with.' She's lost all focus. Her vocabulary wrapped up inside the ball of cotton wool inside her head.

'We love you so much.' Her mum looks despairing. 'We love both of you. All of you. I can't bear it that—'

'Mum, it's okay.' Kate hugs her. Wondering why it is always her holding everyone else together. Offering Beth a peace branch, Tegan a chance to explain. Understanding, if not forgiving that her parents' loyalties are torn in two. They have always been united. Other than when Dad had his accident and had a period in hospital, Kate can only remember them spending one night apart and that was when Mum was having her gallbladder removed. Kate had gone to stay at the farmhouse so he wasn't alone. After he'd gone to bed she had tidied the kitchen and thought that, despite the warmth from the Aga, it had felt colder without Mum. When she had gone upstairs she had noticed the door of the spare room was wide open. Inside was Dad, curled up in his childhood bed with Barney, his threadbare teddy, tucked under his arm.

In the morning a flush had crept around his neck as he told Kate he hadn't consciously sought comfort from his childhood. Must have sleepwalked, had done it before when under stress, and Kate had reassured him that it would stay their secret. Thinking it sweet that even in sleep, he had been aware, on some level, that Mum was missing. Hadn't been able to settle without her.

Although understanding, Kate had felt guilty that her presence hadn't been enough to soothe him.

She feels guilty now.

She *always* feels guilty about something.

She wishes she had the luxury of falling apart, but who is going to hold her together?

As she thinks this, her mobile begins to ring. Thankful for an excuse to leave, she extradites herself from her mum's embrace. Her phone has stopped ringing before she has hurried outside.

The missed call is from Owen.

She takes a shaky breath.

Her future might rest on what he has to tell her.

CHAPTER FORTY

Beth

Tegan's future could rest on what Nicola is about to tell her.

Beth's own future. Matt's. Everyone's.

They're in a café, the coffee machine hissing and gurgling and all around people are eating breakfast. Cutlery chinking against plates. The smell of frying bacon flipping Beth's stomach.

After Nicola confirmed on the phone to knowing Travis, she had suggested meeting before work to talk properly. Beth had suggested a location while she ran up the stairs to get dressed.

'Travis is . . .' Nicola studies the mug of cappuccino she is clasping, making small circular movements from her elbow, watching as the froth swirls. 'Sorry. This is hard.'

Beth waits, fingers playing with the hem of the red and white checked plastic tablecloth because if her hands weren't occupied she'd be trying to shake the truth out of Nicola.

Eventually Nicola raises her head and says, part defiantly, part apologetically, 'Travis is my son.'

'Your son?' Beth spots a lifeline and she grasps at it. 'So you know where he is?'

'No. We . . . we weren't close.' Nicola winces as though that statement causes her physical pain. 'He'd been living with my mum for the past few years. He was accused of . . . of something and I didn't stand by him like I should have done.'

Nicola's eyes fill with tears and, even though Beth knows *exactly* what it was that Travis was accused of, she feels a pang of sympathy towards her because she too could soon be the mother of a child with a criminal record.

'Please.' Beth holds Nicola's eyes. 'My daughter's life could depend on it.'

'Honestly, Beth. I don't know where he is. My mum's neighbour texted me the afternoon following the party to say he'd been back to her house but he didn't stop there. I don't know where he is now. I didn't even know he was here until I arrived at your party. After Mum died he just took off.'

Beth takes a moment to process this.

'You were arguing?'

'Yes. He . . .' Nicola takes a sip of water. 'I never told Travis who his father is. I told him it was a one-night thing. I thought I was doing the right thing but I can see now that it has eaten away at him.'

'Who is his father?'

'It was Aaron.'

'You were pregnant when you left here?' Beth does the maths in her head. 'You were so young. Is that why your mum moved you away?'

'Partly.'

'I thought it was because of that night at ours.' Beth watches shock flicker across Nicola's face. 'When Kate nearly drowned.'

The past drapes heavily around Beth. It's dark and heavy and she shivers, remembering how distraught she was that she had nearly lost her sister.

How distraught she is that she might lose her now.

'Because you thought I was so ashamed I didn't jump in the river and save Kate that I couldn't face her again?' Nicola looks at her so earnestly, so sincerely, 'I was – am – ashamed of myself. I was scared. It was dark, cold, foggy. It happened so quickly. I tried to grab her but my fingers were numb with cold and I couldn't grip her properly. I couldn't hardly see anything. I let her down. I let you both down.' Beth knows that Nicola is speaking the truth and doesn't have the heart to tell her that she hadn't thought shame had driven her away, but guilt. Always harbouring a smidgeon of doubt that, when Kate had felt Nicola's hand on her wrist, she was pushing her rather than trying to save her. A knee-jerk reaction to hearing the news that her beloved Aaron had been kissing another girl. 'I'm sorry.'

'It's okay,' Beth says and she finds that finally it is. 'Why didn't you tell Travis about Aaron?'

'There's no easy answer to that. We do what we think is best, don't we, with our kids? Aaron didn't want anything to do with Travis. I know we were young but . . . Aaron was always so sad he didn't have a family of his own. I thought he'd perhaps be pleased he had a chance to build one,' she sighs, 'but no. By the time Travis was old enough to ask about him, I deliberated how I could tell him that his father had rejected him. I always felt that my dad leaving and never seeing me again was somehow my fault, you know?'

'You know it wasn't, though.'

'Knowing that and believing that are two very different things. Anyway, I googled Aaron to see what Travis would find if I gave him his father's name and . . .' She shook her head. 'He'd been in and out of prison. Assault, theft. I thought . . . I thought it was kinder to tell Travis I didn't know who his father was, that it was better for him to think badly of me for a while than to know he was rejected, his father was a criminal. And, if I'm honest, I was scared that he might track Aaron down, that he might end up hero-worshipping him, get involved in something illegal himself. You read such a lot about nature vs nurture, don't you? I thought I was enough, but I wasn't.'

'I'm sure—'

'No. I wasn't terrible in the way my mum was but parenting never came naturally to me, and Mum was so good with him, as though she was trying to make up for all the times she wasn't there for me. Perhaps I should have told Travis the truth but . . .' She shrugs.

Beth nods. She knows as a parent that sometimes hiding the truth is the easiest thing. The kindest.

'I'd kind of hoped that when I came back, Aaron would still be here.' Nicola raises hopeful eyes to Beth's and Beth knows that it isn't just for Travis that she'd like to find him.

'I haven't seen him for a few years. We've lost touch. Sean stuck by him throughout his troubles.'

'I'm not surprised. He was a good man, the man I thought Aaron could be but . . .' Her voice drops to a whisper. 'I thought . . . I thought love was enough.'

This brings a lump to Beth's throat.

'Do you think it ever can be enough?' She wants it to be. She really, *really* wants to believe that love can conquer all. Everything.

'Are you okay, Beth? I mean aside from everything with Tegan?'

'I'm in trouble,' Beth says quietly. The coffee shop is noisy but she is still scared of being overheard. She is scared of so many things. 'I owe money to somebody you don't want to owe money to.'

'Can you ask your parents for help?'

'They don't have any money.'

He's going to kill her.

Shaking, Beth swallows the fear back down along with the remains of her bitter coffee.

Once she gets home Beth clatters her keys on the table and calls Owen. She's going to tell him that Travis is Nicola's son. Perhaps she will tell him more. Everything. It was a relief sharing that she was in trouble to Nicola, but her debt is only a fraction of what she needs to say.

'Hello, Owen,' she says as the call connects.

'Can I call you back? I'm trying to get hold of Kate.'

'Do you have news?' Beth asks. 'About Caily?'

'I do.' His voice is strained. 'But I have to tell Kate first.'

CHAPTER FORTY-ONE

Kate

'Tell me that again.' Kate sags with relief.

'The good news is that there is no trace of sperm in the swabs Nicola took,' Owen says. 'Caily wasn't—'

'Hang on. When you say "the good news", does that mean there's also bad?' The phone is tightly clutched in her hand. The skin across her knuckles stretching.

'Kate.' Her name is gentle on Owen's tongue. She hears the love he once had for her, the love he has now.

Or the pity.

'My contact in the lab has rushed through the DNA testing.'

Kate inhales deeply.

'We have a match. We know who the traces of skin found under Caily's fingernails belongs to.'

Kate cannot speak. She is still holding her breath. Praying.

Despite Tegan's arrest, it cannot be her.

It just can't be.

For the sake of all her family, let the DNA belong to Travis.

Who does the skin found under Caily's fingernails belong to?

CHAPTER FORTY-TWO

Beth

Tegan's skin has been found under Caily's fingernails.

Beth sinks onto the stairs, feeling the sway of them beneath her. Her whole world. Rocking. She grips her mobile to her chest, almost wishing that Owen had never called her back.

'Beth?' Owen's voice reaches her and she raises her handset to her ear again. 'Did you hear what I said?'

'Yes,' she says but the word is a croak and so she licks her dry lips and tries again. 'Yes.'

She wants to ask what happens now but she is scared to find out. Instead she questions, 'And you've just told Kate this?'

'Yes.'

He offers nothing more. No clue as to how Kate reacted, but then how does Beth imagine she reacted? She'll be shocked. Confused. Hurt. Angry. All the things Beth is feeling now.

Tegan's skin has been found under Caily's fingernails.

She longs to call Kate but she knows she cannot. Her loyalty cannot, should not, be with her sister but with her daughter.

How has it come to this?

The cousins divided.

The sisters divided.

The entire family will be divided.

'What will happen now is that the case will go before the CPS – the Crown Prosecution Service – and they'll decide whether or not Tegan can be charged. I'm going to ask for a decision as soon as possible. I'm pulling strings.'

Beth cannot speak. She clutches at her throat, feeling her fear lodged there.

She cannot swallow.

She cannot breathe.

'Beth? Is there anything you want to ask, say?'

She hangs up the phone.

When Sean was arrested and sent to prison there was a shift in their community. People eyeing Beth with sympathy, with suspicion, lowering their voices when she was near them. She had wanted to grab Tegan and run away with the shame of it all. But she'd stayed, got through it with the support of Kate, her family.

Now she fears she does not have that support.

Again, she feels the overwhelming urge to grab Tegan, to run away.

Is there anything you want to say?

She is bone-tired. Head fuzzy. She can't think straight. She's sick. Sick with fear. Sick of feeling scared.

Whatever happened on the bridge, however Tegan's skin ended up under Caily's fingernails, her daughter has lied about it.

CHAPTER FORTY-THREE

I am a liar.

Nobody knows the things I've done. I'm trapped in a web of my own making and I don't know how to break free.

I touch your hand, expecting it to be cold, but it's warm and dry. I wonder whether anyone has thought to bring in some moisturizer and massage it into your skin.

Can you feel?

Hear?

And if you could, what would you say to me?

What would I say to you?

Because it is all too awful.

The truth.

CHAPTER FORTY-FOUR

Kate

'The truth, that's all I want.' Kate wipes away the last of her tears. There's a low-level buzzing in her ears, which still ring from Owen's news. 'You can't stop me going over to Beth's. Tegan's skin was found *under* Caily's fingernails, for god's sake.' She looks at her parents, pleading. Wanting them to back her up, offer an explanation, but they can't.

'I don't understand how that can be.' It is the third time her mum has repeated this.

'It's okay,' Dad says firmly, and it's shockingly comforting to hear those words aloud – *it's okay* – even when she knows it isn't. 'We'll come to Beth's with you. There's bound to be some sort of innocent explanation.' Kate passes him his crutches. He pulls himself to standing and, numb, Kate leads the way to her car.

Behind her, on the back seat, her parents sit quietly, holding hands, the passenger seat next to her empty. This is how it must have been for her mum when she drove Kate and Beth to school all those years ago. Although they never really fell out they'd sometimes bicker about who would ride shotgun, until one day her mother said if they couldn't agree then they must both stay in the back. Because she treated them equally.

Then.

Now they're still searching for excuses for Tegan, taking Beth's side.

She glances at them resentfully in the rear-view mirror, softening when she sees her mum's worried face. Recalling her distress of a few moments ago when Kate asked her to fasten her seat belt and she hadn't remembered how, Dad gently leaning across, buckling her in as though she is now a child.

But they are still very much her parents and they have insisted on coming with her because they think they can keep the peace, they think they can keep the sisters calm.

Kate feels anything but calm. Her stomach an expanding ball of tension and anger and confusion and hurt.

Beth doesn't want to answer the door. Kate hammers on it with her fists until it opens and she stumbles inside, striding into the kitchen before she whirls around.

'Skin?' she snaps. 'They found Tegan's skin under Caily's fingernails.'

'I know.' Beth crosses her arms over her chest.

Mum plays the peacekeeper. 'It doesn't mean that Tegan had anything to do with—'

'Mum?' Kate cuts her off. 'Just stop it. Don't you want to know the truth? Your granddaughter is lying in a hospital bed.'

'We know.' Mum is shaking, her voice, her hands, as she pulls another tissue from her battered patent-leather handbag. Snapping the brass clip shut.

'She's in a *coma*.' The word is bitter and Kate spits it out.

'Kate, it isn't Mum's fault—'

'Dad, it isn't anyone's fault according to you, is it?'

'But Tegan wouldn't—'

'What, Mum?' Kate cuts in, furious. 'Tegan wouldn't what? Lie? Hurt Caily? The evidence suggests otherwise and if she's so innocent why doesn't she come downstairs and defend herself?' Kate is shouting and when she falls silent, they all hear it.

The creak on the stair.

The sound of someone.

Listening.

Crying.

Kate rushes towards the hallway.

'Kate, don't.' Dad reaches out a hand to stop her but, the second he makes contact with her arm, Kate wrenches hers away as though she has been burned. And that's how it feels, betrayal. Hot. Painful. Wounding.

Kate stands, her hands balling into fists, glaring at her niece. Tegan is perched halfway down the staircase, her knees drawn to her chest. Her face blotchy and tear-stained, the face so like Caily's. The delicate features, the shimmering blonde hair.

The years fall away. She was the first person to hold Tegan after Beth, she was there for her first steps, her first words. She had always wanted to be the cool aunt, the one Tegan could confide in all of the things she couldn't tell her mum. She'd envisaged chats about boys, Kate dishing out advice even though she'd only ever had two boyfriends, but teenage Tegan had stopped confiding in her.

'Tegan.' Kate's voice is thin. She tries to summon the anger of a few moments ago but all she feels is an immense sadness that expands in her chest until she cannot feel anything else. Tegan blurs in front of her eyes and Kate swipes away her tears. 'Please . . .'

She trails off, unsure what she is asking for.

Please tell me the truth.

Please let this all be a horrible mistake.

Please rewind time. Be running around the farm with Caily, pigtails flying behind them, wicker baskets looped over the crooks of their arms as they searched for Easter eggs.

'You don't have to say anything, Tegan.' Beth places herself between Kate and her daughter.

'We know you didn't push Caily,' her mum says.

'It's been a horrible mistake. Owen will sort it all out,' Dad offers.

'Stop. It.' It is back, Kate's fury. 'Will you all just stop it? Beth, I understand you defending your daughter. But Mum, Dad, you have two grandchildren. *Two.* If you can't support me, if you're taking *her* side,' Kate shoots a poisonous glance at her sister. 'Then—'

'Stop it,' Tegan says. 'Stop it.' Louder this time. 'There's something I want to say.'

CHAPTER FORTY-FIVE

Beth

'There's something I want to say.' Tegan's voice has dropped again.

Beth pounds up the stairs and yanks Tegan by the wrist until she is standing. Then she ushers her into her bedroom.

'Jocelyn said you cannot talk to anyone,' she says urgently because she does not know what her daughter was about to say and she cannot take the risk that she might confess in front of Kate and her parents.

Not that she believes that Tegan pushed Caily but . . .

Her skin was under Caily's fingernails.

'But Mum—'

'Your solicitor said.' Her tone is firm. Final. 'You stay here until Kate has gone.'

Beth closes the door behind her and joins the rest of her family downstairs.

'Tegan won't be speaking to you today. I want you to leave.'

'But—'

'Now.'

She stares defiantly at her sister but inside Beth cannot bear it. It isn't the hurt and anger on Kate's face that wounds her but the confusion.

Aside from the usual childhood squabbles, they have always been united. Had each other's backs.

Beth remembers Kate's wedding. Standing to the side, pink dress frothing around her ankles, a posy of cream roses clutched in her hands. She had shed tears as Kate and Matt made their vows, completely engrossed in each other. She had wiped her eyes as her sister kissed her brand-new husband. Her mum had leaned forward, from her pew, and squeezed Beth's shoulder, whispered that rather than losing a sister, she was gaining a brother. But Beth hadn't felt as though her twin was slipping away from her. A fear that everything might change was not the cause of her overwhelming emotion. She was crying because she could feel Kate's happiness bubbling away inside her and she was overjoyed that she'd found someone else to love.

To love her.

As Kate had stood on the steps of the church in the bright sunlight, pastel confetti decorating her hair, her gaze had met Beth's, held her.

I am still your other half, she silently said.

I know, Beth had silently replied.

And that didn't make Kate's love for Matt any less, because love expands the heart, doesn't it?

But now Beth can feel her own heart shrinking because, in an instant, with one withering stare, Kate has withdrawn her affection and all Beth feels now is icy, icy cold.

They are broken.

Whatever happens with Tegan, whether or not she is charged, whether or not she was the one to push Caily, Beth knows as she watches Kate and her parents trudge back to Kate's car that her relationship with her sister is irrevocably altered.

Fractured beyond repair.

The night is endless.

Beth had asked Tegan what she had wanted to say to Kate, whether she wanted to talk to the police, but Tegan had clammed up again.

Unable to sleep, Beth has made countless cups of milky coffee. Letting them cool on the table before her, a skin forming on the surface, until she tips them away, cold and unappealing down the sink, and begins the ritual again. Filling the kettle, boiling the water. Immersing herself in the familiar, trying to keep her mind free of tumultuous thoughts, but to no avail.

Her mind is filled with the bleak. The dark. The horrific.

She wants to google what might happen to Tegan if she is found guilty, but she is too afraid of the answer.

Above her, floorboards shift. Tegan is also awake and yet Beth does not go to her because she is scared she might tell her daughter things she does not need to hear right now.

That soon, Beth will go to the police station and confess to a crime because her confession might fill the police with an urgency to find Travis, which in turn might help clear Tegan's name. In her heart she believes Travis was the one who pushed Caily, not only because he had those newspaper cuttings of her, but because she believes he is capable of anything.

Beth turns it over and over in her mind. Weighing up the pros and cons.

She has to tell the truth if there is even a smidgeon of hope that it might help Tegan.

Will the police detain her? And if they do, then what?

She's had if-anything-happens-to-me conversations with Kate before. Just hours ago she'd have been certain that Kate would take Tegan in if Beth could not take care of her for any reason, but now she is not sure.

What will happen to my daughter?

This is the only thought on Beth's mind as dawn begins to break. The pale grey sky streaked with pink and peach. She sits in the patch of sunlight falling through the kitchen window but it does not warm her.

Nothing can.

She is frozen with fear at what is to come.

Frozen in disbelief by the things she has done.

It is her that Owen should be arresting, not Tegan, but she cannot expect him to unpick the truth when so much has been hidden.

She is tired of lying, tired of the low-level fear that pulses in the pit of her stomach that she will be found out.

It has to end.

Today.

Somehow, she showers and dresses, her mind operating on autopilot. She takes Tegan some breakfast. Weetabix flooded with milk and sprinkled with golden sugar just the way she likes it and a weak tea in a mug proclaiming that Beth is the 'World's Best Mum'.

She isn't.

Beth sits on the edge of Tegan's bed. She takes her hand and Tegan lets her.

'I love you,' Beth says because that simple fact is the only thing that should matter.

But it isn't.

'Do you think Aunt Kate will ever speak to me again, Mum?' Tegan asks.

'Of course,' Beth says, although she knows nothing of the sort. 'It'll all be cleared up soon. She'll realize you didn't hurt Caily.'

Tegan doesn't answer, and Beth does not tell her that she was asking a question because she is her mother and she should not have to ask for clarification. She should not have any doubt.

'Do you think Caily will wake up soon?' Tegan chews the skin around her thumbnail.

'I think . . . Yes. Yes, she will.'

'But you don't know?'

'Nobody can know. But . . . she's strong. Determined. Do you remember when we went on that picnic to Wyeland Forest—'

'The place with the wooden assault course?'

'Yes. And you'd had a growth spurt and they let you through but told Caily she was too small.' Beth smiles at the memory. Her niece, hands on hips, indignant, had recited a Winnie-the-Pooh quote about being small but strong. The man had laughed, 'Okay, but don't come crying to me if you get stuck.'

'She never gave up,' Tegan said. 'She couldn't reach half

the things and I offered her a leg up but she was determined to do it on her own. She jumped and jumped and—'

'Proved everybody wrong.' Beth nodded.

'But I waited for her. I was there to help her and now she's taller than me. Braver than me.' Tegan stares at Beth beseechingly, the bags under her eyes dark against her pale tear-streaked skin. 'What's going to happen to me?'

'You're going to be fine,' she promises because she thinks, she hopes, that this is true. 'I've got to go out for a little while. Will you be okay?'

'Yeah.' Tegan curls onto her side, duvet pulled up under her chin. On the bedside cabinet her Weetabix is congealing. 'When will you be back?'

'I don't know,' says Beth because that is also the truth.

She walks slowly downstairs, pausing at every single framed photograph. Tegan, slightly out of focus, on a swing, head thrown back, laughing. Kate and Beth, holding hands, their other arms high above their heads, punching the sky triumphantly as they breeze through the blue ribbon on school sports day. Later, both now mums, they recreated this pose during the parents' race. This time their cheeks are red with effort, but their grins are exactly the same. Tegan and Caily at the end of the assault course in Wyeland Forest brandishing certificates, the look of pride on their faces immense. She drinks them all in, everything. The pictures, the ornaments, the memories, because she does not know when she will see them again.

She doesn't want to do this alone.

And so she composes a message to Matt, knowing he too

is desperate for a way out. Thinking that he will, perhaps, be relieved.

She reads the text through before she presses send.

I'm on my way to your house. Please come to the police station with me. It's time to tell the truth.

CHAPTER FORTY-SIX

Matt

Truth be told, Matt is close to breaking point. After yesterday's bombshell that Tegan's DNA was a match with the samples taken from under Caily's fingernails, he is incredulous he is doing something as normal as standing in the fruit and veg aisle of his local Tesco.

He cannot process the fact that his niece may have hurt his daughter. He's loved Tegan since the day she was born, treated her like a second daughter. However betrayed he feels, it is a million times worse for Kate because as well as losing Tegan she is so scared she might lose Beth. She had raged and cried and looked to Matt with wounded eyes to say something – *anything* – to ease her pain but Matt had been at a loss to know what to say, what to do.

His words inadequate. Insufficient. The stabbing pain in his chest fast and frequent.

He studies the list in his hand with eyes that are blurry with tiredness, wondering how innocuous, everyday items, can cause an intense wave of sadness to wash over him. Kate has asked for a jar of Cadbury's hot chocolate because she hopes the smell might rouse Caily. Sedation is being withdrawn today and they want to do everything they can to help Caily wake. Matt unscrews the lid and breathes in the powder deeply, his heart aching at the memory of Caily sipping from a giant 'Friends Central Perk' mug, a swirl of whipped cream on the top. He quickly seals the jar and drops it into his basket before seeking out emery boards, wondering whether Caily will ever again coat her nails with brightly coloured polish adorned with tiny stars or moons or whatever she and Tegan were into. He selects a can of Pedigree Chum because, although Twix hasn't been allowed in the hospital, Kate again hopes this smell might trigger Caily's senses.

Bring her back to them.

'Do you have a bag for life?' he is asked by a bored-looking assistant with dyed black hair and multiple piercings as she scans his items, and he feels himself wobble. Whose life is the bag meant to last for, he wants to ask, because some lives are too short, but instead he mumbles an apology and pays for a plastic bag, knowing that this alone would disappoint his environmentally-minded daughter and he has already let her down so much.

He is hurrying across the car park, head down against the pelting rain that bounces from puddles in front of his feet, when he hears his name being called.

He turns, his stomach sinking into his muddy boots at the sight of the man standing next to his Land Rover.

Leroy. One of Victor's henchmen.

He's never spoken to Matt before. He usually stands behind Victor and Victor's brother, Ray, looking threatening.

Matt swallows hard. Leroy is huge, solid. Matt isn't weak,

years of manual labour have defined his muscles in a way his fifteen-year-old self had dreamed of, but Leroy looks like he could snap him like one of the sticks Twix crunches in his teeth during walks.

He glances to his left, he could run towards the main road. He sees the Range Rover, knows that Victor is inside.

To his right the safety of Tesco.

But then what?

In three powerful strides Leroy is in front of him. 'Don't run.'

Matt grips his bag tightly: what would happen if he swung it at Leroy's head? Would the tin of dog food, the jar of hot chocolate be enough to stun him?

But then what?

'I don't want to hurt you,' Leroy says.

'Don't you?' Matt meet's Leroy's dark eyes and sees something in them. Compassion?

'No. Victor and Ray might enjoy that but . . . come and get in the car. Victor wants to talk to you.'

'Why?' There is a constriction in Matt's throat and the word is barely audible.

'You know why.'

'No,' Matt clears his throat. 'I mean why do you work for Victor if you don't . . . enjoy it?'

For a second he thinks Leroy isn't going to answer, but he waits for the clatter of trolleys to pass as the assistant pushes a long line of them back to the shop, then throws a glance over his shoulder as though afraid of being overheard.

'Because I was like you once. I got in over my head and it was this or . . . I have a family. Kids.'

'How old?' Matt tries to find a common ground.

'The eldest was twelve then. He'd started hanging around in a gang, most of the kids in our area did. My missus found a knife in his drawer and . . . It's always on the news, isn't it? Knife crime. We were scared he'd end up in prison or dead.'

'It's a terrifying world we live in.'

'Yeah.' Rain runs down Leroy's face and it almost looks as though he is crying. 'We wanted to move but the bank refused my loan application because my work as a bouncer was through an agency. Victor gave me a loan but then the pandemic hit and the clubs shut and I couldn't pay him back. The interest was . . .' Leroy raises his shoulders in a here-we-are shrug. 'Come on. Keep him waiting any longer and he'll be even more pissed.'

They walk across the car park. Matt's boots pound on the tarmac. The vibration travelling through his body. He is painfully aware that every single cell in his body is trembling.

The door of the Range Rover clicks open. Victor's voice growls.

'Get in.'

It isn't a question.

All at once Matt wants to cry, but he is a husband and a father and a man and he cannot fall apart.

He cannot plead because fear has seized his voice box, and so he doesn't speak as he climbs into the back of the car, his plastic bag rustling as he settles his shopping on his lap. The door slams with a finality, as though signifying the end of something but Matt doesn't like to think what.

The car begins to move and he feels an urge to twist around in his seat and watch as the town grows smaller behind them because he is scared he will never see it again.

Never see anything again.

Instead he bunches his hands into fists, not to fight with, but to try and channel his emotions so he doesn't come across as weak or stupid.

He is both of those things.

Resting his head back on the seat, he closes his eyes and thinks of his wife.

His daughter.

Wishing he could tell them how sorry he is.

Hoping he will get a chance to but fearing that this is it for him.

The end.

Matt's phone trills a text. Beth's name illuminating his screen.

Victor holds his hand out and, when Matt unlocks his mobile and passes it over, Victor reads the message, tosses Matt's phone back on the seat, immediately makes a call.

'Ray, get over to the farm. Beth's on her way there. She wants to go to the police. Shut that bitch up.'

CHAPTER FORTY-SEVEN

Kate

Shut up, shut up, shut up.

Kate tries to block out the negative voice in her head, goading her that Matt isn't answering her calls because he is not coping. He could be stuck at roadworks, Tesco might have been out of stock of some of the items and he's gone further afield. Maybe the ancient Land Rover broke down. Multiple reasons why Matt is taking so long and all of them better than the single spinning thought that he's taking his time because he does not know how to calm her.

Tegan has hurt Caily.

She tries ringing Matt again, her phone cradled in the crook of her neck between her shoulder and cheek, using both hands to zip up the bag she's filled with things for Caily.

He still doesn't answer.

Frustrated, she paces over to the window.

The rain beats against the panes, the sky overhead grey and angry. Kate wonders whether Matt has stopped to do something on the farm. She pictures him, wind pushing his hood down, hair plastered to his head, cold water trickling down his back as he hurries from the shop to the car. He'll probably want a hot shower and to change before they leave for the hospital. A curl of impatience unfurls in her stomach. She's desperate to get back to Caily.

She picks up the bag. She can't wait any longer.

She opens the front door, steps outside. Locks the door behind her.

Kate doesn't sense she's being watched.

Isn't aware of the car parked, not in her yard but on the verge, behind the hedge.

Doesn't notice the figure step out of the shadows.

Doesn't feel the hate.

CHAPTER FORTY-EIGHT

Matt

Matt feels the hate radiate from Victor.

'Don't touch Beth,' Matt says. 'If you do—'

'What?' Victor leans forward, his elbows resting on his knees, fingers steepled together. 'What will you do?'

Matt shifts uncomfortably in his seat, his bladder full, or perhaps it is only fear making it feel that way. He covers his lap with his hands, scared that his urine will leak, staining his crotch and then he'd be . . . what? Embarrassed? Scared? Of all the things that could happen here today, wetting himself isn't the worst. But still, he squirms like a small child, a child on the verge of tears.

'I'm sorry,' he says in a voice that doesn't sound like his, too quiet, too high.

'You're sorry. I'm sorry. But that doesn't make things right, does it?'

'I know . . .' Matt takes a deep breath. 'But you know what happened, though. I've told you about Travis. You could—'

'Uh-uh.' Victor shakes a firm finger in front of Matt's

face. '*I* could? You think this is my fault? Something I should fix?'

'No . . . no, of course not but, I don't know—'

'Luckily for you I know. I know exactly what you need to do. Give me what you owe me.'

'But—'

'On Sunday I gave you forty-eight hours, which I think was reasonable. Now it's Wednesday. That's how generous I am. I'm adding on a little extra interest for the inconvenience. The stress.'

Bile stings Matt's throat. 'But I don't . . . I haven't . . .'

'Then find it or we have a problem. Do we have a problem, Matt?'

What is he going to do?

Matt felt his head shake of its own accord – *no, we don't have a problem* – and he wants to put his hands either side of his skull to keep it still. To stop lying. To stop agreeing to things he cannot guarantee.

'Good. Remember, some things are more precious than money. The safety of your family, for one.'

Matt's chest tightens as he thinks of Caily still and silent in her hospital bed. Her fall was before Victor knew that Matt had fucked up, but just because Victor hadn't hurt her then, doesn't mean he wouldn't hurt her now.

Hurt Kate.

Beth.

Patrick and Mary.

All of them.

There's a roaring in his ears, the edges of his vision beginning to blur.

What is he going to do?

This time the pain in his chest is so fierce he hunches forward.

Matt's phone vibrates again on the car seat. He turns his head. Kate's name lights up his screen. She wanted to leave for the hospital by 8am. She is probably wondering why he is taking so long.

His phone falls silent. He imagines a frown furrowing her forehead but can't decipher whether it will be one of worry, frustration or exasperation.

Probably all three.

There was a time he'd know what she was feeling just by closing his eyes and picturing her, but all he feels in this moment is a low-level fear that pulses deep inside him, causing a nausea to rise that he repeatedly forces back down, his Adam's apple bobbing every time he swallows. He's horribly out of his depth and he doesn't know how to fix this. How to get out of this terrible situation that he has created.

What is he going to do?

He's been such a fool.

He thought it would all be so . . . perhaps not easy but, despite the risks, uncomplicated. But now he is here and his wife is waiting and he has no idea what he can do to make it better. There's nothing he can say but his mouth is too dry to speak anyway. He runs his tongue over his lips. Tastes the salt in the sweat that beads on his upper lip.

The bitter tang of his own fear.

His own stupidity.

'Please don't go to my home.' He tries to rise and immediately hands press firmly on his shoulders, pushing him back onto his chair. 'My wife, Kate, is there.'

What is he going to do?

What will happen when Ray finds Beth?

CHAPTER FORTY-NINE

Kate

'Beth.'

Kate thinks she hears her sister's name being called but she must have imagined it. Perhaps her subconscious is urging her to speak to her sister, talk through the latest developments with Tegan, but she has nothing to say to her.

She can't have heard anything.

She's alone. Isn't she?

Unease squirms through her as she stands under the cover of the porch, phoning Matt again to let him know she's going back to the hospital without him. For the third time it goes straight to voicemail. He must have come back and got caught up with some task or other. His Land Rover is likely outside her parents' house. She scans the landscape for signs of him but he could be anywhere, doing anything. The farm is woefully neglected. The animals still cared for but the plans they'd made for this season have never come to fruition. After this – if there is an 'after this' – the farm will be on its knees. She remembers the struggle of twenty-five years ago, the time Dad very nearly had to sell up, and she feels heavy-hearted that it might come to that, but she can't help: farming isn't her priority right now.

Nothing else is as important as her child.

She gives up on Matt, pulls her hood over her head and hurries across the yard.

A crack of lightning splits the dark, angry sky in two. The wind howling over the flat fields, through the trees. Rain battering down on the car roof as Kate jabs her key into the ignition, throws her bag and phone onto the passenger seat, pushes the boot release button inside the door. She hurries around to the back of the car with the holdall for Caily, mentally checking that, aside from the bits Matt has gone out for, she has remembered everything: some pretty pyjamas, some grapefruit-scented leave-in conditioner for her hair, strawberry hand cream for the skin that is already cracking around her fingernails. Some pale-pink varnish that Caily artistically calls blush, so when she wakes up her nails will be nice.

When. Not if. It could be anytime, Nita said.

Thunder rumbles deep and low.

Kate shuts the boot, is just about to climb into the car. It is impossible for her to hear anyone approach her, but then an arm loops around her neck. For a second her mind is blank, not a single thought in her head. But then terror grips her. She feels it pressing down on her, the man pressing down on her, until she can't tell which are physical sensations and which are caused by her terrified mind.

She can't scream.

She can't breathe.

Who is he?

What is happening?

What is he going to do to her?

She opens her mouth to call for help but the arm squeezes tighter, rough fabric against her skin. The smell of aftershave overpowering.

What is he going to do to her?

Panic bursts into flames inside her, a red-hot desire to escape fuelling every desperate punch to her assailant's arms, every frantic stamp on his feet. Kick to his shins.

What is he going to do to her?

She struggles ferociously but fruitlessly. Not fully comprehending what is going on.

Or why.

Her frenzied attempts to escape slow, her energy depleting, but Kate isn't giving up.

She can't.

What is he going to do to her?

Every crime story she has ever read jabs into her memory, sharp and horrifying. The woman recently bludgeoned to death while walking her dog. The teenager strangled in a local beauty spot. Senseless, motiveless, unprovoked. Kate does not want to become another statistic.

She is afraid, so very afraid. Sweat prickling at her skin. Her bowels loose like she might lose control of them at any given second, and part of her wishes she would. That she would disgust her assailant so much that he would let her go.

He begins to propel her forward, while she leans her weight back, damp hair falling into her eyes. From inside the house she can hear Twix frantically barking and wonders if Matt can hear him. Where is her husband? At the thought of him, of Caily, she begins to fight again. She has too much to live for to let this man . . . *Oh god. What is he going to do to her?*

Something sparks in Kate's brain. An article she'd read once on self-defence. It advised letting your body go limp because then you are a dead weight, harder to move. Kate lifts her feet, forces her muscles to relax but the pressure against her windpipe is unbearable. Her vision quickly filling with shadows.

She sets her feet back down and resentfully, reluctantly, allows herself to be thrust forward towards the road. It is then she notices the vehicle on the other side of the hedge.

Are there others like him waiting in his car?

Where is he going to take her?

In a last, desperate attempt to escape, she bends her arm, jabs her elbow backwards as hard as she can. By some miracle it connects with his groin. With an 'oof' of pain, he loosens his grip on her and she is free.

She is running. Away from the road. Away from his car.

But moments later, he is right behind her.

CHAPTER FIFTY

Matt

He is free. There is nobody behind him.

Matt had made a promise to Victor and Victor had let him go.

He runs back towards town, back towards his car.

He needs to reach the farm.

Reach Ray.

Before he hurts anyone.

CHAPTER FIFTY-ONE

Kate

He wants to hurt her.

Kate knows this as she runs.

She's back at her car. Momentarily she contemplates throwing herself inside it, locking the door, but the man is so close she can hear his breath loud and ragged. She carries on.

He's bigger than her. Stronger than her. Legs longer. But she is fit. Years of farming have honed her body.

She is leaving her house behind now, the frantic barking of Twix fading, drowned out by the rushing of the river as she sprints alongside it. Her only hope is to maintain her lead long enough to reach the bridge. If she reaches it, she'll be visible from the road. He can't hurt her if there are witnesses, can he? Or if there aren't any cars she can run into the woods, she is confident that she can lose him. She is familiar with every tree, every clearing.

Run.

She is beating him, chest burning with the exertion, limbs leaden but the bridge is in sight.

Almost, almost there.

But then she is yanked backwards by her hood. The zip of her coat digging into her throat. Tighter and tighter.

She is choking, her air cut off. Head spinning. Scared he's going to drag her all the way back to his car. For a moment he doesn't move. Perhaps wondering what to do with her. He's tired, she can hear the wheeze of his chest. Smell the nicotine on his fingers.

Feebly, she slaps at his arm, wanting to beg him to let her go, offering him money and silence, not that they have any cash, but the silence? She can promise him that.

Kate wants to ask him why he is doing this. If this is connected to Caily . . . The thought that her daughter might have felt this frightened, that Caily might have experienced this man's hands on her, tears at her very being. She is sorry she ever doubted Tegan for a second. Sorry about so many things she might never be able to put right.

'Stop struggling, Beth.' The voice growls in her ear.

He thinks she is Beth.

Her first reaction is one of relief. She can stop this. Tell him he is mistaken, she is Beth's twin, an easy mistake to make, but then she thinks if he believes her, lets her go, then he will find Beth and then what?

She doesn't know who he is or why he wants to hurt her sister but, despite her anger towards her sister right now, she will not give Beth to him.

'Beth,' he says again, sharply, and she stops fighting against him. Does not tell him that she is Kate.

Beth.

She has much she wants to say to her twin.

She loves her.

She loves them all immeasurably but, although she can feel hot tears rising, her lungs are too restricted and she cannot cry.

'This is a warning. Keep quiet.'

He pushes her forward, towards the river. Her feet stumble over the rough ground, damp grass soaking the bottom of her jeans.

Lightning whips again, making Kate jump, but the man doesn't react, doesn't falter, stalking forward with purpose.

They reach the bank, water flowing fast and choppy under the blustery wind.

What is he going to do to her?

He edges her forward until her toes are at the water. And then she knows.

With sickening clarity she knows.

No.

She clings to his arm again. Tries to shake her head. Tell him that she cannot swim.

No.

No.

No.

And there is a split second of blessed relief when he jerks Kate back and she thinks he's changed his mind, but instead, lighting fast, he moves his hands to her shoulder blades and shoves her with force.

Her arms flail for something solid to hold on to.

Her mouth opens in a scream.

Although she is expecting it, hitting the water is still

a shock, dark and murky under the rain-splattered surface, and she gasps, her mouth filling with stinking water.

Her throat.

Her lungs.

CHAPTER FIFTY-TWO

Beth

Beth's lungs feel as though someone is stamping on them.

It must be because she is nervous.

She barely registers the car on the verge as she pulls into Kate's yard. Parking next to her sister's car.

The passenger door is open, on the seat an overnight bag. The sky illuminates with lightning and Beth remembers the way she and Kate would comfort each other during storms. Hiding beneath the covers, making up stories of giants with rumbly tummies who only ate boys, never girls.

Beth waits, sure that Kate will come out of the front door, knowing that she'll be in a hurry to get back to Caily but also knowing what she wants to say won't take long.

Sorry.

It isn't nearly everything, it isn't nearly enough, but it is all she has to offer right now, until Matt is here at least and then they'll tell her the truth, together.

She, more than anyone, deserves to know.

Beth doesn't know how far Kate's forgiveness will stretch but she doesn't want to lose her sister.

But perhaps she deserves to.

Thunder grumbles, rain firing onto the bonnet, bouncing from the windscreen.

Beth's stomach squirms with a sense of foreboding. She doesn't particularly think it is the thought of facing Kate, or the police, causing the unsettling sensation, but something else.

Something she has felt before.

A sense Kate is in trouble.

Unnerved, Beth unfastens her seatbelt, opens the car door. It is then she hears Twix barking, distressed.

She runs to the front door, boots splashing through puddles.

It's locked.

Kate was clearly ready to leave but she never actually made it into her car. Still, she can't have just disappeared?

'Kate?' she calls and then cups her hands around her mouth so her voice travels further and she calls again, 'Kate?'

Nothing.

Rain drips from the guttering, trickling down Beth's neck, but she doesn't notice the cold because she feels it everywhere. A freezing dread.

Knowing with certainty that Kate is in trouble.

Beth's fingers fumble for her phone. 'Come on, come on, come on,' she urges Kate to answer. Instead she hears the ringing from inside Kate's car. Discovers her handset on the passenger seat.

Kate is in trouble.

All those years ago, when she'd experienced the same deep-seated fear, the same worry, Kate had been in the river.

Then she had felt water filling her own lungs, stealing the air she tried to greedily gasp in. She felt the sense of helplessness, hopelessness.

Panic.

Closing her eyes, she feels it all again. Everything.

Then she sees the man running towards her, coming from the river.

Ray.

Kate is in trouble.

CHAPTER FIFTY-THREE

Kate

Kate is in trouble. She is petrified.

The water is frigid. She plunges under the surface again, her chest tight, her lungs fire. Her legs thrash wildly, feet frantically trying to touch the riverbed, but already she is out of her depth.

There's a choppiness to the water generated by the storm and, although Kate can still see the bank, the current sweeps her further into the middle where it is too deep to stand.

Why didn't she learn to swim?

Her arms and legs flail. The intrinsic desire to breathe forces her lips apart and she coughs and splutters as she breaks free of the surface again.

Everything is grey. The water. The sky. The world has lost its colour. She can't see her attacker anymore and, although he is the one who has put her here, she wishes he'd come back.

She doesn't want to die alone.

Already her body feels leaden, she's tiring. Slow. A chill seeps into her bones.

'Help.' Her cry is feeble, sapping energy she doesn't have.

She tries to think of Caily, kicking her legs again with more force. She can't give up.

She won't.

Move.

Her body screams out for rest. The more she tries to propel herself towards the bank the further away it appears.

A crack of lightning.

Kate whimpers. Water seeping into her mouth as she bobs up and down. She tries to keep her head above the surface but it's hard.

Getting harder.

Her clothes fan out around her, weighing her down. She kicks again, thinks she's still wearing her boots but she cannot be sure.

She can't feel her torso. Her legs. Her feet.

She is the water and the water is her.

Kate slips underneath the surface.

Her movements are frenzied, the urge to breathe painful. Her chest feels as though it's going to burst.

Quickly she tires again.

Stills.

There's a quiet she hasn't experienced before. She can't hear the splash of water. Can't hear her own pulse in her ears.

Everything is dark. Kate can't tell whether her eyes are open or shut but she's shrouded in black and it's oddly comforting.

More than anything, she wants to sleep.

She allows herself to sink.

She surrenders.

CHAPTER FIFTY-FOUR

Beth

Beth won't surrender to the stitch jabbing into her side. She doesn't slow, doesn't falter. Her arms pump fiercely, shoes slapping against the wet grass. She passes Ray, their shoulders almost touching. She half-expects him to grab her but he doesn't.

What has he done to Kate?

This is all her fault.

She throws a glance over her shoulder. He's heading back towards the road.

The river snakes parallel to her, dull and dank. A burst of lightning casts a silver glow across the water. Beth can't see anyone. Anything.

Kate.

Her pace slows, she clutches at her waist, taking deep breaths as she stares into the water, left, right. And then she sees a flash of pink.

Kate's coat.

Without conscious thought, she inhales deeply as she kicks off her shoes, dives into the river. The icy temperature of the water pushes her instinctively back to the surface, stealing her breath, her clarity, but then she gathers herself and propels herself back underwater.

She's disorientated.

Unable to see clearly.

Hear anything.

Kate.

She trusts her instincts and allows her arms to propel her through the murkiness, breathing out slowly through her pursed lips, and then resisting the urge to inhale, ignoring the desperate ache of her chest.

Weeds tangle around her fingers, something catches in her hair.

Kate.

She needs to resurface, to refill her lungs but then . . .

Her hand brushes against something else.

Something solid.

Kate.

Beth propels herself forward, feeling the fingers she has connected with become a hand, an arm.

She grabs her sister, her arms circled around Kate's chest, and she kicks and kicks because their lives are quite literally in her hands.

She doesn't register whether Kate feels heavy.

Whether her own body is screaming with agony.

She doesn't let anything detract her from the movements of her legs, powerful now, frantic.

Desperate.

Above her she sees light now, on the surface of the water, encouraging her, teasing her.

You'll never reach me.

But she knows, despite the painful burn behind her ribcage, she will reach it.

She will save them.

Her lungs cry out as she bursts through the water.

Her sister in her arms.

Her still, silent, sister in her arms.

Please wake up.

CHAPTER FIFTY-FIVE

Kate

It's a slow awakening. Her senses don't roar back into life. Instead, she becomes aware of the cold, hard ground. Of the ache in her chest. The bitter taste in her mouth.

The feel of the rain against her face. The wind blustering against her skin.

The noise of the storm returns, quiet at first, but then growing in volume until the rumble of thunder sounds so close it's as though she could stretch out her hands and touch it.

She should feel relief to be out of the river, to be alive, but instead she feels scared and confused.

Kate forces her eyes to open. Colours return.

An anxious face peering at her.

Beth's face.

A second ago Kate felt entirely alone, but she isn't.

She never will be.

She has a twin and she is loved.

She begins to cry, allows Beth to scoop her into her familiar arms, and they shake with both shock and the force of their tears.

But then Kate remembers how she got in the river, the man, how he was after Beth, not her, and she knows that neither of them is safe.

They need to move.

CHAPTER FIFTY-SIX

Beth

Move.

Unsteadily the sisters make their way back to Kate's house, clinging to each other for warmth and comfort.

Reassurance.

Beth scans the yard for Ray while Kate plucks the keys out of the ignition. They hurry across the porch. Kate's hand trembles and it takes her three attempts before she manages to fit the key into the lock. She pushes open the door and is immediately shoved back with force.

She stumbles and Beth catches her.

'Twix.' Kate turns her face away from his love and licks. 'Let us in.'

Beth and Kate squeeze into the hallway, Twix dancing joyfully around them.

It's isn't until Beth locks the door behind them that she allows herself to breathe. Kate is the same because after a deep inhale comes a shaky exhale filled with tears.

'I don't . . .' Kate covers her face with her hands.

'Shh.' Beth wraps her in a comforting hug. 'Don't think about it right now. We need to get warm and dry—'

'He thought I was you. Why is someone after you? We need to call the police.' Kate wriggles from Beth's tight embrace. 'We need to tell them that someone . . . someone . . .' She dissolves into tears again and Beth's heart breaks for all that Kate has been through.

Knowing that she is the cause of it.

'I'll tell you everything, I promise. But first go and get in the shower and warm up,' Beth urges. 'I'll call Owen.'

Kate could have died today. *Died*.

She places a hand over her chest, feels the thud, thud, thud of her heart, knowing that half of it belongs to her twin, has always belonged to her twin. Matt and Sean have a small piece of them both but the twins complete each other.

Kate turns, she's already halfway up the stairs. She holds out her hand and Beth slips her own into it, their fingers linking together. 'I don't want to be alone,' Kate whispers and Beth answers with a look that says 'You'll never be alone' and 'I'm sorry' and all the things she cannot say because the thing she wants to say the most of all is 'you're safe now', but she cannot promise that.

It would be a lie.

Kate quickly showers while Beth pulls clean clothes from her drawers, yoga pants for both of them and oversized sweatshirts. While Kate is drying herself, Beth jumps into the shower. She kneads shampoo firmly into her scalp until it's covered with foamy, lime suds. But no matter how many times she washes it, she will never get the smell of the river out of her hair.

The taste of fear coating the back of her throat.

She switches the water off and pads into the bedroom, following Kate's damp footprints that have darkened the carpet.

Kate is dressed, sitting on the edge of the bed. 'What did Owen say?'

'I'll call him when I'm dressed.' Beth tugs socks onto her feet. 'I wanted to talk to you first. Let's go and make some coffee.'

Minutes later they are ready.

They stand.

Head out into the hallway.

Kate clutching Beth's arm tightly when they both hear a noise from downstairs.

Somebody is in the house.

CHAPTER FIFTY-SEVEN

Matt

Somebody *must* be in the house.

Beth's car is outside. Kate's too. Where are they?

'Hello?' Matt calls as he runs from room to room. There's an excited bark as Twix hurls himself downstairs, quickly followed by Beth and then Kate. Hair damp, face pale. Anxious.

She rushes into his arms.

'Thank god. Thank god. Thank god.' His knees buckle and he's clinging to her, trying to be the strong one, but crying with relief. Kate buries her face in his neck and he feels her tears trickling past his collar. They remain locked together, he doesn't want to move, he can't.

'I was so scared he'd hurt you,' he whispers into her hair.

She lifts her tearstained face to his. 'How did you know about . . . ?' She takes a step back, wriggles from his grasp. 'Who was that man?'

She shifts her gaze to Beth. 'He thought I was you.' Looks at Matt once more. 'Who was he?'

There's a silence punctured only by the ticking of the grandfather clock.

The Kate in front of him dissolves and reforms as his young bride. Huge trusting eyes that held his from beneath her veil as he promised to love and honour and cherish her, vows that he meant.

He has failed her in the worst way imaginable and he needs to tell her the truth but the words are stuck to the roof of his dry mouth and he cannot force them out.

'Matt?'

But Beth speaks before he can.

'Matt and I have something to tell you. Something . . .' Her voice shakes and Matt knows this is where he should step in, step up, but he doesn't.

He feels no relief that in minutes Kate will know everything, only a sick, squirming dread.

'Let's go and sit down.' Beth is very much in charge, leading the way. He takes Kate's hand. Her palm is clammy, his palm is clammy, so he tightens his grip, not wanting her to slip away but fearing she might anyway.

Matt and Beth sit either end of the sofa, leaving space for Kate in the middle but, instead of taking her usual seat, she sits in the armchair by the window. She crosses her arms as though she knows that the fabric of her universe is about to be torn apart and she has to be the one to hold it together, hold herself together. Twix, sensing the tension in the air, slinks over to Kate and sits next to her protectively, leaning against her leg.

There are twinges in Matt's chest and ridiculously, for a split second, he wants – actually wants – to collapse. To be rushed to hospital away from Kate and those trusting eyes and her questions.

Her inevitable disappointment.

His mouth is dry. He runs his tongue over his teeth, wishing he could find the right words stuck there. The words that could convey the complete and utter despair he has felt these past few years. Brexit. Covid. The fucking weather. Everything has conspired against him. The government giving with one hand and taking with the other, although giving makes it sound so easy. Jumping through hoops for the little funding they offer. He's supposed to feel grateful when, after mountainous paperwork, inspections, phone calls, practically begging, the money lands in his account. He used to be so proud to be a farmer. Now it feels like being repeatedly punched in the face and having to say 'thank you' for the privilege to the people who are punching you.

He'd love their inept prime minister to walk a mile in his scuffed and muddied boots, the stitching around the sole coming undone.

'One of you tell me what's going on,' Kate demands.

'Okay,' Beth says in a shaky voice. 'Okay. But it won't be easy to hear.'

CHAPTER FIFTY-EIGHT

Beth

It isn't easy to know where to start.

'I'm going to tell you everything.' Beth's face burns with the shame of it. 'Please just listen and then I'll answer any questions you might have. Okay?'

'Okay.' Kate crosses her arms, her mouth a thin line.

Beth doesn't want to filter her words, to pick and choose what to tell Kate, what to keep hidden. She has been doing that for the past few months. And so she decides to tell her exactly what happened from the beginning, allowing the day to come rushing back to her in shades of black and white.

Tegan had left for school and Beth had wearily fired up her old laptop, searching for jobs, just as she did every day. She used to be selective. Setting her radius to within twenty miles of her home, typing in keywords, jobs she wanted, but now her search was open and vague. There were new positions available, there always were and, although Beth had initially shied away from zero-hour contracts, thinking them unfair, she filled in the online forms, sent off her CV, not with a feeling of hope as she had done in the first couple of weeks of being unemployed but with despair. Scanning over the automated message that the company had received her application along with a little piece of her dignity. She didn't expect to hear anything else from them.

She never did.

But still she checked her emails. There were no responses from the last batch she had applied for. There were discount vouchers for a theme park, a picture-perfect family advertising fun. Mum, Dad, a boy and a girl. A cliched family that squeezed her heart. She had wanted that, once. Thought she had that. But then Sean was sent to prison and, sad as it seemed, she hadn't been in love since. She'd been on dates, when she was working in the theatre café she'd occasionally been asked out, but none of them were . . . *him*.

There was a knock at the door. Too early for the postman and she wasn't expecting any deliveries. Everything in her body, her bones, her blood, her skin, turned to ice.

It was them.

The loan people who smiled as they demanded more than she could give each week.

Ever since she'd fallen behind on the payments when Tegan had needed new shoes, she'd been battling to keep on top of the rising interest. The balance now over double what she had originally borrowed.

She was short again this week, not by a lot but enough. She'd used more fuel than usual taking Dad to his physio, Mum to the GP, both of them to the opticians, but she could hardly charge her parents for lifts, could she? She'd considered selling the car but it was only fit for scrap and she'd need one if – *when* – she got a job. Everywhere around here was so remote.

The knock came again.

Hesitantly, Beth edged down the hallway. If she ignored them they'd only come back later and Tegan might be here then.

She opened the door and it was as though the clouds had parted and the sun was shining brilliantly upon her again, casting her in glorious technicolour, because there he was.

Sean.

A stripe of anxiety between his eyebrows.

Sean.

He'd been released. She slumped against the doorframe, too many emotions to identify fighting for dominance. Felt the rhythmic beating of her heart, *go-stay-go-stay*.

Knowing that she should tell him to leave. He had let her down in the worst possible way even though she never believed he was the worst possible person, but there was something binding them together.

Something more than Tegan and time and the wonder of first love.

Something more powerful than either of them, inextricably linking them.

Despite it being seven years, she let him hold her with his bright, blue eyes. Knowing what she would find in them.

Love.

She realized that it would always be like this. The sight of him her undoing. He had shattered every happy memory of them that she had and yet she still carried them around in her pocket. She stepped back and let him into the hallway where once photos of them both had lined the walls.

For hours he talked, saying everything she wanted to hear. He was sorry. He loved her. Loved Tegan. He hadn't ever wanted them to visit not because he didn't want them to see him locked up, although that was a small part of it, but because he wanted them to move on. Build a life without him because, more than anything, he wanted them to be happy. They spoke of everything except the terrible crime Sean had committed, because he did not want to speak of it and Beth did not want to hear it, unable to equate the Sean who had been in prison to the one standing before her.

He spoke with a gentleness she remembered from the first time he had tentatively asked her out, aged fourteen, the tender way they lost their virginities together, two years later. Holding her hand throughout labour, not caring how tightly she gripped his fingers. Cradling Tegan to his chest night after night when she screamed with colic, singing as he rocked her.

He told her all this and more and, in turn, she told him that there wasn't, could never be, anyone else for her.

It was only when he reached out to gently rub the pad of his thumb over her cheeks that she realized she was crying, they both were.

It was only later, curled up in bed together, that it dawned on her that all along, she had been waiting for him.

Beth tries to explain to Kate now that she hadn't felt like a pushover as she had fallen back into his arms. She felt there was a strength in forgiveness, in being able to move forward. She wasn't weak. She knew this because, when Sean was taken away from her, she felt like she might not survive it. And yet she had.

They met the following day while Tegan was at school. Not at Beth's – she couldn't risk the neighbours saying anything – but at the small room his probation officer had found him.

'Should we tell Tegan yet?' she had worried.

'I want to wait a few weeks. To come back into her life with something to offer her. To be able to take her places, make it up to her. Make her proud of me.'

'She's used to having nothing,' Beth said, burying her face in Sean's shoulder as she told him about her debt. Her desperation. Today it was her turn to unburden herself.

'I'm so sorry you've been through all of this.' Beth heard the pain in his voice, felt it.

'I'm so scared.'

'We could leave. Start again and—'

'I can't leave Kate. Mum and Dad. It isn't fair to drag Tegan away from Caily. From school.'

Sean curved his body around hers. She felt the tremble in his arms and knew he was fighting back tears.

They held each other.

'I can help,' he said eventually, tentatively. 'I can fix everything.'

'How?'

'I can't tell you.' His voice was loaded with emotion.

Beth shifted away from him. 'I can't take any more secrets. If you can't be honest with me then there's no future for us.' The words spilled from her before she was even sure she wanted to utter them.

The wait was interminable but then, just when she was about to pull on her clothes and leave, he told her, and it was as though the solution he threw her was a rope, but one spiked with sharp points that could send her tumbling back down to a frightening reality.

But still she took it anyway.

And then she offered it to Matt.

CHAPTER FIFTY-NINE

Matt

As though they are running a relay, Beth hands the baton to him and Matt picks up the story.

'Victor Kent offered Sean the chance to make some money.'

'Victor . . . Dani's dad? The girl who's been bulling Caily?' Kate leans forward in her chair.

'Yes.' It is Beth who answers. 'Sean had turned him down. He really didn't want to do anything illegal but then, when he heard how much I owed, how scared I was, he thought it might be a solution.'

'What did Victor want Sean to do?'

'Grow cannabis.' Matt felt the words climb up his windpipe and now they are finally free he feels an immense sense of relief. He's hated lying to Kate. For a moment he cannot say anything else.

'I knew the red barn wasn't being used anymore, and there's still electric there from the old farmhouse,' Beth said. 'But I also knew there was no way of keeping it from Matt. He'd know from the electric bill that something was up, so I took a gamble and asked if he wanted to come in on it with us. The farm was struggling and—'

'You went behind my back to ask my husband to commit a crime?'

'I knew you wouldn't—'

'Of course I fucking wouldn't.'

Matt flinches, Beth too. Kate almost never swears. Any hope that she might have understood begins to trickle away. 'Who do you think you are? Walter fucking White?'

'Haven't you noticed how much pressure your husband is under?' Beth waves her hand towards him. 'How much weight he's lost. How grey he is, and not just his hair.'

'Of course but . . . we're farmers. We've had tough years before.'

'Have you noticed how often he stops moving, presses his hand against his heart?' Beth says softly.

Kate's eyes widen.

Matt feels the pain in his chest now, this time it radiates into his left arm. He feels it all. The despair and frustration and guilt and shame.

'It isn't just a tough year,' he says quietly. 'Everything that could go wrong has gone wrong, and without your dad—'

'Don't blame my father.'

'I'm not blaming him. I love him too, you know? But without his help with the manual work, I haven't been able to cope. We've lost all our casual, affordable workers thanks to Brexit and . . . you know.' Tears break through his voice and Kate's face crumples because she does know and she has tried her best to help but it isn't enough. He has never told her it all because he never wanted her to feel that she isn't enough.

'This farm has been in your family for generations and I didn't want to be the one responsible for losing it. Kate, we've tried to diversify. There . . . There is nothing left. One crop.' He says slowly, shamefully. 'That's all it would have taken to turn the farm around. When Beth told me, I said no, of course I did, but . . .' He's crying now. 'I couldn't sleep. I kept turning the what-ifs over in my mind and when I googled I learned that there are over 500,000 people growing weed in the UK and suddenly it didn't seem so terrible. That's approximately one person in every street. Statistically—'

'I don't care about statistics,' Kate isn't shouting anymore but somehow that is worse as she says sadly, 'I can't believe you've both lied to me.'

'We didn't exactly—'

'Don't.' She shakes her head. 'Don't for one second think that not telling me something is different to lying.'

He hangs his head.

'How could I not have known? Here. Right under my nose.'

'You've no cause to go near the barn and we haven't used it for years.'

'But still . . .' She falters. 'This is my home, Matt. My family's home. You brought drugs here? When we have a child? Does Caily know?'

'Yes.' Matt has never felt less of a father than he does in this moment. 'She found out the night of your party. She came into the barn and saw me and Beth and the plants.'

'But she didn't—'

'I asked her not to tell you.'

'You asked her to keep it a secret? And the next day . . .

the next day.' Kate begins to pace. 'She fell from the bridge.' She fixes him with eyes that are full of mistrust. 'Did you push her to keep her quiet?'

'Kate!' His swallows down his outrage. 'No,' he says quietly. 'No, I didn't.'

'Someone did. You have to tell those men to collect their plants.'

Beth and Matt exchange a glance.

'The plants have gone. We're pretty sure that Travis stole them. We think Caily told him about them the night of the birthday party. They vanished when he did.'

'Does Victor know they are missing?'

'Yes.'

The colour drains from her skin. 'Oh god. Did he or his men push my daughter from the bridge?'

Matt winces as she calls Caily hers instead of theirs, but he understands. 'No. Caily's fall was Friday. I was in the barn, tending to the plants when it happened. Victor didn't know the plants were missing until Sunday afternoon. He had no reason to want to hurt her.'

Then.

'Presumably because you can't give Victor his plants he wants his money?' Kate's voice is steel.

She is standing right next to Matt but he can feel her emotionally pull herself away from him. He wants to tell her that she can still trust him, but he's proven himself to be a liar.

'Who else knows?' Kate is in problem-solving mode now. This is Kate at her most magnificent, and when Matt looks at her now he feels a swell of love but, unlike before, he doesn't know if it's reciprocated. Whether she'll ever love him again.

'Caily, Travis, Sean, me, Matt, you, and Victor and his men.'

'Tegan?'

'I really don't think so.'

'The man today . . .' Kate sits down heavily as though weighted once more in the water. 'That was because of . . .' Matt winces, expecting her to say 'you' but instead she says 'this' and he feels a glimmer of hope that perhaps they are in this together. That she's not about to pack her bags and leave.

'Yes. They've been waiting for their money and I couldn't pay—'

'And you just thought you'd ignore it and hope they'd forget?'

'No. But . . .'

'We've been trying to come up with a way out of this mess,' Beth says. 'Not just Matt and I, but Sean too.'

'But you haven't been able to?'

'No and today . . .' Matt clears his throat. 'Today while I was shopping, Victor . . . he . . . he took me . . . I thought he was going to kill me.' Matt feels his shoulders round and he forces them back. He is not the one who nearly died today, Kate is. 'I've promised him I can get the money in twenty-four hours.'

'What if you can't?' Kate prompts in a breathy voice.

'I . . . I don't know.' He can't speculate. Can't think about it.

'Then we tell the police. Owen?' Kate brightens and he lets her hold this nugget of hope for a moment before he says, 'Tell them what? We've no evidence, Travis took everything. I've no marks on me from today. You can't identify who pushed you. We've no proof.'

'Right.' Kate chews the side of her thumbnail in the way she does when she's thinking. She never gives up, his wife. She hasn't given up on Caily. She won't give up on him. He has never loved her more than he does right now.

'Then . . . then we just pay them somehow,' she says, resigned. 'How much do we owe them?'

He notes the use of the word 'we' and he knows she is more than he deserves. It's more than he can bear. He covers his face with his hands.

'Matt? How much? Beth?' Her tone rises in pitch.

'One hundred and twenty thousand pounds,' Beth says and that is the last thing anyone says for what seems like hours.

Kate is the first one to speak, to move.

'I'm going to the hospital.' Her voice is dull and flat.

'I'll come—'

'I don't want you with me,' she cuts him off. 'Either of you.' She glares at Beth. 'You'd better come up with a way out of this mess because if you don't . . .' She chokes back a sob. 'Neither of you contact me until you've thought of something.' She strides quickly from the room, but Matt can see her wiping tears from her cheeks as she walks and he hates that he is the cause of them.

After Kate has left, Matt makes tea that they won't drink but he's glad of the normality. The process of boiling water, squishing the teabag against the side of the mug, adding a splash of milk. Because that's what they are, a normal family who have stupidly got out of their depth. Thought they'd found a quick fix for their financial problems.

They sit at the square kitchen table, Sean on speakerphone,

going round in circles. There's nothing they haven't suggested and dismissed over the past few days. None of them own property they can remortgage. One hundred and twenty thousand pounds might as well be one hundred and twenty million it is so far out of reach.

There's only one idea he keeps coming back to, but Beth dismisses it again and again.

'Matt, we can't.'

And so he promises her that he won't, but the second she leaves he breaks that promise.

Because there's nothing left to try.

CHAPTER SIXTY

Kate

There's nothing left inside Kate. Her well of hope has run dry.

It had been a long and uncomfortable night. Kate waiting for a call or text from Matt that never came, slumped in the chair beside Caily's bed, holding her hand, afraid that if she let go Caily might slip away from her.

Turn into someone she doesn't recognize like her husband and her sister.

Liars.

She tries to stop her rumination by turning her attention back to Caily but she cannot focus. If Kate thought the men Matt and Beth were involved with had done this to her daughter she would tell the police in a heartbeat but, although she does not know if she can, if she ever will, trust Matt, she believes him when he says the timing is all wrong. That Victor did not know the plants were missing when Caily fell.

Matt may be many things but she knows he is still a good father. If he thought for a second Victor had hurt Caily he would ask Owen for help.

This doesn't bring any comfort, though. It doesn't solve what happened to Caily. What will happen to all of them if they cannot pay what they owe?

'Wake up,' she whispers desperately because if Caily wakes up they could run but, even as she turns this over, Kate knows she wouldn't leave. Couldn't leave Matt and Mum and Dad and Beth and Tegan. The innocent and the guilty.

Despite everything, she loves them all deeply.

Her throat is dry and sore but still she talks to her daughter, not about the things that are on her mind, but about inconsequential details of their lives together, the mundane routines they share, in their normal house as a normal family.

They are not criminals.

Again she runs the conversation of yesterday over in her mind, but it feels like an out-of-reach dream, vague and amorphous, and this suits Kate because she does not want to see this new shape of her husband, her twin, to face that what they told her was the truth.

They are criminals.

Sporadically she googles cannabis-growing in the UK and she sees Matt is right. It is far more common than she ever thought possible. Statistically several people in her village are probably also growing plants, although not to the extent that they – Matt – was. Not that these facts excuse what they have done. Not that they bring any comfort to her because today the twenty-four hours are up and one hundred and twenty thousand pounds seems further away than ever. Her phone remains dark and quiet. She told Matt and Beth not to contact her until they had come up with a solution, and their silence tells her all she needs to know.

Again her thumb hovers over Owen's number.

But she has to give Matt and Beth these last few hours to come up with a solution and if they don't . . .

Her chest tightens. She can almost feel her lungs filling up with water. The stench of it as it ran down her throat.

What if they don't?

She knows Matt is sorry, but his apologies won't be enough to save them.

CHAPTER SIXTY-ONE

Matt

Matt is sorry.

Sorry that yesterday he went behind Beth's back and told Mary everything. Hoping that, despite Beth telling him her parents had nothing, his mother-in-law might hold the solution. Secret savings. Offer to remortgage the farm, perhaps. Anything.

But she had held him as he cried, crying herself that she couldn't help. Urging him to tell Owen. She seemed to think Owen could fix everything, and this made Matt wonder whether she wished that Kate had married Owen instead of him, so he'd straightened himself up and told her not to worry. He had thought of something else, could sort everything out.

Another lie, stacked on top of all the others.

He is sorry for everything.

He cannot think of anything else as he watches the sun rise, dusting the sky with shades of lavender and pink. The light casting a warm glow onto the fields below. The world is so beautiful. Matt chokes back a sob, wondering if this might be his last day in it.

He is a normal man. How has it come to this? They are an ordinary family who have found themselves in extraordinary circumstances and, as much as he tells himself he had been pushed to the limit, he knows that there are many, many families as desperate as him. That the sharp rise in the cost of living has affected so many people, but not everyone turns to crime, do they?

But would they?

If it were presented to them the way it was presented to Matt?

An almost foolproof way to ensure they could feed their children, afford to heat their home. Keep their home. Take care of ageing relatives. What if any average person had a chance to pay off their debt, tuck some away for the future, for little effort?

Would they?

Would they, after endless deliberation, decide that £120k was worth the minimal risk?

He thinks that perhaps, although most wouldn't, some would.

But this brings him no comfort. He's so very tired but there are animals to be fed. The farm he once loved now a millstone around his neck.

He's late getting up.

Last night he lay on the edge of his cold, empty bed, wishing Kate was next to him, their limbs tangled, her freezing feet on his warm legs. Time and time again he picked up his phone and punched out a sorry text but it was insufficient. Inadequate. She doesn't want an apology, she wants a solution and this he does not have.

In the kitchen Twix greets him with gusto, his tongue lolling from his mouth, his tail wagging frantically. He stares at Matt and then stares at his bowl as though he hasn't been fed for days, and Matt can't remember if he gave the dog his dinner last night. It was Caily who always fed him. Matt opens a tin of meat and scrapes it into Twix's dish before heaping a generous portion of biscuits on top. He crouches down and places it on the back door mat, but before he stands he wraps Twix in his arms and buries his face in his neck.

I've done everything wrong.

He mutters the things he cannot say to his wife, but Twix, impatient and hungry, nudges him aside with a gentle butt of his head before he digs in to his breakfast.

On autopilot Matt trudges from one part of the farm to the next, methodically carrying out his daily tasks. He will put the farm in order before he goes and faces Victor.

He has no money but surely he can offer to make it up to him some other way?

Perhaps not like Leroy had because he does not have his build, his menacing looks, but to offer him his life if needs be.

Anything to keep Kate safe, Caily safe.

He is taking one last, slow look around the farm in its entirety, passing the red barn, when he hears a noise.

For one impossible minute he allows himself to believe that Travis has returned with the plants.

That everything will be okay.

If he wasn't so tired he might have dismissed that thought, might have bypassed the barn, bypassed the danger or at least scouted around the perimeter, looking for a car. But instead, stupidly, he stuck his head in the door.

Ray and Leroy are inside.

'We thought you'd have done a runner,' Ray says, a smile on his face.

'No.' Matt feels the weakness in his knees but forces them to lock. 'I take responsibility for everything.'

'Saved us our next job, which was hunting you down then.' He flicks on the heat lamps, which begin to glow. 'It's freezing in here.' He drags a hay bale from the stack near the door into the centre of the barn, gesturing to Leroy to do the same. Matt knows just how heavy the hay is and yet they both make it look effortless. Their strength is terrifying.

'Pull up a pew,' he says to Matt as he sits. It isn't an invitation and so Matt drags another bale, panting, and then sits, gathers his breath.

'We can grow another crop,' Matt offers again. 'The lamps still work—'

'Our lamps.'

'Yes, but . . . I don't understand why we can't try again?'

'I could give you one hundred and twenty thousand reasons. Hands behind your back.'

Matt does as he's told even though it's ridiculous. Something you'd see in a film.

He is just a farmer.

Ray fastens a thick cable tie around his wrists. The plastic cutting into his skin. Matt watches as he stalks over to the door, talks into his mobile.

'The boss will be coming to see you later. In the meantime, let's get your sister-in-law here. Your wife too. Kate, isn't it?' Roughly, Ray pulls Matt's mobile out of his pocket.

'Leroy, please. Not my family.' Matt isn't too proud to

beg. Leroy has a family but he turns away from Matt, taking Matt's last hope with him. Of course Leroy is protecting his own family first.

Of course.

Isn't doing that precisely what got Matt into this mess in the first place?

'I'm not ringing them,' Matt says quietly, defiantly. Firmly.

'Who says anything about ringing?'

Before Matt can register what he's doing, Ray holds Matt's mobile in front of his face and it unlocks instantly. Smirking, Ray composes a text.

After a few minutes there's a beep, followed by another.

Ray doesn't say anything as he reads them, but from his smug expression Matt knows.

Beth and Kate are on their way.

CHAPTER SIXTY-TWO

Kate

She is on her way.

Rising to her feet as she reads.

Matt's text is curt, devoid of kisses, but Kate doesn't care.

He has figured out a solution and relief spreads through her thick and fast, leaving her feeling dizzy and light as she reads the message again.

Thought of a way to sort everything out. Meet me in the red barn.

She stops. Thinks. She doesn't want to leave Caily. Sedation has been withdrawn and she could wake up any time. Kate has to be here.

Has to be.

She glances up and down the corridor. She can call Matt instead. Where can she find a quiet space in a hospital that's constantly streaming with staff and visitors? She'll have to go and sit in her car. Whatever Matt has thought of, he can tell her on the phone, but then she dismisses that thought before it has even fully formed, remembering the way her phone displays adverts for things she has mentioned in passing, fearing it listens to her conversations, which, before this, have been dull and mundane.

Even as this pops into her mind she tells herself she is being paranoid, but is she? She's in a situation she has never been in before and so she has to think in a way she has never thought before. Her husband, her sister are criminals and Kate can't risk anyone, anything, overhearing their conversation.

She feels heavier again as she reluctantly leaves her daughter's side. Hating that she's thinking like a criminal.

Hating Matt too.

But replying that she'll be at the barn in fifteen minutes.

CHAPTER SIXTY-THREE

Beth

Fifteen minutes & I'll be there.

Tears of relief dampen Beth's eyes as she punches out a reply to Matt's text.

Thought of a way to sort everything out. Meet me in the red barn.

She calls Sean.

'Matt has thought of a solution,' she says.

'Thank god. What is it?'

'I don't know. He wants me to meet him in the barn.'

'I'll come.'

'No. I think Kate might be coming too. I told you how upset she was yesterday. I don't want her to see you until everything is sorted out. I want . . . I want us all to have a fresh start. Be a family.'

'Be careful,' he says. 'Please.'

CHAPTER SIXTY-FOUR

Matt

'Please.' Matt is not proud of the way he is begging. Not proud of the snot and tears that stream down his face, into his mouth. He isn't proud of anything he has done these past few weeks, but his shame is nothing compared to the cold, hard ball of terror that expands in his stomach each time he thinks of Kate. 'My wife . . . she hasn't done anything wrong. She didn't even know until yesterday. Please don't drag her into this—'

'Like I dragged her into the river?' Ray smirks. 'What's it like fucking an identical twin? Ever got them confused?'

'I can sort this out if you give me some more time.'

Ray crouches and for one hopeful moment Matt believes he is going to let him go, but instead he roughly yanks off one of Matt's boots, and then the other. He pulls Matt's socks off and stuffs them into his mouth. Matt immediately tries to push them out with his tongue but Ray is tearing off a strip from a roll of tape and slapping it across Matt's lips.

From outside, a car engine.

Beth?

Or Kate?

'Matt?'

At the sound of his name being called, Matt tries to make a sound. Tries to warn her.

But he can't.

It all happens so quickly.

CHAPTER SIXTY-FIVE

Kate

It all happens so quickly the second she steps into the barn. She's roughly grabbed around the waist, a hand over her mouth.

Immediately a burst of heat flames inside her and she grabs at the hand over her lips, her nails scratching his skin.

She recognizes the smell of him. The man who pushed her into the river. Terrified, she struggles, lurching her body from side to side. Eyes widening at the sight of Matt, gagged, hands behind his back.

She hears a car.

Beth.

She forces open her mouth and tries to bite the fingers covering her lips but she can't.

Beth.

She focuses all her attention on her sister. Trying to warn her not to come inside.

To run away.

Fetch help.

Seconds pass. The door doesn't open.
Beth does not step inside.
Does not start her car again.
Where is she?

CHAPTER SIXTY-SIX

Beth

Where is she?

Kate's car is here but there's something stopping Beth from going inside.

An instinct that tells her Kate is in trouble.

Instead of rushing towards the door, Beth creeps around the edge of the barn. Round the back is the Range Rover and her heart pulsates. She pushes her face against a crack. Sees Matt tied up. Ray with his hands on her sister, roughly pulling her mobile from her pocket.

Beth feels the shake in each and every one of her cells, a rage that is absolute, but as much as she wants to rush into the barn and help her twin she knows she'd only be putting her more in danger.

Leroy is telling Ray to take it easy. They don't want to hurt anyone, do they?

Beth turns away, pulls out her phone, almost drops it as she tries to unlock it with hands that tremble. She punches in

Owen's name. Presses dial. But then there's an arm crooked around her neck.

Her handset is snatched from her fingers.

Kicking and screaming, she's dragged into the barn.

CHAPTER SIXTY-SEVEN

Matt

Matt wants to drag both Ray and Leroy outside and kill them with his bare hands. Beth is quietly sobbing as her wrists are fastened behind her back. Kate, already bound and gagged, is quietly defiant, glaring at Ray as he leans over her sister, and Matt knows if looks could kill he would be dead right now.

'Please.' He has never heard Beth sound so vulnerable and his heart cracks. 'We can pay you back. Please don't hurt us. We can—'

'I'm not going to hurt you.' Ray runs his fingers across Beth's cheek and this gentle, intimate gesture chills Matt to the bone.

What is he going to do to her?

To Kate?

To him?

Ray stretches tape over Beth's lips before he stands and studies each of them in turn before pulling out his phone. He stalks over to the door before he makes a call, speaking in a low voice. Words Matt cannot hear. Does not want to hear. But even though he cannot decipher them, they still terrify him.

Ray strides back to them.

'Victor will be here soon. In the meantime don't do anything I wouldn't do.'

He is almost out of the door when he turns back.

'We'd always find you.' He doesn't growl the words as a threat because it isn't. It's a fact, which pierces the escape plans Matt has been scrabbling to formulate. A sharp stab of knowing that, even if somehow they got out of here, there is nowhere they can run.

Not with Caily in hospital.

Not with Kate's parents here.

The sound of the barn door closing, the thick plank of wood being slotted into place, sealing them in, is a nail in his coffin.

But then he looks at Kate, at Beth, and he knows he cannot, must not, give up.

If he can get them out of here he will wait for Victor and face the consequences of his actions. He feels the heat on his face and he looks up.

The lamps.

He told Kate they couldn't go to Owen, the police because there's no proof, but perhaps the lamps are his proof.

But are they enough to convict Victor for a long period? Because if they aren't and he's out there, Matt will never feel free again.

He doesn't think they are. Lamps aren't a crime and besides, they are on Matt's property.

Patrick and Mary's property.

What crimes have been committed here today?

Kidnapping?

False imprisonment?

All he knows of the law is from the ITV dramas they sometimes watch, although Matt generally falls asleep as a result of his early-morning starts. One thing he does know is that if he tells the police he'll be implicating himself, he could end up in prison, but if he can keep Kate and Beth out of it then it's better than the alternative.

He can't bear to think what the alternative might be.

Outside an engine turns over, revs, and then he hears the Range Rover pull away.

In perfect synchronicity, after one worried glance towards each other, all three rise to their feet. Matt jumps towards the door, the tape around his ankles loosening with every jump. He rams his shoulder against the only way out, feels a jolt of pain shoot down his spine. The door doesn't give but he throws himself against it over and over, feeling his teeth clamp around his tongue, his mouth filling with blood he is forced to swallow because he cannot spit it out.

He glances helplessly at Beth and Kate. Beth is leaning against the wall. Kate is inching the tape away from Beth's mouth with her nose. Small precise, repeated movements.

Even if it works, if Beth can scream, there is no one around to hear them. Ray has taken their phones.

The only chance they have is if they can somehow free their hands. Use something to prise the nails from the wood.

Frantically he looks around. There's little here. They never use this barn. He hops around the perimeter, already tiring by the time he reaches the halfway point. Sweat pooling under his arms at the exertion. Remembering the school sports days when Caily and Tegan would compete in the sack race, rosy cheeked, pigtails flying behind them, making it all look so effortless, neither girl crossing the line until the other had caught up.

The memory gives him strength and he keeps going until he reaches a rusty scythe propped against the wall. He knocks it over and rubs his bound wrists over the tip of the blade, his skin raw, blood dripping. There's a give, and suddenly his hands are free.

'Matt!' Beth calls his name at the same time that he smells it.

Smoke.

He turns slowly, horrified.

The heat lamps have ignited the bales of hay. It had been stupid to drag them underneath the lamps to sit on. Orange flames laughing and dancing and crackling and spitting. The sight of it is horrifying but Matt tells himself it's okay. This is such a big space and the fire will burn itself out.

Won't it?

But there's hay littering the floor and this catches. The flames creeping towards the old tractor that broke long ago and was abandoned here. Is there petrol in it?

There's a stack of old petrol cans. They must be empty. *Must be.* This is a real dumping ground. Stacked against the edges of the barn are the oak beams that he had stripped from the old farmhouse next door, intending to sell along with rolls of insulation that he had damaged removing and were no use to anyone.

A heap of old tarpaulins that used to cover the machinery.

Full of holes. Not meeting the modern fire-retardant standards.

He had thought this barn was virtually empty. That there was nothing in here that was a danger, but now he sees hazards everywhere he looks. The pile of logs left here because the log store at the yard was full. The rotting planks of wood he recently replaced but hasn't got around to disposing And there's the building itself. Constructed of wood, not with the reassuring solidity of brick like the main ones they used.

The fire is igniting everything in its path.

Spreading quickly.

Too quickly.

Wildly he looks around, desperately searching for a way out, but other than the door, which is locked from the outside, there isn't one.

They're trapped.

CHAPTER SIXTY-EIGHT

Beth

They're trapped.

Beth stares in horror at the smoke rising from the hay bales. Smells the burning. The tape falls from her mouth.

'Matt!'

Terror descends on his face when he notices the fire.

He almost folds in on himself, crumpling to the floor, and at first Beth thinks he has collapsed or has given up but then she sees him yanking off the tape around his ankles and she realizes his hands are free.

Kate is already jumping awkwardly towards him. She loses momentum and topples hard onto her face, hands still tied behind her back, unable to break her fall. Beth feels her pain, her own nose throbbing as she shuffles over to her, wincing at the blood streaming from both nostrils as she sits up, coating the silver tape around her lips, red.

'Kate's hurt.'

Matt is running now. Gently unwinding the tape from Kate's mouth, dabbing at the blood with the edge of his T-shirt.

'No time.' Kate turns around so he can cut the ties around her wrist, before he stoops, his fingers working the tape around her ankles but she pushes him away and says, 'Free Beth,' and then she sits, running her thumb around the tape, trying to find the edge the way she does when she wraps Christmas presents with brightly coloured paper the girls tear off in three seconds flat.

The thought of Tegan and Caily focuses Beth. She scans the barn. The fire is spreading. Almost reaching the cans of petrol stood lined like soldiers against the wall and, although Beth hopes they are empty, they might contain dregs. Why did they begin dumping everything in here instead of disposing of it properly? They *have* to reach the door before the flames because if the whole wooden structure ignites . . .

'Leave me,' she says firmly, insistently. 'Perhaps the two of you can break down the door. Go and fetch help.'

'No.' Kate's ankles are free now and she crouches in front of Beth so she can help her twin.

'Kate. It's going to be too late if you don't go now—'

Kate glances at the door. 'Matt's already tried to get out that way. We need to think of something else. We stay together,' she says calmly but Beth knows she is not calm. She can sense her panic, detect the tremble in her fingers, but she will not leave her. Beth does not know where Kate finds her strength. Although born only twelve minutes apart, Kate was always the younger, seemingly weaker. The one who needed looking after. Now Beth sees that it is Kate who has looked after everyone all these years.

It has always been Kate.

But Kate cannot save them now.

They are going to die.

'Help,' Beth shouts loudly, knowing that no one will hear them, that they are miles away from the farmhouse, but still she screams over and over again because there is nothing else she can do.

The flames have taken hold. They smoulder now, a hot burning mass that slithers and slides, igniting everything it comes into contact with.

They are going to die.

Beth's knees weaken just as there's a pressure in her wrists and then a release. She is free. Running towards the door, the heat pushing her back.

The smoke curling.

She's coughing.

Coughing.

Coughing.

Kate drags her back into the middle of the barn. 'If we put the tarps over our heads and stay low, we can get out,' she says, but there's a question in her voice and her uncertainty fills Beth with dread.

'I don't know. In the films they . . .' Beth rummages for a memory of the last disaster movie she watched. 'They soak towels in water.' They each look around but smoke is filling the space. Beth's vision hazy as though she has the onset of a migraine coming.

Kate's coughing sounds painful.

Matt slips his arm around her shoulders. 'We'll be okay.' But he doesn't say how.

'We have to try the door again. The three of us.'

They try, ramming against it on the count of three. Once, twice, three times.

It doesn't budge.

'We're never going to break the plank that's holding it in place,' Matt gasps.

'What about the wall over there?' Beth points to the far side of the barn. The place the fire hasn't yet reached. 'Would it be easier to break than the door?'

They begin to run but then there's a bang, the sound of something exploding and Beth feels her heart actually stop beating for a moment.

In slow motion they turn. Thankfully it isn't the petrol cans, but something has fuelled the flames, now high and fierce. Angry. Something else has ignited and the heat is unbearable. The smoke acrid.

'The hay loft!' Kate grips Beth's arm and Beth almost cries with relief. Of course. They can climb up there and jump out of the hatch.

Matt reaches it first. Looking frantically around for the ladder.

'There,' Beth runs to it. It's lying on the floor, flames licking at one end. She begins to stamp on the flames. Matt quickly follows, tugging off his jumper, beating at the fire until the ladder is only smouldering. They take it back to where Kate is waiting, prop it up.

'The rungs,' Kate doesn't say anymore. She doesn't have to. They can see the ladder is missing the bottom few rungs entirely, and some of the ones higher up are missing too.

Matt holds a rung firmly with both hands, pushing down on it, testing its strength. 'It should hold.' He stands it on its end and props it against the edge of the loft entrance. 'Beth, you steady it. Kate, you go first.'

'Beth goes first,' Kate says.

Beth wants to argue with her but Kate's face is set and Beth doesn't want to waste time so she steps into Matt's cupped hands while Kate holds the ladder steady. She stretches until she reaches the first rung. Matt lifts her until she can walk her hands upwards, move her feet, and then she's at the top, where, although the fire hasn't reached it, the smoke feels thicker.

She chokes and chokes and chokes, her throat raw. On her hands and knees she crawls over to the skylight, hearing Kate climbing up behind her.

Her fingers fumble for the catch. The lock is rusting and she wriggles it, yanks it, coaxes it, but it's no use.

The skylight won't open.

She turns, frantically shouting for Kate to head back down, but all she can see down the hatch is black smoke. Orange flames.

They are going to die.

CHAPTER SIXTY-NINE

Kate

They are not going to die.

Kate holds on to this thought tightly even though her heart is hammering from behind her ribcage. Sweat is dripping from her forehead, sticking her clothes to her skin. She should feel terrified – she is terrified – but oddly she feels a strange detachment, as though this isn't really happening to her.

To them.

Beth has reached the top of the ladder and disappeared into the loft. Kate accepts a leg up from Matt and then she too is climbing, feeling the wobble in the ladder but knowing Matt is holding it steady.

Her life literally in his hands.

She reaches the top.

Beth is sobbing. Rattling the skylight. 'Open. Fucking open,' she pleads.

Kate can't help her. Has only the capacity to deal with one thing at a time.

The smoke is thick. Stinging the back of her throat.

It's hot. So very hot.

She lays flat on her stomach and clenches the top of the ladder with both hands.

'Ready,' she calls to Matt. She sees the worry on his upturned face as he gauges the gap between the floor and the first rung.

How is he going to reach it without anyone to give him a leg up?

He stretches, jumps, misses.

Tries again.

Again.

All the while the flames edge closer and closer. The smoke threatening to choke him.

Now Kate panics. Before they were all together but this separation is unbearable, and this is when she knows.

She loves him still. No matter what he has done.

She loves him.

He has to make it.

He just has to.

'You'll have to take a run up,' Kate shouts before turning her head, burying her face in her shoulder so her mouth is covered, her nostrils.

It's getting too much.

'I can't,' comes his reply. Kate hears the desperation in his voice. 'You'll never be able to hold it.'

'I will,' Kate says and she gathers her strength and her resolve and she grips the ladder like she's never gripped anything before. Feeling the strain in her arms, her shoulders, her spine ridged, buttocks clenched, her hips pressing down into the hard ground.

She. Is. Ready.

Matt takes several steps back, runs and leaps. His finger-tips connect with the bottom rung, and then his palms are wrapped around it. Kate feels the strain in every single part of her body. Her muscles screaming, but she doesn't let go.

She. Is. Ready.

Matt swings his body, draws his knees to his chest, ready to stretch with one hand and reach the next rung, freeing up the one he is gripping for his feet.

Pain jolts through Kate as he makes it. Every inch of her hurting as he climbs towards her, but then she sees his face and she can't feel anything except love, but then he slips.

Falls.

Plummets into the swirl of smoke below.

She hears him scream.

And then nothing.

CHAPTER SEVENTY

Beth

There's nothing. No answer as Kate screams again, 'Matt!'

Beth crawls over to her. Acrid smoke attacking her throat, her nose, her chest. Her eyes stinging. 'He's fallen. I'm going back down.'

Beth grips Kate's arm with force. Shakes her head, unable to speak, her coughing violent and painful.

Kate knocks her to one side, swings her legs back down onto the top rung.

'No, Kate,' Beth says but as she protests she's already holding the ladder as steady as she can, knowing that whatever she says won't make any difference.

Kate won't give up on Matt, she wouldn't give up on her and Beth realizes that, despite the recent tension between them, Kate hasn't given up on Tegan. Not really. She just wants to know the truth.

Beth watches the top of Kate's head bob with every step down and she wants to tell her she is sorry.

She wants to weep.

But now is not the time.

There's a movement in the ladder and then Kate has dropped to the floor.

Beth scrambles back over to the skylight. It is up to her to get them out of here.

She lays on her back, bends her knees and kicks the glass as hard as she can. The first kick sends a shockwave of pain through her spine and into her neck, forcing her teeth to grit. She kicks again and again, sweat pouring from her. Her movements slowing.

It's so hard to keep going.

The smoke.

The heat.

The fear.

It's all-consuming. Taking over her.

She summons up every last ounce of energy and puts all she has into one final kick.

There's a crack, a give, her feet flying into the air. She covers her face with her arms, expecting a backdraft, an explosion, but the fire doesn't change.

She rights herself and crawls quickly towards the open frame.

'Help us please somebody help us we are trapped.' Panic joins her frenzied, shouted words together into one long sentence. If it were a rope she could throw it down and reach the ground.

But she does not have a rope and she does not have time to waste.

She sits on the edge of the sill, her legs over the edge.

Closes her eyes.

Jumps.

The impact when she hits the ground leaves her bones juddering.

Later, she will feel the throb of pain, but now she rises, stumbles, heads for the door.

She doesn't stop to think what is on the other side of that door. Whether the flames will rush towards her. Engulf her. It is enough that she knows who is on the other side of the door.

Her sister.

The plank is ferociously hot. She screams and yanks her hands away but then pulls her sleeves down to cover them and tries again.

She has to do this.

Has to.

She grits her teeth, tugs at the plank until it clatters to the floor, wrenches open the door. Billowing black smoke pushes her back, but then she's running.

Running and shouting.

'Kate?'

'Over here. Hurry.'

She finds her twin partly through sound. Partly through instinct.

Matt is leaning heavily on Kate, limping. Dazed.

Beth loops his free arm around her neck and together they half drag him, slowing each time one of them coughs, towards the door.

And then they are out.

Free.

Doubled over, dragging in air that stings their throats, their lungs.

It's over.

Isn't it?

But then they hear a car.

CHAPTER SEVENTY-ONE

Matt

There's a car coming towards them. A jabbing pain in his ankle but it doesn't hurt as much as the searing pain in Matt's heart each time he sees Kate's soot-stained face and realizes how close he came to losing her.

They cling to each other as the car approaches.

Owen climbs out of it, door left open, engine still running.

'Are you okay?' It is Kate he is looking at as he asks and, whereas before Matt would have felt a stab of jealousy, now he is glad that Kate has so many people who care about her, because if he hadn't made it out of here today . . .

'How did you know?' Kate sobs.

'Beth tried to call me and I went to hers but she wasn't there and so I came to the farmhouse and spotted the smoke.' He shouts across to an officer. 'Radio the house and tell Mary and Patrick that everyone is safe.' He turns back to Kate. 'I wouldn't let them come. Christ. What happened?'

Matt can't stop coughing. His ribs feel tender. Bruised.

There's a burst of sirens, a fire engine and an ambulance bumping around the edge of the field.

Soon they are wrapped in blankets, sitting inside the ambulance, and he's dragging in oxygen through a mask.

His pulse is checked. His eyes. Ears. All the while Owen hovers just outside. All the while Matt turns over what he should and should not say.

'We need to take you all in and examine you properly,' he is told by the paramedic.

'What exactly happened here today?' Owen asks when the oxygen is packed away and they are preparing to leave.

Matt exchanges a glance with Beth, who gives a nod.

It is time to tell the truth.

Before he can speak, he hears a shout, Beth's name being called.

Sean sprinting towards them.

'Are you okay? What happened?' He cups Beth's cheeks tenderly with his hand.

'They were just about to fill me in,' Owen says.

'Was this because of . . . ?' Sean's eyes flicker towards the still-burning barn, the firemen arcing water onto the flames.

Their silence must tell Sean all he needs to know because he turns to Owen, looking like a man broken and says, 'There's something I have to tell you. Something that I should have been honest about years ago.'

And in a split second again, everything changes.

CHAPTER SEVENTY-TWO

Beth

There's a change on Owen's expression as Sean says, 'This fire was my fault.'

Everything fades away except the enormity of what he is saying. The pain in her hands where she'd touched the door, the others, everything. 'No—'

'Beth, don't try to protect me,' Sean says. 'I've been using the barn to grow cannabis. Matt, Kate and Beth didn't know. I knew this barn was never used or the land surrounding it. It's shielded from the road by hedges and trees and—'

'No.' Beth shakes her head. 'No.' The sound of the ambulance starting turns her head. She notices, suspended underneath the wing mirror, a gossamer spider's web, translucent in the sun. Fragile. Everything right now seems fragile. Easily broken.

'It isn't true, it isn't.' Beth looks back at Kate, Matt. 'Why aren't you saying anything? It wasn't only—'

'Beth,' Owen says. 'Emotions are running high right now. I'm only going to say this once. As a friend, I suggest thinking very carefully about what you want to say.'

The years fall away, Owen is no longer a policeman but fifteen, on the school adventure trip, holding Kate's hand as he helped her up the mountain, rocks slipping beneath their feet. Stopping to help Beth.

Although his hands remain by his side, he is offering them to her now. Offering her help. Whether he wants her to stay silent for her sake or for Kate's, Beth does not know, but she cannot stand here and let the man she loves carry the blame.

'Owen, the truth is—'

'I've only seen Tegan once since I've been back.' Sean's voice is painful as though his words are sharp, scraping his throat. 'I've been waiting until the right time. I don't know if it's ever the right time, for anything. She was in the post office and . . .' He is crying now, unselfconsciously. 'I couldn't help following her. Couldn't tear my eyes away from her. You've done an amazing job with her.' He hooks Beth's hair behind her ears. 'And you haven't finished yet. She needs you, like Caily needs Matt and Kate.'

'I need you.' Beth gently wipes the tears from his cheeks with her fingertips. 'We both need you.'

'Questions will be asked,' Owen says. 'How you sourced everything, who you were selling to.' He's giving them all a chance.

'I know,' Sean says. 'I wasn't working alone. I was working with Victor Kent.'

'Christ, Sean. I thought . . . once you were out. Aaron mixing with Victor I could understand. He was always in trouble. But you? Still?' Owen is angry at Sean too, for different reasons than Beth, but hurting all the same. On that same school trip Owen, Sean and Aaron had sliced into the pads of their thumbs with a penknife – *blood brothers* – and had pressed them together.

'He didn't want to,' Beth says. 'But I've got myself into debt and we decided . . .' She trails off, unsure what to say. What might implicate her. Take her away from Tegan. She's ten again. Blindfolded. Searching for the paper donkey, his tail in her hand, but she's heading in the wrong direction. She begins again, searching for the right words. 'I mean—'

'Beth,' Sean shakes his head.

'Is he going back to prison?' Beth searches Owen's eyes for the familiar reassurance, *don't worry that you haven't done your homework, you can copy mine. Don't worry that you forgot your lunch, you can share my sandwich.*

'Yes,' he says. 'He's still on probation.'

'Will Victor?' Matt asks and for a moment Beth hates him – *hates him* – for thinking of himself, the money they still owe but then she realizes they are back where they started.

'There's no proof,' she says. 'No cannabis on the property.' For a moment her heart lifts because then surely Sean's confession won't mean anything.

Owen opens his mouth to speak but Sean cuts him off, 'I wasn't driving my car the night of the robbery.'

'But you . . . you admitted it,' Kate says.

'Who was driving?' Owen asks.

'Ray.'

'Why?' Owen stares at Sean helplessly. 'Why did you say it was you?'

'Aaron had got in over his head with Victor. He owed them big time. He asked me to do a job with him to pay them off. I said no, of course I did. But . . . but they'd threatened

334

to kill him and . . .' *Blood brothers.* 'Anyway, I begged him to tell you, wanted to tell you myself, Owen, but he told me some of the things Victor and Ray had done and I wasn't just scared for Aaron anymore, I was scared for Beth and Tegan because Aaron had already told Victor I'd help and he said Victor would be furious if I didn't. Already he thought I knew too much.'

'I'd have helped. You know that—' Owen begins.

'I didn't know anything, only that Aaron promised that once he'd cleared his debt he'd move away. Start afresh. I went through the plans over and over with him. I didn't go into it lightly.' He looks at them all in turn. 'You know how it was with Aaron, he didn't have anyone. We were his family.'

'But still. I'd never . . .' Matt stops himself and Beth knew he realizes that he isn't so different. It's so easy to judge others, to say you'd never do something when you haven't been in that position, felt that desperate. She didn't condone what Sean had agreed to all those years ago, but she understood it.

'Anyway, when we got there it turns out that Aaron was double-crossing Victor and somehow he knew.' Sean links his hands together as though praying, presses them against his lips. Beth rubs his back. When he lowers his hands he is crying again. 'I know where they buried him. Buried Aaron.'

Beth feels her knees buckle. Kate covers her mouth with her hands. Matt is shaking his head.

'What *exactly* are you saying?' Owen asks in a low voice.

'I want to report the murder of Aaron Dixon. I should have done it years ago. Victor and Ray killed him and buried him. They took my car. The next day I received a phone call from Victor, telling me that Ray had robbed that shop using my car. That I was likely to be arrested. That if I admitted it then he'd know that he could trust me. Wouldn't have to . . .' He pulls Beth to him, can't say the words. He doesn't have to. Victor had threatened her and Tegan.

'You should have been honest,' Owen says.

'I was scared. I'd seen my best friend . . . Aaron . . .' Sean pinches the bridge of his nose. 'Victor is a dangerous man, and I wasn't thinking clearly after Aaron. I was terrified and a few years in prison seemed preferable to the alternative because what would have happened? Witness protection? Removing Beth and Tegan from Kate and Matt? Mary and Patrick? Running away?'

'It would have been better than losing you,' Beth said because his actions may have kept Beth safe but they hadn't made her happy. The lie he had draped over the truth to protect it. Protect them. But it had been insufficient, ineffective akin to those rotting tarpaulins in the barn once used to cover machinery, never knowing that underneath the cover there was already corrosion, rust, decay. She'd rather have spent the years running away from Victor, looking over her shoulder if that's what it had taken to keep them together as a family.

But then what about Tegan? What sort of life was that for a child? What sort of danger would they have been putting her in?

But still . . . she should have asked more questions after his arrest. She hadn't believed it, deep down. In the past, when she had watched the news with her parents and there was a weeping wife outside the courtroom, Mum always said that she must have known. *Must have.*

Beth hadn't known, not because she chose not to see what was going on but because it wasn't true.

'He told me he'd look after me when I got out. I told him I wasn't . . .' Sean gives a choked laugh, 'I wasn't a criminal.'

But then Beth had told him about her debt and again he had felt he didn't have a choice.

'I love you,' she says, but those three words just aren't enough.

'There's such a lot to unpack here.' Owen looks visibly upset. Perhaps picturing Aaron, as they all probably were, freckled face and scabbed knees, always climbing trees, throwing himself off walls, never thinking through the consequences. 'We'd better get to the station.'

'No.' Beth sobs. For the past seven years, Beth's heart has been incomplete, searching for its missing piece. Sean has it in his hands and she cannot let him take it away again.

'I can't . . .' Breathe. Cope. Live. 'Without you, I can't . . .'

Sean's kiss is featherlight, lips barely touching as they brush against hers. To those watching, it probably looks like nothing at all but it's everything.

A promise.

'Before we go, I've got some news you'll all want to hear,' Owen says. 'No charges are being brought against Tegan.'

Beth notices Kate take Matt's hands and suddenly it seems that the fire, the way they had come together, has never happened. It's her against them once more, but she is not alone, she glances at Sean, not yet anyway.

'I'm glad you realize Tegan hasn't done anything wrong.' She straightens her spine.

'That was decided quickly,' Matt says.

337

'I've pushed it through. I've literally called in every favour I've been owed throughout my career for Caily.'

He smiles at Kate, and Beth knows he's done it for her. Not for Caily, not for any of them.

'What about the skin? The video?' Kate asks.

'What about you're glad your niece is innocent? What about "Sorry, Beth, that it even crossed my mind for a moment that she was guilty?"' Beth is raging, knowing she is directing all her anger, all her frustration that she is losing Sean again, at the wrong person but unable to help herself.

'Well I'm glad you *think* your daughter is innocent, but mine is still in a coma.'

'Do you have another suspect?' Matt interjects.

'I'm afraid not. Of course, we're still looking for Travis.'

'When you find him, you'll likely find the plants I was growing in the barn,' Sean says.

'But what now?' Kate asks. 'What about Caily?' Kate keeps her eyes on Owen. Beth realizes that her sister can't look at her. Will it always be like this? This doubt hanging between them because the CPS not pressing charges isn't the same as Tegan being proved beyond all doubt that she hasn't done anything wrong, is it?

'The case will remain open but I think perhaps, unless Caily wakes up and tells us herself what happens, it might remain a mystery.'

None of them realizes it then of course, but by the morning there will be a dramatic change in Caily's condition.

And again, everything will be different.

CHAPTER SEVENTY-THREE

*T*here's a change.

Your heart monitor no longer beeping, instead there's one continuous sound. An alarm rings and the room fills with people but it's too late and, although they try, they cannot save you.

You're gone.

I wake.

The sheets drenched with sweat, my blood rushing in my ears, not soothed by the fact that it was only a nightmare. Knowing that this will always haunt me, whether the truth comes out or not.

Whether or not you wake.

CHAPTER SEVENTY-FOUR

Caily

Caily can feel the love in the room as she begins to wake.

Coming back isn't sensory overload, more of a gradual awareness.

Mum's smell. The posh peach soap she likes. The one Caily bought her for her birthday. Wafts of it reminding her of Mother's Days past when she'd clamber onto her parents' bed, a badly wrapped gift in her pudgy hand.

'Open it, Mummy.' Too excited to keep still, she'd bounce up and down on the mattress with anticipation as Mum gently lifted the soap from the gift box as though it was the most precious thing in the world before rubbing the bar against her wrists like it was an expensive perfume before repeating the action on Caily's wrists so they smelled the same. Caily had never felt more grown up, more content, snuggled next to Mum.

But she is not in Mum's bed now.

She doesn't feel safe and secure.

She doesn't feel grown up.

Mingling with Mum's fruity scent is something sharp and unpleasant . . . bleach?

Where is she?

Sound.

She hears a beeping, faint at first but then growing louder. As steady and as regular as the metronome that lurched from side to side on top of the piano when she used to have lessons, when Mum used to tell her she could be anything she wanted to be.

What she wants to be is awake, but there's a darkness that keeps tugging her under.

Physical sensations return, her head throbs, her leg too. Her pelvis. Her entire body pulsing with pain. The mattress is unfamiliar, too hard. Sheets pinning her down. She tries to move but can't seem to coordinate her limbs.

She's scared.

She tries to speak, but there is something in her mouth and it is dry, tongue thick. There's the sensation of falling – Alice down the rabbit hole – and through her dizziness she tries to pick out what's real and what's imagined. Is she falling now? Then? She wants to cry. She wants her mother to catch her.

She tries to make a sound, thinks she does, but she isn't entirely sure that her whimper isn't only in her head.

But then there's a sharp intake of breath. 'Caily?'

Mum's soft hair brushing Caily's cheek as she bends over her, warm air against her ear.

A whispered word. A plea.

'Caily?'

I'm here. Caily wants to say. *I'm here.* But she can't.

'Come back to me.'

Mum begins to softly sing, *You are my sunshine*.

Caily spirals through time, she's a baby being rocked in her mother's arms to this song, later dancing on chubby toddler's legs, clapping uncoordinated claps, hands missing each other. Older still, her and Tegan would perform it on Mum and Aunt Beth's birthday. Caily singing, Tegan harmonizing.

It has always been their family's song, a happy song, but she remembers Dad telling her once that the lyrics were about a person pleading through troubled dreams for the return of their love.

This is the version that connects to Caily the most now, that gives her the strength to cling on to consciousness. Her eyelids flutter. She feels her mother's hand in hers and she gives it a gentle squeeze.

CHAPTER SEVENTY-FIVE

Kate

Kate squeezes the buzzer to summon the nurse with her free hand, her other hand still holding Caily's.

'Squeeze my fingers again if you can hear me.'

She waits, holding her breath until her chest is tight and painful, but then one of Caily's fingers moves. She's sure of it.

Nita rushes over.

Kate's aware of the door opening behind her but she doesn't look around, her eyes fixed on her daughter's face.

'Kate?' It's Nicola. 'I was just passing and thought I'd pop in to see Caily.'

Kate is glad she is here, witnessing something so momentous. She's grateful not to be alone because, although she wants Caily to regain consciousness more than anything else in the world, there is a small part of her that's afraid this girl in the bed might be different somehow. That the fall might have changed her.

Or what came before the fall.

But Kate knows that even if Caily doesn't recognize her,

doesn't know who she is, she will wrap her daughter in love and comfort and memories until she feels safe and secure.

Healthy.

And happy.

There's a twitch of Caily's eyelids.

'Did you see that?' Kate whispers. Nicola is right behind her now. 'Her eyelids moved.'

'Are you sure it wasn't my shadow?'

Kate's hope plummets before she drags it up again. Her daughter *is* coming back to her. She knows it.

'Can you move back from the bed, Kate, so we can check on Caily?' Nita asks.

Kate gives her daughter's fingers one final squeeze before she steps into the corner.

Without waiting for confirmation, knowing in her heart she is right, she types **I think Caily is waking up** into her phone and sends it to her contacts on WhatsApp.

Kate wants everybody to share her joy.

But not everyone does.

CHAPTER SEVENTY-SIX

Everyone wants you to wake. Even me, but I'm flooded with heart-pounding dread.

You're waking up.

What will you say?

What will happen to me?

How can I stop this?

Stop you?

Everything?

It's out of control.

I'm out of control.

Will you remember what happened?

Will you be scared when you wake? As you were scared when you fell.

You used to be fearful of so many things: the dark, thunderstorms, the monster under the bed.

But now that monster is me.

Waiting.

Waiting.

Waiting.

CHAPTER SEVENTY-SEVEN

Caily

Caily waits for the muzzy feeling in her head to clear. Her throat is dry. A thumb lifts her eyelids, a torch shone in her eyes. Her name is called. The door opens and bangs shut. Voices.

Throughout it all, Caily can still hear her mum singing about skies of blue, even though she thinks she's stopped now.

Her cheeks are wet with tears, she's not sure if they are hers or Mum's, but her hand feels empty now, her mum has let her it go, moved away, so it must be she who is crying.

Everything becomes clearer, sounds, smells, before receding again as memories begin to strobe.

I see you.

Her dress slashed.

I see you.

Tegan shaking her.

I see you.

The hate in her eyes.

And then on the bridge . . .

Caily wishes she could slip back into unconsciousness so she doesn't have to face reality.

Face the fact that someone she has loved completely since the day she was born has hurt her.

She cannot breathe.

Panic claws its way out of her chest. It hurts.

She cannot breathe.

She's dying. Her limbs are rigid, a crushing weight on her lungs.

She cannot breathe.

The last thing Caily hears before she plummets back into darkness is a cry for the crash team.

And then, nothing.

CHAPTER SEVENTY-EIGHT

Kate

Fear.

Chaos.

Helplessness.

Hopelessness.

Kate feels it all as she is ushered out of the way, towards the door.

She is not leaving.

The room swims before her eyes as it begins to fill with doctors, nurses. Kate isn't sure who they are, she doesn't care who they are as long as they can help. They immediately rearrange tubes, wires, remove equipment.

Her legs shake as she leans against the wall for support, pressing herself into the corner so she doesn't get in the way of the myriad people now crowding into the ICU, around Caily's bed, barking out questions, performing swift actions with urgency and precision, but Kate can feel their underlying panic. It mixes with her own until this small space has expanded with a terror so thick it presses down on her windpipe, restricting her air.

She's dizzy. Her knees give way, she begins to slide down the wall before forcing herself upright again, not wanting anything to take the attention away from Caily, not even for a second.

'Kate,' Nicola gently takes her arm but Kate snatches it away with a violent shake of her head.

She is not leaving.

Her muddled thoughts tell her that if she leaves, Caily will have nothing to hold on to. Instead, she stares at the bed, catching glimpses of Caily when the team change position, willing her with every ounce of her being, every muscle clenched in concentration, to wake.

'Can we get Mum out of here?' a man calls over his shoulder, and the wrench, deep within Kate's chest, is the same as all those years ago when the midwife whisked Caily away to clean and weigh her only minutes after Kate had given birth.

She is not leaving.

Not just because she doesn't want to, but because she can't. The wall is her support and without its solidity her pipe-cleaner legs would buckle under the weight of worry, and she isn't weak. She can't be.

She has to be strong for her daughter.

Just as Nicola takes her elbow, there's a break in tension in the room. The nurse holding an oxygen mask over Caily's mouth turns and smiles and says, 'She's okay.'

The restriction around Kate's throat lifts, the fuzziness in her head beginning to clear as she takes deep breaths.

'What happened?' she asks Nicola. 'That was terrifying. I thought her heart . . . her heart . . .'

'I think Caily might have had a panic attack. All this must

be very disorientating and frightening for her. The crash team were a precaution. See? We're taking good care of her. She's fine now, look.'

The oxygen mask has been removed. The room emptying of people.

Caily is going to be all right.

And she, Kate, is not leaving her. Not for a second.

Time has lurched and stretched and stopped and, although it feels like for ever since the crash team left, it isn't. The room has emptied save for Nita in the corner and Nicola, who stays but doesn't speak. Caily is stable, she is told, and again Kate is watching for signs, for the flicker of an eyelid, for the squeeze of fingers.

Caily stirs, murmurs and then there is something else, something that Kate has barely dared hope for.

Caily was eleven months when she uttered her first word. Kate remembers it clearly. For weeks her and Matt had been tailing Caily with a video camera, wanting to capture every first, but when Caily gripped a Marmite soldier in her fist and grinned, displaying two white front teeth in pink gums and said 'Dada' there was no camera. Matt wasn't even there, but Kate didn't feel disappointment, all she felt was immense joy that this tiny, perfect child they had created was hitting all her milestones.

Matt isn't here today, but this time it is Kate Caily calls for. She never thought hearing Caily whisper 'Mum' could spring tears to her eyes, a lump to her throat.

Her relieved heart lifts in her chest.

Everything is going to be okay.

She doesn't once leave her daughter's side while she drifts in and out of lucidity. Sometimes murmuring, sometimes crying, sometimes just lying there, staring at Kate. The doctor tells her that this is normal while the sedation wears off. That Caily cannot be expected to wake and be full of conversation, full of life.

But she *is* alive and Kate has never felt more grateful for anything.

Eventually it is the following day.

Seven days.

Seven days since Caily's fall, which has felt like an eternity, and at last she is finally sitting up, groggy but still alert.

She sends a group WhatsApp to tell everyone.

Her daughter is most definitely awake.

PART TWO

CHAPTER SEVENTY-NINE

You're awake.

I don't know how I feel about this.

I don't know what to do.

There's an urge to run away, but however far I go I can't escape myself, can I?

All I'm certain of is that I'm tired of the lies. Tired of it all now.

I want to put an end to it.

It's gone too far.

I want it to stop.

I'm going to tell the truth.

CHAPTER EIGHTY

Now

Tegan

Tegan has to tell the truth.

Caily is awake.

Tegan should feel glad, she *does* feel glad of course that her cousin is alive but . . . Still clutching her mobile in her hand, she pulls her knees up to her chest and rests her forehead upon them, rocking gently backwards and forwards, trying to keep the rising panic at bay.

I'll fucking kill you.

The last words Tegan had said – no, screamed – at her cousin are still loud in her head.

She begins to hum, trying to block them out, but they rattle around her mind and it's all she can hear.

I'll fucking kill you.

Tegan hadn't meant that. She'd been angry, hurt, betrayed, but now her overriding emotion is fear. What will Caily say when she wakes? She balls her fingers into fists, she can still feel them clutching Caily's arms, squeezing into her soft flesh.

Shaking.

Shaking.

Shaking.

CHAPTER EIGHTY-ONE

Beth

Now

Beth's hand is shaking as she stares at the message until the letters shift and blur in front of her eyes.

Caily is awake.

She feels detached from herself, the hand holding the phone doesn't feel like hers. She feels . . .

Nothing.

No, that's not true. She glances towards Tegan's door. She can hear her daughter crying, she can see that Tegan has already read the group message, and she feels a thick dread curling around her heart.

After the arguing and the accusations, the guilt and the blame, it's time for the truth to come out.

Tegan wouldn't have pushed Caily, Beth knows this.

But then she thinks of the video Owen showed her. The anger.

Still, Tegan absolutely *wouldn't* have pushed her.

Not purposefully anyway.

CHAPTER EIGHTY-TWO

Matt

Matt purposefully doesn't waste time searching for a parking space, instead abandoning his car on the grass verge, not caring if it's clamped. Not caring about anything except for reaching Caily.

Reaching Kate.

He pelts towards the hospital, waving away the parking attendant who tells him he can't park there, that he'll have to wait for a proper space.

The first time he came to see Caily he'd got lost twice in these winding corridors, had repeatedly asked for directions. Now his feet automatically guide him, he barely notices the signs, the rattle of the trolley, the smell of fish when he passes the kitchens, the stench of fried oil as he takes a short cut through the café.

He's sweating by the time he reaches the door, and he hesitates, unsure what will be waiting for him on the other side.

Gently, he turns the handle, the soles of his trainers squeaking against the floor as he shuffles inside.

Caily's blonde hair is splayed over the pillow. Although she's still pale, there's a pink to her cheeks that wasn't there before. Her eyes are closed but she looks peaceful.

'She's asleep,' Kate whispers without turning, placing her hand on her shoulder for him to take, knowing it is him.

Matt's throat expands as he watches his daughter, and he has to swallow several times before he can speak.

'Has she . . . has she said anything yet?'

'Only my name, and that she was thirsty.'

Matt sinks into a chair. There's nothing left to do but wait until Caily wakes up again.

Wait for her to speak her truth.

Wait to find out if she blames him.

Wait for his nightmare to end.

CHAPTER EIGHTY-THREE

Caily

Caily feels like she's standing on the edges of some weird dream. She's awake but everything seems hazy. There's the woman from the party, Mum's old friend, she can't quite remember her name, there's something about her that nudges at the edges of Caily's memory. Something she needs to recall.

Mum and Dad are either side of her bed. She's detached from it all as though she's watching herself from high above as she opens her eyes, blinking as though she's illuminated from the glare of a spotlight after standing on a dark, dark stage.

'The performance? Have I missed *La La Land*?' she thinks she says in her head, but Mum trails her fingers across her cheek and says, 'Don't worry about that now, sweet girl.'

But Caily is worried about that.

She's worried about *everything*.

She wants to ask how long she's been here but she isn't sure it really matters. Tegan hates her. She's still keeping secrets for her dad. And . . . she closes her eyes against the memory of that day on the bridge.

Perhaps she could stay here, safe in this room, for ever.

'Caily?' Mum's voice is soft, tentative. 'Do you remember what happened to you?'

Caily casts her mind back, recalling that day. Feeling it again, the pinch of fingers on her arms.

Falling, falling, falling.

Although she doesn't want to, she remembers it all.

CHAPTER EIGHTY-FOUR

Tegan

Tegan remembers it all. Tears stream down her cheeks and she tries to swipe them away as Mum taps on her door, but as fast as she drags her sleeve across her cheek they fall again.

'Tegan?' Mum hovers in the doorway. Not rushing over to comfort her as she usually would. She's wary. Tegan thinks she somehow knows that the conversation they need to have will forever be the divide between the before and the after. The years Mum thought Tegan was wholesome and good and the time when she found out the truth.

Tegan is not wholesome.

Or good.

Tegan raises her face to her mum, her desperate look a plea.

Tell me everything will be okay.

Tell me you'll always love me.

Mum gives a slight nod as though she's read her thoughts, and the way she now approaches Tegan, her brow creased in sympathy and worry, tells Tegan that Mum has not read *all* her thoughts.

She doesn't deserve any sympathy.

Rather than sitting on the edge of the bed as she normally would, Mum swings her legs onto the mattress and shuffles back so her spine is against the headboard as if she needs supporting for the news she is about to hear, or as if she assumes this will be a long conversation when really, Tegan wants to get it over with as quickly as possible. Mum lifts her arm and Tegan wriggles into the space, her body pressed against Mum's, her head on her chest. This is the way they used to lie when Mum would read her Roald Dahl. Their favourite book was *The Twits*. Tegan's shoulders would shake with laughter. Now they shake with remorse.

With guilt.

She takes a juddering breath and then another.

'Mum, there's something I need to tell you. Please . . . please don't hate me.' Tegan's crying so hard she can't hear Mum's reply but she feels the hair being swept away from her face, cool fingers rhythmically stroking her forehead, and she feels love in that touch and she knows that, whatever happens, Mum is on her side.

'I need to talk to you about Caily. About that day . . . and about before.'

There's a pause and she's not sure whether Mum might tell her she doesn't need to say anything but if she doesn't relay what she did then Caily will, and Tegan has made adult choices that she can't blame anyone else for. Now she needs to face up to the consequences.

She doesn't quite know where to start so she goes back to the last time she felt truly happy and takes it from there.

'When Caily got the part of Mia I told her I was really pleased for her, which I was, but I was also a bit jealous.'

She feels it again as she speaks it, the envy whirling around her body, but then she thinks of where Caily is now and she feels ashamed.

She feels ashamed again.

'It's only natural,' Mum says but she doesn't say anything else because she doesn't know anything else.

Yet.

'I was so . . . scared. I guess because everything was changing. Caily might be leaving for London if it went well and I didn't want her to go but I didn't feel I could tell her that because . . .'

'Because you knew she'd stay for you?'

'Yeah.' Tegan wipes her cheeks again. 'And I was happy for her, like if I'd got the part and not Caily she'd have been happy for me.'

'You don't know that,' Mum says. 'You think you know those closest to you, how they'll behave, but you don't. Not really.'

Tegan takes a moment to turn this over but she doesn't believe it to be true. Caily has always supported her, right from when they had their very first performance and Tegan just stood there, shaking and crying like a baby, until Caily took her hand.

'Then Caily started to . . . change, I guess. She was upset because of that Instagram account, all the memes, but more than that, she fancied Travis and always wanted to hang around the farm. I felt I was losing her. Like she'd let me down like I'd let you down.'

'You've never let me down.'

'Yeah? Well, I'd seen all the red bills and I thought if

I could have been the one Eloise noticed I might get rich and help you—'

'Tegan.' Mum's voice is tight. 'You don't have to worry about me. About money and stuff. We're okay.'

'Are we, though?'

'Yes. I'm sorry you've been carrying all this worry on your own.'

'Yeah but normally I would have had Caily to talk to but I wasn't seeing much of her. I tried to talk to her so many times but all she wanted to talk about was herself, how she looked. I know she was trying to build her confidence back up but . . .'

There's a beat while Tegan gathers her thoughts, gathers her words.

'Anyway. I'm trying to tell you about Kofi's party. Caily wasn't there. She said she had a headache but . . .' Tegan gives a small shrug. 'It probably wouldn't have happened if she had been there, but I drank. I drank a lot and . . .' Tegan can't go on. She imagines she can taste the bitterness of alcohol coating her tongue. Hot bile rising in her throat.

'And?' Mum gently prompts.

'I was a mess. I am a mess. Mum . . . I had sex at the party and got pregnant.'

There is a sharp intake of breath. Tegan buries her face against her mum's chest and feels the beating of her heart, and she hopes she hasn't broken it.

There's a beat. Two. Three. A horrible silence stretching until Tegan feels it will snap, that she will snap. But before she breaks, Mum asks, 'Who is the father?'

'I don't . . . it doesn't matter. A boy from the drama club. I don't want—' Her tone sharply rises, along with her distress.

366

'Shh.' Mum holds her but doesn't ask any more questions, instead telling Tegan that it's okay.

Tegan wishes they could stop there, that 'it's okay' could be the last words Mum says about it, but she has to continue.

'After the party I began to suspect I might be pregnant. I was so freaked out. I tried to tell Caily so many times but she was caught up in her own problems. We had a fight because I couldn't get her to listen and then . . . It felt like she didn't care so I didn't tell anyone. On the day of the accident Caily caught me throwing up in the loos and I felt so ill, I told her everything. She . . . she was . . . lovely. Really supportive but said we had to tell you. But I didn't want her to. I begged her to keep it a secret but she said she couldn't. She left the toilets and . . . and . . .' Tegan feels it again, the utter dismay that she's shared the secret she'd vowed to keep, her frenzied desire to prevent anyone else finding out.

'Mum. I . . . I had to stop Caily telling.'

CHAPTER EIGHTY-FIVE

Beth

'Tell me everything. I promise I won't judge you.' Beth holds her shaking daughter in her arms, stunned by everything she has heard so far, scared by what's to come.

Tegan had sex.

Tegan is pregnant.

She doesn't know what to think. What to say. She's choosing her words carefully because she knows that her reaction could for ever change the shape of her relationship with her daughter and she has to get it right, but this will be a conversation she replays in her mind over and over.

She remembers when Tegan was a baby, the smell of Johnson's baby lotion, talcum powder. The warmth of her against her chest. How she vowed then that she'd never let anyone hurt her.

She has let her down.

Tegan has been carrying the guilt, the shame of her actions alone.

Beth will stand by her. Of course she will.

'Shh,' she soothes. 'It'll be okay.'

She doesn't know how or when, but she has to believe that.

She doesn't know the whole story yet.

CHAPTER EIGHTY-SIX

Caily

The whole story is just too horrible to bear, but Mum is looking at Caily expectantly.

'You don't have to say anything if you don't want to. If you're not ready.' Dad strokes her hair the way he used to when she was small. His fingers still smell of the farm, of hay and soil and her childhood. She feels a tear leak down her cheek.

'But Owen will be here soon,' Mum says. 'He'll want to know what happened.'

'I'm sorry, Caily,' Dad says suddenly. Passionately. 'I'm sorry that you came into the red barn and saw me and Beth and those bloody plants. I'm sorry I asked you to keep it a secret. If that has anything to do with what happened to you on the bridge.'

'It didn't. But Dad,' Caily licks her dry lips. Her voice small and weak. 'Travis knows. After I left the red barn I was looking for Twix and I bumped into him when he was on his way home. I was crying and . . . it just all came out. I was really scared. What if he tells? Please. You shouldn't be growing that. It's . . . wrong. You'll go to prison like Uncle Sean did and . . .' She begins to cry.

'I won't. I promise you, it's all gone and I won't ever do anything like that again. It was stupid and—'

'Caily, is there anything you want to tell us before Owen gets here?' Mum dabs at her wet cheeks with a tissue. Mum always has a tissue in her bag. It's familiar and comforting and it makes Caily cry harder. 'He was the one who brought you here after the police had an anonymous call—'

'Anonymous?' Caily is winded, she feels the punch of the word so physically in the gut. 'So . . . was I . . . who was with me when Owen came?'

'No one,' Mum says sadly. 'You were alone.'

A sob chokes Caily's throat.

She can't breathe.

She can't actually breathe. She thought, when she woke, when she remembered, that she must have the details wrong but . . .

Anonymous.

Alone.

Her mind rewinds to her last memories of the day of the accident as she heaves in a lungful of air, trying to calm herself but unable to.

'Shh. You don't have to tell us anything right now,' Dad soothes.

The room is quiet.

Hot.

Oppressive.

Caily tries to compose herself, 'I don't know what to tell you,' she says because that is the truth. There was that horrible, awful row with Tegan. She was supposed to have stayed for the final rehearsal but she'd left school without telling

Miss West. She can still feel the pain of Tegan pressing her fingers into her arms, shaking her. The steel in her eyes as she'd told Caily she hated her.

'The person who was with you must have dragged you out of the water and then used your phone to call the police,' Mum says.

'So . . . they helped me?' Caily sags against the pillows with relief. She wasn't remembering it right, of course she wasn't, they didn't hurt her – why would they? – they saved her.

'Do you remember who was on the bridge with you, Caily?' Mum asks.

'Yes,' she says. She can't look at Mum.

Can't bear to see the anguish and confusion in her eyes when she tells her who was with her.

CHAPTER EIGHTY-SEVEN

Tegan

Tegan can't bear to look at her mum, doesn't want to see disappointment in her eyes. Once, after Travis arrived at the farm, Mum had tried to have the sex talk with her, as though worried she'd be romping in the hay, and Tegan had waved her away, embarrassed.

'*Mum*. We've already covered everything at school and there's the internet and—'

'I just want you to be careful. Be safe.'

Tegan had turned away from her, rolling her eyes, thinking Mum didn't know her as well as she thought she did.

Careful.

Safe.

Two adjectives and she hadn't managed either. Perhaps Mum knows her after all, and Tegan is the one who has done the underestimating because Mum's fingers still stroke Tegan's forehead. Still full of love. She hasn't pulled away, she hasn't so much as sighed.

She's just . . . stayed. Tegan snuggles into her and breathes in the summer-meadow fabric softener that Mum has used for as long as Tegan can remember and it always reminds Tegan of the farm.

Of her family.

She needs to tell Mum the rest, so she shifts until she's sitting upright and, although she still can't look Mum directly in the eye, she continues.

'Caily said I should speak to someone about being pregnant and I didn't want to. I told her that I'd dealt with it alone because she'd been so preoccupied and when she asked what I meant I told her that I'd had an appointment with a doctor for a termination.'

Tegan remembers the shock on Caily's face.

'It won't interfere with the show,' she blurted in the face of her silence.

'It's not about the show. I don't care about the show, I care about you. Don't you think it's too big a decision to make without talking it through properly?'

'I have talked it through.'

'With some doctor. A stranger. What about someone who knows you? Are you sure about this?'

'Yeah. I feel crappy but I am sure it's the right thing.'

Caily studied her. 'You're so strong, Tegan. I do know that you wouldn't be doing this if you weren't sure but I can't imagine not talking to Mum about something this huge. I wish you'd talk to yours.'

'Why? I am certain. I know it's . . . Look, I'm not rushing into this as some quick fix or because I'm overwhelmed or ashamed or anything else but because it is the right thing, for me. I've had time to really consider it and I've thought about it really carefully.'

'Okay, but afterwards you'll need support. Your family.'

'And perhaps I'll tell them but I don't have to decide that right now.'

'But if you tell them and they know I knew then—'

'This isn't about you.'

'I'm not trying to make it about me but . . . I'm out of my depth. I don't know how to support you.'

'By listening to what I want.'

'But I think—'

'Perhaps I don't give a fuck what you think.' Tegan's anger spiked, sick of feeling she had to defend herself and her decision.

Tegan raises her tearstained face to her mum. 'It was awful, we argued all the way to the hall and she said . . . she said she loved me and was worried and, although she never wanted to break my trust, she needed to tell an adult, even if it was only Aunt Kate. I . . . I panicked and I grabbed her by the arms and . . .' Tegan can still feel her fingertips digging into Caily's soft flesh below her short-sleeved shirt. The look of hurt and surprise on her cousin's face as Tegan shook her as hard as she could. The venomous words that spilled out of her mouth.

'You silly cow. I hate you.' But Tegan hadn't hated her, not then, not ever. Certainly not now.

'And after you told Caily you hated her?' Mum asks carefully, her voice neutral.

'I told her . . .' A sickening dread wraps itself around Tegan's throat and she feels the squeeze so physically she pulls away the neck of her T-shirt so she can get the words out.

'I told her I'd fucking kill her if she told anyone. I texted her that too. I was so worried. I hadn't realized Dani had filmed me and Caily and shared it. I literally wanted to die when Owen played that to you, but I didn't want him to know I was pregnant. It wasn't his business, or yours. It was my body, my choice.'

Mum stiffens and Tegan waits to be pushed away but instead Mum takes her hand, though this time she doesn't give Tegan space to find the right words.

'What did you . . . What happened next?'

'Caily left and I . . .' Tegan covers her face with her hand. It's too awful.

'You followed her?'

'No. I didn't see her again. I . . . I went for the termination.'

'You had an operation—'

'No, it isn't like that. It took minutes. I'd already had a consultation a few days before. The nurse gave me a tablet. I had to take it there but I didn't feel anything. But I knew I wouldn't really until I took the second tablet. That's why I knew it wouldn't interfere with the show. I didn't . . . well, not until I took the second tablet the next day like they said.'

'So when you asked for the thick sanitary towels, said you had a really bad period—'

'Yeah. I'm sorry, Mum. I never wanted you to find out. I was sure – am still sure – it was the right thing for me. I didn't know how you'd feel and I didn't want to upset you.'

Tegan places a hand over a stomach where her baby could have grown if she'd given it a chance, but there's nothing there except an emptiness that hasn't left her since that day, even though if she could travel back in time, had to decide again whether to have a termination or not, she would still make the same decision. The right decision for her, even though it did – it does – hurt.

Afterwards, she had come home to the news of Caily's accident and, once she'd concocted her story about where she had been, it seemed easier to stick to it even when the lie grew too big, when she was caught out, she formed another story and then another and she couldn't remember who she'd said what to and it all felt so out of control.

'That was why you didn't want to tell the police where you were? Tegan, you could have ended up in court.'

'I know. If it went much further I'd have had to tell the truth, but . . . what will everyone think of me? They'll say—'

'They'll love you. We all love you. Nobody will judge you. I'm so sorry you've been through this on your own. But I respect your decision and . . . and thank you for trusting me now.'

'But you must think—'

'I love you,' Mum says, three simple words but that is enough. Tegan begins to cry again.

'I can't bear it, Mum, the last thing I said to Caily was that I hated her. I hurt her. She . . . she looked so scared when I shook her. I . . . feel it's all my fault. What if Owen's got it wrong and she wasn't pushed but she threw herself off the bridge because that was the last straw on top of the weeks of misery that Dani had put her through with the Instagram account? She was so upset.'

'She wouldn't have done that.'

'But you just said, we never really know anyone.'

'Yes, but someone was there with her. Someone called 999. Someone dragged her out of the water.'

'Yeah, but who?'

CHAPTER EIGHTY-EIGHT

Kate

'Please, Caily. Do you remember who was on the bridge with you?' Kate asks again gently, ignoring the glare from Matt. Kate knows she isn't being fair but she wants to, needs to, hear who it was before Owen gets here. Because if it was Tegan, perhaps there is a chance they can contain it, figure it out as a family. It's not that she doesn't want whoever hurt her daughter to pay, but her relationship with Beth is at stake. At the very least, she can call Beth, warn her, if Caily says Tegan is to blame.

If.

Caily's distress is written all over her face, her pleading eyes darting between Kate and Matt. Back to Nicola before landing on Kate again. Her chest heaves as she drags in shallow breaths. It's obvious she's remembering what happened, and Kate is torn. She wants to tell her that she doesn't have to think about it, doesn't have to talk about it, but once she has, once Kate knows the truth, she can deal with it and then they can all move on.

Can't they?

'It's okay, I promise. You're not in any trouble but . . . please . . . tell me who was with you on the bridge.' Kate takes her daughter's hand, which is nearly as large as her own, and feels the tremble in them both. And when Caily utters a name Kate's fingers tighten. Caily winces as she tries to pull away but Kate can't unclench the fist she has formed. She can't believe what Caily is saying.

'Grandma. Grandma was with me on the bridge.'

CHAPTER EIGHTY-NINE

Mary

Being a grandma used to bring her immeasurable joy. Caily and Tegan were her world, but Mary does not feel joy as she sits at the kitchen table, her mobile clutched tightly in her hand. The tea she made earlier is untouched. Mary can't drink, can't swallow, can't function.

Caily is awake.

Is she going to be okay? Is she still going to be Caily or will her accident, the blow to her head, have turned her into somebody different, someone with gaps in her mind where her memories should be?

Will she remember?

Caily is awake.

Mary has reread the message so many times that the letters slide around until they rearrange themselves into something else entirely.

Guilty.

This is what Mary feels, this is what she is, and it's only a matter of time before everyone finds out. And then what?

She doesn't want forgiveness because she doesn't feel she deserves it, and she can never, ever forgive herself.

Outside the window a breeze wafts away the clouds, exposing the sun that glares accusingly through the window.

Mary closes her eyes. Once the sunshine held myriad meanings: picnics in the field when Beth and Kate were small; the crops being handed a fighting chance after a relentlessly wet spring; sitting on the bench in the yard with Patrick, soaking up the last vestiges of the day's warmth before the sky darkened and sprinkled with stars, knowing that their calloused hands and aching backs were indicative of them building a future for their family. Now the glint of the sun is sharp and pointed, jabbing into her the memory, the reflection of her panicked face in the river as she dragged Caily to the bank, sweat plastering her hair to her scalp, horror heating her blood. Struggling to move her weight despite her daily yoga sessions keeping her muscles honed.

What had she done?

It's incredulous that the night before there had been dancing at Kate and Beth's fortieth party.

Laughing.

Knowing that, although she and Patrick had health challenges, they were surrounded by love, family.

Friends.

Her thoughts drift back to Nicola, she thinks that everything that has happened can perhaps circle back to her.

She hadn't known it when Matt had found her on social media and messaged her an invitation. But that was before Mary found out.

She knows it now.

Caily is awake.

What has she done?

Is there a way to put it right?

Mary can only think of one possible way to repair some of the damage, prevent future devastation, and the thought of it deepens the painful cracks that already criss-cross through her heart.

CHAPTER NINETY

Caily

Caily's heart hurts. She speaks slowly, carefully, not because she is choosing her words but because she is trying to make sense of them. She's already falteringly told her parents about her fight with Tegan. She tells them that Tegan is pregnant while studying their faces for signs they know, but from their shocked expressions she is certain that this has come as a surprise to them both.

And then it's time to talk about Grandma. She is hit by a sense of betrayal so cold and sudden it's as though she's been saturated with freezing water, which reminds her of the hosepipe battles she'd have in the farmyard with Tegan when they were young and carefree. She feels a desperate yearning for everything to go back to the way it was.

But, of course, it can't.

She picks at a stray piece of cotton that hangs from the edge of her sheet, wondering if she pulls it whether it will unravel the way she feels that she herself might at any given moment, the way that Grandma surely has, because why . . .

'Caily?' Mum speaks tentatively. 'You . . . you're saying that . . . that Grandma was with you when you fell?' Mum's skin is suddenly taut across her face, tinged with grey. However confused and conflicted Caily feels towards Grandma right now, she must remember that this is her mum's mother and so must be a hundred times worse for her.

A thousand.

And she wonders if she should have said anything at all, but she doesn't know what the police and her parents know, what truths have come to light while she's been unconscious.

Who is lying.

Regret pricks the back of her eyes, tears well again because, although there are so many things she doesn't know, she realizes that her family will never be the same again.

Will forever be broken.

'I got the bus back instead of staying for the rehearsal because I wanted to talk to you, Mum. I wanted someone, an adult . . . you, to know that Tegan was pregnant and she was going to have a termination. I was so worried about her and I panicked, I think, because it was such a shock and I was . . . scared. Selfish, I suppose. I didn't want to be the only one who knew. It felt like too much responsibility. What if something went wrong?' She paused for breath. 'I didn't want to tell you over the phone in case anyone overheard, and I knew I had time to fetch you before her appointment. It was so foggy when I got off the bus and began to walk across the bridge.' Caily licks her lips, her mouth is dry, but when Dad asks if she wants a break, a drink, she shakes her head, not wanting the water to slip down her throat and wash away her courage. She closes her eyes and the bright, white hospital room fades away, replaced by the swirling mist, grabbing her with damp fingers. Her head had been swimming with worry and doubt. Was she doing the right thing telling Mum, she had wondered? Being Beth's twin, she was bound to tell her, and Tegan did not want her mum to know. Should she keep quiet?

'Grandma was babbling about a man in a Range Rover. She seemed really scared but she wasn't making sense,' Caily says. 'I can't really remember anything else.'

But this isn't true. She remembers the way she had been hurrying across the bridge, the same bridge her and Tegan would hurtle over after chanting 'Who's trip-trapping over my bridge?' They'd shriek as they ran, poised for a troll to grab their ankles, send them toppling over the railings. Instead, a shadowy figure trudged out of the gloom, making her jump.

'Grandma!'

'Caily.' Grandma forced a smile. She didn't step towards her and hug her like she normally would. She looked exhausted. Last night's party must have been too much for her. Mum said it would be.

'I thought you had your final rehearsal this afternoon? I'm really looking forward to seeing you sing and dance later but I don't think Grandad can come. He . . . he's *sick* and . . . Caily? Is everything okay?' Grandma spoke faster than normal.

'No.' Caily felt a rush of relief. Grandma would know what to do. She leaned back and Grandma took her hand and pulled her forward.

'Careful, the railing is still broken.'

Grandma's fingers were cold and dry around hers. She could feel the bones, but these were the same hands who had held her as a baby, who clapped at every performance. She felt safe.

'Can I tell you something? A secret?'

Grandma gave a small shake of her head.

'Secrets . . . sometimes they're best left in the past.'

Caily shivered. Grandma wasn't herself, acting weird. Mum had said she'd been more confused lately, but Caily hadn't really noticed her getting worse before.

Now she noticed.

Now she was scared.

'Grandma?'

'Sorry. Are you in trouble, Caily?'

'Not me. Tegan. She told me something. She's pregnant.'

Grandma seemed to shrink in front of Caily's eyes. Her shoulders drooping, her head lowered.

Caily felt a pinch of regret. Grandma was too old to understand that times had changed. That young people had sex before marriage and it didn't always mean anything. She shouldn't have told her.

'Grandma?'

She was staring over Caily's shoulder so intently that Caily turned to see what she was looking at, but there was nothing there.

'Grandma, I've got to go. I was on my way to tell Mum but—'

'No.' Grandma jerked upright. 'You can't tell anybody.'

'But?'

'But nothing.' There was something in Grandma's tone that Caily hadn't heard before. That frightened her.

'Tegan needs—'

'I'll talk to Tegan. Find out what she needs. You . . . you can't say anything to anyone. Promise me, Caily. *Promise* me.'

She started babbling about a Range Rover, stressing how Caily shouldn't talk to the man driving it. She wasn't making any sense. She gripped Caily's hand tightly and Caily tried to pull away but Grandma's daily walks and yoga sessions had given her a strength that Caily wasn't expecting.

'I . . . Grandma, you're hurting me.' She stepped back. Closer to the edge. Closer to the broken railing.

Too close.

'I . . . want to go and tell Mum.' Caily took another step.

'No.' There was steel in that one word.

'You're scaring me. Okay. I won't tell. I promise I won't tell anyone.' Caily's voice was high, her breathing erratic as she tried again to yank her hand free, panic rising as she felt the smooth soles of her shoes slip against the damp wooden floor. She began to lose her balance.

She felt a tug on her arm and thought Grandma was pulling her back but, just as she began to fall backwards, she felt a release. Not only a release, did she feel a slight push? Grandma's fingers spayed open, letting her go, and suddenly Caily was falling, arms windmilling, feet fighting for traction.

And the last thing she remembers was the horror on her Grandma's face as she plummeted to the ground.

The scene replays again and again and Caily observes

it now from different angles, wondering if that can really be what happened. Surely Grandma didn't purposefully let her fall, would never have pushed her. But if she didn't, then why didn't Grandma tell the emergency operator who she was?

She can't make sense of it.

CHAPTER NINETY-ONE

Mary

The day of Caily's accident

Mary couldn't make sense of it. Couldn't stay at home, the walls were closing in on her. She stepped out of the farmhouse, into the mist, wishing it could swallow her. Wishing she could disappear entirely. She needed to clear her head. She crossed the yard quickly, unable to bear the sight of the barn with the debris of last night's party. The 'Happy 40th' banner strung between the beams. The table still littered with bottles of fizzy wine that she'd bought to toast Kate and Beth's birthday.

She had been so excited as she waited for the guests to arrive, the glow of gratitude for her daughters and her husband keeping the chill from her bones while she waited for the heaters to warm.

It had been so nice to have something to look forward to. Goodness knows she needed it because, however much she tried to hide it from the family, her increasing forgetfulness was distressing. She's barely into her sixties and feels too young for this, but then does anyone ever feel ready for a health challenge? She might be strong physically with her daily yoga and walks, but what use was a capable body without a capable mind? But still, she wouldn't think of that now. She had been happy as she placed three of her famous apple pies on the trestle table. Crammed pink candles into holders before pressing them into the soft buttercream icing of the cake she had made. She didn't know then that this was the last time she would experience pure joy.

Mary was lost in thought, didn't register how far she had walked, almost to the bridge, she was still immersed in the events of the previous evening. She pulled her cardigan around her thin frame, wishing she'd picked up her coat, but then perhaps she wasn't deserving of its warmth.

All these years and she hadn't been deserving of the truth.

Her heart hurts as she wondered whether her whole life had been built on a lie and not the solid foundations that she thought being a wife and mother gave her. She had thought she was the one who held them together.

She hadn't even realized they had become unstuck.

There were holes in Mary's mind where her memories used to be. Things she used to remember, she now couldn't. Sometimes there were fragments, brief recollections, but the more Mary tried to grip on to them the further the blackness spread, like the ink stain the girls had made on the rug when they were small. The darkness leaching over the colour.

There were also things Mary wished she could forget.

There weren't many guests last night. Family. Some friends. A couple of women Beth works with.

And Nicola.

Mary had helped Patrick out to the barn. He'd been wearing a prosthetic for the party, but it had never fit him properly and it rubbed. He was on the waiting list for a new one. She knew that tomorrow he would be sore. If she could she would take away his pain, hold it herself. Almost fifty years of marriage and she loved him more than ever.

More than anything.

Everyone arrived fifteen minutes before Caily and Tegan were due to bring Beth and Kate, as instructed, and when Nicola stepped tentatively into the barn Mary waved her over to where she stood, behind Patrick's chair, one hand lightly on his shoulder. The other holding the glass of champagne she sipped from, the bubbles fizzing on her tongue.

'Look, it's Nicola Crosby. The girls' friend when they were at school. Do you remember?'

She felt his shoulders stiffen beneath her fingertips.

'Mary,' Nicola stepped forward and awkwardly kissed her on the cheek. 'Patrick. It's so good of you to invite me. I really want to put the past behind me. It's . . . I've spent years feeling terrible about what happened and it's wonderful to have a chance to reconnect with you all. With Kate and Beth—'

'What do you mean?' Mary asked at the same time as Patrick turned to her and said in a strangled voice, 'You didn't tell me you'd invited Nicola.' His face was ashen, his eyes wide. 'How did you find her?'

Mary didn't tell Patrick he hadn't involved himself in the arrangements. It didn't seem important that he didn't know Nicola was coming or that she hadn't told him how Matt had traced Nicola on social media after seeing childhood photos of her with Kate and asking Mary for her name.

What she really wanted to know was why he didn't want her there.

'I'm so sorry, I'll go.' Nicola's voice cracked. 'I should never have come. Mary,' her voice now a whisper, 'I thought you knew.'

'Wait.' Mary grabbed Nicola's arm as she turned. 'I want to know . . .' She trailed off as someone called, 'They're coming,' and then she was on autopilot. Mouth stretched into a smile that didn't reach her eyes, automatically pulling at a party popper as Kate and Beth stepped into the barn, laughing.

And then, after she'd had a brief chat with Kate and Beth, she led Patrick and Nicola into the kitchen.

They sat at the table. Mary ran her fingers over the grooves carved into the wood through the passage of time. Nicola might have made some of these marks herself, she stayed over for dinner often enough. Her mother, Debbie, was neglectful. More interested in boyfriends she thought might support her. Always out for what she could get. Nicola had become another daughter almost, before Kate had nearly drowned, before Nicola had suddenly moved away.

Patrick was stooped in his seat, Nicola studying her lap.

'Can one of you please tell me what's going on?' Mary could hear the tremor in her voice. She gripped the legs of her chair with damp and slippery hands to stop herself from leaving because she never thought Patrick would keep a secret from her and she knew whatever she was about to hear would change everything.

Patrick parted his lips before he clamped them shut again, his eyes watery.

'I stayed over one night,' Nicola began. 'I was fifteen.' She trailed off.

'You stayed over lots of nights.' Mary heard her heart thudding loudly in her ears.

'It was the night Kate nearly drowned. I woke up . . . It was dark. And . . .' She shook her head as though she couldn't possibly go on.

'And I was in her bed,' Patrick said softly.

CHAPTER NINETY-TWO

Kate

Kate lowers her forehead onto Caily's bed. She is back underwater, a sloshing sound in her ears, Caily's words dull and echoey. She must be hearing them wrong.

Mum can't have been on the bridge with Caily when she fell. Her family doesn't keep secrets. She knows her mum, both of her parents, inside out.

Doesn't she?

CHAPTER NINETY-THREE

Mary

The day of Caily's accident

Didn't she know her husband at all? Mary could not believe what she was hearing. It felt as though the floor had dropped, her stomach plummeting, the sense of falling.

Nicola had woken to find Patrick in her bed?

The room blurred and tightened around her, forcing the breath from her lungs.

'It wasn't . . .' Patrick ran a hand over his chin. 'I'd been sleepwalking. You know I sleepwalk when I'm really stressed. Anyway, that night Nicola slept over, when Kate had nearly drowned. Well, that's about as stressed as I'd ever been and I had a couple of drinks. The spare room where Nicola was sleeping had been my room when I was a boy and I must have got confused.'

Mary didn't know what to say, her mind fugged with confusion, the champagne she had drunk bitter in her mouth.

The words punched into her again and again.

Patrick was in bed with Nicola.

The memories she thought she had of the happy marriage

she thought they'd shared were now scattered like strands of hay in the yard. Dirty and worthless.

'I . . . I was scared when I woke up and Patrick was next to me. I leaped out of bed and he woke up and was mortified. He was holding a tatty old teddy bear, was confused,' Nicola said. 'I didn't sleep for the rest of the night, though, and the next morning when I told Mum what had happened she said . . . she said . . .'

'I was one of those child whatsits. But I'm not. I didn't touch her. I didn't even know where I was until she jumped out of bed and then I woke. I felt awful for frightening her. I went to see Nicola's mum, Debbie, first thing to explain and . . .' The despair on Patrick's face broke Mary's heart and part of her wanted to comfort him, but she didn't. 'She said she was going to report me to the police and I'd be locked up and . . .' A single tear trickled down Patrick's cheek. 'I hadn't done anything.'

'But Nicola, didn't you tell your mother that nothing happened?' Mary's tone was more accusatory than she'd like, but she needed to feel she had some semblance of control because everything she thought she knew was slipping away. Patrick was slipping away. Already across the table, he looked like a stranger with his grey skin, his grey hair, his black lies. Where was the man she had married?

'I did, but Mum kept saying there was no smoke without fire and I must be blocking out the trauma and . . . the more she said it, the more I doubted what I remembered. Had Patrick touched me?'

'But you're certain he didn't?' Mary could not look at her husband as she asked that.

'Yes.' Nicola took a deep breath. 'And that's why I wanted to say sorry because I know that . . . that sometimes there *is* smoke without fire. I've experienced . . . my son . . . he's on the sex offenders register because his girlfriend who had told him she was eighteen turned out to be fifteen. She looked so much older and . . .' Nicola cleared her throat. 'It only takes a second to ruin a life, to ruin a family, and we almost ruined yours. I'm so sorry. It's only been since Mum died recently that I've been able to see her clearly. Realize how manipulative she was.'

Mary took a moment to digest this before asking, 'But you must have convinced your mum Patrick was telling the truth, because she didn't report him?'

'She didn't report me because I paid her,' Patrick said slowly, shamefully.

'You . . . how much?'

'Virtually all we had.'

Mary covered her face with her hands. She may not remember things clearly, not all the facts, but feelings. She can remember feelings and the hopelessness, the helplessness, the anxiety, that came when Patrick twenty-five years ago had told her the farm might have to be sold. Those feelings still burned into her. The fear they would lose their home – their daughters' home – and the guilt that she hadn't done more to help, hadn't done enough while Patrick had shielded their financial situation from her. That's what became of playing a role, the dutiful wife. Caily or Tegan would never get caught out like this. Everything's about equality nowadays, joint accounts and joint culpability.

'Mary? Patrick?' Matt stepped into the kitchen. 'We're going to light the candles now, are you coming out?'

Mary slowly scraped back her chair, unsteady as she stood, and somehow she put one foot in front of the other. She was numb as she watched her daughters lean over the birthday cake. Her mouth moved of its own accord, singing happy birthday.

Beth and Kate held hands the way they always did when they blew out the candles, and she wondered what they had wished for.

If Mary had one wish, she'd turn back time.

She glanced at Patrick, sure he was thinking the same thing. He knocked back a whisky, his hand shaking as he poured another. He wasn't supposed to be drinking but Mary reasoned he'd already done the unimaginable. He couldn't do anything worse.

She was wrong.

CHAPTER NINETY-FOUR

Mary

Mary couldn't figure out right from wrong.

Truth from lies.

Long after the guests had gone home and Beth and Tegan had stumbled yawning up to bed, Mary and Patrick sat in the kitchen, warmed by the Aga, and talked about Nicola. She veered between an absolute belief in him to doubting everything he was telling her.

She knew, *she knew*, that he wasn't capable of the terrible things Debbie had accused him of. Nicola had confirmed that much tonight, but why – *why* – hadn't he confided in her? It was this as much as anything that cut deeply. She had always believed they were strong together, a team.

'If I hadn't paid Debbie off then she'd have reported me and—'

'Nicola would have told them it wasn't true, surely? Despite Debbie trying to make her think the worst, she must—'

'Nicola was upset, confused, her mum was telling her I must have touched her and if she had even a smidgeon of doubt then . . . Mary. The girls were still at school. Can you imagine the gossip? What they'd have been subjected to? And imagine if I had been arrested. Convicted, even. I didn't do anything. I'm a grown man and fifteen-year-old girls do not interest me.'

'I was fifteen when we met and I interested you.' She couldn't help it slipping from her mouth.

'Mary.' There was so much sorrow in that one word, so much sorrow on Patrick's face. 'I was young—'

'You were twenty-five. Old enough to know better.'

'So now you think I'm . . . I'm a monster?'

'No. No, I don't.' Tears poured down Mary's cheeks and she brushed them away with the back of her hand. 'But you could have told me. You *should* have told me. You've broken my trust.' Mary thought he had broken more than her trust, he had broken her entirely and she didn't know how she'd ever put herself back together.

'I know and I'm sorry. I . . . I didn't want to ruin everything. Ruin us.'

'And that . . . that woman – Debbie – she's the reason we struggled all these years. You gave her everything.'

'I gave her money, not everything. You are everything. *We* are everything.'

He threaded his fingers through hers and gave them a gentle squeeze. She couldn't help pulling away, and when the hurt spread over his face she used her hand to cover a fake yawn, pretending this was why she had extracted herself from his touch and not because she couldn't bear to feel his skin on hers.

'Why don't you go up to bed?' Patrick said. 'I'll check everything is locked and be up soon.'

Wearily she tramped upstairs, catching her hip on Patrick's stairlift. Passing Beth's childhood bedroom where Beth was sleeping again tonight after too much champagne. The spare room – Patrick's old room – where Tegan was sleeping.

Tonight, Mary didn't wash her face with soap and water or apply a thick layer of Nivea. She didn't brush her teeth. She took off her party dress, which she'd chosen so carefully, and climbed under the cold duvet and somehow fell into a troubled sleep.

Mary startled awake. The room was in darkness, everything familiar and strange all at the same time. This room, this bed, was her sanctuary, her safety, the place where Patrick had brought her as a young bride. Here, she had cried, night after night, conflicted and confused. Happy she was married but missing her father.

Her full bladder forced her out of bed. Mary pushed open the bedroom door and padded out into the hallway, the carpet warm against her bare feet. Through the landing window the moon cast a creamy glow, illuminating the family photo taken last Christmas when everyone was together. When everyone was happy.

She'd almost reached the bathroom when she heard something. A soft voice. Patrick's voice.

All at once she was overcome with a sense of foreboding. A sickness deep in her stomach. She followed the sound until she was standing outside the spare room – Patrick's old room – Tegan's room. The door was ajar and through the crack she could see Patrick standing over the bed – her granddaughter's bed – 'Go back to sleep,' he whispered, 'and don't worry. Nobody will find out about this. This is our little secret.'

It seemed the floor rocked beneath Mary's feet. She covered her mouth with her hands to contain the scream she felt building deep within her. Tegan was quietly crying and Mary did not know what to think. What to do.

Only hours ago Nicola had told her that Patrick had got into bed with her when she stayed in that room and it had all been hushed up, and now he was in there with Tegan, telling her to keep a secret.

Patrick was talking, awake, alert. Certainly not sleepwalking.

He was almost at the door now and Mary scuttled back into the shadows, pressing herself against the wall as she listened to the whirr of the stairlift as he made his way back downstairs. She hesitated outside Tegan's room. She couldn't hear crying anymore. Couldn't hear anything except her own pounding heart. The voice in her head yelling at her to do something. Anything.

She hurried to the bathroom, dropped heavily and painfully onto her ageing knees and vomited.

By the time she pulled herself together she was chilled to the bone.

Consumed with an ice-cold panic that Tegan might have lost her innocence and suffered at the hands of her husband. Selfishly she was also filled with a deep-seated grief for the fifteen-year-old she had been who had chosen love rather than her father. She felt terrible for all of them. Debbie perhaps had been right, Nicola had been blocking out trauma.

She was shaking as she gently pushed open the door to

Tegan's bedroom. Tegan was asleep. Her hands curled around the top of the duvet. Her face was relaxed. She looked so peaceful. Momentarily Mary wondered whether she'd imagined the whole thing. Whether it had been a horrible, horrible nightmare. She tried to convince herself that it had been, as shamefully she slunk back to bed because she wanted to believe that more than anything.

The following day, she could still taste the bitter sick in her mouth as she walked and walked through the mist. Trying to order everything in her already fractured mind.

She was fifteen when she met Patrick and he pursued her.

Nicola was fifteen when Patrick climbed into bed with her.

Tegan is fifteen and last night . . .

What?

The river flowed beneath her feet as she trudged over the bridge, sleep-deprived and ashamed. Ashamed she hadn't woken Tegan or questioned Patrick last night. Ashamed that she still didn't know what to believe.

The doctor had told her that irrational thoughts could be part of her deteriorating health, her mental impairment, and she wished she had someone to talk to. Someone who could help her decipher reality from the imagined because her husband, her beloved Patrick, could not be what the signs were pointing at him being, could he?

She was so deep inside her head she didn't notice Caily approaching until her granddaughter was right in front of her. They had a brief conversation and then she had listened, with mounting horror, as Caily told her that Tegan was pregnant.

Who was the father? It couldn't be . . . It just couldn't be Patrick.

Could it?

Caily's worried face was before her, but all Mary could see was Patrick creeping out of Tegan's room.

Caily's lips were moving but all she could hear was Patrick.

Nobody will find out about this. This is our little secret.

Tegan had been so snappy and withdrawn these past few weeks and they'd all put it down to losing the part in the musical, but what if it wasn't that at all?

What if last night wasn't a one-off?

What if Patrick had been abusing Tegan for weeks? Months?

What if he was responsible for her falling pregnant? She didn't have a boyfriend. Men of his age could still be fertile, just look at Clint Eastwood, Mick Jagger, Rod Stewart. They all fathered children in their sixties and seventies.

'Grandma?' The way Caily spoke her name made Mary realize that she had been trying to get her attention.

Mary tried to focus her gaze on her granddaughter but it was pulled to the road by the sound of an engine.

Through the mist she saw that a black Range Rover had crawled to a stop.

The tinted window opened.

A bald man with dark eyes and thick lips locked eyes with her.

His engine revved. He glared at her with utter contempt before slowly pulling away.

Mary watched as the taillights grew fainter but, before

they could become swallowed by the weather, there was the right blink of an indicator. He was turning into the lane.

He was going to the farm.

Who was he?

Something slithered down Mary's spine. She covered her heart with her hand, frightened. He must be a policeman. He'd come to take Patrick away. Tegan must have gone to school and told a teacher that her grandad had behaved inappropriately last night.

Mary felt sick. The driver of the Range Rover was going to tear their lives apart. She needed to rush home.

'Grandma? Are you okay?' Caily's voice was coming at her from far away. 'You're hurting me.'

Mary wasn't consciously aware of gripping Caily's arm. She wasn't fully present as she held her tightly. She was frantic with it all.

'You can't talk to him.'

'Talk to who?'

'The man in the Range Rover.'

'I don't know what you're talking about.'

'You can't tell him.'

If he was a policeman, and Mary was convinced he must be, Caily mustn't tell him that Tegan was pregnant. But then he might already know that if Tegan had said something.

Mary couldn't make sense of it. She couldn't make sense of anything.

No, Caily mustn't tell him anything, she mustn't confide in Kate either, until Mary knows exactly what that man had come to the farm for.

And then . . .

What?

She didn't know. A pressure was building and building in her chest. She just didn't know what to do.

Her mind was full of bees, buzzing-buzzing-buzzing.

She needed to figure it all out because, as Nicola had said last night, *it only takes a second to ruin a life, to ruin a family.*

Would Patrick be sent to prison to die, infirm and alone? Would she lose her home? Her family? Would they blame her?

How much did Caily know?

'Grandma? Let go of me. I didn't see a Range Rover. It's so foggy. You're imagining things again.'

But it had been there, hadn't it? Or had she fabricated it? Was the driver real or was he like the rats she could hear in her head, scratch-scratch-scratching? A manifestation of her guilt. Of what she thinks Patrick really deserves.

Or was she crazy?

Caily was still talking. About Tegan. Kate. She was trying to pull her hand free. The hand Mary didn't realize she was gripping. Her shoes slipping on the floor.

The last words Caily uttered were her promise that she wouldn't tell, and then she lost her balance.

There was the briefest moment of complete stillness before Mary began to pull her back but, unbidden, she felt her fingers open, and then Caily was falling. Arms propelling wildly. Feet trying to gain traction against nothing but air.

A terrible, terrible scream.

Now Caily is awake.

Mary sits alone now, elbows on the kitchen table, her head in her hands. As she has a million times since that day, she replays the scene again and again, incredulous that she's remembering it correctly. She can't, hand on heart, say that she wanted Caily to fall to stop her sharing what she knew about Tegan with anyone. She can't say that she might, out of fear and confusion, have gently pushed her backwards. What she can say, with certainty, is that she was filled with the type of panic she had never experienced before. That she could, perhaps, have stopped Caily from falling.

But she hadn't.

By now she knows that no one has come for Patrick.

But knowing that does not eradicate the problem.

He is a problem and, although it pains her to even think it, Mary has the solution.

He hasn't long left for this world anyway.

CHAPTER NINETY-FIVE

Kate

The world has stopped making sense.

Kate may know what happened on the bridge but she doesn't understand why.

Explanations jostle inside her head but she dismisses each one as incomprehensible. Improbable.

Mum's mental impairment has worsened and she didn't know what she was doing.

Mum didn't recognize Caily and thought she was in danger.

Mum had no recollection of being on the bridge.

Caily has imagined the whole thing, some side effect from being in a coma.

What Kate doesn't do is link it to her father at all because he wasn't there.

That is, until her phone vibrates with a message from Mum to her and Beth.

I'm so sorry about your dad. I'm going to make it right.

CHAPTER NINETY-SIX

Mary

Mary is going to put everything right. She is still slumped over the kitchen table. Still has her head in her hands. She raises her face and slowly scans the room. Taking in the empty chairs that used to seat wriggling toddlers, chubby-cheeked children, awkward teenagers. She'd hoped that one day there'd be another high chair, another generation.

This room had once been full of laughter and love. Now it is lifeless and lonely.

Her eyes are drawn to the family photo on the dresser. Beth and Kate on the edge of an emerald-green field, identical grins, holding Tegan and Caily out to the camera like a prize, both babies swaddled in matching pink and mint crochet blankets Mary had made.

She wishes she could see Caily one last time. Tell her how sorry she is. She has visited her often in the hospital since that first visit when she had skulked around in the shadows until Caily was alone, certain that if Kate or Matt had been there they would have immediately known something was wrong because Mary couldn't help breaking down, whispering her apology over and over like a mantra. Telling her that she didn't mean to leave her there, hurt, alone. Willing her to recover. And she did want her to recover, whatever the price. Mary knows this on a deep level, for she had fished Caily's ballet shoes from the water after she had fallen, wet and bloodied from the wound on Caily's head, and she'd taken them to her hospital room because they were Caily's good-luck charm and, goodness knows, she needed some luck.

For the last time Mary tries to unpick fact from fiction. Stack what she knows to be true against theories. She can't swear that she believes Patrick is a . . . a . . . She can't even think the word. But she isn't certain he hasn't done anything wrong. After all, Nicola herself says she can't remember anything untoward happening and Debbie, her mother, always was a money-grabber, but the cold, stark fact is that he had climbed into bed with a child and the night of the party he was in that bedroom again. And not just any child, his granddaughter. Their darling Tegan, who had been withdrawn and moody for weeks now, which they'd all put down to losing out on the part to Caily, but what if it wasn't the show, or even the pregnancy, but something else?

Something worse?

It's too much. Too coincidental.

Tegan is fifteen.

Nicola was fifteen.

Mary had been fifteen.

It's all getting muddled in her head. Often nowadays she is confused, unable to recall the events of the day before, the week before, but what she can recall is her father's disgust all those years ago.

'Patrick is a grown man and you're a child, Mary.'

'I'm not a child. I'm fifteen.'

She had felt so grown up. It was a different time. Although her father didn't approve, it really wasn't unacceptable in the way it would be nowadays.

Bile rises hot and acidic in her throat. She rushes from the table and retches over the sink but there is nothing to come up. She rests her forearms against the stainless steel where she'd washed out baby bottles, birthday cake tins.

Her head feels fuzzy, heavy.

There are a lot of things that Mary can't remember. But love, love for her family is ever-present and all-consuming and, no matter how her mind deteriorates, her heart will always be full of her family and that will never fade.

What she does know is that she and Patrick have had a long and happy life, perhaps him undeservedly so, and whatever, whoever he is, if she has been married to a monster all these years she had had no idea. And although the very notion is unimaginable, unthinkable, there is one thing wives of monsters seem to have in common: they don't know, or they choose not to know. She had always commented when she saw them on the news, tearful and protesting. No, they didn't know their husband was a murderer, rapist, or a man perhaps like Patrick.

They must have known.

Now she knows and she cannot ignore this. She can't subject her family to it, potentially an arrest, a court case, the media. Whatever Patrick may have done, she can't subject him to it either.

Or herself.

Her beloved family has been through so much.

She casts her mind back to earlier that week when Matt came to see her. Patrick had been napping. Her son-in-law had stood before her, broken. Sobbing. She had listened in horror as he told her in a strangled, shameful voice she barely recognized about the incomprehensible amount of money he owed to Victor Kent. About the cannabis he had tried to grow. He told her that neither Kate nor Beth had any idea and that it was entirely his fault.

Could she and Patrick remortgage the farm, he had begged? Lend him some money?

But it was impossible. They had tried after Patrick had his accident, and the banks wouldn't lend them anything. Their pensions were meagre and there was nothing left in their savings.

'Please don't tell anyone I came here and asked.' He had wiped the tears from his cheeks, ashamed.

She promised she wouldn't tell his secret, didn't tell him that she had been keeping one of her own. Knowing that if Matt discovered what had happened on the bridge with Caily he'd be justified in blaming her.

Hating her.

It was all tangled together, inextricably linked. Travis stealing the plants. His grandmother responsible for the financial hardship of the farm because it had never really got back on its feet again after she had demanded money in return for her silence.

That one night when Patrick had climbed into bed with Nicola had changed the course of their history. Ruined so much. If it weren't for that, they'd have money in the bank,

Matt would never have needed to grow cannabis. Would never be indebted to Victor Kent.

Nicola would never have left, her mum would never have been paid off, Travis would never have turned up on their doorstep, curious and entitled. Of course, if it hadn't been for Nicola then Mary would never have suspected anything untoward between Patrick and Tegan, and Caily, poor Caily would never have . . .

Fallen.

Been pushed?

Been on the bridge in the first place.

If.

If.

If.

The butterfly effect. A tiny flutter of wings that changes everything.

When Matt had stood openly crying in front of her, asking if there was any way they could remortgage the farm, lend them money, she hadn't been able to help. There was nothing left.

Nothing.

Because Nicola's mum had taken it all.

But now . . .

Their life insurance might be the thing to save them, to pay back Victor. She cannot rewrite history. Cannot go back to the night Kate nearly drowned and stop her daughter going out. Break the chain of events that led to this. But she can, perhaps, change the future.

Give her family enough money to set them back on the right path.

Inside her head she hears the scratch, scratch, scratch of rats but knows it's only the guilt. It's always the guilt.

She can make it stop.

She can help her family.

She texts the girls and then she pulls on her apron and assembles apples and sugar; as always, there is a ball of homemade pastry chilling in the fridge.

And then, with a heavy heart, she lifts down the rat poison, thankful now that, to save money, Matt had imported a cheaper one that isn't coloured blue.

Patrick will never know.

CHAPTER NINETY-SEVEN

Beth

Beth will never know how Tegan has found the strength to keep everything to herself. She gives her one last hug before she unfolds herself from the bed, shaking out the pins and needles in her arm.

'I'm going to the hospital to see Caily. Coming?'

'Yeah.' Tegan rubs under her eyes with her fingertips, mopping up the mascara that has run.

'You look like a panda. Let me.' Beth leans forward, pulling a tissue from her pocket.

'Mum. I'm fifteen, not five. If you spit on that, I swear I'll—'

The buzz of Beth's phone interrupts Tegan.

'Odd.' Beth is puzzled as she reads. 'It's a text from Mum to me and Kate.'

I'm so sorry about your dad. I'm going to make it right.

'Sorry about what? I'm getting more worried about her. She gets so muddled lately. You haven't noticed Grandad has done anything he needs to apologize for?'

'Nah. Not like you. You and Aunt Kate should apologize to everyone's ears for subjecting them to "I Will Survive".'

'Don't be cheeky. I can't think what Grandma means. I'll call her later. I didn't get a chance to speak to either of them much at the party, did you?'

'No. I did later, though, when I was trying to sleep. Grandad heard me crying and he came in and sat on the chair by my bed.'

'Did he seem okay?'

'Yeah. Normal. He asked me what was wrong and said I could tell him anything. I nearly told him I was pregnant but in the end I just said it was boy trouble.'

'Oh, Tegan. I wish I'd known you were upset. I was only in the room next door.'

'Yeah. But you'd drunk enough gin to—'

'It *was* my birthday.'

'I know. It's fine. Grandad was really kind. We chatted and I felt so much better. He may not be a cuddler but he's wise with his words. I asked him not to say anything to you about me being so upset and he promised me it would stay our secret. I hope he's okay, Mum. He's so kind.'

They began to get ready to go but, before they could leave the house, the second text came through.

Please forgive me. I love you all so much. Goodbye, my darlings.

CHAPTER NINETY-EIGHT

Mary

Please forgive me. I love you all so much. Goodbye, my darlings.

Mary texted the girls again once the apple pie was ready. She unfastens her silver wedding pendant and places it inside a drawer where she cannot see it, cannot feel the weight of her husband's love around her neck like a noose, before walking into the lounge, where Patrick is sitting in his favourite armchair by the window, staring out over the fields.

For a moment, she is transported back in time to watching him cradling one of the twins in each arm, telling them his own version of the story of *The Very Hungry Caterpillar,* eating their crops, visiting the other animals. He'd spot Mary watching him and he'd begin to softly sing 'You Are My Sunshine' to the babies but his eyes would be locked on Mary's and she would join in because Patrick, the girls, her little family were her sunshine. The sun, the moon and the stars.

Her everything.

It takes her several attempts to swallow down the lump in her throat before she can gently tell him, 'I've made a pie.'

'You've forgiven me?' He looks at her with watery eyes. Hopeful eyes.

'I love you,' she says because, despite everything, she does.

They walk through to the kitchen, where they sit in their normal seats as though this was a normal day, but it isn't.

It is their last day.

Mary feels such an incredible sadness swell inside her, weighing down her limbs, rendering her incapable of stopping Patrick as he loads his fork and takes his first mouthful.

She holds her breath, waiting for him to notice a bitterness, an unusual texture, something.

Instead he smiles as he wipes a dribble of custard from the corner of his mouth before he digs in again.

Mary takes hold of his hand and she hopes her eyes convey it all, her sadness, her shame, but most of all her love, not only for him but for the family they've created.

He looks at her enquiringly but she doesn't speak because the time for talking is over.

She keeps hold of her husband's hand as she slowly picks up her own fork and ladens it with moist apple, crispy pastry, thick creamy custard.

And poison.

CHAPTER NINETY-NINE

Beth

A poisonous panic seeps through Beth's veins.
Hurry.
Hurry.
Hurry.

CHAPTER ONE HUNDRED

Kate

*H*urry.

Kate feels an urgency to do *something* as she reads the text.

Please forgive me. I love you all so much. Goodbye, my darlings.

She has a thick, curling dread that something unimaginable, incomprehensible is happening at the farm.

Goodbye, my darlings.

She whimpers. After forty years and across the miles, Kate can feel Mum letting go of her hand. Her mobile slips from her grasp, onto Caily's bed.

'Kate?' Matt's face swims in and out of focus. She cannot speak. He takes her mobile from the bed and she allows herself a split second of hope that he'll offer a rational explanation, but instead he is reading it out loud and his voice sounds as though it's coming through a tunnel, faint and echoey.

'What does Grandma mean, "Goodbye, my darlings"?' Caily asks, panic in her voice, but nobody answers her. 'Mum?' Caily pleads, and Kate is torn between her daughter's needs and the fierce desire to reach her parents.

'Caily, it . . .' She takes a moment to pull the fragments

of what she wants to say together, to pull the fragments of herself together, to remind herself that, although right now her overriding feeling is that of a daughter, she is a mother too. 'It'll be okay. I'll be back as soon as I can.' She drops a kiss on Caily's head. 'Dad will stay and look after you.'

'I'm coming with you, Kate,' Matt says but he's torn, she can see that.

'I'll be okay. It's probably Mum having one of her . . . Please, stay with Caily. I'll call you as soon as I'm there.'

She runs out into the corridor, ringing Beth as she pounds towards the car park.

'I'm on my way,' is all Beth says, hanging up before Kate can tell her to drive carefully.

Incessantly she calls Mum's mobile, the landline, Dad's phone.

All remain unanswered.

Kate hares down the rutted track, her teeth knocking together with every bump. Past the old yellow tractor that Caily and Tegan used to pretend to drive. Past the charred barn that burned down.

And then they are there.

Before the car has fully stopped, she sprints into the farm-house, calling out to her parents.

She is greeted by a chilling sight.

CHAPTER ONE HUNDRED AND ONE

Matt

Matt feels a chill deep in his bones but he chatters about inane things, trying to take Caily's mind off Kate and her grandma. Trying to take his own mind off his wife and Mary.

They were used to Mary saying odd things, doing odd things, but uneasiness squirms in the pit of his belly. This feels different somehow. This feels wrong.

'Dad?' Caily says. 'Do you think I can have a hot chocolate and perhaps something to eat?'

'I'm sure that will be okay, won't it?' He looks to Nicola for guidance.

'Yes, of course. Now you've been moved out of ICU you can have a feast in bed. I'll go and fetch you something from the canteen,' she offers.

'Can you go, Dad?' Caily asks. 'You know what I like.'

The last thing he wants to do is leave his daughter's side, but she has been through so much and is asking for so little. The least he can do is go and see if the coffee shop has any of her favourite cakes.

'I'll stay with her,' Nicola promises.

'I'll be back before you know it.' Matt kisses Caily and then hugs her too tightly. Feels her squirm to be free. Wonders when he'll ever stop feeling this immense gratitude that she is alive. He will never take anyone for granted again.

He slips out of the room. As he walks, he hears his name being called. He turns, Owen is coming from the opposite direction.

'How is Caily?' Owen asks.

'She's . . . awake.' It's the best Matt can do. He has no idea how she is feeling. Christ, he has no idea how he is feeling.

'Is she up to being questioned?'

'Perhaps best wait until Kate gets back.'

'Where is she?'

Matt explains about the text.

'Right. Perhaps I'll go to the farm and check it out,' Owen says.

'Thanks. I am worried. I'm sure it's just Mary having one of her turns, though.'

'Probably. Anyway, we've arrested Leroy and Ray,' Owen says. 'Victor was there but he got away, but he's running scared. It's only a matter of time before we catch up with him.'

Matt's head spins. He remembers the way his mobile had been taken, texts sent to Beth and Kate pretending to be from him.

'You don't think that Victor—'

'I think he's long gone by now,' Owen says but he's already retreating. 'I'll call you as soon as there is news.'

On the day of Caily's accident Matt had stood in this very corridor with Owen, torn apart with jealousy, anger, feeling utterly inadequate as Owen played the white knight, promising to sort everything out.

Now he knows Owen was not playing at anything. He cares for them all. This time he is grateful to him as he watches him disappear around the corner, towards Kate.

Despite Owen's assurances that Victor will be long gone by now, Matt sees, from the window, the way Owen sprints towards his car.

He tries to tell himself that Kate is fine. She's at the farm and it's the last place Victor would be.

Isn't it?

CHAPTER ONE HUNDRED AND TWO

Caily

'You were there at the farm. At the party,' Caily says to Nicola. She's struggling with it all. She can't comprehend anything that is happening – from the memories of that day, to the text Mum has received, to this virtual stranger sitting beside her bed and holding her hand. Part of her questions whether she has actually woken up or whether this is a nightmare where members of her family take on different shapes and nothing makes sense. But there is something she remembers.

'You were talking to Travis. Arguing with him?'

She feels Nicola's fingers tighten around hers, hears her soft intake of breath. There's a beat. Outside Caily's room the wheels of a trolley squeak. 'I was.'

'Why?'

'He's my son.'

'You're his mum?' Caily studies Nicola carefully for the first time. Noticing the curve of her lips, the angle of her cheekbones, seeing the similarities. 'Does he know I'm here? Can you tell him to come?'

'Travis has gone, sweetie.' Nicola brushes the hair from Caily's face. 'I'm so sorry.'

'What do you mean . . . gone?' Caily's stomach flips at the word.

'Left town.'

'He wouldn't do that.'

Nicola reaches into her pocket and pulls out a white envelope folded in half. 'He left a letter for you.'

Caily tentatively takes it. Turns it over in her hands. It isn't sealed and she wonders if Nicola knows what it says. Once she reads what's inside she won't be able to pretend anymore that he loves her, the way she loves him. But she can't help carefully hooking her finger under the seal, opening the envelope.

Dear Caily,

When my grandma died I was lost, confused. She took me in when I'd been accused of something terrible. My crime had been falling in love with a girl I believed to be eighteen.

She wasn't.

Grandma offered me a refuge. I'd never been close to Mum. She'd never told me who my dad was, only that he was someone from her home town, and I resented her for that.

After Grandma had gone, I was sorting out the house when I found some newspaper cuttings. Cuttings about you and Tegan and your family. I also found a bank statement showing a large cash sum paid from your grandfather to my grandmother.

I wondered why Patrick would have paid so much cash six months before I was born, why Grandma would have been keeping tabs on you, and I began to wonder if, somehow,

I was related to you. If Patrick was my father. If it had been covered up.

I came to the farm to find answers.

I had wanted to prove that Patrick was my father and then ask him for some money, but I found something I hadn't been expecting.

Love.

Compassion.

A family.

All I had wanted was to get some of Patrick's DNA and send it off for a paternity test, but something I hadn't figured was how much I liked your grandparents.

Your family.

You.

Caily, I knew you had feelings for me, I felt those feelings too. That connection. I told myself it was because you could be my niece but . . . I don't know.

Patrick isn't my father. I did eventually do the DNA test and when the results came through a couple of days ago I was gutted. Not because I wouldn't be able to ask for money but because I felt as though I'd lost you all when really you were never mine.

Tonight, at the party, the last person I expected to turn up was my mum. She was horrified I was there. I explained why and she told me that my father was a boy called Aaron. She never told me about him because he was what Patrick would call a wrong 'un.

Like father, like son perhaps.

She said she had tried to contact him but he'd never replied. She thought he'd moved on or was in jail.

There is nothing left for me here anymore. Your family weren't my family. My father was no longer around.

Caily, when I found you crying near the red barn after the party I helped you look for Twix. You told me what your dad and Beth were growing and I realized that it gave me the chance to start over. Make some money.

I'm not proud of stealing and I hope that one day you can all forgive me. I hope to make it up to you all.

Caily, you are so young, so beautiful. In other circumstances, if there wasn't such an age gap, I could have loved you.

In my own way, I do love you.

Remember, no matter what anyone says, your star shines brighter than the rest.

Keep shining.

Travis

Caily wipes her tears. 'You should have told Travis about his dad.' She pushes herself up against her pillows, trying to put steel in her spine and her words.

'I know. But I honestly thought Travis was better off without him. I thought . . .' Nicola's voice cracks. 'I thought I was enough. But I wasn't.'

They lapse into silence. Caily thinks she should feel broken-hearted but, although she's sad, she feels a strange sense of relief. Travis didn't reject her when she tried to kiss him because she was ugly or unlovable or any of the things Dani had told her she was on Instagram, but because he thought he might be related to her.

'Why did my grandad give your mum money?'

'Because she accused your grandad of doing something that he hadn't and she was threatening to expose him. He paid, even though he was innocent, because he didn't want to bring any shame on your grandmother and your mum and aunt. Because she convinced him he would go to prison. I think she felt guilty later. That's why she kept cuttings of you. Perhaps trying to convince herself that she hadn't really hurt your family, that you were doing well. Your grandad is a good man, you know.'

'Yeah. Tegan said he was great when she was upset after the party. Why do you think Grandma is apologizing for him? What do you think is going on at the farm?' Suddenly Travis, who had been her entire world, didn't seem quite so important.

'I don't know. But I'm sure your grandma won't do anything rash.'

Caily isn't sure. Nicola didn't see the wild look in Grandma's eyes that day on the bridge.

Beth

There's a wild look in Kate's eyes as she bursts into the kitchen. Takes in the remnants of apple pie on the kitchen table. The half-drunk mugs of tea.

Victor.

Beth tries to stand up from the chair she has been forced to sit on but Victor roughly yanks her head back, ripping hair from her scalp. Tears leak from her eyes onto Victor's hand, which still covers her mouth to prevent her from calling out a warning to Kate. She isn't only crying because she is in pain and afraid but because she is frustrated and angry, desperate to reach her parents.

So horribly, horribly worried about Mum's text.

Please forgive me. I love you all so much. Goodbye, my darlings.

'Let her go,' Kate demands.

'You bitches,' he growls. 'I know what you've told the police, you and that worthless piece of shit you married.' He tugs Beth's hair again. 'But they can't—'

'We'll find out what they can and can't do when they get here. They're on their way,' Kate says firmly, defiantly as she stares Victor down. She makes no move to back away but isn't as calm as she appears. This Beth knows because there is an almost undetectable tremor in her voice, from her stance. Her legs wide, hands on hips, the way they'd stand when they played superheroes as children, Kate always Wonder Woman, Beth Superman.

As she used to during their games when she adopted a different persona, Beth feels a surge of power, she straightens her spine. As though she has willed him with her mind, Victor lowers his hand from Beth's mouth but she can still feel his fingers there, still taste the nicotine from his skin. She smells the sweat emanating from his armpits as he leans over her to pick up the plate of apple pie. He tries to act nonchalant as he shovels forkful after forkful into his mouth, golden pastry crumbs falling down the front of his shirt, but the way his foot tap-tap-taps against the tile floor betrays him.

'I don't give a fuck about the police. They can't touch me,' he says, but Beth knows he is lying. The sheen of sweat on his face, the tremble of the fork as he directs it towards his mouth again, says that he isn't just worried. He's terrified. He must know that the police are after him.

'What have you done with our parents?' Kate asks.

Has he hurt them? Beth's stomach plummets. She had felt as though she was on a fairground ride, cruising on the flat once more, as scared as she could get but certain the surprises were now out of the way, but then from out of nowhere there's another steep drop and she's free-falling, grappling to hold on to what she knows. Her brain struggling to make sense of the situation.

'Did you . . . did you text me from my mum's phone.

Pretend to be her?' As this occurs to her, Beth's fear amplifies. The desperation she felt a moment ago is nothing compared to now.

What has he done to her parents?

She opens her mouth to shout their names but Kate gives an almost imperceptible shake of her head. A 'Don't call them because they could be hiding. They could be safe.'

'Wouldn't you like to know?' Victor sneers but Beth noticed the hesitation before he answered. And she thinks, wherever her parents are, Victor does not know.

But they *are* in trouble.

Please forgive me. I love you all so much. Goodbye, my darlings.

Did Victor send that text? Or them? She *has* to find them. The ticking of the grandfather clock reminds her that time is passing. Time is running out.

Victor is close to her, too close. She hears the grind of his teeth against the pie, feels his hot breath on her neck.

'Let's make a deal,' he says, a slither of wet apple spraying from his mouth, landing on Beth's lap. Disgusted, she flicks it onto the floor. 'Give me cash and your car keys and—'

'Do you really think that if we had any money we'd have been growing for you?' Beth gives a hollow laugh.

'If I were you, I'd run,' Kate says. 'Owen will be here any minute now. Sorry, that's Inspector Bartlett to you.'

'Your parents must have something here.' There's an edge of panic to Victor's voice. 'I know their type. That generation. Big house, family money, don't believe in banks.'

'Why don't you ask them?' Kate asks wearily, crossing her arms, as though she's tired of this game. As though there is no rush, but in reality she's figuring out her next move.

Beth watches Kate carefully, sees her give the briefest of glances towards the draining board.

Towards the knife.

She knows what Kate is going to do.

Beth knows what she has to do.

CHAPTER ONE HUNDRED AND FOUR

Kate

Kate knows what she has to do.

Victor thinks he has the upper hand. But he is older, slower, predictable, and he does not possess what Kate and Beth have: the frantic desire to find their parents and the ability to communicate without words.

It happens simultaneously, so perfect it could have been scripted.

Beth suddenly stands, distracting Victor by sweeping her hand up under his plate, knocking it out of his hands, smashing it on the floor. By the time he registers what is happening, Kate already has the knife. The blade cold and hard in her hands. Her heart cold and hard when she thinks about what this man has put her family through.

She can still feel the heat of the fire, hear the crackle, smell the smoke. She will never, ever forget the panicked look on Matt's face as he fell from the ladder, back down into the barn. As she remembers, her adrenaline rises.

She hates this man.

Hates him.

She tightens her grip on the handle, the afternoon sun glinting from the blade.

She has the knife.

But he has her sister.

His forearm wrapped tightly around Beth's neck.

CHAPTER ONE HUNDRED AND FIVE

Beth

Beth cannot breathe, her throat crushed. Black flecks dance in front of her eyes. Her vision blurs at the edges. Sound becomes muted. She can see Kate's mouth move but she cannot make out what she is saying. Her knees buckle. Her body wanting to give up.

But she will not give up.

She will not leave Tegan without a mother as well as without a father. Thinking of Sean, the reason for his absence these past seven years, the reason he cannot now, still, come home, her resolve hardens.

This man . . .

This man with his hands on her is the cause of everything that has gone wrong in her life.

Missing husband.

Missing father.

The danger she, Kate and Matt have been in is all because of Victor.

And now he dares to come into her parents' house with

435

his anger, his demands and his toxic energy and think that he can bully them.

He cannot bully them.

Her eyes meet Kate's. Kate's are wide, a frightened expression on her face. Her sister is whimpering. Has backed up against the wall. Against the cellar entrance. Spine pressed against the faded picture of the wardrobe. Beth remembers it all so clearly, Dad carefully papering the door with the image from the girls' favourite story. Mum recreating the great feast of Narnia. Tegan and Caily disappearing through the door, stepping into the pages of their beloved book. The den they made at the bottom of the steps. The adventures they'd share with the rest of the family when they returned. It was here they always headed, both together and separately. Here one of the girls would hide, while the other sought them out, making a pantomime of covering their eyes and counting to ten before *coming ready or not*. They'd look under the table, in the kitchen cupboards, knowing all the time that the other would be in the cellar, their Narnia. Giggling, the seeker would head down the stairs.

I see you!

Saw you first!

Beth watches the memory play out in Kate's mind too, it's written all over her face. And that's when Beth knows, that although Kate has one hand behind her back, the other with the knife limp at her side, it may appear as though she's given up. Cowering.

But she hasn't.

She isn't.

Beth raises her eyebrows – *I am ready* – and then Kate

begins to move. Circling around the outside of the room, brandishing the knife, blabbering, begging Victor not to hurt Beth, but to hurt her instead.

Beth makes it easy for Victor as he moves in time with Kate so he remains facing her, their steps matching.

She feels his grip relax.

He thinks he's won.

But he has not won and Victor should not underestimate them. Should not underestimate the force of the love they have for their parents, which engulfs any fear they may otherwise feel. Should not forget that he has ruined Beth's marriage, her life.

Twice.

That she will do anything to ruin his.

Beth knows, from the way Kate sets her mouth into a straight line that Beth and Victor are directly in front of the cellar door.

Kate had *not* been cowering in front of it.

She'd been unlocking it.

Victor groans, lets go of her.

Beth turns. His face is pale, coated with a sheen of sweat. He folds himself in two, clutching his stomach as though gripped by a painful spasm. His face is raised, eyes still on Kate.

It is time.

He moans again, arms folded over his stomach. He screws up his face in pain. Lowers his head.

As if there was any doubt over what Kate had planned, she looks directly at Beth and says, 'I see you.'

'Saw you first.' Sharply and suddenly Beth pushes with all

her weight. She feels Victor lose his balance, his grip on her falling away as he thumps back against the door that still has the faulty catch. Feels the draught as it swings open. And then Kate is holding her arms, as Victor falls backwards. His expression is one of shock, horror, despair.

It shows that he is human.

It shows that he is scared.

Beth doesn't care.

She makes no move to help him as he thud-thud-thuds down the stairs. The darkness swallows him up.

A scream.

And then nothing.

Silence.

Kate's hand finds Beth's. Their fingers linking together. Beth gives three quick squeezes but then she lets her sister go and lurches forward, slams the door shut, Kate twisting the key.

And then they are running.

Running.

Running.

Calling out for their parents.

Wondering why they won't reply.

Or whether they can't.

CHAPTER ONE HUNDRED AND SIX

Kate

'Mum? Dad?' Kate calls as she pounds up the stairs two at a time, Beth on her heels. Automatically heading for their parents' bedroom but . . . when she reaches it she comes to an abrupt stop, her arm out to prevent Beth from entering the room, wanting to protect her from . . . this.

There are images burned into Kate's memory that will never fade: Caily lying in a hospital bed, hooked up to machines, the flames devouring the barn she and Matt were trapped in, and now this.

Her parents lying together on their double bed, foam gathered at the edges of their mouths, Dad's eyes wide and glassy. Mum's closed.

There's a black border framing Kate's vision. A sense that at any moment the ground will give way beneath her feet.

'Dad?' She shakes him frantically before she races around the other side of the bed. 'Mum?'

Beth is by her father's side now, her fingers pressed against his wrist, searching out a pulse.

Kate does the same to her mum.

Beth's eyes meet Kate's full of sorrow, she gives a swift shake of her head just as Kate says, 'Mum's alive.'

Kate climbs onto the bed, sweeping Mum into her arms as Beth garbles into the landline, pleading for an ambulance, the police, everyone.

'Mum. Please wake up. Please.' Kate's sobbing, her tears streaming from her face and dripping onto her mother.

Mum opens her eyes, just a crack, licks her lips and tries to speak but Kate cannot hear her.

'Shh. You don't have to say anything.' She rocks her the way her mother used to with her.

'Victor Kent,' her mum whispers.

'Don't worry about—'

'Matt told me about the money we owe.' Mum draws a ragged breath. 'The life insurance policy is in the dresser.'

'No.' Kate cries harder. 'I don't want it. We just want you.'

'I'm making everything right.' Mum's eyelids flutter before they close.

'Open your eyes,' Kate begs but her mum is still and silent. Kate *has* to bring her back. She begins to sing, 'You Are My Sunshine.' Her throat has narrowed and her voice is thick with tears. She feels the mattress dip, another pair of arms wrapping around her.

Her other half.

Beth joins in with the song and they are a tangle of limbs, a ball of love, as they repeatedly sing about blue skies and happiness and things that seem so utterly out of reach.

Kate and Beth remain locked together as Owen arrives along with the paramedics who usher them away from their mother, their bodies shaking with the force of their combined sobs.

They watched as their dad is examined, their mum.
Fingers pressed against Mum's neck.
Her wrist.
A glance exchanged.
An apology uttered.
A time of death recorded.
Their sunshine taken away.

EPILOGUE

Thirteen months later

Kate anxiously scans the crowd. The theatre is almost full. She sits alone, empty seats either side of her. On the row in front, three generations of the same family. Two young girls sitting on the laps of their grandparents. Their parents smiling fondly as they pass them sweets, a carton of orange juice.

Again, Kate feels the searing pain of grief. Her parents should be here.

It brought no comfort to Kate when she was told that if they had been younger, healthier, weren't on the specific medications they were taking, then they'd likely have survived the rat poison.

If anything, knowing this made it worse.

The poison hadn't killed Victor, although he'd eaten as much, if not more, of the pie as her parents had. It had made him sick, though. Owen had found him at the bottom of the stairs, lying in a puddle of his own vomit, and Kate knows if he hadn't eaten the pie, been gripped by stomach cramps, they might never have overpowered him. Her mum, in her own way, had saved them.

Sometimes Kate wishes the fall had killed him. That plummeting down the stairs had broken his neck, but she gets some satisfaction knowing he's in jail. That he won't be released for a long time.

The police had located Aaron's remains and they'd held a funeral. Kate and Beth supporting Nicola as she wept for her first love. She hadn't been able to track down Travis to tell him that the father he longed to meet had been dead for the past seven years. The almost-empty crematorium a direct contrast to how full it was when they'd buried their parents. Then the small space had been crammed with locals who had known and loved them.

At least Mum and Dad went together. She was offered this phrase time and time again with sympathetic eyes and a pat on the arm, and sometimes this does momentarily ease the ache in her heart. If her dad had pulled through he'd have been utterly devastated that Mum thought the worst of him because that is how she felt when the facts were slowly slotted together and it all fell into place. She tells herself time and time again that Mum wasn't herself these past few years. That often she didn't know what she was thinking, doing. But how tortured she must have been feeling to think that baking that pie was her only way out. It's unimaginable the guilt Mum would have felt if she'd survived and Dad didn't. How would Kate have felt then? When she thinks of her parents it's with a mixture of sorrow and regret and, if she's honest, anger.

Anger that Dad didn't fight harder to clear his name if Nicola's mum had sullied it rather than giving her their money, even if he did that to protect them all.

Fury that Mum had watched Caily fall and then left her.

If.

If she fell.

Each time she's asked Caily exactly how she fell Caily's face has closed. She says that Mary was babbling, distressed about a man in a black Range Rover.

Victor.

If only Matt had never got involved with him. He'd never have been around the farm. Never have scared Mary and perhaps Caily would never have fallen.

If she fell.

But Caily still insists that she cannot remember the actual fall, and perhaps she can't.

Perhaps she doesn't want to.

So yes, there's myriad emotions connected to her parents.

But love, there's always love.

She tries to remember the good in them both, cherish the memories she has. She knows they adored her, adored the whole family. She is certain that Mum did what she did partly so Kate could claim the life insurance, get the farm back on its feet.

The insurance company hadn't paid out, though.

'I'm sorry, we don't cover death by suicide,' the flat, faceless voice on the end of the phone had said, not sounding sorry at all.

As it turned out, they didn't need the money anyway. When probate came through on Nicola's mum's estate Nicola had paid back all the money her mum had taken from Dad.

She hasn't seen Nicola since Aaron's funeral. For a while she had thought Nicola was the beginning and the end of the chain of events. If Kate hadn't wanted to talk to Nicola alone, crossing the fields in the dark and the rain, she wouldn't have fallen in the river. Her dad wouldn't have been distressed, drinking. He'd probably never have sleepwalked into his childhood bedroom. Into Nicola's bed. Nicola's mum would never have had a reason to demand money. The farm would have been in better shape financially when Dad had his accident and Matt took it over. He'd never have needed to agree to the red barn being used to grow cannabis. He'd never have got involved with Victor, and if Victor hadn't been near the bridge the day of Caily's fall . . . It's an endless circle.

Everything inextricably linked.

And then there was Travis.

His curiosity piqued by his grandmother's bank statements, by her cuttings of Caily and Tegan. Coming to root through Nicola's past. Breaking Caily's heart in the process. Stealing the plants. And then . . . then . . . Kate places her hand across her throat. She can still feel the choke of smoke. The smell of soot. The sound of crackling flames.

'I want to pay your family back,' Nicola had said.

'Okay.' Kate eventually agreed, wondering but not asking whether Nicola would have offered the money if Mum and Dad were still alive. If Mum hadn't taken both their lives, thinking she was saving them from Victor.

If everything began with Nicola then taking the money had been an ending.

But also, in its own way, another beginning.

As well as being able to update some of their ancient equipment, which allows Matt to use his time more efficiently, they had intended to use a big chunk of the money to pay off Beth's loan, but then Owen had investigated the company that had loaned her the money and found that they didn't meet the FCA rules and, after getting the financial ombudsman involved, Beth's debt, along with many others', were written off. Instead, they had used the remainder of their funds to open a farm shop with a café.

Once the planning permission came through they'd built on the land where the red barn had stood. Beth completed the relevant food hygiene courses and now runs the café, and they'd quickly built up a reputation for wholesome, homecooked food. They were booked for Sunday lunches weeks in advance.

At the moment most of the profits are ploughed back into the farm so, to save money on rent, they are all living in their parents' farmhouse. Her and Matt, Caily, Beth, Tegan and Billy. Billy who had shocked them all with an emotional confession by the side of Caily's bed while she was recovering.

'It was me,' Billy had said, swiping away tears. 'It was me who set up the Instagram account and posted those photos, not Dani. Me who ruined your dress.'

'Why?' Caily asked, her own eyes welling. 'You are . . . were my best friend.'

'I know. I just . . . I'm so unhappy at home, Caily. My parents are so bloody awful and I was sure that I hadn't been picked for Sebastian because I'm shorter than you. I thought if you pulled out of the performance then Tegan would play Mia and I'd get Sebastian because our voices blend together in a way that hers and Kofi's wouldn't. Height-wise we were perfect too. I wanted that scholarship. I wanted London. Not even because my dream is to be on stage, because it isn't, but I can't keep living at home, I just can't. My parents don't accept who I am, they don't try to understand me.'

'But . . .' Caily had looked helplessly at Kate. Kate's hands had pulled into fists. She was furious.

'Billy, you should leave.'

'Wait,' Caily called as Billy turned towards the door. 'Why target me? Not Kofi?'

'Because . . .' Billy took a deep breath, exhaled. 'Because I know you. I know your weak spots and how to chip away at your confidence.'

'You think I'm weak.'

'God, no. I think you're strong, Caily. The strongest person I know. I was really desperate. I don't expect you to forgive me but I am really, really sorry.'

Kate watched as Caily stared at her hands, thinking. Eventually she raised her head.

'I see you, Billy Vaughn.' She began to cry. 'I see your talent and your kindness and your heart. You've done something horrible and hurtful but I understand why.'

'Caily, you don't have to—' Kate began.

'But there's been so much loss already,' Caily whispered. 'So much.'

And so she led by example, her brilliant, beautiful girl. Kate can't say she was thrilled when Caily asked if Billy could move in once he'd turned sixteen, but she'd once been so judgemental about Sean after he was sent to prison, so quick to condemn him, and she didn't want to make that mistake again. If she could help turn a life around, she wanted at least to try.

After all, she had forgiven Beth and Matt for lying to her, hadn't she? Perhaps not easily, but hours of conversation, raw with honesty, had peeled back the layers of deceit until all she was left with was love. And ultimately, when everything is down to the wire, love is everything, isn't it?

Billy waves at her now from the side of the stage. She waves back. It's Billy's musical that the group are performing today. Miss West had been really supportive after she'd read the first draft, and Billy hopes the local press will be kind with their reviews. That this first performance might lead to bigger things, a career as a writer, a West End show, Broadway even.

'Hey you.' Matt drops a kiss on the top of her head as he settles into his seat. Twix is with him, smart in the same tweed bow tie he wore to the party.

'How on earth did you talk them into letting a dog in here?'

'Charm,' Matt grins. The same Matt she first fell in love with.

'Caily will be pleased he's here.' She fusses Twix, taking the lead that Matt hands her, gripping it tightly so he doesn't try and bound onto the stage. 'Everything go okay today?'

'More than okay,' he smiles, his eyes crinkling at the edges. He's happier now. Healthier. He'd been for an ECG, a cardiac MRI and an angiogram, and his chest pains had been attributed to stress. Now they had disappeared altogether. 'The auction at the Norris farm was quiet. I've got us a new cultivator and drill and . . .' he drums his hands on his knees, 'a tractor.'

'Very sexy.'

'It is. 150 horsepower.'

Marsh Farm has turned a corner. They have too. There'll be no more secrets because, in that burning building when they were convinced they'd lost each other, they found each other too.

They'd always been a team, they'd just lost sight of that for a while.

'Have I missed anything?' Beth slips into the seat on the other side of Kate.

'Nothing's happened yet. I was getting worried about you.'

Since their parents' funeral Kate and Beth had spent hours repairing their fractured relationship. But this time it is different. Equal. Kate is no longer half of something, she is entirely whole.

'Had to wait for Sean to call.'

Sean is back in prison. Owen had tried his best to cut him the best deal possible but it was unavoidable. His sentence is short, though, and Beth visits often. Kate too. She's had a lot of time to think and she sees why Beth loves him now. Sees the good in him.

They'll be there for him when he gets out next week.

Because that's what families do. They stay. They endure.

Suddenly the auditorium is plunged into blackness.

The darkness is absolute.

A ragged breath.

The wait excruciating.

A whimper.

Light floods the stage.

Kate's hand finds Beth's. She squeezes it three times.

Two girls – their girls – stand shoulder to shoulder. They turn to each other and hug and that hug says more than any words possibly could. It says '*I love you,*' '*I'm here for you,*' '*I can't wait to audition for theatre companies together once we've sat our A levels.*'

Before they've even begun to perform, the audience is on

their feet, clapping, cheering, dabbing at damp eyes with scrunched-up tissues, knowing what this local family have been through.

The girls smile as they pull apart.

'I see you,' Caily mouths.

'Saw you first,' mouths back Tegan.

And then the music begins, Billy's opening lyrics get an instant laugh, and they are leaping and twirling and Kate's heart is right up there, spinning with them.

Kate had been fearful that a broken pelvis meant broken dreams; it sounds so terrifying, doesn't it? But it didn't. There were weeks where Caily couldn't support her own weight, impatient while she waited for her bones to heal, but understanding that the less she pushed herself initially, the quicker and more complete her recovery would be. Then came the months of gruelling physiotherapy. It was shocking how quickly Caily's muscles had lost strength in the period she wasn't using them, but she was young, healthy and followed all the recommendations of the physio, never once complaining and now she is . . . she is . . .

Everything.

Kate's tears roll down her cheeks but she doesn't wipe them away. She can't move, can't take her eyes off her daughter. She doesn't look at the audience.

But she knows she isn't the only one watching those girls. Everyone is.

THE FOLLOWING LETTER
CONTAINS SPOILERS

Hello,

Thank you so much for joining me for *The Fall* – my eighth psychological thriller, and my eleventh published book. If you've enjoyed reading about Marsh Farm I'd be incredibly grateful if you could pop a short review or star rating on Amazon. It really does make such a difference in increasing a book's visibility.

This story came to life after a period of despair. With the pandemic and the skyrocketing cost of living, life has seemed gloomy at times. So many families are struggling to make ends meet.

I thought about taking an ordinary family, putting them in a desperate situation and throwing them a lifeline that, although illegal, seemed too good an opportunity to miss. Would they take it? What would happen if it all went wrong? Could I take a close-knit family and tear them apart and see if they would come back together?

I'd wanted to write about cousins for a while; my cousins were such an integral part of my childhood. Caily and Tegan were a joy to write. Unusually, when I began to construct *The Fall* I had an idea where it might go but that was before Mary and Patrick whipped the story away from me and changed it into something else entirely. I've grown really fond of the whole family and, although I'm sad to let them go, I'm loving working on my thriller for next year set in Newington House, which is so creepy and unsettling I've begun locking my study door before I write.

I do hope you can join me again and, in the meantime, do come chat to me on social media.

https://twitter.com/fab_fiction
https://www.instagram.com/fabricating_fiction/
https://www.facebook.com/fabricatingfiction/

Louise x

ACKNOWLEDGEMENTS

It takes so many people to bring a book to life and I'm immensely grateful to them all. HQ Stories have such a wonderful team, from production to marketing to PR, my fabulous editors Manpreet Grewal and Cat Camacho headed by the powerhouse that is Lisa Milton.

Thanks as ever to the team at TBP, my agent, Rory Scarfe and to Hattie Grünewald.

Big thanks to Stuart Gibbon from GIB consultancy for advice on police procedures. Any mistakes are purely my own.

Natasha Haddon for her ongoing support.

My cousins Tori, Mark, Lee, Dean and Paul, who inspired me to write about those special childhood relationships. It's been fun to revisit old memories.

My friends, particularly Natalie, Sarah and Hilary. My family, Mum, Karen and Bekkii.

My husband, Tim, who has seen me through yet another 'I can't possibly write a book' stage during the tricky first draft, along with supporting me through everything else this past year has thrown at us. I couldn't love you more.

My children Callum, Kai and Finley, who are a source of infinite wonder and pride.

And Ian Hawley. Always.

BOOK CLUB QUESTIONS

1. Matt felt immense pressure not to ruin Kate's family business, and complete desperation following the effects Covid and Brexit had on top of climate change and the myriad difficulties British farmers already faced. Can you understand why he agreed to work for Victor? What could he have done instead?

2. '*When everything is down to the wire, love is everything, isn't it?*' Kate loves her family unconditionally and forgives them at the end. Do you think that broken trust can ever be repaired?

3. Caily lost her self-esteem and confidence because of the Instagram posts. Did you grow up with social media? If not, how different do you think your life might have been if you had? Should more be done by the platforms to protect users, particularly with trolling and the use of filters casting unrealistic expectations?

4. Beth fell in love with Sean aged fifteen and today, aged forty, believes that he is the only man for her. How rare is this? Why do you think we often grow apart from our first love but they have stayed together?

5. Nicola kept the truth from Travis about his father not wanting to meet him because she didn't want Travis to know his father had rejected him, and if Travis had Aaron's name she was scared he would google him and learn about his criminal past. She was worried Travis might hero-worship Aaron and embroil himself in something illegal. He ended up breaking the law anyway. Are adults ever justified in keeping the truth from a child? What do you think about nature vs nurture?

6. Matt and Beth never admitted to Owen what they did, although they hinted they had been involved. Owen told them, 'As a friend, I suggest thinking very carefully about what you want to say.' Should he have offered this chance to his oldest friends or did he have a duty to formally question them?

7. Caily, Tegan and Billy have the chance of a scholarship that would mean missing out on A levels. Do you think it is good to have an education as a back-up plan or should you follow your dreams if an opportunity presents itself?

8. Miss West not only teaches drama but also encourages Billy in his writing, giving him the opportunity to see his musical performed. Some schools don't offer many,

if any, creative subjects nowadays. How important are they for children?

9. Mary thought she was making the ultimate sacrifice to save her family from financial ruin. Patrick thought he was saving his family from shame and humiliation and was scared that although he hadn't done anything wrong he could be prosecuted. Did you feel any sympathy towards either of them?

10. Who was your favourite character and why?

Turn the page for an exclusive extract
of *All For You*, the nail-biting and
shocking thriller from Louise Jensen

Can this family ever recover when
the truth finally comes out?

Available to buy now!

PROLOGUE

Something is wrong.

I've a deep, primal instinct screaming that I need to get home to Connor. It isn't just because of the row we'd had. The horrible, hurtful things he had said, it's something else.

A knowing that, despite being seventeen, I should never have left my son alone.

Hurry.

The flash of neon orange cones blur through the window as I gather speed until the roadworks force me to a stop. The candle-shaped air freshener swings from the rear-view mirror – its strawberry scent cloying.

My fingertips drum the steering as I will the temporary traffic lights to change to green. The rain hammers against the roof of the car, windscreen wipers lurching from side to side. It isn't the crack of lightning that causes my stomach to painfully clench, or the rumble of thunder, even though storms always take me back to a time I'd rather forget, but a mother's instinct.

I've felt it before. That bowling ball of dread hurtling towards me.

Drawing in a juddering breath, I tell myself everything is

fine. It's only natural that worry gnaws at me with sharpened teeth. Every mother in our town is on high alert right now after the disappearance of two teenage boys. I have more reason to be on edge than most.

It's not as though I'm thinking Connor has been taken, but it's one thing for him to ignore my calls, he'd never ignore Kieron's.

Never.

Particularly when he had asked Kieron to call him after his hospital appointment.

Why didn't he pick up?

In my mind's eye I see him, bounding down the stairs two at a time, balancing on a chair to reach the snacks he doesn't realize I know he hides on the top of his wardrobe.

An accident, or something else?

Something worse?

My stomach churns with a sense of foreboding.

Calm down.

I've been under so much pressure lately that I'm bound to be anxious. Edgy. But… I jab at my mobile and try Connor once more. My favourite picture of him lights the screen. We took it five years ago during an unseasonably hot Easter. Before Kieron was diagnosed, before everything changed. We're on the beach, the wind whipping his dark curls around his face. His grin is wide, traces of chocolate ice cream smudged around his mouth.

We were all so happy once. I don't know how, but I have to believe that we can be again. The alternative is too painful to bear.

The phone rings and rings. Fear brushes the back of my neck.

Frantically, I try calling again, from Kieron's phone this time. He still doesn't answer.

The lights are taking an age.

Next to me, Kieron sleeps. His head lolling against the window, breath misting the glass. The dark sweep of his lashes spider across his pale skin. The hospital visit has exhausted him. The red tartan blanket I always keep in the car has slipped from his knees and I reach across and pull it over his legs. The passenger seat is swallowing his thin body. At thirteen he should be growing, but his illness is shrinking him. It's shrinking me. Sometimes I feel as though my entire family is disappearing. Aidan barely talks to me, never touches me. In bed there's an ever-increasing space between us. Both of us teetering on our respective edges of the mattress, a strip of cold sheet an invisible barrier between us. My head no longer resting on his chest, his leg never slung over mine, his fingers not stroking my hair anymore.

Connor is monosyllabic and moody in the way that seventeen-year-olds often are but he never was, before...

But it isn't just that, it's also this sickness that isn't just Kieron's. It's everybody's.

The lights turn green.

Hurry.

Before I can pull away there's a streak of yellow. Through the rain a digger trundles towards me, blocking my path.

Kieron sighs in his sleep the way his brother sighs when he's awake. Sometimes it seems the boys only communicate through a series of noises and shrugs. But that's unfair. It's hardly surprising Connor's mouth is a permanent thin line as though he's forgotten how to smile. It's not only his concern

3

about his brother on top of everything he went through before the summer that has turned my sweet-natured son into a mass of guilt and unhappiness, but the sharp truth that out of his friendship group of three, two of them have disappeared.

'The Taken', the local paper calls them, reporting that out of those who were there that tragic day, Connor is the only one left.

But Connor knows this as he hides in his room, too scared to go to school.

We *all* know this.

Tyler and Ryan have vanished without a trace and the police have no idea why.

It's up to me to keep Connor safe.

I glance at Kieron.

I'll do anything to keep both of my boys safe.

The driver of the digger raises his hand in appreciation as he passes by me. Before I can pull away, the lights revert to red once more. Frustrated, I slam my palms against the steering wheel.

Calm down.

Rationally, I know Connor hasn't been taken.

He's at home.

The door is locked.

He's okay.

But still…

He never ignores Kieron.

Never.

Hurry.

Despite the lights being red, I pull away. There's no approaching traffic. I snap on the radio again. The newsreader relays in

4

cool, clipped tones that the missing boys haven't been found but police are following several lines of inquiry. Nobody else is missing. The unsaid 'yet' lingers in the air, and although I know Connor is safe, my foot squeezes the accelerator. Home is the only place my anxiety abates. When we're all under one roof and I can almost pretend everything is exactly how it was.

Before.

Visibility is poor. Frustrated, I slow, peering out through the teeming rain. If I have an accident I'm no use to Kieron, to anyone. My heart is racing as there's another crack of lightning. I count the seconds the way I used to with the boys when they were small.

One.

Two.

Three.

A grumble of thunder. The storm is closing in. Everything is closing in, crashing down. My stomach is a hard ball, my pulse skyrocketing as a sense of danger gallops towards me.

Hurry.

The urgency to be at home overrides the voice of caution urging me to slow down. I race past the old hospital, which has fallen into disrepair, the white and blue NHS sign crawling with ivy, and then the secondary school. I barely register the figure cloaked in black stepping onto the zebra crossing but on some level I must have noticed him as I blast the horn until he jumps back onto the path. He shakes his fist but I keep moving.

Hurry.

My chest is tight as I pull into my street, my drive-way. A whimper of fear slithers from my lips as I see the front door swinging open.

Without waking Kieron I half fall, half step out of the car, my shoes slipping on wet tarmac as I rush towards my house.

'Connor?'

The table in the hallway is lying on its side. My favourite green vase lies in shattered pieces over the oak floor. The lilies that had been left anonymously on the doorstep are strewn down the hallway.

Funeral flowers.

'Hello?' My voice is thin and shaky.

Blood smears the cream wall by the front door. Lying in a puddle of water from the vase is Connor's phone, the screen smashed. My feet race up the stairs towards his bedroom. A man's voice drifts towards me. I push open Connor's door just as shots are fired.

Instinctively, I cover my head before I realize the sound is coming from the war game blaring out of Connor's TV. His Xbox controller is tangled on the floor along with his headphones.

His bedroom is empty.

The Taken.

It's impossible.

'Connor?'

He was here.

He was safe.

The front door was locked.

Quickly, I check every room in the house until I'm back in the hallway, staring in horror at the blood on the wall, trying to make sense of it.

Connor has gone.

ONE PLACE. MANY STORIES

Bold, innovative and
empowering publishing.

FOLLOW US ON:

@HQStories